Lost & Waiting

Amanda Read is a novelist and short story writer. She graduated from the MA in creative writing programme at Bath Spa University, with distinction.

In an earlier life, she was awarded a Royal Horticultural Society Fellowship through which she trained as a plant systematist at the University of Reading, the Royal Botanic Gardens, Kew, and the Natural History Museum, London.

Amanda lives in the UK in rural Wiltshire. She works as an agricultural research programme manager for international development.

Advance Praise for
Lost & Waiting

'I was held, I laughed, I marvelled … this is such a winner!'

'Joyful, sensual, funny writing.'

'A tremendous force and energy and a sharp wit.'

'Tantalises.'

'A wonderfully "big-budget" panoramic feel … very assured.'

'Such command, and depth and richness of detail.'

'A big story, well-imagined, with strong characters.'

'Compelling…visceral and real.'

AMANDA READ

LOST & WAITING

First published 2020 by
Independent Publishing Network

ISBN 978-1-83853-411-0

Cover Design by Clare Stacey at Head Design
www.headdesign.co.uk

Printed by Amazon UK Limited

Visit **www.amandaread.net** to read more about the author.

for Carlos and Carmen

A glossary of botanical terms appears on p.331

'There's no sense in going further—it's the edge of cultivation,'
So they said, and I believed it—broke my land and sowed my crop—
Built my barns and strung my fences in the little border station
Tucked away below the foothills where the trails run out and stop.

Till a voice, as bad as Conscience, rang interminable changes
On one everlasting Whisper day and night repeated—so:
'Something hidden. Go and find it. Go and look behind the Ranges—
'Something lost behind the Ranges. Lost and waiting for you. Go!'

Rudyard Kipling
The Explorer (1898)

1. Green in Buenos Aires

Evangeline

First impressions: green, Parisian, satellites of dogs orbiting super-handlers. Evangeline could lose herself in a place like this.

In the taxi, her attention fell on the photo of two children taped to the dash—a serious girl with plaits and a younger boy grinning gap-toothed. Unmoored, as ever when caught off guard, she pulled away from the picture and fixed on the passing frothy torrents of violet-blossomed Jacarandas washing the city with new beginnings.

Showered, changed and kitten-heeled, it was early evening by the time Evangeline went in search of a drink and Wi-Fi. A sultry rhumba spilling from a bar off the main drag beckoned to her. Seated near a tiny stage, and with a beer on the way, she recognised *Libertango* played with brio by an elderly accordionist, a lanky cadaver on double-bass, and a pianist in denial of a receding hairline. Evangeline twitched her shoulders obligingly along with the music and stretched her legs beneath the table. Before she got too carried away, she reached for her phone.

Her inbox had been busy while she'd been offline. She opened the first email as more loaded.

> Thank you for your interest in working with Asklepion to develop your preliminary study 'Project World Tree *(Yavuea morganii)*: a Taxonomic Framework and Distribution Map.'
>
> Asklepion regularly reviews its projects to ensure a robust pipeline and accelerated delivery of the next generation of medicines in meeting global health challenges.
>
> After careful prioritisation, we have concluded that investing in Project World Tree is not the right direction for Asklepion—

What?

There must be some mistake. She was already here. A knot tightened inside her as she re-read the email. They couldn't do this: they signed an agreement.

Surely, the other project partners—the Royal Botanic Gardens, Kew, and Universidad de Santiago de Chile—would be up in arms over Asklepion's renegade behaviour?

Evangeline read in horror as they decided the project's fate without reference to her at all. Didn't they have to involve the project manager in such discussions? Apparently not. From there, the three partners moved on to horizon scanning and potential areas of mutual interest to them, of zero interest to her.

In among the high-level stuff, one email was to Evangeline alone.

> I'm sure you are absolutely fuming right now. I know I am. I asked around here at Kew and it looks as

> though Asklepion are within their rights to back out even at this late stage. Obvs. this has to be a knee-jerk over the scandal.
>
> I'm super sorry I can't now join you on your expedition. Perhaps you could get some funding from another source? At the very least, make a holiday out of the trip.

Find alternative funding at this late stage? The botanist would have known just how remote that possibility was. And what scandal?

Trending on Twitter had the answer.

> AmazonBio: 'We all have a global responsibility to put an end to unethical bioprospecting.' Foreign Pharma Giant criticised over attempts to patent the knowledge of indigenous people in the Amazon without consent. **#Asklepiongate**

All this had exploded while Evangeline was asleep in the air over the Atlantic. By now, everyone would have left work for the weekend. She should have looked in more detail at Asklepion's business practices, but the offer of money and escape blinded her. What were her options? A minute or so staring at the pristine tablecloth drew a blank.

How different an experience it must have been before the advent of long-haul flights and the global village. Edwin 'Chile' Morgan's account of his travels in the region during the mid-nineteenth century was full of adventure. Plant hunter, raconteur, philosopher, and with such a lust for life as to sweep Evangeline along in his enthusiasm, Morgan was the reason she was here.

Her best friend, her only friend, was a dead man. Long dead.

If Morgan was here, he would know what to do. She rubbed her earring between finger and thumb. It was one of a pair she had made up from Morgan's cufflinks. Gold, the size of small coins, they bore a well-worn relief of four radial lines ending in crows' feet, with a star, sun and crescent moon in each of the four segments.

Lost and waiting.

'What was that?'

The waiter was pouring her beer. 'Holiday?' The insistence of his voice suggested this wasn't the first time he had asked the question.

'No, not really.' she felt slow, as if in need of cranking up her gears. She squeezed the earring, warm from the heat of her hand. 'No, I'm on my way to Chile.'

Now the words were out there, the knot slackened between her shoulders. She didn't have to go home straight away, the flight to Chile was booked and paid for. Why waste it?

One project member had yet to comment on the project's meltdown: the Chilean anthropologist, Jesús Dorador. Had he not seen the emails? Perhaps he thought enough had been said on the subject and wanted to avoid being tarnished with the whole sorry mess. If this was the case, she hoped it wouldn't prevent him meeting up for a coffee while she was in Santiago. Now they were unlikely ever to meet in person, she realised how much she had been looking forward to putting a face to the calm presence that came across in the project's conference calls. While the other participants joined by video, Jesús only ever used audio. Something about bandwidth, he explained in that voice of his. It wasn't just his accent, although the way he r-r-r-rolled his 'r's always sent a thrill through her. His voice had the perfect timbre, not too soft, not too deep, but like honey dripping from the comb and ideally suited, she just knew, to bedtime stories.

And now she would have to break the news to him that the project wasn't going ahead. Then she should let Will and Mum know she was alive.

'What are you planning to do in Chile?' An accented masculine voice came from the next table.

Subtly expensive, olive-skinned and with the first signs of grey, the man wore his shirt cuffs folded back with clinical precision. He was alone. He must be on business, then, but what? It had to be something more exotic than IT. A wine dealer?

He carved into a steak that dwarfed his plate.

'I was planning to do a tour,' she said. 'Starting from Santiago and driving down to Villarrica—'

'The town?'

'The volcano.'

'You are interested in geology? Volcanology…?'

'I'm interested in plants.'

'A hunter of plants, then.' He nodded his approval, then waved his fork in the air, rewinding a spool. 'You say you *were* planning to go. Does that mean you're not now going?'

'I…don't know.'

His not knowing her was a freedom of sorts. There was no fear of hitting up against the double brick wall of Mum and Will that always happened when any talk of her plans arose. A strange alliance, that one: until Effie was born, Mum didn't have much time for Evangeline's ex, now she was forever urging Evangeline to get back with Will.

'The thing is, I intended to find a particular tree. This tree has only ever been recorded once, and that was almost two hundred years ago. If the tree still exists, it is hugely important. But I've just had news which makes it look like the trip's off.'

The fork went in while she spoke. He ate with his mouth closed, the muscles in his jaw efficient at dispatching the meat. He nodded, whether in acknowledgement of what she said, or a judgement on the steak, she couldn't tell.

He swallowed his food. 'I hope your news was not so serious. It is a pity for you to have come all this way for nothing. This tree you speak of. It is medicinal, no?'

'That's what we think, yes. A tree from the same family has ethnobotanic value among the Mapuche.'

'The relationship between people and plants goes back to Eve and the apple,' he said under his breath. He pointed to her empty glass. 'Can I get you another drink? Perhaps some wine? Argentina prides itself on its wine.'

'I'd love one, thanks.' If she sounded a little too keen for a drink, what did it matter? After Asklepion's bombshell, a drink was exactly what she wanted.

He beckoned the waiter over, ordered, then turned back to Evangeline. 'So, for now, you are thinking you might as well go to Santiago, because the flight is booked, no?'

'Something like that, yes.'

'And this will buy you time while you consider your options.'

'Yes,' she nodded. 'Yes, I think it will.'

'You have already taken the first step on your journey. Santiago will bring you one step closer to your especial tree. After that the road will not be as impossible as it now seems.'

She sipped her red wine and allowed his words to sink in. 'You might be right.'

He smiled with his eye teeth. 'How do you like the wine?'

'It's lovely, spicey.' To prove it, she raised the glass to her lips again. 'Do you live in Buenos Aires?'

'No, like you, I'm here to explore a business prospect.' He brushed a crumb from his table. 'But it didn't work out.'

'What is your line of work?'

'You could describe me as a collector.'

'Of art?'

He pursed his lips. 'It's just a hobby really. I can't resist beautiful things.'

'I was thinking of fitting in some sightseeing tomorrow before I head off to the airport. Which galleries and museums do you recommend?'

His look gave the impression her stock had risen.

'There I can help you. Buenos Aires has many.' He reeled off a list of institutions any one of which she might have wanted to visit given the time. At his mention of the museum of ethnography, she wondered whether she might find out more about the tree.

'If you did want to go, it would be my honour to be your guide,' he said. 'That way, you get to see the most important pieces and I'll make sure you catch your flight.'

The wine really was very good, it ignited a cheerful hearth within her. She tried to fathom the colour of his eyes. 'Are you sure I wouldn't be putting you out?'

'Not at all.'

What else was she going to do? On her own, she would spiral around her dilemma. Hadn't she come to South America to change her life? His company would keep her mind occupied, he seemed harmless enough and, anyway, they'd be in a public place. 'Then I'd love to.'

'I should introduce myself,' he half-rose from his seat in a slight bow, 'Victor—Victor Ríos.'

'Victor? I'm Evangeline.'

⁂

The twisted strap of the rucksack dug into Evangeline's shoulder. She must have taken the wrong turn as she left the hotel. The ten-minute walk drawn in biro by the concierge on her map soon became three quarters of an hour. She still hadn't managed to contact Jesús, and she should at least have texted Mum to let her know she was here in one piece. Had Mum already got on the hotline to Interpol, convinced her daughter—at this very minute—

was in the employ of a drug cartel?

Victor was leaning against the museum railings with a phone against his ear and a folded newspaper under his arm. His aviators glinted in her direction. He pulled languidly away from his support and twitched the newspaper by way of greeting.

As Evangeline drew close, she wasn't sure but thought she heard in Spanish, 'Here she is, I'll call you later.'

Victor pocketed the phone and opened his arms. 'Evan*ghe*line. It is good to see you again,' his accent implied so much more of her name, but was he overdoing it?

'Sorry I'm late.' She radiated heat.

Taking her by the shoulders, Victor kissed each cheek. His cologne put her in mind of a summer brook flowing over mossy pebbles. In denim shorts with dust sticking to flip-flopped feet and her T-shirt hot and damp beneath the rucksack, Evangeline felt a little inadequate. She wondered what passers-by made of the contrast: his Club World to her Traveller Class.

Inside the museum, Victor waved away her contribution to the entrance fee and took charge of stowing her rucksack in a locker. Meanwhile, she stood in the middle of the empty foyer blissing out on the frigid air-conditioning now flowing beneath the T-shirt she held clear of her back.

'Shall we go?' Victor appeared alongside her.

Evangeline dropped her hand and grinned, 'Ready.'

He led the way up a broad staircase. 'Vale, I will limit our visit to exhibits from south-central Chile, in the region around Villarrica. This is the region you are travelling to, no? You must say if anything else takes your interest.'

'Perfect.'

The sienna walls, discreet lighting and smell of wood-polish quieted Evangeline's breathing. She allowed herself to be guided by Victor, observing him as much as the objects he called to her attention. His voice was hushed, reverent even, and all the more dramatic.

Coming upon pottery, painted with birds, serpents, felines, anthropomorphised animals and plants, in functional forms of drinking cups, bottles and bowls, he said, 'Andean culture incorporated the animals of the jungle in its belief systems. In particular, the power and cunning of the jaguar was most…venerated? Iconografías of feline-human hybrids were common, always portrayed with fierce-looking fangs.' Victor's teeth gleamed. 'Sacrifice, both human and animal, was practiced, often by—' he put his hands around his neck as though wrenching open a jar, startling a laugh from Evangeline. 'As this redware shows.' He pointed to a figurine. 'Do you see the hands bound behind the back and a cord around the neck is also tied to his…pipi?' He raised his hands in apology and moved on to the next cabinet.

'Here we have Mapuche musical instruments. The cullcull, there, made of ox horn, is used to sound the alarm.'

'These instruments are still used, then?'

'Si,' he said, as though it was obvious.

He was already sloping around the cabinet to another exhibit, when Evangeline's attention was drawn to one of several tall cabinets lining the wall, each one housing a life-sized mannequin in traditional dress. The male figure, designated Huaso (Cowboy) by an info stand, was dressed in a broad-brimmed straw hat (chupalla, according to the label), a woollen natural-dyed poncho (chamanto) and leather riding boots with silver spurs. Morgan had taken to wearing this style of clothing during his time in Chile. It was the closest Evangeline had got to the plant hunter since she came across his journal.

She put her hand to the glass. 'If only you could come with me.' She wondered at the dull ache in her chest. Was is possible to miss someone she had never met?

'I believe this is something which will be of more interest to you.' Victor was leaning over a wooden kettle drum. His expression was neutral as she joined him, but she caught a glimpse of something prowling in the depths of his eyes.

The drumskin was decorated with a design of four radial lines ending in crows' feet. Crescents, circles and daisy-like symbols decorated each quarter. The design was familiar but where had she seen it before?

'My earrings.'

When had he noticed them? Yesterday evening in the bar, or just today?

'Si, they have the same design as this kultrún.'

'I have the earrings, but I don't know much about the design.'

'This is Rewe, it is the World Tree. But, tell me, how did you come by the earrings?'

She looked up at him. 'Say it again, slowly.'

She studied his mouth as he repeated, 'Rey-weh.'

'Rey-weh?'

'Güeno, Plant Hunter.'

She fingered her earrings and was taken back to the first time she held Morgan's journal. Its worn leather binding, densely lined with sailcloth, had concealed proof of its author. 'They came to me from an old friend. They were cufflinks originally, but I had them made into earrings.'

'The design is much replicated on the kultrún, it even appears on the Mapuche flag, but it is rare to find it so finely wrought in jewellery.'

'Rewe is...the World Tree.'

He raised an eyebrow. 'This is the special tree you look for?'

'Yes, but...' She studied the design on the drum closely. 'I don't see it.'

Close behind her, so close she was enveloped in his mossy-pebble cologne, Victor pointed over her shoulder. 'The lines are the branches of the tree. They connect the points cardinal. In

10

between are sun, moon and stars. Rewe links the sky, the earth and all life—you and I—and the underworld.'

'All part of the same cosmos,' she said, gazing at the design with new insight. She stepped away from Victor. 'Is it a myth, or does it really exist?'

He nodded, as though weighing up her words. 'Perhaps both.'

They pushed through the exit and the heat pressed in around them. She blinked in the sun's glare while Victor flagged down a taxi.

Through the open passenger window, he instructed, 'Al aeropuerto.'

He stowed Evangeline's rucksack on the backseat, then turned to her. Once again, she received what she took to be his habitual social kiss, his jaw grazing her cheek.

'Evan*ghe*line, I'm certain we will meet again.'

'Thank you for this afternoon, Victor. It's been fruitful.' She climbed in beside her rucksack, feeling she wanted to say more, but what?

'Fruitful, yes, I have a feeling your search for the tree will yield ripe reward.' Victor held the car door. 'Take care out there, Plant Hunter. Hasta la proxima!'

Victor nodded through the window and straightened. Two taps sounded through the roof, the car pulled away and his white slub-weave shirt, embroidered leather belt and hips of tobacco linen trousers receded from view.

The afternoon had brought Morgan's journal to life, but there was something about Victor. His eyes. Yes, his eyes. They were tawny—like the jaguar.

2. Finding Jesús

Evangeline

The official flicked through a few pages of Evangeline's passport, glanced at her once more, then handed it back. She headed for the exit. Automatic doors slid open to release her into the world.

Those waiting, leaning over waist-high metal barriers, straightened to scan the arrivals. Children sprawling on the floor were hauled to their feet. Eyes flicked to her then away. She wished someone would smile in recognition, wave.

Who was that? There, in the jam, blue eyes set in cloisons of black lashes. Evangeline shook her head, no time for distractions. Jesús had said he would be here, but that was before #Asklepiongate. The description he gave her, dark hair and jeans, was proving inadequate, faced as she was with a wall of people all dark-haired and in jeans. The cards held by some of the crowd—men, shortish, stocky-ish, in scuffed, black leather jackets—bore names: Alonso, Gutiérrez, Rojas... Then, a card with no name, just two curved, vertical lines topped with curly green: a tree. She smiled, looked up into cloisonné blue eyes, and smiled more. She felt she had found home.

He broke free from the herd. The raw-necked, faded T-shirt might have borne a design once, the hole in the jeans looked genuine.

'Evangeline?'

'Jesús? I was beginning to think you weren't coming.'

He looked confused. 'Is good to meet you at last.'

His lips brushed against either side of her face, so gently, as to make her drowsy.

'For tonight, you stay with my friend and his girlfriend, Cristóbal and Catalina. You'll like her. OK, yes? Tomorrow we start—'

'But—'

'Give me your bag.' He unhooked the rucksack straps from her shoulders and, carrying the bag by its handle, led her out of the terminal.

A warm, evening breeze, laden with conifer and diesel, rippled her T-shirt. The sense of real air melted the tension in her back. Jesús guided her towards the multi-storey car park.

Jesús zig-zagged a ticket across the face of the pay machine and found the slot. Overhead lighting put him in stark relief. His skin was flawless. Evangeline guessed the stubble was a ploy to look less boyish. He brushed his curls from his eyes and bent at the knees to read the charge.

'Vale. Let's go.' He slung her rucksack over his shoulder and headed for the lift, trailed by Evangeline.

'Wait a minute. You haven't read your emails over the weekend, have you?'

'No. Qué talca?'

'Where do I start.' A lump caught in her throat. She allowed her eyes to follow the hazy outline of the Andes. 'Asklepion backed out.'

'¡Chucha!'

'It gets worse. Once they threw in the towel, everyone else

jumped ship.'

'But you are here?' Jesús said.

'I guess so.'

Jesús was quite for a moment. 'And me.' He rested a hand on her shoulder until she met his eyes.

'No, honestly, you don't have to…' She stopped talking for fear she really would cry.

'Better this way. We answer to no one.'

It was true, she had been apprehensive about Asklepion's interference. 'But don't you want to think it over?'

Jesús looked like he was doing a quick mental calculation. 'No.'

'So, you still want to come with me?'

'Why not?'

Why not, indeed.

⁂

The wooden table bore all the hallmarks—sickle-stains of wineglasses, scorch-marks, and dents and scuffs and pen-smears—of being the axis for all who passed through the house. Four faces reflected the candlelight from this table.

Evangeline found the table comforting. She'd often found that some objects resonated across time and place such that, in a strange environment, their likeness was a welcome friend, the anchor to her world. The table, then, was her axis.

Before dinner was served, before much wine was drunk, the introductions and polite questions—Did you have a good flight? Have you been to Chile before?—were in English. As the meal got going and the conversation ricocheted faster across the table, those who could, often lapsed into Spanish. She only managed to pick up the odd word or phrase. When Catalina, a pocket-sized pharmacologist with expressive hands, called the men to order and told them to speak English for the benefit of our guest, her sideways glance—claiming territory—left Evangeline feeling less, not more, included.

It wasn't the first time this evening Catalina had marked her place in the pack. Earlier, Jesús and Cristóbal had taught Evangeline the essentials of Chilean swearwords, cracking up as her English mouth was coloured by conchatumadre (literally: shell of your mother), ándate a la chucha (go fuck yourself) and ahuevonado (balls-for-brains). This last one translated to large eggs, its evolution making it Evangeline's favourite. In the process of bringing the meat to the table, Catalina seemed compelled to explain that no Chilean woman would use such language. She punctuated her statement by thudding the cast iron casserole in place on the table. The merry-making paused: all eyes fell on the chili con carne performing a Chilean-Mexican wave around the pot, the unctuous, smelter-red oil cresting to release spice-wood vapour.

Jesús guffawed and the conversation resumed.

And then, later, when Catalina observed of Evangeline's travel plans: you're very brave, what she meant was: what ahuevonado idea is this?

Cristóbal, a Led Zeppelin fan—not bulky exactly, but more than willing to take up a whole lotta space—took it upon himself to broaden Evangeline's knowledge of Chile.

'Eva, to understand how Chilenos think, first you must know our myths. And the myths from the Norte Grande—in the region of the Atacama Desert—are very different from those along the coast, or from the forests and mountains—the Araucanía, or the Zona Austral. The myths reflect the different environments in which our people live and their history.' He pushed his empty plate aside, a move taken as a signal by the others to clear their places also, forming an unstable tower of used crockery and cutlery.

'But let's start at the beginning: the legend of the Battle of the Pillan.

'The Pillan were good spirits who lived in Paradise. Their brave king, Antu, was as golden and fierce as the sun. Antu's queen was the beautiful Kueyen, she of the flowing midnight hair that glistened with all the stars in heaven. The Pillan defined the laws governing Man, written for all eternity in the Book of the Admapu, and all was well in the world of Man. The land was so rich and fertile, that golden maize stretched as far as the eye could see. Llamas produced wool so soft, it was said, that even the clouds used the wool to rest their weary heads during the heat of the day. Great, silvery shoals of fish would spring from the sea into the waiting nets of the fishermen, while the women gathered fruit in the abundant orchards.

'But then one day, a man refused to give thanks to the Pillan for his food. Antu, enraged, unleashed the Wekufe from their cave in the West. The earth trembled with fear at their approach and vomited a torrent of bright hot, sulphurous bile. Day turned to night, the rivers turned to salt, and winter's bitter claws strangled the maize in the field.

'The man, repenting his transgression, tried to run away. But no man can outrun the Wekufe, for they have no soul. His last cry, before they ripped open his belly, was: Kueyen, save my dear wife and innocent children.

'Kueyen was touched by his plea, for wouldn't she want Antu to think of her to his last? In tears, she went to her husband. Crushed to see his woman cry, Antu promised to do her bidding.

'In haste, Antu set off to the world of Man, his valiant generals beside him. They met the Wekufe on the mountain of Rucapillán. The clash could be heard all across the peaks, down in the valley and even as far as the sea. As the day wore on, the Wekufe were forced to retreat to Netherearth where, it is said, they live still. They venture out from time to time and, when they do, they bring destruction, disease and death.'

16

Cristóbal reached for the bottle on the table, drained it into his glass, rocked back on his chair and added it to existing empties on the counter.

'And now you, Eva,' Cristóbal said. 'Tell us your story. What are you doing here?'

Evangeline withdrew the journal from her bag. Cristóbal's flat-palmed drum-roll on the table prompted an accompanying rattle of the leaning tower of plates.

'This is the journal of Edwin Morgan, more widely known as Chile Morgan,' she said. 'It was written during his last exploration of Chile—a journey from which he never returned.'

Cristóbal pointed to the book. 'That there is the original?'

Jesús butted in, 'Si, si. Tell them how it came to you.'

His enthusiasm would win anyone over, Evangeline smiled. 'Well, I was in Kew's library. That's the Royal Botanic Gardens, Kew. In London.' People nodded as though they might have heard of it, but perhaps they just wanted her to get on with the story. 'Anyway, every now and then, the library sells off some of its collection, the ones by lesser-known authors. Kew staff have first dibs—'

'You work at Kew, then?' Catalina had heard of it.

'No.' Evangeline laughed that this might be a possibility. 'I was just lucky I happened to be in Kew for a lecture—'

Catalina was about to ask another question when Jesús jumped in, 'But tell them what happened.'

'So, I went to this book sale at Kew,' Evangeline said. 'And got into a bit of a fight.'

'What?' Cristóbal barked with laughter. It wasn't that funny, but the wine helped.

The look he exchanged with Jesús relaxed her. It felt like a seal of approval. Cristóbal said, 'Tell us more.'

'There were loads of books laid out on tables but tucked away beneath the tables was a whole stash more in crates. I went in. I wasn't the only one, either. Can you imagine a bloom of botanists in search of a bargain?'

'The books never stood a chance,' Jesús said.

'Nope. I dived into the depths. Grappling around, I felt a notebook.' Holding the journal between both hands, she remembered first feeling the heft of it, so full of character. 'Just as I got my hands on it, the book was wrenched away by the stink of a sour dairy with dry rot.'

'What was it?' Cristóbal said.

'A man with a comb-over,' she said, but saw the need for elaboration. 'You know, short-sleeve shirt alien to an iron, waistband at mid-chest?'

Nods of recognition around the table.

'What did you do?' Jesús said. Even Catalina looked like she was, at least, listening to the story.

'I grabbed the nearest book—a huge thing about halophytes in the Kalahari—and hurled it at Comb-over. You should have heard the crack. He was Comb-over no longer: the unwashed straggle unpeeled itself and was now bobbing about like a front row-theatregoer with haemorrhoids.' Playing to the crowd, she was louder, more animated.

Catalina held her hand to her throat.

'He dropped the book, I pushed off, threw my arm out, caught it, and touched down with a sideways roll—'

'Good save.' Cristóbal clapped.

'Yes.' Evangeline held up her hand. 'But the only thing is, as I rolled, my feet were sticking out from the tables like knives on chariot wheels. I took down quite a few more than Comb-over alone. By the time I finished, the room looked like a pitch-full of Italian footballers when things aren't going their way.'

'Very amusing, Evangeline.' Catalina didn't look amused. 'What does this have to do with your journal?'

'Chile Morgan's journal,' Evangeline said.

Catalina shrugged: semantics.

Jesús chipped in, 'You know there's a portrait of him in the University—in the main lecture theatre,' adding, 'Era pelirrojo.'

Catalina wrinkled her nose.

Turning to Evangeline, Jesús translated, 'He had red hair.'

Catalina gave a mischievous little smirk. Evangeline's high spirits of moments before, evaporated.

'So, Eva, you are taking my gancho, here,' Cristóbal clapped Jesús on the shoulders, 'to follow an old pelirrojo on the road of no return. One question: why?'

'There's a mythical tree that crops up in different cultures and religions. It goes by all sorts of names: World Tree, Tree of Life, Yggdrasil…' Jesús turned his chair towards her, Cristóbal nodded in encouragement, but Catalina raised an eyebrow. Evangeline persevered, 'It's thought by some that the World Tree is a collective memory held in the human unconscious going back to when we were apes in the trees.'

'Then you've got the right earrings for the job,' Cristóbal said.

Evangeline fingered her earring, feeling the design of Rewe, the World Tree.

Catalina, silent, looked as though she was weighing up the conversation in her head, her lips a doubtful compression.

'To answer your question,' Evangeline continued, 'if his journal is to be believed, Chile Morgan found the World Tree, but his discovery never came to light.'

'Tell them about your research,' Jesús prompted.

'Oh, yes, so, Morgan's description of the tree is identical to an unlabelled plant specimen I came across in his collection at Kew,' Evangeline said.

'And what did you discover about the plant specimen?' Jesús chipped in.

'And the plant specimen,' she nodded with a smile in his direction, 'appears to contain yavuacin, known for its regenerative properties, effective in repairing damaged tissue and organs of the body. This is the same compound as found in other plants of the Yavuaceae, but far more concentrated and in greater quantities.'

A shadow descended on Evangeline's mind, with the image of a hospital room, dark but for the blueish image on the ultrasound monitor.

'It's still early days, of course,' said Evangeline.

'But it looks promising,' said Jesús.

Catalina acknowledged, 'Pues, increasing lifespans have led to a prevalence of age-related diseases. Healthy ageing is a key priority at Asklepion.'

Jesús explained, 'Catalina works for Asklepion Pharma. Their South American headquarters is here in Santiago.'

'I didn't realise you worked for them, Catalina.' Evangeline filled her mouth with food.

'Yes, I understand you applied for one of our preliminary research grants. Funding is highly competitive. Only the very best proposals—by the most highly-qualified investigators—get funded.'

The mouthful stuck in Evangeline's throat.

The candles sputtered out.

Jesús jumped up and came back to the table clutching four tumblers, a shaker of ground cinnamon, a carton of milk and a bottle of Kappa pisco.

The glass jars which, until recently, emitted candlelight remained dead.

Jesús slapped his forehead, 'Ahuevonado!' and turned back to the kitchen cupboards.

'Bring some of that coffee over as well, while you're about it.' Cristóbal had assumed charge of mixing the cola de monos.

'I can see how Jesús will contribute to this "fieldtrip" of yours,' Catalina did not quite do the inverted-commas thing with her fingers, but it was there in her inflection. 'Not to mention the loan of his Department's Land Rover, but what do you bring to the party?'

'I'm sort of a plant person,' said Evangeline.

'A botanist?' Catalina said.

'Yes, well, no, not exactly. Not by profession.'

'This is your PhD project, then?' Catalina persisted.

'No, not that either. I'm a postgrad.'

'OK. So…you are—how do you say—an amateur?' Catalina held her eye.

Heat rose to Evangeline's face. The atmosphere felt hostile, but she soon realised the antagonism came from only one quarter. The men remained in the happier mood of earlier, apparently oblivious to any point scoring.

Jesús restored light to their world and joined the exchange. 'You should see all the data this girl got together. She's convinced me. Anyway, what else would I do with my summer vacation, apart from bumming meals and cola de monos off you two?' He raised his glass to the group, 'Al seco!'

Beneath the table, Jesús' free hand found Evangeline's knee and squeezed lightly.

3. Way, Haul Away

Morgan: Swansea, 25 October 1842

I arrived early, many hours before we were due to embark. As I unfolded from the Hansom, I clamped my chupalla[1] to my head and pulled tight the chinstrap. My trunk was set on the ground with me, but that was it; the echo of the horses' hoofs on cobbles receded. I was left to negotiate my belongings and myself to the next stage in my journey.

I expected no more and took account of my surroundings. The block of warehouses, their grey walls rising high over the street, held back the full force of the Westerlies. Even so, a moist chill stung my face and whipped tendrils of my hair into fiery eddies. The bracing tang of Swansea Bay masked an underlying trace of

---

1. This straw, broad-brimmed hat originates from the noble breed of Chilean horseman known as the *huaso*. Most interesting to me, and I hope to you also, reader, is that the word derives from *achupalla* the name given to a bromeliad (the Pineapple family) used for the manufacture of chupallas. And, as if that isn't enough to whet your appetite, the common Chilean interjection, *'por la chupalla'*, loosely translated, means 'what the—?'

feculence. If this were a summer's day, I might have been less inclined to breathe deeply. I drew around me my chamanto. In this, the Chileans have perfected the dual-purpose covering: the darker side is worn upwards during the day to reflect light, the lighter reverse is revealed at night. Its silk and alpaca wool make this my preferred outerwear for warmth, yet, should temperatures rise—an unlikely event in Welsh October—it may easily be cast over my shoulders for greater ventilation.

Pale against a drab sky, gulls yawped as they battled the elements. Earthbound, I was in a similar predicament. A huddle of men, like a colony of penguins, blocked my passage. They regarded me with curiosity. I'm familiar with such scrutiny and can hardly blame them, my travels among different cultures have left their mark. Not just in my choice of attire, but I believe I must look as foreign to them as they to me. With their downtrodden shoulders, hollow cheeks and vacant eyes, and their greasy, threadbare clothes, they were barely human. And yet, they were my fellow man.

They came here, every day. These dockers would work for ten pence per ton, but the foremen, ever watchful of profit and cost, take on the barest minimum. Some men have a score or more years' experience in all kinds of porterage. But experience can serve as handicap; an old busheller is rarely to be met with. Entombed in the hold from dawn to dusk, the dust settles on their lungs. Heavy labour induces the desire for hard drink. The bars here sap up any earnings before the men, empty-handed, make their way home to wives and ragged children. These were broken souls.

My trunk didn't require a whole colony for its transportation, but I could at least provide one of the men a small remuneration for services rendered.

One enterprising fellow, broad and with a low centre of gravity, stepped forward, 'Bore da, syr,' he touched the brim of his weather-worn Bowler. 'Where are you headed?'

'The Abraxas,' I handed him some coins.

'The Abraxas, is it? I've got you.' He pocketed the coins, swung my trunk onto his shoulders and made to head through the unemployed.

The invisible force of the jobless, which hitherto had bound the mass as one, gave way. This was no biblical parting of the waves. All the same, we were permitted to continue unhindered.

Dockside, the hulls of schooners, clippers and barques jostled in a restless line, their masts swaying in lively fashion. Men from all corners of the globe were present here. They wore pea jackets, short jackets or waistcoats; check shirts, linen shirts, Guernsey frocks or tunics; breeches, pantaloons, wide-legged shorts or slop hose; cocked hats, Monmouth caps, Mandarins or fezzes; sea boots, buckled shoes, sabot or, as on the day they entered this world, they went bare foot. There were sideburns, moustaches, pigtails and queues, and even one swarthy djinn without a hair on his head. Many an arm or hand displayed inked lettering and dates, or symbols of sea, patria and love. The sailor species has a certain swaggering wide gait and a singular vernacular that distinguishes him from genus Homo. *Homo marinus?*

Men strode along gangways, hauling loads on board or forming mountains of ore, grain and guano on the quay. The orogenic process was held in check by stevedores shouldering their load from quayside to warehouses. This ceaseless industry would continue throughout the day, driven by the bellowed oaths of the foremen.

I stopped in my tracks. In all the hurly-burly, I'd lost sight of my porter—and my trunk. The last I saw of him was when he deftly sidestepped two barrels careening side by side across his path. The barrels had been propelled by the mighty hands of the glabrous djinn. I think I must have been in awe of the djinn's inhuman strength. It was then, while I was distracted, that my porter was swallowed into the throng. I began to wonder whether I'd seen the last of my trunk. Stock still, I wasn't making myself popular with those around me, where continual motion was the order of the day. I spied a port in a storm. Head and shoulders above the crowd, returning from whence he came, the djinn cut a colourful figure. I hailed him and approached. It was a rare experience, indeed, to find myself wanting in size against another. Despite the chill, he was bathed in sweat; a white semi-circle of crust, like beach spume, glimmered around the pits of his red pea jacket. His shorts, loose at the knee, appeared to be made of discarded sail cloth.

'The porter you nearly knocked over, just then. Did you see which way he went?' I asked.

'Me no knock over no one. Look around you, man, dere many porter here.'

I surmised my opening gambit had not gone well, 'He was heading for the Abraxas.'

'So, de Abraxas you wanting, now?

'Can you point me in the right direction?'

He held his chin in his hand and frowned, 'Let me tink on it.'

I began to think I was wasting my time but, suddenly, he clapped me on the shoulders. He threw back his head and roared with laughter. A deep belly-laugh. The kind of laugh that could only come from a man on an even footing with the world.

'I just teasing wit you, man. I know Abraxas well. She in Pier Seven.'

I thanked him and set off again after my quarry.

The barque Abraxas was chartered by Antony Gibbs & Sons and was destined for Iquique, Peru. The Guano King—to wit, Gibbs minor of the aforementioned Sons—was somewhat of an admirer of mine. While in London, he had been kind enough to describe my *Travels in Patagonia*[2] as essential bedtime reading. Indeed, his cordiality did not stop there; it was he who underwrote my imminent expedition to Chile, by way of the Peruvian port. Whatever anyone else says of Mr Gibbs, I have found him to be true to his word and most efficient in his dealings. I suspect those that sneer at his success in business would have less issue in sanctioning a fortune made on guano, if that fortune filled their own coffers.

The truth of the matter was, the sales of my books, *On the Flora of the Andes, Evergreens of Chile and their Uses* and the popular *Travels,* brought in a less than exceptional income, at best. Lectures at the Royal Society may have raised my profile, but they did little to elevate my pecuniary stature. Then there are my teaching duties at Kew. I'm not immune, as anyone will surely testify, to the rapt attention of half a dozen students of the fairer sex as they are guided ever so gently to an appreciation of the perfect synergy between stamen and stigma and style. Be that as it may, these delights are as nothing to the discovery of a new plant in its natural habitat.

Now it may well be that Mr Wm Gibbs, E^sq., proud purveyor of guano, has endeavoured to increase his own social standing on the back of my celebrity—he has, after all, been described in crude circles as a parvenu. Nevertheless, I was forced to conclude the Learned Societies allow more credence to former glories[3] than tomorrow's prospects. Such resting on one's laurels, as the Learned Societies are prone to do, does not support the work, as I say, of tomorrow's prospects. I do not believe I'm immodest when I suggest that such a prospect is none other than your humble servant, Edwin 'Chile' Morgan. In short, therefore, if it were not

---

[2] Written after my last botanical exploration in 1838
[3] Indeed, they continue to favour the work of gout-ridden Banks, despite his extinction some time ago.

for Gibbs's interest, my latest venture would not be on the verge of setting sail.

In the course of my ruminations, I had counted off Piers Three, Four, Five and Six. I was now at the bow of a glorious vessel, a three-masted square-rigger. Her varnished body warmed the pallid sun's reflection as if the gleam arose within the woodgrain's depths. Her forepeak arched and extended from the body like a shapely arm, to hold the jibboom aloft. Like the best of women, she was broad in the beam, built for comfort not speed. I considered myself fortunate to be making her acquaintance on the outbound leg of her journey. Her cargo: textiles out, guano home. This goddess of the seas was Abraxas. She was to be my world for the next three months.

The ship was alive with activity as the modest crew, twenty-eight all told, made final preparations. A shantyman, with a clear strong voice, led the crew in a rousing call-and-response which espoused the allures of various nationalities of women. On the beat of the chant, hand passed over hand. On the off-beat, load ascended in rhythmic bursts.

'Way, haul away. We'll haul away, boys. We'll haul her on together.'

As I sang along under my breath, a hand tapped me on the shoulder. I swung around to identify my accoster. An adjustment to the lesser of my vertical line brought me face to grimy face with my porter. I was delighted to be reunited with him and, even more so, with my trunk. My faith in human nature restored, I sought out and introduced myself to the captain, a good-natured fellow by the name of Trask. By general standards, Trask was tall enough. His fair hair and blue eyes gave him a youthful appearance, though I guessed he was around thirty-five. I was relieved to learn Gibbs had sent word to expect me—it wouldn't have been the first time I'd been brought up short at the very threshold of my journey. Captain Trask confirmed we would set sail in two hours.

Trask addressed a presence over my shoulder, 'There you are Solomon. All the provisions aboard, I hope? This is Mr Edwin Morgan. Please see to it his trunk is stowed in his cabin.'

'Aye, sir. We acquainted, sir,' said my bass-voiced friend the djinn, otherwise known as Solomon.

'Very good, Solomon,' he turned back to me. 'Mr Morgan, is there anything you need for the moment? Perhaps Solomon here could fetch you a bite to eat?'

'I'm fine, thank you.'

'If you'll excuse me then, I have my duties to attend to. I look forward to welcoming you aboard shortly.'

The good Captain and Solomon boarded the barque together, the gangway bouncing violently under the magnificence of the djinn. For a while longer, I remained on the pier to enjoy the spectacle of the ship and her diligent crew.

At length, the last chest of cargo was hoisted aboard. A boy, no doubt the smallest of the crew, jumped upon the load. Up he went, high up among the rigging. He lifted his cap, filled his lungs and piped for all he was worth: three cheers for the captain, officers and crew. He was rewarded by a clang of bells from the neighbouring vessels.

The first mate, a Yorkshireman by the sound of things, signalled for me to embark. I took my cue and soon after joined the crew on board.

From the foredeck, Captain Trask addressed his first mate, 'Mr Bathgate, call all hands.'

Loud enough to raise the creatures from the deep, 'All hands on deck.'

'Prepare to set sail, Mr Bathgate.'

'Lay aloft and loose all sail, men.'

The crew went aloft and cast off the gaskets. A rousing shanty started up again.

'Sheet home lower topsails.'

In unison, the topsail sheets were hauled tight.

'Hoist up the topsails.'

The crew hauled the halyard, heaving yard and sail. The gallants and royals were set in similar fashion. Swiftly, cleanly, the crew set sail. Just as swiftly, the light—which, today, had never been assured—lost heart and turned to dusk.

Captain Trask took the wheel, 'Prepare to weigh anchor, Mr Bathgate.'

'Brace up fore and aft,' roared the first mate.

At their stations, a team of men took hold of the braces, and leant back with all their weight.

'Weigh anchor.'

A third detail, Solomon among their number, took to the capstan, three to each shaft. It hadn't occurred to me before, but the shanty required for heaving, such as against these capstan bars, was distinct from that for hauling. While I entertained this thought, Solomon's voice rang out good and true. The anchor chain soon rattled home and the Abraxas fell off. The order to set the courses was given.

We were on our way.

The land of song receded into gloom. The void weighed in upon me. Waves unseen clawed against the beams. Ageless Abraxas, you are beginning and end, life and death, creator and destroyer. Power above all, keep us safe on our voyage.

Not one to dwell long on intangibles, I left my station aft to stagger to the mizzenmast. Like Vice Admiral Nelson before me, I plotted my strategy, identified my target and aimed, setting my course for the main mast. I came a cropper amidships: a swell on the port beam caused me to lose my footing. I grasped for the main. Like a drunken man with his bottle, my arms wrapped round the mast. The forward momentum sent me spinning twice around my anchor before I ran aground. I hauled back to an even keel, found my bearing and continue onward in a crabwalk to foremast.

First mate Bathgate clapped my back as I took on board my reward, a tot of rum.

To the merriment of the crew, I was not yet in possession of my sea-legs. But have no fear. I was made of stern stuff. No green around the gills, here. No holing up in a cabin for me. The adventure was under way. Ahead: Chile. My aim, to discover new flora, new horizons. Whatever lay ahead, I was ready.

4. Dispatch of the Warriors

Buenos Aires

Victor didn't have to wait long for the phone to be answered by Tomoe's soft voice.

'I'm extending my collection,' Victor said.

'When might we expect delivery?' Tomoe said.

'Wheels down at eight-thirty.'

'I welcome its arrival.'

'Take the Hummer.'

'This is greatest honour.'

'And take Hippolyta with you,' he said, noting the pause on the other end of the line. He imagined Tomoe's carmine lips pressed together. Ordinarily, he would give her the responsibility alone, but this was too important a job.

'Please, your onna-bugeisha go alone,' she said.

'I said, take Hippolyta with you.'

'Please to excuse my insolence, Victor-san. What is the nature of package?'

'A strawberry blonde. She's my Lilith.'

'The tracker is on her?'

'Of course. The song of Bachuéte'e will sing loud and clear

with this one.'

'I look forward to it.'

'Here she is, I'll call you later,' he said watching the long, pale legs stride towards him. The legs walked with purpose, contrasting with the strawberry blonde head which turned in wonder at all she beheld. He waved his newspaper and her pond-green eyes looked primed for adventure. There was something almost reckless about that look. Good.

'Sayonara,' came the voice on the end of the line.

'Hasta luego,' he replied.

5. The Toll Before Temuco

Evangeline

Every time they went over a bump Evangeline's queasiness threatened to decorate the four-by-four. She wound down the window, but a copper brown dust settled on the dashboard and caught in her throat, forcing her to close the window again.

They joined Route Five an age ago when the concrete of Santiago levelled to fields and its rusty smog cleared to intense blue sky. Mountains either side of the valley bracketed the patchwork of fields. Evangeline had covered a huge distance airborne over the last few days, but now on the ground she felt her journey had started for real. Rewe was waiting.

Lost and waiting.

The whisper, or the thought of a whisper, was the same as before. Male or female? Female, most likely, yes, a woman's voice. She sensed it not just with her ears, but through her skin, her flesh, across the membranes of the vessels and, sap-like, flowing within her, connecting with her.

Beyond the confines of the car and the endless Route Five, a solitary estate car sped along a local branch of the road network, snarling up dirt. The reddish-brown cloud hung suspended, faded, disappeared. Before long, the estate, too, faded from sight. The minor road sheared off and was replaced by a broad, fluvial floodplain strewn with boulders and minerals wrenched from mountain peaks and abandoned by storm surges too intent on finding their way to the ocean. At this time of year, those same boulders baked white as bones. At this time of year, also, the river all but clogged up with red sediment, and faltered to complete the cycle. It occurred to her that the minor roads and the highway, the floodwater, river and ocean, the boulders and silt—all the elements of the landscape—connected as one system to which she, too, belonged.

Driving one hand on the wheel, elbow leaning on the door, Jesús fine-tuned the radio. He greeted the static-free reggaeton with a nod, which she took to mean that's more like it. Despite his outward calm, from the way he blithely swayed his shoulders she suspected that inside he was singing with gusto. As travelling companions go, he was proving to be one of the better ones: just going with the flow, no forced conversation or sing-alongs. That said, on a different day, with a clearer head, she'd quite fancy hearing him sing.

Was it a coincidence he knew someone from Asklepion? The pharma giant had been the only partner without an operative on the ground. Maybe they were expecting him to give a second opinion of the project's progress.

She glanced sideways at her driving buddy. What was going on behind that easy-going exterior?

Evangeline offered Jesús an Extra Strong Mint then took one herself, but wondered whether she ought to ration them, this being her one and only tube. The smell, reminiscent of Mum's handbag, brought to mind a scuffed knee and a meeting with the headmistress. Turning the mint over on her tongue, the chill-fire cleared her head.

'Jesús.'

Eyes still on the road ahead, he tilted his head towards her. 'Arbolito?'

Arbolito? Had he forgotten her name? 'You know what Catalina was saying last night?'

'What did Catalina say last night?' he said.

'About what you bring to this expedition.' Just saying the word *expedition* made her feel all H. Rider Haggard.

'Ye-es?'

'Why did you agree to come, when everyone else pulled out? We've never met before. I'm not a scientist. I'm a student. This is just the hare-brained scheme of someone who's, quite likely, bitten off more than she can chew. Why are you doing this?'

'This is why you've been so quiet today, Arbolito, yes?' His eyes now gentian blue, a rarity in the southern hemisphere species, observed Evangeline. She nodded. Hearing Arbolito a second time, she worked it out as Little Tree, and felt special. He continued, 'Remember your first email to me? Very serious with "Estimado señor". But below the formal was passion. Is like finding water in the desert.' He nodded and glanced across at her. 'True, with no Asklepion, is difficult. But your determination is why I am here, your faith in a thing that is not rational is what convinces me. Tambien, you think I let you find the World Tree without me?' He grinned, then his face became still. 'And now you're here.' He glanced across again. 'Is good.'

'Jesús.'

'Yes?'

'Can we stop for a coffee?'

'OK.'

'Like, right now.'

'Understood.'

≷

Taking the driver's seat, Evangeline built up speed to re-join the highway. A black Hummer loomed in the rear-view mirror.

'Do you get a lot of Hummers in Chile?' she asked.

'What?'

'There was one just like that, this morning.'

The Hummer drew alongside. Its tinted windows blanked Evangeline's inspection of the driver. Taking in the bull-bars and searchlights, she conjectured he—it had to be a he—would have a buzz-cut, thick neck and clunky gold in a rings–chains–teeth combo.

Jesús whistled low with approval. 'A Black Chrome! Only thirteen-hundred of these bad boys were built.'

Evangeline suspected Jesús had been watching too many re-runs of *Top Gear*.

'Our Defender has the more classic styling and delivers performance where it's needed.' She defended their Tonka toy in her best Jeremy Clarkson. All the same, she hadn't bargained for this kind of shenanigans when drawing up her Project World Tree risk register.

The Hummer accelerated and cut in front, forcing her to swerve from slip lane to highway. The passing near-miss hooted in middle-aged rage.

'Hey! What do you think you're doing, sunshine?' Evangeline flicked her lights in rapid succession at the Hummer's rear-end.

In tandem, Jesús gestured and yelled, '¡Conchatumadre!'

As though the Hummer had heard, it slowed to fifty. Evangeline was blocked in by heavy traffic and forced to toe the line. Cars behind sounded their horns and overtook when they could. Evangeline fixed her eyes forward but sensed irate drivers with things to say as cars passed.

The Hummer accelerated in a cloud of exhaust. Evangeline picked up speed, but the Hummer moved to the hard shoulder, slowed and drew level, its blank windows malevolent. It veered into the Defender. Metal crunched on metal.

'What the—?' She gripped the steering wheel.

'¡Ni cagando!' Jesús said.

Evangeline pressed the accelerator to the floor, sucked in her breath and slid the car through a gap into the next lane.

The Hummer followed. Evangeline returned to the inside lane. And back to the outside. Each time, the black bulk loomed in the rear-view. She wove in, out. The Hummer remained on their tail. Then closed in. Nudged the bumper. Receded. Only to hustle again. To shunt with more force. Clank. Rear bumper: first casualty.

Jesús shouted, '¡Puta!'

The surrounding traffic—a fume of non-signallers, lane-hogs and Volvo drivers—too hell-bent on individual missions to permit others to overtake. Jesús' arm reached across hers and blasted the horn. Cars retaliated likewise but soon pulled in: Evangeline meant business.

In its own way, the Hummer also proved adept at road clearance. In her mirror, the predator sliced between two cars. Their side panels buckled under the battering ram of bull bars. A Toyota in the wrong place at the wrong time was given short shrift. Shunted from behind, it spun across the highway and continued over the grass verge, hopping from side to side like it couldn't stand the heat. Its front-left hubcap flew off in a trajectory that took in the roofs of several cars before careening off into oncoming traffic. The Toyota finally ground to a halt amid a billow of dust.

'¡Huevón culiado!' said Jesús.

Ahead: a toll plaza, a traffic barrier, lane closures. Rear-view confirmed the Hummer closing in. Eyes forward on the road, Evangeline spotted the hi-vis jacket of a workman. She screamed. He froze. She swerved the car. Framed in rear-view the Hummer slammed into hi-vis. The force catapulted the man's body into the air. Hi-vis tangled in Hummer searchlights. Body draped windscreen.

Accelerator flat to floor, Evangeline aimed towards a clear toll lane. As the Land Rover smashed through the barrier, the bonnet sprang open and eclipsed her line of sight. She hit the brakes and the rear wheels burnt their mark on the tarmac. The bonnet clanked down. Disorientated, Evangeline took a moment to realise she was looking at the way they'd come.

The alternating toll booths and lanes formed a triptych of blinded predator and movement and destruction. A deafening crash. A plume of smoke signalled the end of the Hummer.

Evangeline and Jesús stared through the windscreen. The wipers had sprung to life of their own accord, sweeping arcs in the dust; the wipers' thunk-thunk out of beat with her heart. Her white-knuckled grip of the steering wheel was the only thing registering as real.

'OK,' breathed Jesús, one arm braced against the door, the other rubbing his temple.

Hesitantly, Evangeline turned her head to the voice that came at her as if through water.

His eyes questioned her. 'OK?'

Some way the other side of destruction, a police siren sounded.

She nodded, tight-lipped. 'Let's go.'

She put the car into first, turned the wheel and the toll booths glided out of vision. The open road lay ahead. Pulling away, she glanced in the rear-view. Flames engulfed the wrecked tollbooths and billowed black smoke into the sky. A slender figure, with flowing hip-length black hair, wielding a narrow, curved sword, limped through a toll lane and stared after them. A woman? The figure made off for the cover of trees at the roadside.

This was no random case of extreme road rage. Whatever just happened, they had been targeted. But, why?

Wood for the trees. Wood for a tree. If someone wanted to intimidate her into giving up her search for the World Tree, they had another thing coming. She was made of sterner stuff.

The memory of Morgan's words was like a motivating arm around the shoulder. For the moment, however, they needed a place to lay low for the night.

6. Hotel Paraíso Suite

Evangeline

The motel they'd checked into was cheap enough, clean enough. All wood-panelling with faded orange candlewick bedspreads, brown tartan carpet and a bulb missing in the bedside lamp. Only one lamp between the single beds: a sign in the bathroom made it clear the Hotel Paraíso Suite prided itself on its energy-saving policy. Evangeline rationalised the room-share as minimizing expenditure. Frankly, after a seven-hour drive and a highspeed chase by the Hummer from Hell, the room presented itself as a haven in a time-warp.

Any minute, she expected the police to be knocking on the door. Someone must have seen the car chase and reported it. The police could trace their car to Cristóbal and, from him, identify Evangeline and Jesús as drivers. Then it would be an all-too-simple matter of pinpointing their whereabouts through their mobile phones. They'd left the scene of an accident that she was sure was no accident at all. Were Chile's traffic laws the same as back home? Could she be deported? Her search for the World Tree over before it began.

Sounds from outside—the lid slamming on a dumpster, a car

decelerating—stopped her in her tracks. She needed to be doing something.

She checked her phone. A red dot signalled WhatsApp activity: five days of Mum.

Sat 13 Oct
Mum: Let me know you arrived safely. Mum xx
22:05

Sun 14 Oct
Mum: Did you manage to get some sleep on the plane? Love, Mum xx 10:50
Mum: Poldark back on tonight. Zowee!! All my love, Mum xxx 19:36
Mum: Don't worry. I'm buying the box set. Missing you, Mum xxx 19:38

Mon 15 Oct
Mum: Don't eat the shellfish. Just watching a programme. Raw sewage straight into the sea. Not nice. Take care. Mum xxx 16:17

Tue 16 Oct
Mum: At the hairdressers. They're having a revamp. Chaos! They've gone for the retro-futuristic look. It's not me. All my love, Mum xxx 10:51

Wed 17 Oct
Mum: Hope all's well, my lamb? All my love, Mum xxx 02:06

Evangeline tapped in her reply:

Hi Mum. Sorry not contacted sooner. All go here.
Met up with Jesús. You'd like him. Would love to
hear your voice.

She read through the message, deleted the last line, and sent:

Hi Mum. Sorry not contacted sooner. All go here.
Met up with Jesús. You'd like him. Love you, E
xoxoxoxox

No point worrying Mum.

The sound of the shower in use called her back to the moment. Jesús was in there. Silver rays gleamed around the ill-fitting door shielding the bathroom. Beyond the door, the gushing of water—which Evangeline knew, having had first use, to be just shy of blistering heat—suggested concealing swathes of steam. She imagined the door buckling under the pressure.

In need of keeping occupied, she took the opportunity to fine-tune the contents of her rucksack. Up to now, zipped pockets aside, she'd only skimmed the upper mantle of the sixty-litre capacity main compartment, unconvinced by the value of dual access (top and side), a feature highlighted with a bullet-point in the manufacturer's online description. So far, she hadn't been that impressed by the lightweight, comfortable suspension system (ENDURANCE-X®). The whole thing felt like a spirited but reluctant llama on her shoulders. There was something in there that got her in the back, just above and across from her kidneys, that was going to have to come out.

She delved in and pulled out a sarong and poncho. Next, was the billy can with ergonomic knife and spork. Then, Swiss-rolls of clothes selected for their suitability for layering—Mum championed the layer and, in this, despite herself, Evangeline was a chip off the block—along with an SLR camera and assorted lenses. Further down, the fleecy top-halves, kitten heels, walking boots and something else. Deep to the elbow in rucksack, her fingers scuttled around the object. First one way, then the other. Feeling but not recognising. Cool but not cold. Curvaceous yet, occasionally, angled and pointed. When stroked, it rang hollow. Her thumb sought out and found the cavity. With fingers working opposed to thumb, she established the density of the shell as being as uneven as an artisan Easter egg. Her fingers and thumb held fast and drew this bonus to the surface.

Angled from her grip was the naked body of a woman. To be more precise: an anthropomorphic earthenware jug, the size of an Oktoberfest stein. It had the texture and underlying colour of a speckled hen's egg. The earthenware was overlaid by a linear design marking out facial features, hair and sleeves of geometric tattoos. A patina of dust had gathered in contours. Most prominent, the gravity-defying, exaggerated breasts. Ripe. Succulent. Dark areolae surrounding erect nipples as though anointing devotees. The buttocks, enormously rounded, counterbalancing. The thighs, a highway to hidden, fecund pleasures, all-encompassing. Hands braced on thighs, stimulating. Generous lips parted, mouth anticipating. Proud.

Evangeline could see the problem straight away. Projecting from between shoulder blades – its angles and gnarls at odds with the voluptuous figure – returning to insert between the cleft of buttocks: the handle. Formed as the bough of a tree. As robust as the figurine appeared, Evangeline wondered how it had survived this far. She had a pretty good idea where it came from and who, unzipping the main compartment's secondary (side) access, stowed it among her scanties. Victor! What is it with men? This must be the most impractical present ever.

And yet … and yet. She couldn't bring herself to discard it in a waste bin of the Hotel Paraíso Suite. She imagined it, in years to come, a talking point while she hosted a dinner party in a gentrified corner of London. Her guests would be intellectual, arty types, amused and secretly impressed by her exploits, the women wanting to know more about Victor the Jaguar.

Wasn't she too old to be daydreaming about her future? That sleek network of life wasn't hers and never had been. Any step forward she'd made so far, she managed to balls-up to astronomic proportions.

Keep busy.

Before she changed her mind, she packed the figurine's cavity with socks, wrapped it in a fleece jacket and placed it back in the rucksack. The essentials layer next, then after drawing tight the toggled fastening cord, all that was left on the bed were the kitten heels.

The bathroom door opened, a rectangle of brightness flooded the economic mood lighting of the room, and Jesús emerged in clean shirt and jeans from clouds of steam.

'Ready?' he said.

'Always. I'm just going to change my shoes.' She stepped out of her flip-flops, grabbed her heels and hopped into them as they headed for the door.

7. Of Superstition, Sirens & Squalls

Morgan: the Atlantic Ocean, 18 December 1842

The fog enveloping the South Wales coastline cleared when we reached open water. Captain Trask set a course south by southwest to skirt the Azores before heading west towards the Americas.

Life on board the Abraxas soon fell into a routine. I believe it must have been Mister Gibbs's[4] influence that had secured me a most commodious cabin, well-stocked with books and furnished with a large bureau at which I could write and draw.

The djinn, Solomon, turned out to be ship's cook. I would be hard-pressed to find a more dexterous or, for that matter, a more creative chef on water or land. Out of a galley stocked with the usual ship's fare—salt beef and pork, cheese, flour and hardtack—in addition to the one dozen geese and two goats on board, the meals he conjured up defied supply and means of preservation in equal measure. I should know, I've had more than my fill of rancid

---

4. He of the Guano fame

fat, weevils and meat so grey as to have surely gained its sea-legs long before the ship set sail. Food prepared by Solomon embodied his warmth, his love of life and the very spirit of the man. In short, it was as though a corner of the Caribbean was presented on the plate each time dinner was served.

And not a man could mistake when the mighty Solomon filled the galley. For fill it, he did. Wherever I was, on deck taking some air, or in my cabin reading, I could hear Solomon whistling like a canary. From voyages past, I knew that mariners' lore held whistling to be a challenge to the wind itself. For this reason, whistling on board was considered bad luck. Intrigued to know why my shipmates accepted Solomon's warblings without fear of the wrath of Zephyr, I determined to raise the question over dinner.

That evening in the captain's cabin, Solomon presented the officers and me with a beef stew or, to put it his way, brown stew beef.

'Dis 'ere,' Solomon announced as he lifted the lid from the pot, 'Jamaica's finest.'

We smiled at the familiar endorsement—dinner wouldn't be dinner without it, then leant forward and breathed in the unfurling fronds of aromatic steam rising from the pot. Solomon waited, as we all did, until Captain Trask had tasted the first bite.

The Captain's freckled skin flushed and his eyes watered, but he nodded and managed a hoarse verdict, 'Piquant and flavoursome. There is certainly some heat in this.' He reached for his wine.

'Yes, sir. I use some of me 'abañero, an' a lickle bit of allspice. The thyme I picked before we left Swansea.'

'Well done, Solomon. Very resourceful. It's delicious.'

Solomon beamed and left us to enjoy the meal, whistling as he went. I waited until he was out of the cabin and we had all started on our stew.

'The whistling,' I said. 'Why is it, of all the crew, Solomon is the only one who can whistle without censorship?'

Mister Bathgate, the ship's first mate and resident Yorkshireman, put it thus, 'If t'cook's fleps're whistling, 'e no fugglin' us on us snap.'

Now, as much as Mister Bathgate can be depended upon to tell it as it is, it doesn't necessarily follow that someone from beyond the hallowed vales of Yorkshire can track his drift.

The good Captain explained, 'If the crew can hear the cook whistling, they're assured his mouth isn't employed in eating the provisions.'

Mystery solved, the conversation turned to our voyage. We'd been at sea for three weeks. To me, other than changes in the weather, each day was the same as the next. Yet, to the crew, the ocean had distinct regions—each with its own character and climate—in much the same way as a continent. First Mate Bathgate mentioned we had today crossed the thirty-fifth parallel north. By the way he nodded in my direction, I suspected an important detail had eluded me.

Captain Trask came to my rescue. 'Mister Morgan, the Abraxas is now sailing on the Sargasso Sea. It's the only sea in the world not bound by land.'

'If I'm not mistaken, the sea's name comes from the seaweed, *Sargassum*,' I said.

'That's true,' Captain Trask said and turned to his First Mate. 'You see botanists such as our Mister Morgan here, may be as well-travelled as ourselves.'

'Theer's tales o' ships gone missing,' the First Mate said. 'Just two- mebbe three-year ago, t'*Rosalie* vanished into thin air. When she reappeared, there were nowt aboard.'

'Well, that's as maybe,' Captain Trask said. 'But what we do know is that Colombus was the first to record the sea. Apparently, he took the mat of seaweed as a sign he was close to land. In fact,

47

he was still hundreds of miles away.'

Bathgate persisted in his role as harbinger of doom, 'Aye, when t'Spanish fetched up 'ere, t'wind failed and they were stranded for weeks int' doldrums. Threwt' 'orses o'aboard to save t'supping water.'

⁂

I awoke next morning, in Aurora's first light. Something was different. At first, I was unable to discern the cause of my unease. Not unease, exactly. In fact, quite the contrary. We were on an even keel. Unusually even.

I shaved without mishap. As ever with my toilet, I paid attention to my teeth – as should one and all. To my mind, there is nothing more abhorrent than a smile blighted by decay. If eyes are the window to the soul, I propose the mouth is the mirror on a man's health. Not quite on a par with Shakespeare,[5] I'll warrant, but the gist is there.

Cleansed to my satisfaction, I dressed and presented myself on deck. I found all was ship shape but the crew out of sorts. The sheets hung limp, the braces slack, the ocean a millpond. I thought back to Bathgate's warnings of yesterday evening: the doldrums! We had no equids, so I looked to the goats. For the moment, they were alive and well, one balanced on the capstan, the other chewing the end of the main brace.

'Eyup, what did I tell thee?' Mister Bathgate greeted me then presented his full and honest appraisal of the situation. "Appen us fast 'ere.'

The lack of forward motion weighed heavily on us all. As one day merged into another, Mister Bathgate was hard pressed to maintain morale. He set the men to carpentry, to oil the masts, repair the rigging, and sew the sheets. By evening, those of a

---

5. Or Cicero, for that matter, *ut imago est animi voltus sic indices oculi,* if we're talking eyes being the interpreter of the soul.

musical bent entertained us with accordion, fiddle, pipe and drum.

During this enforced period of torpor, I often felt the fetid atmosphere surrounding the Abraxas lacked the necessary oxygen to keep us mortals alive. It was also true that what little energy I possessed seemed insufficient to draw in the much needed lungfuls of that which enriches a man's blood, helps him to function, allows him to think. Even my clothes weighed me down. I succumbed to wearing a skilt,[6] less restricting than breeches, and adopted the sailor's practice of going without shoes. I also spent as much time as possible on deck. Occasionally, some exotic vegetation—a seed pod with a durable shell, for instance, or a tangle of *Sargassum*—would be borne to me on the currents. Then I'd lower a pocket of old sail tied to the end of a fishing rod— much in the style of a butterfly net—and, in this way, catch the floating treasure. I welcomed the opportunity to copy its likeness to the pages of my journal.

If all else failed, I would dangle a line over the gunwale. When I managed to catch anything of worth, I'd convey it, with all pomp and ceremony, to Solomon in his galley. On a voyage such as this, fresh fish, of any description, was more than manna in heaven. In his turn, Solomon would make much of bringing the dish to the table, where Captain Trask would commend both fisherman and chef—in addition to Our Lord Provider—for making the meal possible.

Late one afternoon, as the sunlight glimmered in a drowsy haze over the ocean, I was fishing off the port beam when I felt a tug

---

6. The skilt, a hybrid of the skirt and the kilt, I bought from the purser's slop chest at a price inflated by the economic principle of supply and demand in an imperfect market: *viz*. while demand for the item increased in line with the rise in temperature, supply of said item within a radius of three hundred miles plus was at a premium. The canny purser recognised at once his monopoly and duly hiked up the price.

on the line. I held fast. The line pulled again. I braced one leg against the gunwale and pulled back. I heard no splash from the end of the line but rather a murmur, a giggle? I was unsure whether to continue to haul or to slacken my line to investigate. A further—musical—sound and my mind was set. I leaned over the gunwale. Initially, the watery facsimile of my Titian head peered back at me atop a dilute Abraxas. But there, behind my reflection, was the face of another—and yet it was like no other.

In the water, that is, immersed below the surface, was what looked like a woman. Her skin was amber, her full lips the colour of a succulent plum. Her sea-green eyes held a stormy glint, but they were playful and, more importantly, directed at me. Without effort, or so it seemed, she maintained her position. The only movement was that of her long, blue-green hair which undulated with the wash of the ocean around her. Her neck was adorned with strings of pearls that hung between her small breasts.

I stared at her. Surely, this was a trick of the light, a mirage. Either that, or the heat had got to me.

I closed my eyes. When I reopened them, she was still there, a half-smile on her lips. And then. She winked.

I jumped away from the gunwale, but my curiosity pulled me back.

'Edwin Morgan at your service, madam.'

'Edwin Morgan. Come with me. Quench yourself in me water.'

My blood was up. I heard ringing in my ears. Dizzy, I wiped my brow. I wasted no more time but plunged into the cool waters below. As if from far away, a shout followed my descent. I thought no more of it. All that occupied my mind, if I thought at all, was to possess the tawny maiden.

My feet hit the water and the ocean closed over my head. Shafts of sunlight refracted through the submarine world and bounced off the bubbles which strove for the sky above. As I rose to the surface, a flash of silver caught my eye. I emerged and filled my lungs.

Laughing beside me was the beauty with viridian tresses.

'Me fiery-headed man.' She tousled my wet hair. 'Me wager you have fire in your bone to match the fire on your head.'

My aim in life is not to disappoint. I pulled her close and tasted her mouth. In turn, she wrapped her arms around my neck and pressed her body against mine. At her touch, I seemed to share in her buoyancy and felt no fear of drowning. Something smooth brushed against my thigh. Then coiled around my hips. Then writhed in pulsing, perpetual motion around my lower limbs. The water boiled around us, as when a shoal of fish is drawn into the net. A further coil landed around my chest. This time, not smooth but fibrous. It tightened. The stormy glint flared in her eyes. A tug on my ribs forced the air from my lungs and her arms from my neck. Against my will, I was hoisted clear of the water.

A scream pierced my ears. It continued, in one long, inexorable note. High but not dry, I dangled from a rope which swung against Abraxas's shapely beam. Below me, my paramour was in a fury, the writhing coil of her silvery tail visible in the now-turbulent water.

A strong arm took hold of me.

'Be gone, Erzulie,' a rich voice shouted to the fury below.

I was hauled aboard and immediately turned on my saviour.

'Solomon! What the hell are you playing at, man?'

The crew clustered around us. Mister Bathgate had me by my arms for I would surely have struck the djinn, giant as he was.

'You no wanna mess wit de watery Erzulie,' said Solomon bracing himself.

'You know her?' I asked.

'She La Sirène,' he said. 'She beautiful. But she sometimeish. One day calm. Nex' like tropical storm. Man follow her to her cave on sea-bed, he tink he wid her one year, but he dere sixty, seventy, eighty year or more.'

'Solomon, I owe you an apology, my friend. I hope I can repay you some day.'

By the exasperated look on Captain Trask's face, I felt he was unimpressed by my exploits. The crew, on the other hand, were most eager to hear as much detail as I could provide, this was a story they would tell until they were called to meet their maker. With skilt clinging to me like a scratchy limpet to a rock, I dripped on the deck, to create a puddle around my feet. A breeze dried my skin. The sheets, latterly so dejected, ruffled. Then they caught. Then they filled. We were on our way.

The sky, clear moments before, was now host to a gathering of dark clouds. Barbs of rain began to drill against sails and deck. The battering pulse descended before long into a continuous cacophony. Captain Trask, ever alert for the safety of his crew and ship, called for discipline.

'Secure all loose gear,' the Captain commanded.

Mister Bathgate took note and yelled, 'Heave to, boys.'

The crew jumped to order. Solomon told me to get to my cabin and stay out of the way. As I followed Solomon's advice, spray over the starboard bow drenched me once more.

'Strike the royals, Mister Bathgate,' Captain Trask ordered above the wind.

My last sight, before I ducked into my cabin, was of the ocean. In so short a time, the tranquil waters had become a grey and raging mass. Erzulie's reputation was just.

In the violent motion of the barque, it took me some time to change into dry clothes. With one foot in my hose and one foot out, I found myself buffeted between cabinet and bunk and back again. Books I'd left open on the desk, my writing materials, this journal, were cast around the cabin like flotsam. Over the course of the next few days, Solomon's culinary skills were wasted on me. I could barely hold down a ship's biscuit. I took to my bed and throughout it all the song of La Sirène wailed above wind and swell, to worm its way into my ear and coil around my intestines where its very pitch induced waves of nausea.

8. El Trauco

Evangeline

The man behind the bar lifted his chin as Evangeline and Jesús entered the stale-sour fug, the soles of their shoes scuffing on the bare concrete floor. The man pursed his lips in the direction of a table for two, quite probably the smallest available, in the rear corner. Other than themselves, the bar was empty. Ordinarily, Evangeline would have asked for a better table, but this was no ordinary day. To ask might incur animosity and she didn't have the energy for barkeeps with issues. So, when Jesús asked if she'd prefer to sit elsewhere, she shook her head. They sat where indicated and accustomed to the dim lighting—the gloom a decorator's ploy to recast the all-expense-spared tavern as atmospheric. They soon learned to keep their elbows off the table to avoid the clank of its uneven legs against the concrete.

Over the bar a relief carving of a hobgoblin stepping out in woodland, fronted a stemware rack. Suspended from the rack hung branded beer tulips, pokals, flutes, goblets and snifters. Some way below these glass stalactites, obtrusive yet deep within his lair, the barman faced Evangeline. His Neanderthal brow loomed over watchful eyes and a bulbous, hooked nose. He watched her now. As he held her gaze, his tongue extended from his mouth to lick the lower, more protuberant, of his astonishing red lips. The gloss of saliva gleamed in the neon of pink and blue lettering over the till: El Trauco. Evangeline was transfixed.

Jesús picked up a printed sheet from the table, flicked it over quickly, then asked the man for the menu.

The man nodded.

Jesús turned back to Evangeline and leaned over the table. 'Do you know what you want to drink?'

She leaned in and said in a low voice, 'A craft beer?'

'A craft beer.' He gave her suggestion the nod of approval. 'Why are we whispering?'

'I don't know,' she whispered.

The man shambled to their table, a forest green bartender apron covering his girth, and thrust two menus in front of them. Standing, he was the same height as they were sitting down.

Jesús asked, 'Qué cerveza artesanal tiene ustedes?'

'Humph!' The protuberant lip indicated a blackboard the width of one wall, chalked with Germanic script.

Jesús questioned the man and turned to Evangeline.

'There's a *Newen's Rewe Ale,* from Villarrica, which is brewed with the piñon, the fruit of the Araucaria,' he said. *'El Duende,* The Dwarf, a local quinoa beer which is a bit like a wheat beer; *Lupulus,* hoppy and strong—'

'I'll go for *El Duende.*'

The man turned to her with the suspicion of a smile.

Jesús ordered.

The man nodded, eyeing Evangeline's scooped neckline, then returned to the bar.

Evangeline brought her hair forward of her shoulders and crossed her arms, 'What is it with goblins and dwarfs in this place?'

'There's a story behind it.' Jesús' hand reached across the table.

'You OK here?'

'It's different.' She widened her eyes. 'So, what's the story?'

'The story. El Trauco is a dwarf of legend who lives in the woods. Always, he is dressed in green and a hat like…like Gandalf. Also, he has el hacha?' He mimed chopping.

'A hatchet?'

'A hatchet. His clothes are made from the quilineja vine. Now, El Trauco has no feet. Legs, yes. Feet, no. And he is ugly. Ugly. But all the women say, "Mijito rico!"'

'Delicious … honey?'

'What a hunk! He is ir-res-*ist*-ible. When El Trauco makes a move on a girl, he appears in her dreams and seduces her. After that, all he needs to do is to transform himself into the quilineja. Then, as the vine, he is carried into the house, waits for the night and seduces her again, but this time in his true form.'

Jesús' hand rested on the table. His long fingers were relaxed and slightly apart. If she were to extend her hand, her fingers would so easily slide in between, and interlock with his. Their eyes met.

Kerrang!

Jesús' eyes widened in alarm: pummelling heavy metal music had burst from matt black speakers. Post-shock, their laughter concealed emotions unspoken. Just as abruptly, Slipknot's volume muted to a lullaby. A chuckle came from behind the bar.

Their beers were delivered on a tray. The man placed cardboard beermats with deliberate care in front of them and transferred drink to table with an arc of his arm. After each glass was safely on its mat, his stubby fingers held the stem briefly, his nails long and yellowed. Up close, his mannish smell surged over Evangeline like a cloud of fungal spore.

The man nodded at the menu.

'You are ready to order, yes?' Jesús asked Evangeline.

'I think so. What are you having?'

'Chorrillana.'

'Chorrillana,' the man nodded, 'y para la gringa?'

'Ceviche de Corvina, por favor,' Evangeline declared, the words having leapt off the *Pescados y Mariscos* section of the menu.

As the man left them, Evangeline was almost surprised to see he did in fact possess feet, two of them, just like most people. The folklore of Chile was more convincing now that she had experience of the country. It made sense of the world surrounding the people who first told the stories. Evangeline had dismissed Morgan's tale of an encounter with a mermaid as pure fabrication, now she was not so sure.

She sipped her blonde beer and wondered how to recover the pre-Slipknot intrusion mood with Jesús. Why was their food taking so long?

'That business this afternoon with the Hummer,' she blurted.

'Uh-huh?'

She lowered her voice, 'Do you think we should go to the police?'

'And be held up for hours?' He shrugged it off. 'Is nothing. I send Cristóbal a text.'

She sat up. 'Do you mean you have sent him a text already, or you intend to send him one?'

'I do it when you was in the shower.'

'Why?'

'Is his car, the University's car. If the police want to speak to us, they trace the Discovery to the University. Cristóbal will take care of it.'

'I suppose.' That was one way of looking at it. 'But could you check with me before sending any more texts.'

'Bacán, tú mandas.' He raised his hands in mock surrender and looked away.

He was right. She was the boss. But the air had become a little frosty. Maybe Jesús was in league with Asklepion—a honey trap—using her to find Rewe. The pharma giant had already shown itself capable of dirty dealing. What about him?

Across the table from her, Jesús traced a tear of condensation on his glass with all the focused attention of a child watching the progress of a ladybird across his hand. Everything he did was so unaffected, so…guileless. Not a word she used habitually, but it fit him perfectly. His skin, the paler skin of his inner arm, mystic, immaculate, more him, somehow.

Jesús lifted the glass to his lips and caught her eye. His look quizzed her, then as though he found the answer he sought, his face broke into a smile. From his back-pocket, he pulled out a local map and spread it open on the table.

'You have the journal here, yes?' His voice had lost the edge from moments before.

'Never without it,' she said, returning his smile as she pulled the journal from her bag.

They leant over the table and attempted to interpret the landmarks Chile Morgan highlighted along his route. Not so easy, when the landmarks tended to be of the 'deformed tree at the pass' or 'rotten timber bridge' variety. If such features still existed, they hadn't made it onto the map. Yet, the descriptions were so rich in detail, just reading his words placed the two in the landscape. If the landmarks were there, they would find them. They were sure of it.

Evangeline read aloud from the journal:

> 'The Silver Rush has seen the area grow rapidly since I was here last. Indeed, I was hard pressed to recognize Iquique when I went ashore. But when a man journeys away from this barren landscape—hostile to all but the toughest of species—heading south to Chile—'

'Iquique belonged to Peru in Morgan's time,' said Jesús. Evangeline nodded and continued:

> 'The pace slows, and the region is less prone to influxes of Europeans—for the time being at least. Here, the people are of a darker hue, they have distinct customs, they speak their own language. Here, the climate is mild, the forests temperate, and the wildlife plentiful. It is here, in this land of crystalline lakes and lofty peaks, that I commenced my search for the rare, the exquisite, the outstanding. I arrived at a fishing village on Lake Mallalafquén, where I intended to spend two nights. As good a place as any, I thought, to re-stock my supplies and to acquire a guide.'

'Mallalafquén is the Lake Villarrica,' said Jesús, pointing to the map.

Evangeline inspected the section he identified, 'Chile then says that during his stay, he takes part in a Mapuche ceremony. After that, he doesn't make another entry in his journal for a week. But, when he does start to write again, he's talking about a tree he saw in a vision.'

'So, he took something interesting at this ceremony.'

'Looks like it. But, from then on, he seemed to have a very clear idea of the route to take.'

'Well, I'm sure the guide would have helped.'

'But that's the thing. After his soul is liberated—that's how he describes it—he says he didn't need a guide. He went off into the wild with just his mule for company.'

During their discussion, their meals arrived and, with plates on the edge of the map, they continued their research.

Evangeline became aware of a low rumble. Not constant, but steadily rising to a crescendo, tailing off, only to rise again moments later. She looked across the table: Jesús was scrutinizing the beer list on the blackboard. She looked under the table: Jesús' legs were absently knee-jigging. She looked beyond the table: a glimmer out of the shadows caught her eye. The dull glow, no more than the size of a peso, rose and expanded. She guessed it was moving towards her. She grasped Jesús' wrist.

'Arbolito?'

'Can you see something there?' she pointed into the gloom.

Jesús' hand gently enclosed her wrist as he turned in the direction she pointed. The low rumble escalated to a growl. The growl was accompanied by the jingle of metal and tapping as of fingernails on piano keys. From out of the shadows, a broad snout appeared above a drooling mouth. Then the huge head, with ears—surely in the wrong place—projecting almost at right-angles from the head. Its muscular shoulders, cloaked by a mane of black bristles, were higher than—and twice as broad as—the head. Steely claws protruded from paws, all sinew and bone. Bowlegs accommodated the girth of the chest which tapered to the waist. Beyond that, the powerful hindquarters with tail hanging between legs. Its skin, warty in places and with a glaucous sheen, exuded despondence.

The thought flitted through Evangeline's head that she ought to call the barman over to—well, to do something. On balance, however, she decided to take her chances with the hound.

Its claws clicked on concrete as it crossed the floor to Evangeline. For all its threatening presence, just above the ear and woven in its wiry hair it bore a scarlet faux flower. The hound sniffed the back of her hand tentatively, then stepped closer with a hopeful wag of its tail. She patted the hound's side, it pressed against her. Under her fingers the skin rucked up in large, velvety folds. The hound, its eyes on Evangeline, rested its chin on her lap and sighed.

Jesús pushed his plate of Chorrillana—a heap of fried potatoes, sausage, chicken, steak and three eggs—across the table for Evangeline to try. The move didn't go down well with the hound which expressed its disapproval with a low growl. Apparently, the hound favoured the female of the species who was quick to learn its sweet spots. A rub of the ear reduced his breathing to slow and deep. He remained at her side all evening.

Chorrillana was good! Evangeline might have regretted not ordering it, had not Jesús offered her more, and then insisted she have more still. Her own Ceviche de Corvina, made with the freshest fish, just wasn't doing it for her this evening.

As the evening wore on, their talk drifted to other things. There was nothing like sharing an extreme experience to bring two people closer.

Now and then, Jesús would lean across the table. He was emphatic with his words—his arms made full use of the space around him. But if he went within a certain radius of her, the hound growled. At one point, Jesús reached over to sweep a lock of hair off her face. The growl escalated with a display of teeth, after which Jesús, chastened, remained on his side of the table until they paid the bill.

As they rose to leave, she was surprised by how busy the bar had become. Sorry to leave the hound, she held each side of its head and planted a kiss on its forehead. It licked her hand and retreated into the shadows.

Evangeline and Jesús said good night to the man behind the bar. It took until they were out on the street for her brain to translate his reply:

'Sweet dreams.'

9. Catalina on the Prowl

The glass office-building door swung close as Catalina made her way to the cafe where she'd arranged to meet Cristóbal for lunch. They had lunch together in a different place each week. It was good to keep things fresh. When you've been together five years you've got to work at keeping your relationship alive. And how do you do that? Well, that's obvious. Numero Uno: have interests (plural) you're passionate about—he'll work harder to be one of those interests. Numero Dos: have a killer bod.

This was the one lunchtime in the week when Catalina didn't go to the gym. She used Asklepion's gym. Staff perk. In the gym, the equipment was always bang up to date. She worked at keeping her body toned. She was proud of the definition of her arms: deltoids, biceps and even radials were all well-defined. Her biceps moved up and down like little chinchillas under her skin. Not all sinew like Madonna. Catalina had natural thigh gap, of course, but it couldn't hurt to include exercises in her gym regime to maintain that perfection. The treadmill helped. As she jogged, she checked her reflection in the wall to wall mirror. The two orbs of her ass were firm as steel with just the right hint of womanly quiver. In the mirror, she clocked the appreciative glances of the gym rats as they walked past. To the furtive and the brazen alike, her neat little ass said: these puppies could whack you all the way to Wonderland. When she came across the same men in the labs or in meetings, she knew what they were thinking and she sure as hell knew how to make it work for her.

She caught sight of Cristóbal striding ahead with his usual walk that never looked hurried but covered some ground, even so. Her man certainly filled his jeans well. Not one of those guys with skinny butts and saggy, excess denim.

He'd already ordered the wine by the time she arrived. That was another thing she found sexy. He was someone people noticed and paid attention to. She'd never have the patience with someone who waiters looked through, or who other men talked over.

'Guess who I've just heard from.' Cristóbal leaned over and kissed her as she settled into her seat.

'Tell me,' she said.

'Jesús!' he said.

'Oh? Is he still with that what's-her-name?'

'Eva. Yes. Anyway, you'll never guess.'

'Probably not, but I'm sure you're going to tell me.'

'They've only gone and been involved in un ahuevónado car chase! Jesús is our very own Bullit.'

'What?!'

'Yeah! They're both OK, don't worry.'

'Oh, right, yeah, hope they're all right.' Catalina was amused Cristóbal assumed they shared the same thought processes and concerns. It would never occur to him that the gringa's welfare didn't come top of the list, when presented with a juicy titbit like this. 'But give me details. Where? When? What happened?'

'Somewhere on the Ruta Cinco just before Temuco. This after-*puta*-noon! He's only just texted me. He says a conchatumadre came out of nowhere and chased them all down the ruta de los cojónes.'

Alarm bells were beginning to ring. This sounded like a professional hit.

'Go on.'

'So, they get to the Temuco Tollbooth, they zip through by the seat of their jodido pants and maldito Hummer crashes into the puto barrier. BAM! The mother of all infernos. Entire section of the huevón road closed.'

'Did they see who was after them?'

'Don't think so.'

'So, the driver's dead?'

'Nope, he was seen running away.'

☙

Back at work, Catalina phoned the Head of Business Development, 'Ignacio, I need to see you this afternoon. ...Well, what time does your meeting finish? ...OK, I'll come to you at three.'

At five to three Ignacio de Soto was rounding up a progress meeting in his office. The pocket-sized powerhouse that was Catalina Torres swooped into his office and truncated the conversation with a glare at the person in the hot seat. The unfortunate individual scuttled out of the office and Catalina closed the door.

'It's about Rewe. We need to move quickly,' she said moving quickly to his desk.

Ignacio had the memory of a clam. With this in mind, Catalina judged she needed to start from the top to ensure he understood why action was needed and needed now. She filled Ignacio in on the details.

'As you know, material from the Rewe sample has been shown in the lab to stimulate damaged animal tissue to self-repair.'

'Catalina,' Ignacio said raising his hands as though to defend himself. 'You know we pulled out of that project.'

'What might be a groundbreaking drug is within our reach. The

Rewe expedition went ahead without us. I've just heard they're in possession of Chile Morgan's journal.'

'*The* Chile Morgan?' Ignacio leant forward.

'Yes, he's the one who discovered Rewe.'

Ignacio let out a whistle that sounded like a firework going up.

'The journal will lead us to Rewe, the World Tree.' Catalina didn't bother sitting down. She'd found that by placing her knuckles on the desk and leaning towards Ignacio, he shrank back into his chair and agreed to anything she suggested.

'I've been keeping an eye on the expedition's progress. Why? Because Asklepion needs this and because I care.' She allowed a moment for the idea of a caring, sharing Catalina to formulate between Ignacio's cauliflower ears—he only recently gave up rugby, but he'd already piled on the pounds.

'I've received information today that the amateur team in search of the tree is in trouble.' Catalina saw from Ignacio's expression that 'trouble' could mean a great many things, not necessarily related to Asklepion's business. 'This opportunity is about to be swept from under our noses by a competitor. We need to get in there and get that journal before someone else does. We can't afford to leave this project in the hands of amateurs any longer.' Her words were beginning to take effect.

'But, you know, since #Asklepiongate, we've had to follow the process by the letter,' said Ignacio.

He rolled his eyes and let out a stale, coffee-infused sigh. Since Asklepion's shares took a three-billion-dollar nosedive after the company's attempts at biopiracy in the Amazon, even the smallest expenditure had to be signed off at director level or above. Catalina watched him mentally wrestling with following due procedure versus getting the goal come what may.

'C'mon. A bit of good news such as finding the source of a game-changer might just make the Powers That Be relax the ban on business class travel,' she said.

Ignacio sat up. 'What do you need?'

'It won't cost much. Just one resource. Temuco. Tonight. In, get the journal, and out.'

Ignacio picked up the phone and hit a speed-dial number.

'Vargas? I've got a job for you. …Tonight. …Temuco, …hang on…' Ignacio's bulldog eyes enquired of Catalina.

'Hotel Paraíso Suite,' she supplied.

'Did you get that? OK. It's a journal. No, not a newspaper. A book. Like a diary.'

10. In absentia

Evangeline

Evangeline opened the motel room door, flicked the light switch and her heart stopped.

She had the terrifying sensation of reliving the moment when the black Hummer rammed into the tollbooth.

She was shunted forward when Jesús failed to brake in time. 'What's up?' he asked the back of her head.

She pushed the door open further.

'Puta.' His voice barely a whisper over her shoulder.

With effort, she turned her head to the room number on the door. Yes, this was their room. But the room that had been seventies kitsch only a couple of hours before, now looked like a disaster movie: mattresses and sheets torn from beds, cabinet drawers in splinters, two rucksacks caved like dehiscent fruit.

'Nononononononono…this can't be happening. Tell me I'm not being paranoid,' she said.

'If you mean it looks like the whole world is after you, then, no, you're not being paranoid,' he said. From out of the debris, he picked up a flip-flop and looked at it vaguely.

'First, the car chase, now this,' she said.

Jesús picked his way to the minibar.

She closed the door. 'What's going on?'

He stopped in his tracks. 'I'm getting us a Piscola.'

'Not you, you turnip.' Still incapable of coordinated movement she stood stock still amid the T-shirts, her halterneck dress, a knifed sleeping bag all haphazardly strewn across the floor. 'This isn't coincidence.'

'You leave anything valuable in here, no?' he asked.

She rifled through her handbag and checked off items, 'Morgan's Journal. Passport. Money. I always keep them with me.' She pressed her hand to her forehead. 'But my camera and stuff were here. You?'

'The same.'

'We'd better see what's missing,' she said. Action, she grasped at it, to hold at bay the thought that someone was trying to stop them from finding the World Tree.

Before their inventory, they cleared the floor by restoring mattresses to divans and returning sheets to mattresses. Then, they set about making two piles of their belongings. Evangeline gathered her things into categories: technology, toiletries, and so on, with sub-categories for clothing (organised from top to bottom and from outer- to inner-wear). For the second time that evening, she made Swiss-rolls of her clothes and formed a neat pile in front of her on the floor. Jesús was less methodical, his heap of belongings more haphazard, but the result was the same. Finishing before her, he resumed his mission to the minibar.

Jesús handed her a plastic beaker filled to the brim with what looked like Coke. Her hand shook as she lifted the beaker to her lips and sipped. She spluttered. It was more than Coke, much more. A snake of nausea shifted inside her but was quelled by a second glug. Drinks in hand, they sat on a bed and surveyed the piles before them. Nothing, not one thing, was missing. They clacked their plastic beakers together and took a slurp of Piscola.

Whoever was after them hadn't got the better of them, yet.

'Hang on. Nothing's missing.' She had a creeping sense of a critical detail being overlooked.

'This, we established.'

'But, why break in and take nothing?'

'Perhaps, el ladrón says there is nothing worth stealing here,' he said.

In silence, they raised their Piscolas to their lips and stared at their gear.

He picked up a voluptuous object the colour of a speckled hen's egg. 'What's this?'

'It was a present.' She reached for the object.

He dodged her grasp and scrutinized the totem. 'A present, eh?'

'I like it.' Her hand reached out again.

He held the totem high out of reach. 'I hope you do. You know how valuable this is, yes?'

'What d'you mean?'

'Arbolito, this representa Bachuéte'e, the earth goddess. Is maybe from the Late Horizon—'

'Qué?'

'Don't be cheeky. Is Andean Civilisation. The period from… la aparitión of the Incas to the arrival of los conquistadores.'

'But, what do you mean?'

'I don't know how you came by this, and I don't want to know. But this, Arbolito mía, is an original.'

'No, it's not.' She looked at the totem anew. 'Is it?'

'If we put its value to one side for a moment, you know that soon we walk eight to ten hours a day, in all types of conditions?'

Tears sprang to Evangeline's eyes. She picked at a thread of the candlewick bedspread. She would not cry. She hadn't shed a tear over the fall-out of #Asklepiongate, nor at the car chase, so she bloody well wasn't going to have any Niagara Falls over a totem she only discovered a few hours previously.

'I just say is too big to carry.'

She nodded. Suddenly, her head felt heavy.

He put a hand on her shoulder. 'I no say is not bacán. Maybe we—I don't know—put it in a safe place?'

She smoothed a non-existent crease from her dress, mentally ticking off things to avoid when travelling:

1. high speed car chases;
2. motel rooms prone to ransack;
3. being an unwitting mule of cultural artifacts for anyone called Victor.

'Jesús?'

'Arbolito?'

'Before anything else happens, let's go to bed.'

11. Of Dwarfs & Dreams

Evangeline

Wearing an outsized T-shirt from a sponsored 10k around
Richmond Park, and PINK® logo boyshorts (Heather
Anthracite/Neon Coral), an ensemble which said
casual loungewear for a sleepover with friends, Evangeline
climbed into one of the two queen size beds. Jesús, in black Calvin
Klein boxers, jumped into the other.

After mile upon mile of the Pan American Highway in
companionable silence, punctuated, it had to be said, by the odd
ordeal, their chatter now was within sight of filling the great
divide.

Eventually, Jesús yawned and said, 'Arbolito, you drive like
Ayrton Senna.' He slid down in the bed, pulling the candlewick
bedspread over his shoulder. 'You've been through a lot today;
you get some sleep.'

With that, he rolled onto his other side and, not long after, his
breathing became rhythmically heavy.

Evangeline lay awake for some time more. A dog howled in
the distance, as though on the scent of its quarry. The sound mixed
with the memory of the day's events.

She must have fallen asleep at some stage, because she found herself in a vivid and unsettling dream. She was cold and walking over claggy, uneven ground in dank woodland. Bare branches clutched at her coat.

Behind her, just a few steps behind, a dog panted. Although constant, it remained out of sight. She'd turn, only for the dog to fade into the gloom.

The shocking sulphuric yellow of aconites tricked the eye into believing they were closer than the watching, waiting trees whose ivy-veined trunks resembled flayed saints. Deeper in, shaggy moss smothered the woodland's fallen. The wind boomed through the tunnel of branches, filling her ears, whisking her hair, and casting ganglions of grey-green lichen to plague her path. Her foot caught on a concealed wiry sucker. She tripped, regained her balance, but her heart pounded long after the culprit was left behind. Her kitten heels stepped into black ooze, releasing the smell of slow decay, forming footprints which soon drowned in oily water.

Jackdaws gathered overhead, cawing above the wind. Evangeline focused on the dog's panting. While he was there, she would not be afraid.

And then,

The panting ceased. The birds fell silent. The air stilled.

A hand caught hold of her arm. She turned and Jesús was with her. Without a word, he stroked a strand of hair from her lip then placed his mouth on hers. The flesh of his lips, questioning, responded to hers. Slowly, he drew away. She savoured the way he looked at her, lingering over her eyes, her mouth, as if captivated. They kissed again, this time hungry, tasting, probing, wild as kindling. The feel of his body through clothes not enough. She pulled his shirt free of his jeans. Her hand swept up, following the soft midline of hair to his chest, his nipples grazing her palm. He was struggling with an obstinate belt buckle to get her out of her clothes. Impatient, she withdrew her hand from the soapy closeness beneath his shirt to pull open her belt. He slid her top up and over her head. A slink of her hips and her jeans fell to the floor. His fingers hooked under the elastic and guided her underwear down her thighs to leave her bare. She pressed against his body, him, Jesús, aching with the need to be closer. Her hand gripped his waistband and they stumbled backwards until bark, cork-like and pliant, imprinted her spine. He fumbled with his fly; the zip ripped open. She pushed his jeans over the curve of his rear. Her legs tensed. So tense she was on the balls of her feet. His hands cupped her buttocks, lifting her off the ground. She wrapped her legs around him, reached between them and guided him in.

A creeping vine spiralled around and between, binding lovers and Tree, lanceolate leaves licked and flickered succulent heat teasing evading catching igniting from core to skin, sap rising within Tree as gasps rose to mingle with canopy thrum, buds bursting, stamen pollinating sticky receptive style fleshily ripening, clusters of fruiting bodies erupt over the O horizon, the hyphae of milky mycelium massing deep deep deeper.

A howl echoed throughout the woods.

≋

Evangeline woke breathing heavily and heart thumping. Vine-like, the sheets wrapped around her and clung to the sweat of her body. Her leg had cramp. She pulled it from the tangle of sheets and flexed out to the edge of the bed. Her calf brushed over a rumple of base-sheet, then the satiny surface of exposed mattress and something that felt like a length of power cable, just as pliant but not as synthetically smooth. She bent sideways at the waist, felt for and found the thing under her leg. In her hand was a piece of vine with dark green lance-shaped leaves and pendants of starry white flowers: quilineja.

She turned her head on the pillow. In the half-light of dawn, Jesús was not so far away. She climbed out of her bed and slid into the warmth beside him. He woke, smiled, picked a leaf from her hair and pulled her close.

12. The Return of the Hound

Evangeline

Later than planned, Evangeline and Jesús carried their rucksacks down to the car park. The sight of Jesús' rear brought a smile to her face. His hand coasted on the wooden rail, as he jogged down the stairs and leaped from the bottom towards the parked car.

Whether by the prickling of the fresh air in her nose, or the lingering aftershocks of wild happenings, Evangeline felt invincible. As for the small matter of finding the World Tree, while it was never going be a walk in the park, they would get there, she was sure of it.

The Land Rover wriggled. She hadn't expected that. A dark bulk moved in the passenger seat. The window was opaque with smears of viscous froth, like bird spit, just a whole lot more of it, and condensation. Moving in, the condensation appeared in regular, two-patch, bursts.

She reached for Jesús' hand. Whoever it was on their tail since before Temuco wasn't going away. Yesterday's faceless thug-in-a-Hummer with a sideline in trashing motel rooms was relentless. Who was he? What did he want?

Her need to know the who and the what, forged her initial terror into a white-hot rage and a third question: How dare he?

Wanting answers, she bore down on the vehicle, now in hyper-animation, and wrenched open the door.

Two forepaws landed on her shoulders, a tail in full throttle.

'How did this get in here?' Jesús asked.

She didn't have an answer. 'Isn't he the best?'

Her pleasure mingled with relief, such that the mechanics of how the hound from last night happened to be in their vehicle were less significant—for the time-being at least.

'He's not coming with us!' Jesús said.

'Well…we should at least take him back to the bar.'

'Perfecto, we drop him off at *El Trauco* and say chavela.'

The hound continued to honour Evangeline with his full devotion.

'Who's a bea-u-tiful boy?' She rubbed the hound's head.

Squeezing into the passenger seat, she wrapped her arms around his bulk in an approximation of a seatbelt. Soon, his panting filled the car. His legs pressed alternately into her lap, often sliding in a skirmish of excitement, his brown eyes never leaving her face. She kissed his velvet forehead and drew his warm body closer.

Yesterday, when they arrived, she'd been so focused on finding a bolthole, she hadn't taken in the character of Temuco. In the new light of morning, Temuco was a peaceful town of tree-lined avenues. Ahead, a couple of traffic cones stood on the camber.

Jesús turned up the volume on a news report.

As the car drew closer to the traffic cones, a trio of workmen in blue overalls, fluorescent vests and hardhats, and knee-deep in what so recently had been canopy, wielded pole saws in the remaining branches of an acacia.

Jesús frowned, then returned the volume to low.

'What is it?' Evangeline's attention was only partly diverted from the line of trees, as she watched the rough amputations. Beyond, sunlight flooded the road. 'These men don't know what they're doing. They're mutilating the trees.'

'Shezmu, the oil company, wants to build a trans-Andean oil pipeline. Close to Villarrica.'

'What? What's going on? There won't be any trees left. Anywhere.'

'Pues, they're at the consultation stage. That will hold them up, at least.'

'We've got to crack on. If we each take another shift behind the wheel, we should finish the driving leg tonight. We can sleep in the car and start the hike first thing in the morning.'

'Bacán,' he said, and clicked the car sound system from radio to a playlist on his phone, already plugged into the audio port.

'Bacán,' she said.

The sign of a hobgoblin with *El Trauco* writ large in Germanic script, loomed into view. A fragment of her dream flashed through her mind.

'What vine does El Trauco turn himself into?'

'What, what?' Jesús pulled on the handbrake before turning to her nonplussed.

She nodded at the sign. 'What vine?'

His eyes crinkled. 'The quilineja.' He brushed her fringe from her eyes, just as he'd pulled a leaf from her hair earlier this morning. Her insides felt like they were being steeped in a balm. Then he said, 'Stop playing for time, the dog has to go.'

He got out of the car and hammered on the bar door before opening the passenger door.

'Come on, perrito,' Jesús said. 'Home.'

Evangeline looked at them both in turn. The hound's brown eyes appealed to her. She couldn't be sure, but Jesús' expression implied let's not make this harder than it need be.

She squeezed the hound tight, his stocky body leaning into her. 'Home. This is where you belong,' she said without conviction.

The hound whined.

'Go on, puppylicous. This is where you live.' She tipped her lap.

The hound slid from the car to saunter, à la John Wayne, into the opened door of *El Trauco*.

She couldn't see within, but sensed the dwarf was there, watching her.

Jesús looked like he was in the middle of explaining the situation through the doorway, when the door shut abruptly. He slammed the heel of his hand against the unyielding oak, and got back in the driver's seat muttering, '¡Huevon Cuilado!'

Before leaving town, they stopped off at a coffee bar Evangeline liked the look of: *El Café del Copihue.* In the half-hour since leaving the motel, the temperature on the tree-lined avenue had risen. All set with two coffees to go, they crossed the pavement to the Discovery.

She squealed, 'Florito!'

In the passenger seat once more, the hound was beside himself with joy at the sight of her. The vehicle lurched side-to-side on its axle, juggling chunks of foam around the interior.

'¡Ni cá!' Jesús said.

Her rational mind knew this was highly irregular. Hounds shouldn't keep cropping up out of nowhere. Then again, this was no regular hound.

'A dog would be good for security,' she said, thinking aloud.

'He's eating the car!' Jesús' arms were in the air.

'I'm not going back to that, that…'

'He's not ours.'

'I'm not convinced he belongs to *El Trauco,*' she said.

'We've got no dog food,' Jesús said.

'We'll get some.'

'He's got personal hygiene issues.'

'He just smells a bit doggy.'

'Florito? Seriously?'

Florito, who seemed unfazed by his new moniker, watched their exchange with an air of expectancy.

'Look, if we went back to *El Trauco* now,' she reasoned, 'it'd only waste time and would probably be more trouble. We're trying to find a tree here, but there's some madman on the loose hellbent on sabotage. Who knows when he's gonna strike next? I'd really feel much safer if we had Florito with us.'

Looking a little put out by her last comment, Jesús accepted defeat. 'Perfecto, but Florito travels in the back.'

Evangeline patted the hound. 'Sorted.'

13. Iquique

Morgan: Peru, 16 January 1843

We had first sight of land in the early morning. It was pre-dawn or, more precisely, given that we were still seaborne, nautical twilight. As Mister Bathgate had explained it to me, nautical twilight is the moment when the sailor can first distinguish between the horizon and the sea. To my mind, it was still night: I needed the light of the lamp I carried to find my way across the deck. But to be more precise still, the four bells of the morning watch were sounded as I leaned against the gunwale and looked across the sea.

Solomon, just relieved at the watch, came to join me to enjoy the spectacle which unfolded before us. As if the sounding of the bells itself was the cause, and not the revolution of the Earth around the Sun, the centre of our field of vision became washed with violet, gradually seeping upwards in the residual night sky. The lower half of the picture was sharply defined. In contrast with the unbending line which greeted us every morning for the preceding twelve weeks, this time when the horizon separated out from the sky, it peaked and curved. Like a giant wave bearing down upon us and yet it had none of the motion of the sea. No, it didn't move at all, but was solid and grounded.

As we drew closer, a hazy layer of vermilion underscored the violet, and the area below the horizon began to separate out between hills, a town and a port, and the gentle waters on which the light glanced. Perched on the crest of the ridge, and looking over the town and its inhabitants below, a solitary cross stood in silhouette. The first glimmers of the sun rose behind that cross. With the exception of the cross, a feature often seen on the coast of South America, and—it has to be said—the sun, the ridge reminded me of home, of Swansea.

By the time the chromatic drama of the dawn muted to an unwavering blue over a sea of Nile-green, the rising sun had ripened the bald flanks of the hills surrounding the town to *terra rosa,* a colour of earth rarely found in the British Isles. The town itself looked to be just waking up. People, at this distance specks more ant than human, moved about on the wharf.

It was midday by the time we dropped anchor offshore and I was able to plant my feet on dry land. Not just dry but dusty and sweltering: the hilly stockade stewed the town it contained. I had arrived in Iquique.

The crew's work was not complete until they'd unloaded the barque. I, on the other hand, was at liberty to explore. I entrusted my trunk containing my belongings and equipment—including a telescope, a compass, a rifle, two pistols and thirty quires of paper—to a porter who put it in store. Then, I made my way through the throngs of stevedores, all stripped to the waist, their skin glazed with a grimy sheen of sweat. The town had expanded since I was here last. Growth had been in a ramshackle, ham–fisted, hustling kind of way. The aimless streets twisted this way and that with little discernible purpose other than to shelter and serve. It was possible, in places, to stretch out one's arms and touch the buildings either side. I say buildings, but they were no more than adobe shacks.

I ventured into the marketplace, a little wary of whom I might encounter. On my last visit, I'd had a misunderstanding with an English trader who lived here. It appears he thought I was romantically inclined towards his daughter. A silly thing, really, I'd merely wished her a good morning as I would to anyone, but I barely escaped with my dignity—and my physical being—intact.

Somehow, I found myself in the butchers' quarter. In the airless alleyways, the stench was cloying. Carcasses hung from hooks, while jointed limbs and viscera lay on slabs, and blood dried in the dust saturated with the blood from yesterday and the day before and the day before that. Butchers dripped sweat on the meat as they carved—their knives clotted with blood and sinew and fibres—and shouted out their wares. Flies settled on the flesh for sale and oviposited, rubbing their fecund abdomens into the meat which would feed the white larvae as they emerged from their eggs in continuation of the dypterid's lifecycle.

Flies zipped around my head, settled on my shirt, found their way into my mouth. Surely, this was Hades here on Earth. I pushed through the women crowding the street, all there to feed their families on the cheapest cut of meat they could bargain, and held my breath until I reached the end of the road.

Putting some distance between me and the meat vendors, I found myself in a street which led directly from the port, and which housed a number of hostelries. I was in dire need of a restorative libation.

That first draught. Oh! Nectar. My glass emptied, I called for another. The proprietress was a homely woman by the name of Lourdes, with a lined face and two plaits down her back. She used a gourd to ladle the murky orange brew from an earthenware vat into my glass then returned to her assiduous production of this local beer called chicha. She made it in the traditional way. Every so often, she fed kindling into a clay oven, a low-level affair which had darkened the nearby wall with soot. A pot of water simmered on top of the oven. Then, as she sat on a small three-legged stool beside the oven, she chewed the main ingredient, germinated corn, to a paste. When sufficiently saturated in saliva, she'd spit the bolus into her cupped hand and drop it into a pail at her feet. To this, she added the boiled water, then filtered the mixture through hay. Each new batch, Lourdes informed me, would be ready in two days. Given her industry, I little wondered at her want of teeth.

The room, an oven itself, smelled of sweet, warm hay. I'd taken a seat on a bench near the opening. The odd, droning fly became less of a nuisance the more of the brew I drank. No, I don't believe the chicha acted as a fly-repellent, although I could be wrong. Rather, the fermented nature of the beverage made me more inclined to look kindly on such small concerns.

Two old men, regulars I'd wager, had nodded to me when I'd dipped through the entrance but remained mutely watchful since. I fancy Lourdes may have been more forthcoming with conversation, if these two hadn't exchanged a glance when she greeted me.

Now on my third glass of chicha, and with no one willing to talk to me, I became philosophical. When I was a greenhorn, I might have been put out by this silent, judging, company. But I can do no more than be myself. People do judge, it is only human nature. But to bend over backwards to please others will only lead to a broken spine.

And so, with this in mind, when another customer ducked through the entrance, I made way on my bench for him to join me and bought him a drink. I shall be eternally grateful I did. The man, dressed in not much more than rags and with a bandage over his left eye, gave his name as Silva and asked me what brought me to Iquique.

'I'm a botanist,' I replied. 'I plan to travel to the Andes in search of the rare and the beautiful. Plants which would grow in the English climate.'

His one eye scrutinised me, taking in the hair on my head, my physog, and back to my thatch.

In a low voice he said, 'Go south of Concepción. There is where you must start. There is something there. Something hidden, its meaning lost in time. A mighty tree. Its branches reach to heaven, its roots delve to the place we all find, eventually. The tree, the sovereign of all trees, the being to which we, and all the creatures who walk and plants that take root—all of us on Earth—are connected with the spirits in the sky and those who dwell in the realm below. We are all part of the one. The one is the World Tree. It is Rewe.'

'But this is pure myth, surely?' I had to ask, he was so sure of what he said, and yet it was fantastical.

'The wingkas[7] say so. But wingkas know nothing.'

I took no offence—why would I?—at the term 'wingka'. 'Why are you telling me this?'

'Legend has it that Rewe will be found by one with red hair. Rewe, the World Tree, is waiting for you. Go!'

'But how do I find this tree?'

'To reach the tree, you must pass through the mountains of fire and ice. It is beyond civilisation. Find the place above the clouds. Go, Rewe waits for you. Go!'

We were interrupted by a hullabaloo coming from outside. I jumped to my feet and ran through the opening to investigate the commotion. Seeing that it was nothing more than a mule very sensibly refusing to go to the butchers' quarter, I turned back to the shack. But Silva had gone. I asked the two men if they saw which way he went, they exchanged a look and said nothing.

The response from Lourdes concerned me more. 'What man, Señor? There's only been the three of you in here all afternoon.'

---

[7] Wingka: a derogatory term, literally 'thief' in Mapudungan, used to refer to non-Mapuche people, their habits and customs.

'The man who looked no more than a beggar. He had an eye-patch,' I said, miming a patch across my eye.

Lourdes shook her head, looking affronted that I should suggest a beggar had been permitted anywhere near such a respectable establishment as her own.

'He was right there.' I pointed to the bench.

Lourdes shook her head more emphatically and looked at me as though I'd taken leave of my senses. I must admit, I was beginning to wonder the same.

I staggered out into the street not sure what to make of events. Had I drunk too much of the local brew? Had I fallen asleep and dreamt some fantastical delusion? Maybe, the heat had got to me. I was forced to put the matter out of my head because, right then, the stubborn mule kicked over a basket stack of poultry and a waggon of vegetables, all the while braying to high heaven, and sank his teeth into my elbow. The pain brought me back to the moment with a jolt.

To give the beast his due, the man on the other end of his tether was a brute. A beast can only behave in the way nature intended. Mules are stubborn. That is their nature. But their stubbornness is borne of intelligence and a sense of self-preservation. It won't do, therefore, when leading him to his death, to beat the mule with a stick until its flank bleeds. Surmising the elbow incident was a plea for help, I wrenched the stick from the ignominious fellow and gave him a dose of his own medicine. Thrash!

By this time, we had quite an audience gathered around us. A fine distraction from the day's work. The man, a weasely, shifty-eyed character in ill-fitting clothes, babbled at me I don't know what. I stood my ground and raised my fists. The mule chose his corner and nudged me forward with his muzzle in the small of my back. The man threw a basket of fowl my way. I fended it off with a jab of the fist. The basket shattered, releasing the terrified birds in a flurry of beaks and squawks. With feathers snowing down upon us, the man went for his potatoes. As he bent forward, I grabbed him by the nape of his greasy shirt, pulled him eye-to-eye, then punched him to the floor with a body blow.

'Morgan, what you at, man?' The rich baritone of my shipmate, Solomon, rang from the crowd.

Solomon joined me in the ring. Two—and a mule—against one. By this time, the crowd wanted a piece of the action and lobbed the upturned vegetables—that is, those vegetables they hadn't already secreted away in pockets and the like—at the man. The mule-beating brute looked like he knew he was beat but wouldn't give up. I had no intention of prolonging the skirmish, but I couldn't in all conscience return the mule to his owner. I reached for my purse and gave the man some coins.

At the sight of the money, he was all toothless smiles, as though the altercation had never happened. He even offered to buy us a drink on the back of the deal. We declined; I didn't want to spend any more time in his company than necessary. He didn't persist with his offer, however, for at that moment, his attention was diverted by the indignant cackle of one of his chickens as it was grasped by the neck by an opportunist of a young urchin. We left him about his business.

'Solomon,' I said, clapping my arm around my friend's shoulders, 'I've been reacquainting myself with the marvels of Iquique.'

'C'mon, man. Stop wasting time on fightin'. We be at sea so long. We got better ting to do.'

We were deciding which direction offered the most entertainment when the mule, who had been tidying up a few discarded carrots, nudged me in the back, once more.

I turned to him, 'But what to do about you?'

Agitated no longer, the mule batted his long lashes. I sensed he had chosen me for a companion. If I was to go through the mountains of fire and ice, to travel beyond civilisation, to find the place above the clouds and, thence, the World Tree, I would need just such a plucky companion.

'From this day forward, I will call you Paco. Will you join me in my quest?'

Paco raised his head and whinnied.

With that, Solomon and I sauntered down the street with Paco between us, looking for adventure, however it might meet us.

14. The Bridge

Evangeline

Broadleaves and conifers overhung sections of the unmarked road, the mosaic of leaves filtered the light and soothed Evangeline's eyes. Beneath the canopy, the lush ferny understorey was restful and cool. At times, the trees pulled back from the road to give way to grass verges, ankle-deep or more, yielding to the breeze to shine in ripples, springing back, green, fresh. Overhead, backlit white clouds softened the ultra-blue sky. It was almost English. It could have been a late spring day; a day when rosebuds hint at the summer to come.

Almost, but not quite. This was grander, fiercer.

Most often, the road was only slightly more than single track. Its surface, all potholes, cracks and dust, gave the Discovery's suspension a thorough workout. She reminded herself that when Chile Morgan made this trip, his only transport was a mule.

Driving beside a creek, a view opened of a mountain range of snowy peaks and forested ridges following one after the other, seemingly to the end of the world. The Mocha-Villarrica Fault Zone, their destination.

Somewhere, among those many thousands of trees, was the

one tree. And all they had to go on was Morgan's journal. The unlikelihood of achieving the task took her breath away. She imagined him, one man, a mule and limited resources trekking through the ranges. The hardships he had overcome were the Victorian equivalent of funding being withdrawn, and an unscrupulous competitor. Morgan had written the journal so that others might find the tree. She owed it to him to complete the expedition.

The road followed the creek around a bend.

'Stop the car!' she yelled.

Florito barked.

Jesús slammed on the brakes. 'What?'

Evangeline wound down her window. 'Look!'

Half the mountains were green and as they should be. But the forest stopped abruptly in a jagged vertical line. Across the line, a brown scar puckered and gaped. Rich, living green one side, stumps and clay the other.

They climbed from the car and surveyed the view beyond the creek.

'The pipeline is accelerated,' he said.

'What? What happened to exploration and consultation?' she said.

'Looks like talk over.'

'What about Rewe! Can't we get a Preservation Order or something, anything, whatever you do in Chile?'

Jesús took his phone from his pocket, 'I see if Cristóbal can help, yes? Maybe he talk Catalina into pulling the strings at Asklepion.'

Not keen on the prospect of involving Catalina, Evangeline paced about beside him and listened in on the conversation. 'Tell him, these thugs don't know what they're doing.'

Jesús nodded in acknowledgement.

'¡Pucha!' Jesús spoke to his phone in Chilean, 'When will she be back?'

Evangeline stopped pacing.

'Is there anything you can do in the meantime?' Jesús asked Cristóbal. 'Uh-huh … uh-huh … uh-huh.'

She got the impression Cristóbal was in his office, googling their options. She recommenced her pacing.

'Tell him, it's really important medically, no, commercially. Tell him, they're murdering wildlife,' she added. 'And heritage. This is the World's Heritage they're hacking down.'

Jesús said into the receiver, 'Did you get that?'

'And lungs. This is Earth's Lungs they're throttling. Don't they realise that?' she said.

He nodded again.

'They could hack Rewe down without knowing.' She paced some more. 'It might have been destroyed already!'

Evangeline clutched Jesús' hand holding the phone to his ear. 'Cristóbal, please help us!'

Jesús put his arm around her.

'¡Bacán! Give us a call when you've got some news. Will do. Chavela.' He pocketed the phone.

'What did he say?' she pressed him.

'Catalina's away on business for a few days. But Cristóbal thinks he might be able to get the University to do something. Put a temporary hold on activity on scientific grounds.'

Evangeline squeezed Jesús tight.

'And Cristóbal sends his love.' Jesús kissed her forehead.

'If there's even the remotest chance Rewe still exists,' she said. 'We've got to try.'

'We will.'

'What are we waiting for?' She held her hand out for the car keys.

She rammed the key in the ignition, shifted the gearstick and pressed her foot on the accelerator. The vehicle kicked up a plume of grit and dust, and they were on their way again. Each time she glanced across the creek, she was shocked by the extent and brutality of the scarred landscape. Would they get there in time? Were they already too late, Chile Morgan's discovery lost to humankind, for ever?

Some way ahead, a wooden truss bridge crossed the creek. At Jesús' direction, she steered the car through the bleached wood arch, slowing to a crawl, and minding the wing mirrors as they cleared the structure, just. The car passed under the shadow of the arch. The tyres rumbled on timber, then they were in sunlight once more. Evangeline gripped the steering wheel as the bridge swayed under their weight.

'I'm not sure about this,' she said.

'Is been here for years. Many, many traffic cross safe.' Jesús' voice remained as calm as ever, but Evangeline couldn't resist looking through the creaking cross-slats, to the giddy, foaming waters surging around the boulders below.

She inched the car forward. Stones, cast-offs from the tyre-treads of all those vehicles to have gone before, bounced on the timbers as on a trampoline. One, seemingly enjoying its moment of vitality, picked up momentum and leapt overboard. She watched it plash—the sound only imagined through the windscreen—and disappear in the engulfing white water.

Movement on the opposite side of the gorge returned her attention to bridge level. A figure in black stepped out. Small, compact, the figure wore a military cap, shading the eyes, and a scarf across the mouth. The figure faced them on the bridge, standing legs apart, knees loose. An arm raised and pointed a gun.

The dawning horror of what was happening was confirmed when Jesús yelled, 'She's got a gun!'

Trapped on the bridge, they were sitting ducks.

Three deafening bangs—Evangeline noted none hit the car—followed by a crack, followed by a snap.

Like falling timber, it began slowly, almost as though it wouldn't happen at all, but once started, it could only have one end. The bridge joists gave way. This couldn't be happening. What was happening? Heart and car lurched together. With a cannonade of metal and wood, they plunged into the surging waters below. Icy, numbing water gushed around. All breath jolted from her as they hit the riverbed. The rapids dislodged the car from its landing site, tail first. They surged forward. She felt blinding pain as her nose smashed against the steering wheel, the blood in the back of her throat tasting of rusty fenders. Her head hit the headrest as they were thrown back, the force of water having lifted the front tyres and propelled the car through the torrent. Hands sticky with blood, she tried steering, but the wheels failed to gain traction in the rapids.

Ahead, the river ended abruptly at the sky. Her brain took moments to process what this signified. By the time she understood the danger, it was too late for any action other than to brace for impact.

White fear gripped her as the car heaved and dipped over the fall.

Sounds came to her of water crashing, of Florito barking, of her screams coming at a distance, not belonging to her. Her breath punched out as Jesús' arm swung across her chest like a barrier on a fairground ride. Then the foaming water below came up to meet them, smashed into the hood and gushed through the open window. Florito, now in front with head in footwell and hindquarters splayed against windscreen, wriggled upright and forced his way through the open window. Her seatbelt was jammed. Jesús tugged at it. Something was wrong. He pulled at the cross strap for more give. It did the trick: the lock released. He pushed her through the same way Florito had taken. Outside the car, the water stung, its cold seeping through her flesh. She fought to keep her head above the surface, but the current forced her under. One moment above and the next below, she couldn't orientate herself. She would catch hold of a rock, a branch, only to lose her grip and be swept away again. A struggle for breath, then her mouth filled with water. The muddy taste. The mineral smell. The water so cold. Her feet, hands, head: numb.

Something punched the small of her back. Forcing her deeper below water, expelling her last breath.

I don't want to die like this. Oh, dear God! Please, I want to live. Just let me breathe. Let me live.

The freezing water numbed her body and mind. It would be so easy to let go.

Then, she felt, what? In the small of her back, a nip? As it gained purchase, it hauled her free of the water. It dragged her, coughing and spluttering, onto the bank. It dragged her back to life.

She drew breath.

Warm licks on her face. She opened her eyes. Inches from her nose was Florito's muzzle. He gave her another lick. Just for good measure.

The warmth of his body and his devotion seeped through her skin, melted angst and wrapped its way around her heart. She sat up and looked around. Apart from Florito, she was alone.

'Jesús?'

No reply. Helpless, she watched a flotilla of their supplies, clothing and equipment tumble downstream. Reaching from the bank, her hand grasped futilely on air. The only thing she managed to rescue was the earth goddess totem.

'Jesús!'

She listened, alert to all the sounds of the river, rustlings of wildlife on the bank, birdsong. She staggered to her feet.

Holding the rushes like guy lines, she screamed, 'Jesús!'

The white waters frothed and churned, but no human response came.

She stumbled along the bank in the direction of flow. Some way further on, a flash of teal in the centre was out of keeping. As she came alongside it on the bank, she realised it was her dress, which lay like a flag on one of a crop of six boulders strewn across the river. Other belongings had been similarly trapped. She made out items of clothing and, forming a dam between the middle stones, a tangle of sleeping bag and tent poles. Caught within that tangle was a plastic pouch, its contents Havana brown: Chile's journal. At that moment of recognition, a well-defined yet slender figure, clad in black—the bandit on the bridge—leaped from the opposite embankment and landed on a boulder. The bandit's face was concealed by the peak of a military cap. The angle of the peak, directed downwards, made clear the bandit wasn't looking in her direction at all, but at one thing only, the journal.

Evangeline had to reach the journal first.

She jumped to the nearest boulder. Her foot slipped and she crashed awkwardly on one knee. The sudden pain shot through her but there wasn't time for that. Her opponent had made it to the next slab. She scrabbled to her feet and launched herself at the nearest rock landing on hands and feet. But as she lifted her head, the bandit reached a third boulder and stretched down to grab the sleeping bag. Evangeline made a running jump for her third rock. As she flew through the air, the journal slid towards the seething water. On rock once more, she threw herself at a corner of the sleeping bag and pulled. The journal flipped back into the tangled equipment: she saved it from the water. On the other boulder, the bandit lay prone, upper torso and arms at full stretch over the equipment. Another inch forward and a finger and thumb pincered the journal. Hand and arm retracted. The figure stood. It really was very neat. Almost pocket-sized.

From across the divide, the bandit faced her, hip thrust to the side, holding the journal up high.

Evangeline knew that petite figure. 'Catalina?' she shouted.

The woman shouted back, 'Face it, Eva, you never stood a chance of finding Rewe.'

'But you, you—Asklepion—weren't interested,' Evangeline said.

'We were always interested. Just not interested in partnering with an amateur,' Catalina yelled above the tumult.

'You wouldn't have known anything about it if it wasn't for me,' Evangeline yelled back.

'What do you want, a round of applause?' Catalina stashed the journal down the front of her jumpsuit and clapped sarcastically.

'You can't do this.'

'Man up, Ginge!' Catalina shifted her slender weight to the other hip. 'Talking of which, where is Jesús?'

Evangeline gasped as though slapped in the face.

Catalina laughed. 'You gringas can't even get that right.' With that, she pivoted on her heel and leaped nimbly from one boulder to another until she reached the bank. Without turning, she waved and shouted over her shoulder, 'Chavela,' as she sashayed into the thicket and was gone.

Evangeline continued to stare at the space so recently vacated by the other woman. What was she going to do?

She had no idea where she was, nor how they'd ever find Rewe, now. They'd come all this way for nothing.

They?

Jesús. Christ! Where was Jesús? Had he made it out of the car? He may have been washed further downriver. He must have survived. He had to. But maybe he was lying unconscious among the rushes.

'Jesús!' She scoured the waterline for any signs of denim held captive within the rushes. The rushes shook their heads in denial.

Movement was slow-going, it hurt to put any weight on the injured knee which had swollen and stiffened. Florito joined in the search with an intermittent, sharp bark that ricocheted between the banks and would surely rouse even the most comatose.

She wasn't thinking. She'd assumed Jesús would make it to this side of the river. But there was no logic behind the assumption and there was every chance he was on the opposite bank. On the same side as Catalina.

Wait a minute.

Was he on the same side as Catalina? What was it he'd said back there on the bridge? 'She's got a gun.' It hadn't registered, at the time. After all, on a dilapidated bridge when looking down the barrel of a gun, the first thoughts are for self-preservation. She replayed the moment, over and over. The assailant was dressed in black, face covered by a hat and scarf. Seen from a distance, it wasn't obvious it was a woman. Yet he knew straight away. If he knew, he must have guessed it was Catalina. And what did that mean?

But Jesús would never do that. Would he?

Then, just now, Catalina hadn't been concerned he was missing. No, she'd been more concerned about getting one over. Was that because she knew where he was? Was this their plan all along?

She couldn't believe he'd be that cruel, to simply disappear and allow her to think he was dead.

Water, surging this way and that, held her attention. In the cupped palm of her hand, she felt the reassuring nudge of Florito's muzzle. 'Well, my pupper,' she said, stroking his head. 'I know you didn't always see eye-to-eye with Jesús, and maybe you were right to be cautious. But I was just beginning to think…'

What to do?

Here they were, just she and Florito, on a riverbank somewhere in the depths of Chile.

Florito ruffed. It was a soft vocalisation. A sound not to cause alarm but meant as a stand-by-your-beds alert. He trotted to the water's edge.

'What is it, boy?' she asked, wary of the return of Catalina to finish them off.

Coughing—spasmodic, spitting, coughing—arose from the undercut. With difficulty, she got on the ground and, lying on her front, she shuffled forward army-style. When she reached the lip of the bank, she pushed her head and shoulders clear of the margin.

An arm hooked around her neck. She shrieked and tried to wrench herself free, but it hung fast. Having anchored itself to her, the arm hauled its body from the shallows.

'Jesús!' Seeing its owner rising from the water, wet hair stuck to his forehead, shirt clinging to his torso, she latched on and didn't let go.

15. Victor's Vexation

Morning shone through the sliding glass door. The door was open, North had seen to it, allowing the air in the room to circulate, to draw in the outside fragrance of orange blossom and cut grass. The early morning chatter of birds in the garden added a bustling atmosphere. By midday, the room would be cast in shade, a respite from the heat.

Even so, the sun did not shine directly on the surface of Mati Klarwein's *Annunciation.* Victor had taken great care to select the precise spot on the wall to emphasize the mischtechnik of the artwork, as he did with everything in the room. Just so.

The room served as a study and as a salon. But it was more than either of those spaces. There was an element of the boudoir about it also.

Things in which Victor took pleasure were gathered here. Objects from his travels, treasures really: pre-Colombian ceramics, an effigy vessel of Bachuéte'é, fertility goddess; stone bas-relief tablets of staff-bearing figures; a hammered gold pectoral; a tumi ceremonial knife with gold and turquoise handle.

Victor enjoyed an early start to the day. It was when his head was at its most clear. He rose at six, then bathed and dressed in the clothes North—his housekeeper and second-in-command—had laid out the night before. He would have some fruit for breakfast, a nectarine from the garden, perhaps, or figs drizzled with honey, rosewater and pistachios. This he would eat on the balcony of his bedroom, overlooking the unfettered exuberance of the garden and the mountains beyond. Then he would come here, where North would greet him with a coffee, a wet shave and await Victor's orders for the day.

On this day, Victor sat, as usual, in the reclining chair North used to perform the delicate operation of his grooming. Ordinarily, the rhythmic throck of razor on leather as she honed the blade, soothed him with its metronomic precision. But things were not going to plan. His warriors, Tomoe Gozen and Hippolyta, stood before him.

The two women were a sight to behold. Tomoe, narrow-hipped, wore leather armour which bound her breasts and broadened her shoulders. She had a sword at her waist that just cleared the ground, and a bow strung across her shoulders. Her lacquer-black hair was in the taregami style: unbound, straight to the knees. Her pale face was exquisite, but which feature stood out most? Was it her lips, painted startling carmine and which were, at this moment, phrased in the most perfect of pouts? Or, the almond eyes, elongated with red shadow? Or was it the courage he knew resided in those deep brown eyes, currently concealed by the lowered lashes?

Hippolyta towered over her stablemate. A magnificent specimen, with square shoulders and straight back. The girdle around her middle emphasised her firm breasts. Athletic and good-natured, Hippolyta had a tendency towards infectious high spirits.

Victor pushed the arm holding the razor away from his chin and slammed his cafecito onto its saucer. A tongue of coffee shot out of the cup to soak his shirt cuff. From over his shoulder, North proffered a hot towel.

Victor dabbed at the stain and asked, 'Why is she not here?'

'The honourable Amazon was driving.' Tomoe scowled at her statuesque partner.

'Why can't Tomoe learn to co-pilot?' Hippolyta shot a glance at her comrade and crossed her arms in defiance. Looking at Victor, she said, 'Anyway, I wanted to see if your Lilith has any spunk.'

Victor raised his hands. 'Enough. Do you realise, the incident was televised?'

He picked up the remote control and aimed at the *Annunciation* on the wall. The painting slid aside to reveal a plasma screen. A newsreel appeared on the screen, an aerial shot of a busy highway on which two vehicles dodged in and out of traffic. From bottom-right of the screen a white structure the width of the highway came into view. The first car, a Land Rover, passed beneath the structure, a tollbooth. The car spun around to stop, facing the way it had come. The second, a black Hummer, slammed into the tollbooth and was engulfed by flames.

'I'm not just talking local TV,' Victor continued. 'Imagine my surprise—and, believe me, this was a huge but hideous surprise—when I'm in a bar in Buenos Aires and see you, Tomoe Gozen, wielding your sword in front of a raging inferno at the Temuco tollbooth.'

The camera had zoomed in on a slim figure whose long hair billowed in the backdraft.

'Looking good, Tomoe,' Hippolyta said.

Tomoe's smile was short-lived.

'Your job was to keep an eye on the girl,' Victor growled. 'Not to prance about like a show pony at the Hipo Chile.'

Tomoe's straight-backed ojigi, her closed hands held to the thighs, was contrite.

'Victor-san, I had her in my sights. She travels with a male.

But those that carry wailing blue eye were upon us.'

'Tomoe, the police don't take kindly to citizens in possession of Shogun weaponry,' Victor said. He adjusted his position. 'But this male. This is news to me.'

'He's very pretty,' said Hippolyta. 'Can I have him to play with?'

'A moot point, my warrior princess, considering you've returned empty handed.'

'Victor, we'll get them next time. We promise.' Hippolyta put her arm around Tomoe's shoulders.

Victor couldn't remain vexed with his girls for long. After all, they were devoted to him. North saw her opportunity and drew him back in the chair to continue the shave. Victor breathed in the lavender perfume synonymous with her.

'North,' he said.

The face leaning over him was an upside-down and more angular version of her compatriot, Queen Victoria of Britain. Her gold-rimmed glasses framed watery blue eyes that were focused entirely on him.

'Sir?'

'You're going to love this one. She's a plant hunter, like you.'

A Northern eyebrow rose above the frame of her glasses. 'Just as you say, Sir.'

No longer able to see Tomoe and Hippolyta, Victor raised his hand loosely in their direction. 'Where are they now, coriñas?'

'The totem's signal is brighter day-by-day. They draw closer,' Tomoe said.

'They will reach the River Gihon in three days,' Hippolyta said.

'Vale, we will be waiting.'

Victor dismissed them with a shooing flick of his fingers. Arm in arm, the girls made for the door.

He called after them, 'You were testing her ...spunk? What did you make of my Lilith?'

'Lilith's got spunk in spades,' Hippolyta said.

16. Reunion

Evangeline

Bruised, still shaken, Evangeline and Jesús took the mountain path with Florito snuffling at their heels. Curls of steam rose from their shoulders, while moisture collected in the folds of their muddied clothes, close and uncomfortable.

She filled Jesús in on what had happened, ending with the news that the bandit on the bridge and the new possessor of Chile's journal was none other than Catalina.

'Arbolito—Evangeline,' he held her hands in his. 'I would never have let her anywhere near you or this project if I'd known what she would do.'

Jesús looked like he'd taken a sucker-punch. It would have to be a shock to find out that someone known as a friend was out to kill them. Did he feel responsible for what happened on the bridge? She found no deceit in his eyes.

'Bacán,' she said. 'I believe you.' That established, she needed to clarify one other niggling issue. 'Look, I know Cristóbal is your friend, but can we trust him?'

'Cristóbal? I trust him with my life. Is a brother to me. Know him from student.'

'Well, the fact we've lost all forms of communication with the wider world, may not be such a bad thing.'

They'd lost everything: the car, their belongings and Morgan's journal. All that knowledge, all that heritage of the Welsh plant hunter gone in a gunshot. But worse, far worse, was the knowledge that someone she knew, or, at least Jesús knew, had tried to kill them. That same someone, Miss-self-proclaimed-queen-bee-Catalina, was most likely stealing a march Amundsen-style in a race to Rewe right this very minute.

But if Catalina thought she already had them beat, she was wrong. Evangeline had nothing to go back to, nothing left at all. Now she had the bit between her teeth, she would seek out the World Tree, and she bloody well would not yield, not now, not ever.

She braced her shoulders. 'Come on, we've got a tree to find.'

Jesús saluted, his chin raised with pride. Of her. She felt her face grow warm. As for Florito, he set off as soon as he received his marching orders, head alert, sweeping from side to side. Evangeline and Jesús followed in his wake.

'The thing with Scott of the Antarctic was that when they found their bodies, alongside them was the equivalent weight of around thirty-five bags of sugar of Glossopteris fossils.' She looked for confirmation that Jesús followed her thread. He smiled, she wasn't convinced.

'Glossopteris were tree ferns,' she continued. 'They only exist in fossil form now. Those found by Scott were the first fossils ever discovered in the Antarctic. They proved the theory of Gondwana.'

'How?'

She guessed the question came from kindness more than curiosity. 'They showed that Antarctica had once been warm and connected to other continents.'

In the silence between them, the warm breeze rustled the dry leaves of the bamboo, whose culms plonked gently together like a xylophone.

'Jesús?'

'Arbolito?'

'Our expedition.' She pulled at her earring that had been Morgan's cufflink. 'We're not going to end up like Scott, are we?'

He stopped walking and turned her by her shoulders to face him. 'You, my woman valiante, must believe it is possible.' The warmth of his eyes melted thoughts of that fated polar trek. He kissed her forehead.

Over the course of the afternoon she came to walk with a lighter step, almost a bounce, with her shoulders back and head up. True, one most likely two (counting the Hummer from Hell) attempts had been made on their lives. True, also, the loss of equipment would hamper their endeavours to find Rewe. But most other people would have given up by now, and no one would think any the less of them for that. The car chase and the ambush made it clear to her that the World Tree was worth fighting for. Maybe it had something to do with being in the open air, or that her feelings for her friends had deepened, or, simply, that the need to focus on the here-and-now lessened the weight of the dank pelt that had hung around her for the past year. It wasn't going to be easy. Who knew what would come their way next? But with just the three of them, in search of their goal, she felt more hopeful of the future than she had for a long time.

≋

Her abstinence from music—for fear of reminders about Will and, and all that—had come to an end. She was ready to revel in it. So, in the absence of cosmic rock to entertain them, they made their own music.

Jesús started things off with *Despacito.* Evangeline joined in with an approximation of the words, her voice rising in confidence on the -ito line endings. And they didn't stop there. They tackled *These Boots Are Made for Walking*; he was Marvin Gaye to her Tammi Terrell for *Ain't No Mountain High Enough*; but it was when they got onto *You Should be Dancing* that Florito came into his own. He nailed the Bee Gees' falsetto.

Thickets of bamboo and ferns closed in, barring their way, clawing at legs and arms. Cobwebs laced hair; flies zipped past ears. They climbed for hours. At first, they barely noticed the incline. But now, in single file, they leaned forward over the path, concentrating on each step.

For the most part, Jesús filled Evangeline in on the political struggles of the largest group of indigenous peoples, the Mapuche, in Chile. Florito panted like a traction engine. Even though he was running on vapours, his instinct—he couldn't not—was to cock his leg on carefully chosen tussocks and other, seemingly random, landmarks. From some way ahead, they could hear the roar of a waterfall. Energised, they picked up their pace.

The path opened to a clearing. Twin falls cascaded over slanting ledges of reddish-brown rock, to mist the lush green shrubs bursting from every nook, and plunge into an aquamarine pool.

Florito led the charge.

The pool, so clean and cool, washed their lacerations and soothed bruising. Their splashes, laughter and shouts, the torrent of water, cancelled any noise that might be heard in this isolated place.

Until, from a ledge above them, 'Well, well, Plant Hunter. Quite the family unit you have now.'

17. Iron Sharpeneth Iron

Morgan: Peru, 24 January 1843

I spent longer in Iquique than I had intended. The plan, that is, my original plan, was to equip myself with non-perishables, porters and pack animals—after all, I couldn't expect mule Paco to manage the load alone—before I crossed the border into Chile. That country's climate and terrain, extending over some thirty-nine degrees latitude, ranges from arid desert in the north to the ice fields in the south, as readers of my most popular publication, *Travels* &ᶜ,[8] will no doubt recall. I needed to be prepared for all eventualities. The shared wisdom of those who knew the country, and my own experiences and intellect informed me that the one thing of any certainty about the landscape and weather of Chile was that nothing was certain.

But there was more to my sojourn than that. I'd been mulling over the story relayed to me by Silva, the ragged beggar I encountered in a chicha bar when we first touched into port. I wouldn't normally entertain such talk of my being in any sense the Chosen One. After all, I'm a man of science not superstition.

8. Morgan, Edwin (1838) *Travels in Patagonia*

But his conviction that the World Tree[9] was real and growing in Chile had piqued my interest. My Titian hair had marked me out before—and not always for the good, I hasten to add—but, in this instance, I was grateful that a mere physical characteristic could be the portal to a new discovery or, if not that, at least a new adventure.

I'd determined to find out what was known about the Chilean version of the mythical World Tree. While in Iquique I had the questionably good fortune to be a guest of the English Consul. On handing him a letter of introduction from my sponsor, William Gibbs E[sq.], he couldn't have been more hospitable. The Consul, an affable former army major by the name of Whitman, bore an outward appearance that implied a fondness for fine port and good food.

The consulate was equipped with an extensive equestrian facility. A hobbyist horse breeder, the Major acquired neighbouring land as soon as he and Lady Whitman took up residency in Iquique, on which he built stables fit for a king. If he had not anticipated hosting a mule along with his thoroughbreds, he was too well-bred to show any sign. While I was the Consul's guest, I was pleased to know Paco enjoyed a bed of clean straw and a fresh bag of oats every day.

On that first evening, over an excellent grilled lobster dripping with butter, I asked my host whether he knew of the myth.

He wiped his shiny mouth on his napkin and replied, 'Sorry,

---

9. As I'm sure the enlightened reader will be aware, the World Tree or *Axis Mundi* is a universal archetype featuring a tree which sits at the centre of the Cosmos and joins the realms of heaven, earth and hell. Our Norse forebears called it *Yggdrasil*, the Persians, *Gaokerena*. The Mayans know it as Yax Imix Che, in Buddhism it becomes Bodhi, in Hindi Akshaya Vata, &[c]. The concept's resemblance to the Biblical Tree of Life is surely more than coincidence.

old boy. Myths aren't really my thing. If you can't race it, hunt it or bed it, it's all Greek to me, what?' At that he barked with laughter, such that the dome of his belly heaved against the lip of the table, threatening to upset my wine. 'All Greek! Do you see, my boy? Greek! … Myths! Ha!' This explanation set him off again in a paroxysm of hilarity heavily laced with a phlegmy cough. As he slapped the table with mirth, a reflection of the candlelight glinted from a smear of grease on his chin which had escaped the ministrations of the napkin.

'Very good, Major,' I said, chuckling along as best I could.

As though disappointed by my lukewarm appreciation of his humour he continued, 'You'll have to forgive me, old boy. With Lady Whitman visiting her sister in Lima, I am bereft of a civilising influence. While the cat's away, what?'

'Indeed, sir,' I said, wondering how to get the conversation back on track. 'Can you recommend anyone who may have knowledge of indigenous Chilean folklore? Silva mentioned the Pewen mapu. They're of the Mapuche people, I believe.'

He stabbed the air with a finger. 'You're talking about the araucanos, eh?'

I nodded in reply at his adoption of the Spanish for these people who have inhabited, since long before the Conquistadors' arrival, a tract of land now within the political boundaries of Chile and Argentina.

'If that's where your journey's going to take you, you need to take care. There have been some rum goings-on at the frontier, of late. But they can handle a horse, those araucanos, I'll grant you that. Tell you what, old boy…' He glanced at his plate and shovelled another load of lobster in his mouth.

He leant back in his chair to savour the seafood. 'This lobster is magnificent.' For a man of his stature, his voice was too small, as though it had been through a meat grinder.

'The best,' I said. 'My commendations to the chef. But you

were saying … about the Mapuche—the araucanos?'

'Was I? Oh, yes, that's it. You need to track down old what's his name. He'll know, if anyone will, this side of the frontier.'

'What's-his-name?' Slow progress, but I clung to this breadcrumb.

'What? Oh, yes. German fellow. Came out in 'thirty-six for the saltpetre. Married a Spanish girl—built like a Cheltenham filly…' His eyes glazed over.

I interrupted his reverie. 'Can you remember his name?'

'Grimm? Piper? Hamelin!' He slapped the table. 'That's it. Johann Hamelin.'

'Do you know how I might find Herr Hamelin?'

'You're in luck, my boy. He's coming into town on Monday for the horse fair. Hamelin's interested in my Smoky Sultana for his wife.'

I choked on my lobster. 'I'm not sure I follow you, Major?'

'My mare, Smoky Sultana. Fourteen-point-four hands of half-Arabian, grey perfection. Hamelin's wife needs a new horse.'

'How might he be able to help me?'

'He employs the araucanos in the mines.'

I was keen to know more about the World Tree from the German. But, in some ways I was pleased to have a reason to stay in Iquique for a couple more days. In the three months or so on board the Abraxas, Solomon and I had struck up a firm friendship. I would be sorry to lose his company. After the incident with the watery Erzulie, I knew this was a man who could be relied upon in a crisis: I owed him my life. Due to a skirmish on the Peru-Chile border relating to the guano destined for home, he was enjoying extended shore leave. I felt honour-bound, therefore, to entertain my saviour as best I could in the short time he had ashore.

Solomon was staying in a hostelry in the centre of town. The kind of establishment that catered to the mariner. A lively bar below, equipped with cheap, strong spirits and welcoming women, a latrine out back, while several—let's say, competitively priced—shared rooms were up the stairs. Everything, in fact, a sailor might need within easy reach. The bedfellow, bedbugs and vermin were issued gratis.

I found my friend in the saloon, where else, the following day. On seeing me come through the door, he unbound himself from the attachment of a honey-skinned, merry-looking, waitress—they always swarmed to Solomon. For these women, more often than not from families at the bottom of the social heap, or the result of a shore leave dalliance, their living was hard won. In Solomon, they found a warmth and kindness they rarely experienced in their lives.

'Long time no see, man. Me tinking you forget your friend, Solomon, now you has bigger fish to fry,' he said rising to greet me in a bone-crushing hug. The few people in the bar glanced in his direction: perhaps it was a seafaring habit he'd acquired, but his was never an indoor voice.

'All of two days. Looks to me like you weren't even aware of my absence.' I jabbed him in the ribs and was as awed as ever by the resistance of solid muscle beneath his skin.

His laughter filled the room. 'Maite, some rum for me friend,' Solomon said. Whether his beaming face was suggestive of the effects of the rum in question, or of the presence of his Aphrodite, I couldn't be certain.

With an exaggerated flourish, he pulled out a chair for me, and landed with a bump in the opposite seat.

Righting himself, he said, 'How goes it, man?'

'I have a proposition for you, my friend.'

I waited while Maite placed a glass in front of me on the table and filled it with liquor. She topped up Solomon's glass.

He handed her considerably more than the value of the rum and said, 'Me see you later.'

'If you're lucky,' she laughed and left us.

He chuckled as he watched her hips swaying in retreat.

'She a good woman,' he said with certainty.

This was playing in my favour. 'Perhaps she'll make an honest man of you, yet.'

He smiled but said nothing for a while, gazing into his drink. Then, shaking his head as though erasing a thought, he said, 'You have proposition?'

'Solomon, what say you to leaving your life on the ocean waves to join me on my land-based expedition?'

'Man, the sailor's life is all I know.'

'If you're so set in your ways, then it's all the more reason to do something different,' I said. 'You've got to push yourself in new directions. If you do not, you will never know of what you are capable.'

He drew back from the table. 'You saying me afraid?'

'You're the bravest man I know. But, yes, even you're afraid.' At this, he crossed his arms across his chest and scowled. I had to think quickly. 'What is it you want in life? If you don't want to set down any roots, then fine. Continue in your seafaring meanderings. But Maite won't hang around forever waiting for your ship to come in. And what will you have achieved? Do you really want to roam the oceans blue into your dotage—a dotage in which you have no wife or children to fill your home, or…' I pointed at his glass. 'To pour you a tot of rum?'[10]

I could see he was mulling over my words. At another table Maite was serving a group of sailors when one of them grasped hold of her by the waist and tried to pull her onto his lap. Her dark

---

10. Esteemed Reader, you may well be wondering at this point whether my assertions were a case of the proverbial pot calling the kettle black. Indeed, you might have a point. But is it not the case that we all too often see our own faults most clearly displayed in the actions of others?

eyes flashed across to Solomon but missed their mark, so deep in thought was he. I was preparing to go to her aid when something she said set the sailors off laughing at their comrade. The lout's face soured but he made a show of being able to take the joke: for is there no worse crime among men than that of taking oneself too seriously? His Ha-Ha-Ha—all noise and no heart—alerted Solomon to the altercation who, seeing Maite in the thick of it, leapt to his feet. With difficulty, I held him back: the crisis had passed already. I couldn't be certain, but I had a suspicion the spirited Maite winked across the room to Solomon to let him know all was well. Certainly, his straining against my hold eased. We both watched the woman saunter away from the crowd. Her wit had saved her, as I'm sure it had on many occasions before.

Reassured as to her immediate welfare, I said, 'Maite deserves better than this.'

It turned out that the oaf had done me a favour. Having witnessed the peril Maite no doubt experienced daily; Solomon decided he needed to be closer at hand. In lieu of any better offer, he accepted my proposal to join me as Chief-of-Staff on my expedition. That is to say, he would look after the running of things, and ensure mule Paco and his fellows didn't step out of line, freeing me up to do what I do best: to seek out new plants. For him, this, at least, was a start in the right direction. Then, once he'd got used to the idea of being on *terra firma* for longer than it took to fix a leaky keel, he could contemplate a suitable occupation with which to support a wife and, God willing, family.

I'm well aware that my position in this account could be taken as meddling in others' affairs, not to say self-serving. For my part, however, I was rather pleased with my attempts at helping out my friend, and on playing Cupid into the bargain. It's not often such opportunities present themselves to me, being the solitary plant hunter that I am. While I'm not unconscious of the benefits this course of action would undoubtedly have for my comfort, I do believe it is the duty of good friends to bring out the best qualities in each other[11], as Solomon has in me on many an occasion.

Over the course of the next few days, the plans and the equipment with which to carry them out, came together. Major Whitman willingly gave up more stalls in his stables for a team of mules to join Paco, the self-appointed team leader. He, that is mule Paco, had taken to his temporary quarters as if to the manor born. Stabled with thoroughbreds, he showed not the slightest sign of inferiority. On the contrary, when Solomon and I turned him out the following Monday, a grey mare with long lashes in the neighbouring stall whinnied at him, dare-I-say, coquettishly. It has to be said that since my first encounter with the mule, he had metamorphosed from the sorriest bundle of bones caked in muck, into a glossy, well-honed, buckskin in possession of a sense of humour and a certain rakish charm—a diamond in the rough, if you will. Indeed, it wasn't just female equids who succumbed to his charisma: for Maite, also with us on this occasion, took to whispering in his ear as she brushed his coarse upright mane free of the mud-dust of the paddock in which he cooled himself.

Aboard ship, Solomon had been in charge of the livestock. After all, a healthy animal produces healthy meat. Therefore, in his new role as Chief of Staff, or gang-master if you prefer, he took it upon himself to inspect the dung of our mules for lungworm. It was approaching mid-afternoon and the combined smell of straw, horse sweat—and dung freshly-pulled apart—was heavy. Light shafted through knotholes in the timbers, illuminating dust dancing in the air. Footsteps and conversation outside heralded the barn door opening, and the gangway being flooded with light.

---

11. A case of 'Iron sharpeneth iron; so a man sharpeneth the countenance of his friend' Proverbs 27:17

'Ah! Morgan, my boy, there you are. Allow me to introduce Herr and Frau Johann Hamelin,' the forcemeat-voice of Major Whitman cut through the drowsy barn.

The Hamelins were a conspicuously fashionable couple. He sported mutton chops, cane and a frock coat cinched in at the waist. The Frau wore ink blue shot silk chosen, no doubt, to set off the black ringlets visible beneath her bonnet. It would be ungallant to comment on the veracity of the Major's assessment of her build, but suffice to say, this was no mere slip of a girl. Accompanying the pair, silhouetted against the opening, was a dark-skinned fellow with high cheekbones and an air of insouciance.

The Major announced, 'Good news, my boy. Herr Hamelin here has brought the mountain to Mohammed.'

'Delighted to be of service, Mr Morgan,' the German said. 'The Major tells me you're interested in tracking down the Vorld Tree.' He spoke English with just a hint of the clipped syllables of a German accent.

'That's the plan,' I replied.

'Antiman here has knowledge of the myth of Rewe.'

As Hamelin named the tree, Antiman's eyes flashed interest, giving my companions and I the once over.

'But first, Major, I want to see this beauty you've been telling me about. Show me your Smoky Sultana,' Hamelin said.

The barn had become somewhat crowded and not wanting to get in the way of the serious business of horse trading, Solomon, Maite and I waited in the yard to speak with the new arrivals.

In due course, the barn door opened on a groom leading the grey coquette, for Smokey Sultana was she, followed by the major and his guests. We all trailed towards the paddock, where the groom let out the length of lead rope to put the horse through her paces. Circling the inside of the fence, she showed us her pedigree. The major didn't fail to draw our attention to various aspects of her gait, her rhythm, her temperament. Frau Hamelin was ecstatic. It was just a matter, then, for Hamelin and the major to agree the terms, and for sherry to be served to secure the deal.

Horse business over, we got on to the more important matter of discussing the World Tree. Hamelin informed us that Antiman spoke no English. 'But this is of little matter,' he said. 'For I will translate from you to him, and from him to you. This is good, ja?'

In this way, Antiman confirmed that the Mapuche have a myth of the World Tree which they call Rewe. He said the tree was at the heart of their culture as it was at the heart of the cosmos. But, when asked if it existed in earthly form, he denied it categorically. Obviously, I couldn't understand his mother tongue, but there is a whole lot more to communication than the language of words. The language of his body was unequivocal: the snort of derision, the lifted chin of defiance, both barriers to open dialogue. I was sure he wasn't telling us all he knew. Once or twice, however, his eyes wandered quizzically to my hair. I had to try a different tack.

Through the mediation of Hamelin, I told him I was a plant hunter, interested in the discovery of new plants. I explained my intention of travelling with Solomon and my pack animals south through Chile to the region popularly known as the Lake District to explore the Andean foothills in search of the rare and the beautiful. Did Antiman have any advice on finding the safest route?

Some extended incomprehensible dialogue ensued, then Hamelin turned to me with a sigh, 'While the climate of the coastal road is more comfortable, there are political incursions at the border with Chile. Before you reach the border, you'll need to go inland but don't go without being fully prepared: you'll be travelling across the driest desert in the world. By day, the Atacama can reach 40°C but by night it drops to below zero.' He paused to make sure the message got home. 'If you manage to survive the Atacama, you must travel through the Central Valley to Concepción—'

'No!' Maite interrupted.

'What is it Maite?'

'Mr Morgan, Antiman said to avoid Concepción. He said there has been unrest in the area and you will not be safe,' she said with a glance at Solomon. It was clear whose safety was most on her mind.

'You understand Mapudungun?' I asked.

'Yes, my grandmother was Mapuche,' she said.

Solomon chuckled to himself at this revelation.

'Did you listen to all Antiman had to say?' I said.

'Yes, sir,' she replied.

'Do you remember his directions?'

'Of course.'

'Would you thank Antiman for his advice. Tell him it is very welcome.'

As Maite relayed my gratitude to the Mapuche, his demeanour relaxed. I wouldn't go so far as to say he broke into a smile, but he certainly presented a more benign countenance.

'One further thing, Maite. Just out of interest, could you ask your friend whether there is anything in the Rewe myth about a man with red hair?'

Antiman looked me full in the face when he replied.

As though the first to share an item of glorious gossip, Maite relayed the answer, 'It is said the redhead from over the seas will know Rewe.'

'Maite, you've been most helpful,' I said. 'I wonder whether I might prevail on you a moment longer.'

She nodded.

'It strikes me that you're a woman who knows who's who and what's what in Iquique. We're currently recruiting for our expedition. Isn't that right Solomon?'

Solomon, initially confused, met my eye.

'That's right.' He beamed.

'Yes, I was wondering whether you might have knowledge of a translator willing to accompany us.'

Maite, whooped with joy.

'Can I take it that you are able to help our endeavours?'

'Yes!' said Maite and Solomon in unison, as he swept her up in his arms.

Herr Hamelin had been left on the sidelines and his mouth was now drawn into the finest of lines.

'I see you have no further need of me, Mr Morgan,' he said.

'Herr Hamelin,' I said with palms outwards in placatory fashion. 'Your services have been much appreciated. Thank you.'

The good major dispelled the frostiness by topping up our sherry.

'To the expedition!' he cried.

18. Time for Tea

Evangeline

Evangeline shaded her eyes and looked towards the ledge above the falls.

'Victor?' She felt pulled up, as when texting while walking and finding a lamppost in the way. 'But you're in Buenos Aires.'

'I think it's plain to see that I'm not, Plant Hunter,' Victor said.

He was flanked by two striking women who might have been engaged in some kind of historical re-enactment. What era they were recreating, exactly, was a little confused: one was dressed in a short Grecian-style toga, the other in Samurai battle-gear.

'Arbolito?' Jesús looked between her and the trio making their way down from the ledge.

'Jesús, this is Victor,' Evangeline said.

'Late Horizon totem Victor?' Jesús asked out the side of his mouth.

'Yes, Late Horizon totem Victor,' she said in similar fashion.

Assembled poolside, introductions were made, then Evangeline gave Victor a potted history of events since she'd left him in Buenos Aires. The offer of a bed for the night, where they could refresh and take stock, and transportation closer—by Victor's reckoning—to their destination would dig them out of this hole. What were the alternatives: decline and spend the night on the mountain, their equipment gone well and truly up the creek? After all, relying on the hospitality of those of bare acquaintance, friends of friends, or government representatives overseas, was something Chile Morgan had done as a matter of course. He never travelled without letters of introduction. Well, if it was good enough for Chile Morgan …

⚜

The car was some kind of understated luxury, sleek, spacious and silent. Outside mirror-black, inside champagne leather. It looked and smelled like it had just come from the showroom—not a sweet wrapper or grungy chammy in sight.

The Japanese woman with hair down to her knees—Tomoe?—was in the driver seat. The armadillo style shoulder caps of her leather armour were way out of proportion with the rest of her body. Victor was upfront beside her.

Cosplay's a big thing, now, even here, thought Evangeline. She had to hand it to her: Tomoe did look good. Victor was the last person she'd have down for that kind of thing. She wondered whether his linen trousers and perfectly ironed white cotton shirt were him being the Man from Delmonte. She didn't want to be around if he went any more adventurous.

The dog tag jingled as Florito scratched his ear. His bulk took up most of the ample legroom on Evangeline's side of the car, the weight of his body bouncing heavily against her legs at each pothole in the road.

'Victor, we really appreciate this,' Evangeline's voice filled the void. 'We don't want to put you out, or anything.'

'Evan*ghe*line, for you, it is my pleasure.' He glanced over his shoulder.

She was struck again by the likeness of his tawny eyes to those of a jaguar. A minor jolt of the car provided an excuse to brace her arm against the door panel, the chrome of the door-lock cool beneath her fingers. Florito rumbled somewhere in his chest, the vibration a chainsaw against her leg.

She'd have been more at ease if Jesús was next to her. But when they climbed into the back of the car, Hippolyta the Amazon got between them. At the time, the move came across as considerate. After all, no one likes to sit in the middle if they can avoid it. All the same, Evangeline suspected an ulterior motive.

Hippolyta's legs splayed carelessly either side of the floor's central moulding and pressed against those of her companions. The heat from the woman's long thigh radiated against Evangeline. Hippolyta possessed an enviable lack of inhibition. This was neither aggressive one-upmanship nor showing off, she was simply devoid of the self-consciousness so often instilled into girls from an early age. Her tunic had ridden up her leg to show a glimpse of sporty navy underwear. Evangeline turned her head to focus on what was out the window, a blur of red road and rampaging green. That is, when she wasn't looking at where the Amazon's hand was positioned on Jesús' knee, thigh, or, hang on a moment, his crotch!

Evangeline cleared her throat. Of course, any man would be flattered by the attention. There was something to be said for the direct approach, after all. She could see how the Amazon's opening lines—'You look as frisky as an unbroken steed. Do you like women?'—would sort the men from the boys. Evangeline was relieved his leg flinched away from Hippolyta's advance.

He muttered, '¡Pégate la ascurría!'

Hippolyta instantly withdrew her hand, suggesting a rebuff. All the same, when the Amazon turned to Evangeline, she seemed unperturbed. 'Eve-Evangeline—no, I'm going to call you Eve. As soon as we get there, I want to show you Victor's garden. You're going to love it. I mean, really *love* it. You can't not. You a plant hunter and all.'

'Hippolyta, our guests may like to freshen up first.' Victor glanced round. 'And don't slouch.'

Hippolyta straightened up, brought her knees together. 'OK, freshen, then we go see the garden. All right, Eve?'

Evangeline felt like things were running away from her. Then again, the alternative—stumbling around Chile with no map, no kit, and a torn ligament—didn't appeal right now. If they could just tidy themselves up and sort themselves out.

'If there's time,' she said. They had to be on their way as soon as possible.

'Here we are, *La Menagerie*, a French word, I think, no? I so want you to enjoy it with us.' Hippolyta squeezed her hand again.

The car turned into a driveway. A driveway with a security gate.

'Welcome home, Señor Ríos.' The female guard with dramatic eyebrows was dressed in khaki topped with a black beret.

Victor leaned across Tomoe's arms resting at ten to two on the steering wheel. 'Sanchez, call up to the house, will you, and ask North to prepare tea.'

'Yes, sir.' The guard pressed a button and the barrier arced upward.

'Hi, Celia. You coming tonight?' Hippolyta called through the window.

'Wouldn't miss it.' The guard waved.

Tomoe's shoulder-cladding hunched and fell as she released the handbrake. The car purred forward and up the sweep of the driveway. The incline cut into the bedrock, such that the house was hidden from view.

The car crested the rise and there, reclining in the sun, was the house.

La Menagerie appeared drowsy but alert, like a gorged big cat guarding the remains of its kill. It was the kind of house which demanded, should it choose to be photographed, a wide-angle lens. Composed of long, clean lines of single-storied concrete, it was fronted by an open veranda, and framed either side by Araucaria.

From the veranda, stone steps, like bracket fungus, appeared to hover over the slope of the garden: all rolling mounds of greenery and gentians, studded with cacti starbursts and puya spears. The vegetation moulded the underlying geology, which graced the garden with an appearance here and there; the Mars-red haematite shocking in the green.

The car came to a rest in front of the house.

Tomoe opened the rear door and bowed as first Florito, then Evangeline climbed out.

'Welcome, Evangeline-san.'

Florito swaggered off to the nearest shrub and cocked his leg.

'Evang*he*line and … Jesús, I want you to make yourselves at home here,' Victor said as he and the others joined her in front of the house. 'Welcome to *La Menagerie*.'

'Thanks, Victor. I still can't get over running into you back there. It was some kind of miracle.'

What were the odds of it being a coincidence? But, if it wasn't that, how did he find her?

'Not quite that,' he said.

Evangeline felt the figurine in her hand. Such a fulsome object. How had it survived the river, when all else perished?

'You've been so generous, already,' she said.

Since Jesús had identified the totem for what it was, she'd been wondering why a man she barely knew would stow it in her rucksack. Her initial conclusion, that it was an act of largesse, was appearing more naïve by the minute.

'No problem. Our house is yours.'

'Well, we need to get on our way as soon as possible. But,' she glanced at Jesús, whose eyes closed-opened in compliance. 'If we could stay for the night, we'd really appreciate it.'

'You stay as long as you need. Take your time to regroup and recharge.'

A woman, in a long black dress and lace cap, incongruously Victorian, came out to meet them. 'Tea is ready, sir.' She had a stuff-and-nonsense tone which elevated her above the position of an attendant.

Under the woman's unsmiling gaze Evangeline felt she was in the sale ring at a horse auction. This woman would be very exacting about conformation and bloodline.

How had she ever washed up here with Victor?

'Shall I serve it on the veranda, sir?' The loaded tray in the woman's hands implied her intention to do just that.

'Bueno, North.'

Master and servant, then.

The travellers stepped from sunshine to shade and took seats while North served tea.

☙

Evangeline was aware of the woman's eyes on her as she put porcelain to lip. The tea's colour, green—proper green, not some mealy-mouthed, off-colour dish water—was disconcerting. The smoky aroma, intriguing. On the tongue, an initial zest was replaced by a grassy freshness balanced by tannins, not a hint of dust. Then came a spicy hit, not too strong, just enough to zing. The sensation, heat without fire, as tactile as the tongue of a she-cat with her cub, spread from throat to core, to fingers, then eyes: invigorating. Evangeline's vision adjusted; all was brighter and more colourful. The tension in her shoulders relaxed.

'Is the tea to your satisfaction, Plant Hunter?' Victor asked next to her, his voice low as ever, yet, just as ever, commanding attention.

North, serving Tomoe the other side of Victor, tilted her head ever-so-slightly.

'It's tea, but with a kick,' Evangeline said, her eyes widened by the tea's afterburn.

She glanced at North who almost smiled. Not so much with her mouth—no, for surely that would have killed her—but the woman's shoulders pulled back a fraction from an already straight posture. North gave Evangeline a strange look, hard to figure out, at first, because so unexpected.

The look was a warning shot, but it had a touch of resignation about it, a hint of Jackie Kennedy: it was the look from the wife of a serial adulterer.

North was in love with Victor?

Really?

Before Evangeline had a chance to analyse this revelation further, Hippolyta's voice muscled its way into focus. She and Tomoe were telling Jesús something about the party that evening.

'Once we get you out of these things.' the index and middle fingers of Hippolyta's perfectly toned arm slid through the button gap of his shirt. 'You'll scrub up. Oh, yes, you'll do just fine.' She nodded, as though absorbing the image of Jesús au naturel. Her eyes lingered over his torso.

Evangeline coughed on her tea.

With the poise of a javelin thrower, the other woman ran her hand through her honey blonde hair as if to see him more clearly. But in the withdrawal, with head facing her target, the Amazon's body turned as well, thrusting her cleavage in his direction.

Jesús laughed as though the joke was on him. 'These clothes are all I've got.'

Victor's resonant voice glided over their side-conversation. 'North takes pride in her tea. It's made from an ancient recipe.'

'Props to you, North,' Evangeline said and met the woman's eye with a grin. She hadn't a clue how anything she might say would be received by North but had an urge to be kind to her.

The woman stared back, with as little apparent interest as if

Evangeline was an ear of wheat in a field of poppies.

Evangeline looked at her lap. She had a creeping sense that an assumption had been made about her. About her and Victor, if she had to put names to it. Yes, Victor was enigmatic. People deferred to him. They did his bidding. He emitted a pull much like that of a dark star, eclipsing the light of those around him. Yet, the thing with assumptions was they were hard to shake. It wouldn't do to try to correct the error; others would only say the lady doth protest too much. All the same, she didn't want North thinking the wrong thing, nor anyone else… no, especially not anyone else.

Jesús' knee came to rest against hers. She felt connection, magnetic, allowing her to breathe again. She looked up and quizzed the face that searched hers. He nodded with a smile meant for her alone, then looked for her hand and took it in his.

He'd not been offered tea. Instead, without explanation, North placed a cafecito in front of him. Perhaps the woman had assumed he, not of British stock, wouldn't understand tea. Evangeline noted his bemused expression. It was as though he could rise above all these interactions and connections, the trivial and the injurious, and would remain untouched by the politics, no matter what. Just the way they'd arranged themselves around the table when they arrived, was a microcosm of human behaviour— particularly of the female variety—in social groups. Thinking about it now, an inappropriate giddiness welled up in Evangeline. Hippolyta had seamlessly manoeuvred herself to be next to Jesús, while Evangeline, not as skilfully, sat the other side of him, and Victor settled into the chair next to hers. Tomoe slipped between Victor and Hippolyta so gracefully as to be barely noticed, her serene face opposite Evangeline. And North's presence wove around them all.

A bee, heavy with pollen, flew in a drunken line low across the lawn on which the dark bulk of Florito chased viscacha in his sleep. Disturbed, the hound snapped; his hollow bite echoing in the pregnant air. The bee, as if conscious of her error, took refuge in the tissue white flowers of a nearby ulmo *(Eucryphia cordifolia)*, now trembling, and buzzing like a comb harmonica. Florito stood, turned and settled down once more, with a heartfelt sigh. Evangeline allowed herself to chuckle.

She'd placed the earthenware figurine on the table when they arrived. It sat there, naked and tattooed, brazen. Victor hadn't given any signs of acknowledgement. But it must have been him who stowed the thing in her bag.

'This.' She nodded at the jug. 'Was all we salvaged from the ambush.'

'It is most fortunate that you did,' Victor's eyes darted between Hippolyta and Tomoe. 'This is a piece collectors would go to great lengths to hunt down.'

He wasn't giving anything away.

'Well, yes.' She turned to Jesús. 'How much did you value it at?'

'Exact value in dollars, I don't know,' Jesús replied. 'But she is very rare. My guess is Late Horizon.'

'She has a certain charm,' Victor said.

'Bachuéte'e is symbol of fertility and protector of crops,' said Jesús.

'She was just a minor character,' Victor said.

Jesús leant forward. 'Is muy significativa in indigenous Chilean culture.'

Victor shrugged. 'Yet, in many circles, she is not even recognised.'

'Prizing money over Earth and humanity is symptom of the patriarchal society we live in.' Jesús flicked his hand in exasperation. 'Is imposible to put value on an artefact that pre-dates the conquistadores?'

'You value it on its importance to you.' Victor's smile was close-mouthed. 'But let's not talk in such crass terms as pesos.'

'You value it, how?'

The women had fallen silent.

'Good question.' Victor picked up the figure and held it between his outstretched hands over the table. 'Is its worth equal to a creation of another kind? A masterpiece, for instance?'

'Possibly.' Jesús nodded. 'But this has religious importance. So, we need to compare it with other iconografías.'

'Even though the masterpiece might be better executed?' Victor pursed his lips. 'And does time really have any significance when everything forged by man has been, at one point in time, new?'

'Pues, Bachuéte'e's significance is she represents a time when women were venera—revered, yes?'

'You say it is rare,' Victor's smile showed his teeth. 'But is it as rare as love? Or the life of a beautiful woman, perhaps?'

Jesús looked at Victor. The moment lasted an eternity.

'On that, it does not compare,' Jesús said quietly.

As they sat on the veranda, Evangeline felt they were waiting for something. Like when standing on a station platform, she'd count down the minutes for the train to arrive. And when it pulled in, the time spent waiting would be forgotten, erased by the next stage of a journey.

Now and then, Evangeline would catch Victor watching her, deliberately, then his gaze moved on to Tomoe or Hippolyta. When he looked at them, his head inclined a little and he leant further back in his chair, breathing in through his nose in a proprietary way.

Evangeline sipped her tea, and then sipped again.

Colours in this Mediterranean climate were boisterous. The hues of fruits and flowers yelled out, competing like vendors in a farmer's market.

Most of all, the garden rang with vibrant green foliage.

But there's green, and then there's green. The ripe, zesty,

yellow-green of the orange *(Citrus aurantium)*, the spiky, virile green of taique *(Desfontainia fulgens)*, the puckered, Hooker's green of chaquihue *(Chrinodendron hookerianum)*, the poised, mantis green of the South African *Strelitzia regina*, the red-tinged, poison green of *Gaultheria insana*, the leathery, jungle green of canelo *(Drimys andina)*. Each green with its own, unique fragrance, texture, vibrant heat and memory. And then again, there was the tea.

'You've got an amazing place, here,' she wasn't saying it out of politeness. She didn't know, until now, that real people lived in such luxury. It was more than that, though. She felt dizzy, as though she couldn't take it all in at once, as though the garden was an entity, ancient and knowing. 'It's… it's overwhelming. It's—'

'But this is nothing compared to what's out back. You wait,' Hippolyta said.

'Though, really it is at its best in spring,' Tomoe said softly, viewing the garden over her shoulder. 'When all the blossom is out. I hope you see it then.'

Unlikely, they'd be on the road again tomorrow.

'You were about to say?' Victor leant sideways towards Evangeline.

'Was I? Oh. Maybe.' She ran her finger around the rim of her cup and sunk in her chair. With a demi-shrug, she said, 'It's just that all these plants, so perfect, so perfect together, so, I don't know, so primaeval. It's like the Garden of Eden.'

Victor's jaguar eyes studied her face, as if divining her innermost fears and desires. When he smiled, she felt he was satisfied, as though she had corroborated some hunch he had about her.

He nodded and said under his breath, 'Ya lo creo.'

'More tea?' With a creak of whalebone, and the rustle of countless unfathomables, North bent over Evangeline's cup.

'Thank you.'

Jesús' finger stroked her inner-wrist. 'Victor, we won't intrude on your party tonight. We can entertain ourselves, out of your—'

Victor raised his hand. 'I won't hear of it.'

'That's really kind of you.' Evangeline laughed self-consciously. 'But we'll look like the poor relations.'

Tomoe laughed discreetly, covering her smile with her hand. 'Onegaishimasu. It is our honour to have you with us, Evangeline-san.'

'We can take care of whatever you need, can't we, mis corazóns?' Victor said.

'Of course. We'll find you some fresh clothes,' said Hippolyta as though organising teams for lacrosse. 'Really, you've got to join us.'

Jesús drained his coffee. 'We have to leave first thing in the morning.'

'No rush on our account,' Victor continued as the congenial host. 'However, I'm afraid we've too many valuable pieces of art to risk having a dog in the living area. With your permission, we can house Florito in the mud room. He'll be quite happy there. North will do him a steak.'

Florito lifted his head from his paws.

It was a reasonable request—inhuman—but undeniably reasonable. But the charge of betrayal in Florito's eyes was clear.

What could Evangeline do?

In her peppiest voice, she sang, 'Steak! You'll love that! Won't you? Who's my boy?'

Victor clapped his hands together. 'Vale, Tomoe and Hippolyta will show you to your rooms.' He looked at her teacup. 'But do have your tea first, of course.'

The tea really was very refreshing. She'd go so far as to say therapeutic. The swelling in her knee had all but gone and any misgivings were melting away. She lifted the cup and drank the last drop.

19. Reflection

Evangeline

A sensual, Mediterranean fragrance—spicy wood, night-flowering blooms and citrus—enveloped Evangeline as she was shown into the room.

Against a backdrop of jade coloured walls, the furniture—an ocean of a bed, a dressing table and an armoire—dazzled. Carved in the darkest wood of all, its scrolling elaborations were picked out in gold. The soles of her walking boots squeaked on the wooden floor when she moved in for a closer inspection. The bedpost was decorated with garlands of deeply lobed leaves and fruit. Twisted within the garlands was a serpent whose head, so detailed with scales and eyes and forked tongue, served as a finial.

Tomoe, her graceful movement silent, followed Evangeline into the room.

'We are honoured to have you to here,' Tomoe smoothed the pristine covers on the bed and placed a white trumpet-shaped flower on the pillow. 'I'll run you a bath.'

The bath stood in the middle of the room on golden feline feet, the claws of which were sunk into the surface of the floor. The bath's sides were black with a gold serpentine design, its cavity gleaming white with a gilt lip. At the turn of the tap, the water cascaded into it, the metallic ring deepening as the volume of water increased.

At this very moment, somewhere hidden and unknown in this house, was Hippolyta being as gracious a hostess to Jesús? Or more?

'May I help you with your clothes?' Tomoe continued.

Evangeline stepped back. 'No. I'm good. Thanks.'

Tomoe bowed, held open a barrier of a towel and turned her head to the side. Evangeline undressed and Tomoe wrapped the towel around her.

'Please, Victor has selected dress for you to wear this evening,' Tomoe picked up Evangeline's discarded clothes and took a dress from the armoire. 'I hope you enjoy the sandals, product and perfume, but let me know if there is anything further you require.'

'You don't have to go to all this trouble.' Evangeline reached out for the dirty clothes in Tomoe's arms. 'Please don't bother about my clothes, I'll need them in the morning.'

'No trouble. Your things will be ready when you want them.'

Next to the bath, a small carved table offered Oribe Shampoo for Beautiful Color with matching conditioner. So precise. But what was it doing here, miles from anywhere? Neither Tomoe nor Hippolyta had red hair. Back in the days of making her name as an account planner, Oribe had been her favourite brand for hair. Since leaving the extravagances of Schneider & Schneider, the B2B comms and advertising phenomenon, she'd been forced to cut back on luxuries.

'This is…unbelievable. Really.' Evangeline held her towel around her. 'Thanks.'

Tomoe bowed. 'I leave you now.' She reached the door and turned back. 'When you are ready, come and play party.'

Alone, for the first time since arriving in Chile, Evangeline attempted to take stock. All her cells fizzed with the exertion of assimilating recent events. Ambushed, left to drown, all their belongings washed away, the journal stolen and with it, Morgan's directions and experience—nothing she could have done would have prepared her for what happened. But they had survived, Jesús, Florito and she. With friends such as these, all was not lost.

She soaked in the bath and tried to figure out what to do next. Their equipment they could replace, albeit with time and money they could ill-afford. Worse was the loss of the journal. Without Morgan's directions, their chances of ever finding the tree had shrunk to the chances of finding a pencil shaving in a lumberjack's turn-ups. More disheartening was the loss of Chile's advice and experience. His words had been like those of an ebullient and slightly wayward uncle, leading by example.

She had taken his 'push yourself in new directions' as a mantra, but where had it got her?

She had to consider abandoning the project. Spend a couple of days R&R here, dependent on Victor's continued hospitality. Then, if Victor was willing to lend them the means to get back to civilisation, from there she'd go home, tail between her legs.

Home, to emptiness and reminders of what might have been.

The alternative was to see the mission through to the end. To find the World Tree, save it from destruction by the oil company, and protect it from overutilization by Asklepion. Exactly how she would do it, she had no idea. What she did know, with a certainty running deep inside her, was that she and the tree needed each other.

On balance, then, there really was only one option: to stay and find out what she was capable of.

And now, they'd landed in the middle of some bizarre costume party. Victor was what? Eccentric? Certainly wealthy. He seemed to love the company of women—or maybe the power dynamic between him and 'his' women? Then there were his eyes. Even when he seemed most relaxed, his eyes were watchful, appraising, waiting.

She rested the back of her neck on the gilt rim of the bath and allowed the water to soothe her. The dress, now hanging from the door of the armoire, was pale green, what Mum would call eau-de-Nil. It didn't look like it belonged to Tomoe (too big) or Hippolyta (too small), nor North (no, just, no). There didn't seem to be a Mrs Victor around. Odd that Victor had women's clothing available for when he just happened to come across a damsel-and-friends in distress. Maybe he was a designer. An uber-exclusive clothes designer. That would explain it. Tomoe and Hippolyta were wearing his new collection. What would the collection be called? Valour Vogue? Kick-Ass Couture? Feisty & Fearless? And the branding would do something with the ampersand, so it would look like a sword and shield.

It had been a while since she'd thought in terms of advertising. Getting the job was her door to a different world. Mum never understood what it was she did; parents never do. It irritated her at the time but thinking back now, Evangeline had to agree the advertising world didn't make a whole lot of sense and, anyway, she'd always felt a bit of a fraud: as though she wasn't supposed to be there. To get people to want things, brand-messaging must make them believe they lacked things. There was an acronym bandied around at Schneider & Schneider: FUD. It stood for Fear, Uncertainty and Doubt. It had been her role to seed anxiety. Status, income, appearance, achievements: all were fair game. Banish wrinkles with this must have anti-aging serum! Yummy mummies! Display that neat little bump in a cool, sexy new wardrobe—just for you! Men! Underperforming? Take this blue pill and you'll have a rocket in your pocket!

Playing on people's anxieties made a lot of money. Funnily enough, at the time, she didn't recognise she was just as susceptible as everyone else. She'd been blind to her desire to use her career as a symbol of success. To be accepted in the world, especially the world of her father. But, just like Alice, she only existed in the Red King's dream. In the waking world, of course, she had gone out—Bang!—just like a candle!

Was that why she was drawn to Jesús? Because he wasn't part of that life? Maybe, it was more than that.

While she'd been musing, a beat insinuated its way through the closed windows. More a feeling than a sound, the beat amplified slowly. Now, the surface of the bathwater radiated ripples from the island of her raised knee.

Out of the bath, dried and anointed with lotions and perfume, Evangeline stepped into the dress and sandals and dimpled at her reflection in the gilt mirror. The Grecian-style swathes made her look taller. The colour emphasised the redness of her hair. Both dress and sandals could have been made to measure.

She loved her reflection in the mirror—she couldn't remember when she'd last looked so alive, but...

Taking a deep breath, it was time to make her presence known.

20. Lilith

Evangeline

Evangeline opened the solid wood panelled door of her room into a tidal wave of Latin American music and laughter and conversation. Yet not a soul to be seen.

Etruscan red Marmorino walls reflected the glow of uplighters. A series of Japanese woodblock prints, depicting a mounted female warrior with long hair, lined the wall, the colour of the walls picking out the red in the prints. Evangeline put off the urge to take a closer look: she wanted to find Jesús before doing anything else. They needed to discuss how they were going to continue their quest. But what if he wanted to call it a day? What if, after two attempts on their lives, Jesús decided finding the tree wasn't worth the hassle? Would she be returning along this corridor knowing she had to go it alone? She had to know how he felt.

The carpet was soft on her open toes and transmitted the pulse of the beat as a buzz against her skin. Following the music brought her to the head of a broad staircase.

Contrary to her first impression, the house was on different levels. But rather than rising upwards, its second storey descended from the ground floor. In the car that afternoon, the car had climbed steeply. Had Victor built this house? Yes, there was something very Victorish about the place. It was secluded, he must have chosen this precise spot. Why?

The party noises rose from below. Conversations tinkled up to meet her, they flirted and competed, but the words themselves remained opaque. With one hand on the banister and the other holding her dress clear of her heels, she descended the stairs. The rise of each step so shallow, the tread so deep, she felt as though she were gliding into a scene revealed one step at a time.

A gallery opened before her. Clusters of feet and ankles extended to legs and torsos. Bodies came together, either by accident or design, in hugs, nudges, bumps. Sometimes in greeting. Sometimes with magnetism, drawn skin to skin as though bewitched. An arm stroked the small of a back, a hand touched a waist then slipped to the curve of a rear. The women's clothes were playful but never frivolous, and the men's suits, in the main, were stylishly low key. She was dressed for the part. That was something. But what part? If it was a game, everyone seemed to know the rules, but her.

Finally, the heads came into view: they became people. Most were dark haired but there was a smattering of chemically assisted blondes, ranging in shade from bombshell platinum to old-money amber. Make up was dramatic. Eyes were smoky, smouldering, appraising and acquisitive. Lips shone bright and voracious. All were animated and glamorous and in the moment.

More than a few heads turned towards her. Eyes cruised the full length of her, before their owners were called back to the conversations they'd abandoned.

If the glare of attention had unnerved her, she'd also straightened her shoulders and lifted her chin. But now the spotlight had faded, and she wondered where to go.

'Arbolito!' Jesús' voice came out of the crowd.

Turning to the voice, she saw him, so beautiful in a cream, loose-fitting suit, break away from a group including Hippolyta at the far end of the room.

He came to meet her at the foot of the stairs, kissed her neck and said, 'Guapisima.'

She grinned. 'Nice threads. Victor's?'

'Not my usual thing, but is not bad. Come, you have to see this.'

'We need to talk.'

But he had already taken her by the hand and was leading her through the crowd, shaking hands in passing with a flashily dressed man with a Mohawk and a nicked eyebrow, whom he greeted as Arturo.

'La Piraña,' Jesús said. He checked her face for signs of recognition, then elaborated, 'Arturo Vidal, plays for Barcelona.'

'Got it,' she said.

Jesús rescued a couple of glasses of something sparkling from a passing tray and handed one to her.

He touched his glass to hers. 'Al seco!' His lips brushed her cheek. 'You not say how you know Victor.'

'I don't. Not really. I met him in Buenos Aires. I was going sightseeing and he offered to show me around a museum.'

'Is clear you made an impact,' he said.

'How do you mean?' she said.

'Expensive gifts and rescue missions, is how.'

'But there's no way he would've known where to find us.' She paused her glass mid-air. 'Nor that we needed rescuing.'

'No sé. But there *is* something you need to see,' he said.

'Sounds ominous. Look, we need to discuss—'

'I think I know why our man Victor take such an interest in you.'

'Oh? Now I'm really worried.'

'No, do not worry. Is … pues, you see.'

Like Clytie with Apollo, she felt as though a cloud had passed before the sun as his eyes strayed from her to follow an impossibly sultry beauty, all cheekbones and full lips, who slunk past them. 'Celine Reymond,' he whispered in awe. 'You can't move for all the celebs here. Come on, they're waiting for you. Be close.'

Be close! Chance would be a fine thing, Evangeline thought. He's got Hippolyta all over him like a rash and now there's a room full to the rafters with out-and-out hotties—minas, as Jesús would say—to contend with.

She followed him as he pushed through the crowd, aiming for the group he'd recently left. Hippolyta was there and Victor, also. They were gathered around a painting.

'Señors and Señoras.' Victor raised his glass in Evangeline's direction. 'I present to you, Lilith.'

Confused, she was met with gasps of appreciative surprise and 'Amazing', 'Uncanny', 'Mira tú!' Glasses were raised in unison.

'Viste!' Hippolyta clapped, then grasped her by the shoulders and turned her towards the picture.

Evangeline was confronted by a Pre-Raphaelite painting of a naked woman, with loose, fiery hair tumbling down her back, eyes closed in ecstasy, her passion-blushed cheek caressing the head of a serpent whose tongue flicked towards her breast. The gleaming serpent writhed around her leg and lower hips.

As beautifully rendered as the painting was, it was disquieting: it was her.

A glass shattered at her feet. Her hand was empty. The air was close, she couldn't breathe.

'North,' Victor's voice came from beside her at his usual purred volume. 'Please be so good as to fetch our guest another drink.'

How did he expect North, wherever she might be, to hear him above the crowd?

Evangeline was barely able to pull away from the painting. She glanced at Jesús who replied with a see-what-I-mean tilt of the head. She ought to respond to Victor and the group, all leaning forward in anticipation of something gracious or humorous, or both, but she had no words.

Victor smoothed over her silence, 'This is the original from 1892 by John Collier.' His eyes roamed over Evangeline's head. 'See how the forest setting accentuates the colour of her hair.'

'The fern crosiers look real,' she managed.

Victor inclined his head, watching her response all the while.

North approached with a tumbler, ice chinking in the leaf green drink. Tea. Made to North's special recipe. It wasn't what Evangeline wanted. All the same, it might be better for her than champagne. She drank it down.

The painting *was* so lifelike. Almost as though, before her eyes, the snake tightened his coil.

Her glass had been refilled. She hadn't seen it happen but guessed the culprit. Really, North was like a female Jeeves. Super-efficient, anticipating, discreet and precise in execution of duty. What secrets did she keep about Victor and his goings-on?

'Excuse me, I need to grab some air,' Evangeline caught Jesús' eye. He nodded in comprehension.

'Yes, of course,' said Victor. 'It will do you good. The garden has a special character at night. I'm afraid I've a little business to attend to now, but Hippolyta will show you around—I know she wants to.'

Before Evangeline had time to work out a way of saying she wanted to be left alone without causing offence, Hippolyta linked arms with her and said, 'At last, the Grand Tour! Bring your tea with you. Jesús, let's get you one more champagne for the road.'

'While you're out there, see if you can find Abraxas,' Victor said. 'I know how much she wants to meet our guests.' He glanced at Jesús as he spoke, and Evangeline felt a sense of foreboding. Hippolyta nodded as though understanding something that wasn't immediately apparent to anyone else.

'I'll leave you now but will join you as soon as I can.' Victor bowed to Evangeline.

※

Under the cool evening sky, light from the house cast a yellow arc on the terrace. Away from the houselights, ultraviolet spots and kaleidoscopic beams cut through the dark. A salsa band played. As they struck up *Oye Como Va,* a wave of revellers pushed out through the open patio doors to the terrace, to join the dancing vanguard and let loose their salsa moves: all matadors and sunbursts. Ordinarily, she would have been in this moment. But nothing about this evening was ordinary. In the centre of the dancefloor-cum-terrace, a statuesque dark-skinned woman with a corkscrew extravaganza of hair was giving it lots of cha-cha hip action. She flashed her teeth as she caught sight of Hippolyta, and took in Evangeline and—especially—Jesús, then flounced her head away and turned slowly, her white macramé dress glowing under the UV, her hips in a twitchy jiggle on the beat. So confident and exciting to watch. Outshining, obscuring. And wasn't that Tomoe, there, joining her? Resting her hands on the other's pelvis, moving as sinuously, but not as freeform. The swarm of dancers pulsated and throbbed as one, like a massive pupating beetle. Shrieks of laughter and the relentless percussion combined in a pitch that thumped in Evangeline's chest. Multi-coloured lights moved over the faces, the bodies, accentuating movement. Slick limbs reached out to her, laughing mouths loomed up close, to pull away into the dark: claustrophobic and empty at once. She was an outlier. From the group, yes, but she also felt strangely detached from her own body. It wasn't *her* skin that tingled as the hairs on her arms responded to a brush of air.

Beyond the terrace, the garden was only hinted at. Erect, paddle-shaped leaves, silhouetted against the night sky, jostled around the terrace, their wax cuticles bouncing light. Deeper into the garden, among the growth, and the smell of damp earth, static structures also. Organic in form but so rigid as to be distinctly unnatural.

Hippolyta guided Evangeline and Jesús through the dancers to a cobbled path which led away from the terrace. Once on the path, the vegetation rose around them filtering the music until all that was left was the son clave beat. Within the abundance, here and there, green spotlights marked out an ornamental plant, the giant umbrella leaves of a *Gunnera tinctoria,* a *Eucryphia cordifolia* heavy with white, scented bloom, the rusty trunk of *Luma apiculata.* Perhaps she might see something from the Yavuaceae, the plant family to which Rewe belonged, if she was lucky. The moon was particularly clear tonight. Colours were vivid, intense, jangling against each other, to vibrate behind her eyes.

Their way was lit by flame torches. Either side of the path, curvilinear pillars formed a guard. As she passed them, Evangeline saw they were stone snakes, covered with glass mosaic sparkling in the torchlight.

'Hey, wait for us,' a voice came from behind. It was Tomoe and the woman in white macramé.

'What took you so long?' Hippolyta said.

'My fault,' said the macramé-clad woman, planting a kiss on Tomoe's mouth. 'When this lovely throws her moves, how can I resist?'

Hippolyta pushed Evangeline and Jesús forward in introduction. 'Guys, this is Abraxas. Abraxas, meet Eve— Evangeline, and Jesús.'

Abraxas greeted Jesús with a kiss on both cheeks, lingering on the second with an audible inhalation.

'Mmm … Jesús,' said Abraxas stroking his cheekbone with a cherry red fingernail. 'Great look. What brings you here?'

'Our car went through a bridge. We ended up in the river,' the way Jesús said it, anyone would think it was an everyday occurrence.

'How very reckless of you.' Abraxas gave a throaty chuckle. 'We can be grateful to Victor for finding you when he did.'

She turned her head to Evangeline while her eyes lingered on Jesús. Abraxas bestowed an air-kiss to her cheek then held her at arm's length. 'You look fabulous in green, Lilith.'

'Will people stop calling me Lilith. My name's …?' Her mind was blank. No, not blank, it was caught as if on a spider's web.

An expression flickered across Abraxas's face to be masked by a diplomatic smile. But there, in that moment, was expectancy: the spider waking at a vibration of her web.

'Arbolito? Are you OK?' Jesús patted her back.

She rubbed her temple and attempted a laugh she didn't feel. 'Just tired, I guess.'

'Fresh air is what you need.' Hippolyta took her by the hand and set off again.

Not being on home turf, Evangeline opted for smiling politely and saying little as the best survival technique. It was her default when she didn't know how to behave. She couldn't help it: from an early age, Dad had instilled into her not to talk back. As a result, she found people didn't realise they'd overstepped the mark until the volcano erupted.

She reckoned that if she and Jesús played their cards right, they could have a good night's sleep, with a spot of breakfast thrown in, and be in with a fighting chance of the loan or otherwise of replacement supplies.

The path was too narrow for all five to walk abreast. Evangeline found herself flanked by Hippolyta and Tomoe, who explained the stone snakes were guardians.

'You see,' said Tomoe, 'the serpent holds her ground. She rises in a threatening display. If the danger persists, she will strike.'

It wasn't clear what the snake-guardians were defending here in the garden.

'Snakes are often associated with women,' Hippolyta said. 'Before the Classical Greek era, they were both considered holy as they embody the power of life.' Her arm pushed back an overhanging festoon of *Mandevilla laxa*, its white trumpets of saffron-throated flowers saturating the air with the scent of vanilla. 'And because snakes live in fissures in rocks or among the roots of trees, they symbolise chthonic beings—those of the underworld.'

Somehow, Jesús had ended up in the back row with Abraxas. Snatches of their conversation reached her through the tour-guide patter of Tomoe and Hippolyta.

'An expedition?' said Abraxas.

'We look for Chilean plants,' said Jesús.

'Is there money in that kind of thing? Plants don't make great TV.'

'You ask Evangeline, she is botanist.'

'And you're involved because…?'

'Am anthropologist. Is the people-plant relación which interests me,' said Jesús.

'Ah! Now that's a lot more interesting,' said Abraxas.

Through gritted teeth Evangeline muttered, 'Cheeky mare!'

Despite her earlier resolution, she wasn't concerned whether she was overheard; people never gave plants their full due.

From what she could make out of their conversation, she was relieved to hear he wasn't telling the full story to a complete stranger.

Hippolyta had stopped and was looking at her as though she expected an answer.

Evangeline could only say, 'Uh-huh.'

'Great, we'll go this way then.' Hippolyta steered them left at a fork in the path.

Flirtatious laughter came from some distance back.

'You're so funny,' Abraxas's voice reached her.

What were they talking about?

Either side of them, smooth, olive culms of *Chusquea culeou* bowed beneath overhanging foxtails of leafy branches. The sentry of bamboo restricted the path, forcing Tomoe to walk behind where she continued to supplement Hippolyta's commentary of the garden. Rising through the greenery, Evangeline made out columns topped with spiny whorls, open-sided towers supported on segmented culm-pillars, freestanding gothic windows, flights of stairs climbing to nowhere, footbridges like vines linking the structures, all luminous in the moonlight, all giving the appearance of having been grown not built. The path opened to a junction. At its centre was a stout column marked by sulphurous yellow lichen. As they drew close, she made out a frieze chiselled into the stone. A tumult of characters in battle spiralled around the column. Men against women. The men, naked but for plumed helmets. The women, on horseback, bare-breasted. A tangle of arms rose in assault, a clash of double-edged short swords, some caught up to the hilt in a torso, a thigh, an embossed shield thrust out towards the observer, so many women and horses lay trampled on the ground. Hippolyta was uncharacteristically silent and pressed her palm to the pillar.

Tomoe put her hand on Hippolyta's shoulder. 'This is the Amazonomachy,' she said softly to Evangeline.

Hippolyta's hand stroked across the relief to a female figure whose head was smashed beneath the foot of a soldier.

With a voice full of emotion, she said, 'this is where I fell.'

Evangeline couldn't have heard right. It sounded as though Hippolyta said she was there. Yet, she had to admit, the figure in the bas-relief did bear a striking resemblance to Hippolyta. What was going on here? In need of reassurance, she turned around. Jesús was no longer with them. Abraxas likewise.

She pulled away from the women and fled. Stumbling on the cobbles, she kicked off her heels. The sting of cold stone on the soles of her feet was a stimulant. As she ran, the colours, which moments before had been so vivid, muted to a more natural nightscape. A broken cobble, sharp as flint, gashed her foot. The pain rocketed to her brain. Ahead of her, a dull cloud hovered head-height above ground. Distinct from the black of night, and yet it was dark itself, shrouding the way beyond. There was no way around it. She ran through the cloud and got a mouthful of midges.

At the end of the bamboo path she recognised the stone snake-guardians of the main path, the Snake Path. She had to find Jesús—whatever he was up to—then they'd leave at once.

Which way? Left led deeper into the garden. Right would be back to the house. She went left.

Glinting in the torchlight, something slithered across the path. Yellow with a black zigzag along its length, the snake stopped and reared up, its forked tongue flickering, sensing her. Its emerald green, intelligent eyes locked on hers as though assessing her. Slowly, she bent to pick up a stone. She had no intention of harming the creature, but she needed to get past. Rising cautiously, she hurled the stone at a sculpture.

Crack. The stone had met its target. The snake hissed, swung its head in the direction of the noise then retreated into the undergrowth. Her path clear, she moved forward.

She heard someone calling her name some way ahead.

'Jesús!' she shouted.

'Evangeline!' It was Jesús' voice.

Hopeful, she dashed in his direction. As she rounded a bend in the path, she caught sight of him alongside the macramé-clad saucy strumpet. They stood in front of a Grecian-style temple.

Jesús rushed forward and hugged Evangeline, then held her by the arms for inspection. 'Bacán?' His examination of her was thorough. 'What have you done to your foot?'

'I cut it on the path.' Having been drawn to her attention, the gash in her foot resumed throbbing.

'Where did you go? We were following you then you disappeared.'

'We ended up at the Amazon-a-thingy.'

'The Amazonomachy,' Abraxas said. 'It's Hippolyta's imprint. We all—'

'There you are.' Victor emerged from a path on the left. 'The girls said you'd been upset,' he said to Evangeline. 'They were worried about you.'

'Victor, what exactly is this place?'

'This is my home.' Victor looked the picture of courteous bafflement. 'Is something wrong?'

'What's going on here?' said Evangeline.

'We're having a party.' In a bemused tone, Victor waved his arm to encompass the people they could see, those they couldn't, the music, his estate.

'But that's not what—' Evangeline said. Was this a case of lost in translation? Was she overtired? Or was there something more sinister going on?

'What's happened, Arbolito?' said Jesús.

'Jesús, there's something…' Evangeline faltered. 'I don't know what it is. I can't make it out. Something's not right. I don't like it. I want to leave,' she said.

'Of course.' Victor held up his hands in a placatory gesture. 'You can leave whenever you like.'

'OK, come on Jesús, we're leaving,' Evangeline said.

'It's late at night, you've no means of transport and you don't know where you're going. Is it really such a good idea to go now?' Victor said. No one could be more reasonable.

'Victor has a point,' said Jesús. 'Let's stay overnight and get your foot cleaned up. We can go first thing in the morning.'

'You're just tired,' Victor said. 'Let's get back up to the house and North can make you a nice cup of tea.'

21. Morning Light

Evangeline

Evangeline swung her legs over the side of the bed and put her feet on the floor. She winced. How was she going to clamber around in the mountains with a gammy leg?

A fresh set of clothes hung on the outside of the armoire: white wrap-around shirt, jodhpurs. She didn't doubt the clothes would fit like a glove.

Downstairs, all signs of the party had disappeared. Instead, a clear blue sky beckoned through open doors, birds sang with every ounce of energy their tiny bodies contained, and the garden was zealous in its abundance.

She found Jesús having breakfast on the patio. He looked up and smiled at her approached.

Everything was going to be all right.

'Buenos días, Arbolito.' Jesús' wrought iron chair scraped on the paving as he rose to kiss her in greeting.

'Buenos días,' she said shyly. No matter how often she saw him, Jesús had the kind of beauty that always surprised her, as though seen for the first time.

His touch drew her to him. 'Is good to see you,' he said.

The table juddered, rattling crockery, breaking the spell. Florito burst from under the furniture, sending a chair over with a clang. The hound lurched towards her, tail wagging with gusto, none the worse for his night in the mud room.

Florito! How could she have forgotten about him?

Jesús righted the chair and drew it closer to his own, tapping it as an indication to sit. She took the seat designated and curled over Florito, now with his head in her lap, to give him the fuss he deserved. 'My handsome boy. Look at your little rudder going.'

Jesús mopped at coffee in his saucer. 'Florito and I walked this morning.'

'I would have come with you if I'd known.' Then rubbing Florito's head, she said, 'Did you have a good walk? Did you?'

'Did you sleep well?'

'In a way. How about you?'

'Uh-huh. You have a good room, yes? With a view?' He waved expansively towards the garden.

'Yes, it was gorgeous.' She twisted around to gauge her bearings. 'I think it looked out the other way, though. Over the front.'

'There are many rooms here,' he said. 'I didn't know where you were. I—'

A tray clattered on the table. Evangeline jumped.

'Good morning.' North busied herself with unloading the tray of a basket of bread, a plate of cheese and a pot of tea. While she poured Evangeline a cup of green tea, Jesús stirred his cafecito.

'Your foot today is good, no?' He asked.

'Sore,' Evangeline said, taking a sip of tea.

When would North's rustling, creaking and clattering leave them alone so she could find out what he'd been about to say?

Jesús stroked Evangeline's shin. 'I know you want to be on the road, but—and this is just a suggestion—you think maybe better if your foot has a day to heal, no? We have a lot of ground to cover and you will feel it, with a poorly foot.'

She gulped down the tea, her first of the day. Tea, not time, is the great healer.

'Jesús, I think I owe you an apology.'

'What for?'

'Last night. I don't know what got into me.'

Something had spooked her last night but now her fears seemed stupid, and she dreaded to think what everyone, especially Jesús, thought of her behaviour.

'Pues, your foot—so much blood—is no surprise you were upset,' he said.

Before she had a chance to mull over his suggestion, he nodded in the direction of the patio doors.

'Here's Victor and Tomoe now. We ask, yes?' he said.

'Buenos días. Would you have any use for this?' Victor handed Jesús a folded map.

'Güeno! Graciela. Just what we need,' Jesús glanced across at Evangeline.

'And how's the invalid, this morning?' said Victor.

'Morning, Victor. Morning, Tomoe. I'm all right, I think,' she said.

Had she had too much to drink last night? Too much tea? Had someone spiked her glass? For the life of her, she couldn't work out how her foot came to be sliced up.

To cover her confusion, she poured another cup of tea.

'Let Tomoe take a look at your foot,' Victor said.

'I'm sure it's fine,' Evangeline said.

Tomoe said, 'Your dressing probably needs to be changed, anyway.'

Bowing to pressure, Evangeline turned her chair to face the Samurai warrior and removed her boot. Tomoe knelt, resting back on her heels. She placed Evangeline's foot on her lap and gently unwound the bandage.

'Don't let this stop you having your breakfast,' Victor said. 'Your tea will get cold.'

The tea was refreshing. She would normally have coffee for breakfast—as Jesús was doing right now. But the tea was part of *La Menagerie.* At each sip, she had the impression of a tendril circumnutating, binding her to the garden.

With a tug, the bloody end of the bandage came away from her foot.

Tomoe drew her breath. 'The wound is deep. You should not walk on it for a few days at least.'

'I know you want to get going this morning,' Victor said. 'But if Tomoe recommends rest, both of you are more than welcome to stay as long as you need.'

'What do you say, Arbolito?' Jesús added.

The wound stung in the fresh air. She looked from Jesús to Tomoe to Victor. Before replying she took another sip of tea. The soothing warmth of it washed through her, dispelling anxiety and pain. Jesús was right, they wouldn't get far with her hobbling about. What was the rush? The garden was so vivid in the morning light.

'If it's OK with you, Victor?' she said.

22. The Kiss of Nahuel

Morgan: The Atacama, 2 February 1843

With three times more retinue setting off on the journey than my original plan, and half a dozen pack mules loaded with all manner of equipment and provisions, we formed something of a royal procession as we left Iquique. The lovebirds, Solomon and Maite, were lively company: their conversation and song a welcome novelty. Paco, at the head of the mule train, took little time to recover his equanimity after the departure of Smokey Sultana. If truth be told, I suspect that particular romantic interlude had been one-sided to the detriment of the beautiful grey.

The Atacama region is one of the driest coastal deserts in the world. So dry as to be almost lifeless. So dry, in fact, that decomposition does not occur; vegetation may be dead for thousands of years, yet still intact. But the region is host to an atmospheric phenomenon which, for some pockets of land, negates the need for rain: the Camanchaca. From the port, therefore, we opted to head inland under the creeping mantle of the Camanchaca, the fog that butts against the steep, coastal slopes and dwells in gorges. Rampant forests of olivillo[12] lorded it over Peruvian pepper (*Schinus molle*),[13] gripping epiphytes, tangling vines, and ground smothering ferns and mosses—all hydrophilous plants—and crowded around us, dripped on us, barred our way. We pressed on; our clothing soaked through.

When we stopped for water, Maite gently touched my arm. 'When did that happen?' she asked.

My shirt sleeve was ripped and, through it, a gash in my arm was beaded with thickening blood. 'I've no idea,' I answered. So intent on forging forward, a small thing like a ripped shirt could go unnoticed. Swiftly, I doused the wound and we went on our way.

Filling our ears was the song of the forest. The incessant, high pitched stridulation of crickets to which the ear soon becomes inured, blended with the cackle of birds guarding their nests. Over the course of the day, the timbre and counterpoint of the forest song ran through a number of variations. It was evening and time for the crepuscular fauna to come to the fore. Now, the barking chatter of chinchillas[14] vied with the haunting whistle of the Chilean tinamou, that stocky, ground-dwelling bird with stunted, neatly tucked tail. Not for the first time, I was convinced I heard the rumbling bass of a jaguar, more of saw-toothed breathing than vocalisation, but to hear it is to know you are within its sights. I was reassured, however, that Paco and his squad were untroubled: not a twitch. That being the case, I told myself to stop behaving

---

12. *Aextoxicon punctatum* a canopy tree more commonly found in the Valdivian rainforests. The fruit, a drupe, resembles the olive, hence the common name.

13. Solomon collected some of the pink berries with which to spice our meals.

14. Named, I have it on good authority, after the Chincha people of the Andes.

like some hysteric before I was locked up in Bedlam.

The day faded in an instant and we had to set up camp by the eerie, diffuse moonlight that permeated the fog. Solomon and I had potted several small birds which he set about preparing to roast on the fire Maite got going, while I hobbled the mules.

My bones ached. Was I getting too old for this game? I should have pitched in when the others busied about, clearing the ground and opening out the tarpaulins for shelter. But, for the life of me, it was all I could do to sit upright. Their voices came at me in dizzying bursts, disconcertingly muffled, then overloud. I jumped as a log cracked on the hungry fire, the flames licking towards the arboreal vault above. And there, on the horizontal limb of a tree, two amber specks glimmered in the light of the fire.

'Man, you need to eat.' Solomon handed me a spoon and a plate piled high with game. 'You look like you see a ghost.'

'Eat,' I repeated, the smell of roasted flesh churning my stomach. 'Yes, it eats the fire.'

I was alone. The dark was absolute. Nothing existed in the cosmos apart from my hunger and me. My hunger was ever present. It was there in the pit of my belly, driving my thoughts. I saw nothing but the need for sustenance. I heard nothing but the demand for food. I smelled nothing but the metallic stench of my own hunger.

In the depths of nothing sparked a bud of fire. When, I don't know. In darkness, space and time are hard to gauge, but within the darkness, a glimmer drew the eye. In time, the bud grew into Sun. Sun rose in an arc above my head and descended behind me. But in its rising, I felt substance form beneath me. The claws of all four of my feet drove into soil, the very soil that gave forth the forest. The forest sheltered me, hid me, fed me. And my hunger grew. Dark became night. Sun brought the day. I watched Sun cross Heaven. So full of life. My hunger ached. I waited where Sun fell to Earth. I opened my jaws wide and felt the fire burn my tongue as Sun slipped inside. I swallowed. All at once, all was dark. But within me fired a chaos of life.

I was alone, my path ahead unclear. The fire inside me grew and gave me courage.

From out of the forest, Jaguar came. His name was Nahuel.

Nahuel approached me and we stared eye to eye. He opened his mouth wide and, with a roar that bent the trees and shook the ground, his breath seared my body. In that moment, he gave me the gift of strength.

'That which you seek is protected by its people,' Nahuel growled.

'I mean them no harm,' I said.

'Their only concern is for Rewe. What would you do with the tree if you find it?'

'The tree must survive. With its seed and its root, I will ensure it continues in my homeland.'

'The progeny may produce strong, long lived trees which bear fruit and give rise to their own saplings, but they will never be the one you want. There is only the one Rewe.'

'I want to see it with my own eyes.'

'Within you are the gifts of courage and strength. You will find the tree and look upon it. But you will never return.'

'So be it. Tell me what I need to do,' I said.

With that, he licked my face, my chest, my arms and legs. He licked the clefts, the curves, the prominences. He licked the hair from my head. His coarse tongue scoured the skin from my flesh. I lost myself and was renewed.

I was not alone. I jolted astride a mule. Light glared, my eyelids slammed shut. Even so, the light was relentless, flashing a river like network on a reddish background. The air was clear but parched. Water, I needed water.

155

The woman supporting me said, 'He's come back to us.'
In that moment, I knew what I had to do.

23. Garden Days

Evangeline

The colours at *La Menagerie* were brighter than elsewhere. Whether due to altitude, or latitude, or clean air, Evangeline had no idea, but she held on to the hope of a logical explanation. For if not that, what? All in the mind? But while colour was sharper, time somehow was fuzzier. Often, it folded over itself, such that Evangeline had no memory of days, weeks? At other times, a moment might stretch as though melting, to seep between the cracks in reality.

On this afternoon, Evangeline and Victor took the snake path through the garden, a walk of which she never tired. She enjoyed their time together, the walks especially, when it was just the two of them. His attention undivided, he would talk about all sorts of things, but he seemed to instinctively know what would interest her.

Victor caught sight of a plant he called hierba loca—maddening plant. It was a sprawling, inconspicuous shrub with small, glossy, myrtle-like leaves, and waxy white flowers resembling its sister-species, the heaths. When eaten during shamanic rituals, the fruit of this plant, he told her, would invoke magic. Further along the path, he pointed out the bushy taique, about her height, with flame red trumpets for flowers. An infusion of its holly-like leaves was used by medicine men to achieve transcendence, he said.

Victor was knowledgeable about such things. When it came to plants he sought and valued her opinion.

'What inspired you to become a plant hunter?' he said.

'My mum has a lovely garden. She always had a way of bringing glamour and fun into even the ugliest of situations. Not a gardener, as such, but plants just seem to zing up around her. I took home some seedlings I'd cultivated at school and she put the terracotta pot on a saucer on the kitchen windowsill,' she said.

'What about your father?' he asked.

A bird she knew to be a ground tyrant took off from a slab of exposed bedrock; a flash of white breast shooting across her field of vision. 'Not so much.'

The memory of seedlings, plant pot and saucer as they struck Mum's face replayed in her head in the same slow-motion as when she first witnessed it. She thought the saucer had smashed on impact, but it wasn't that. Blood, lots of it and caked in John Innes No 2, streaked across Mum's cheek. The white shard flying from Mum's mouth was now embedded in the pine-laminate MDF wall-cabinet. As Dad's fist drove home the advantage, Evangeline-the-child skidded along in his wake, tugging the rear of his cable-knit out of shape. His rage, a constant stew beneath a tight lid, vented with yelling and force. This time, it had been about the phone ringing while the cricket was on. Mum, on the other hand, set her shoulders as she washed her mouth at the sink.

She bent to hug Evangeline, and lisped in the girl's ear, 'We're better than this.'

Victor and Evangeline came upon the temple.

Eccentric and overgrown, a surreal hybrid between nature and artifice, backcrossed and inbred, a recombination of the building blocks of life, this temple was one man's dream.

In size and proportion, eight columns across by twelve deep, the temple was of the golden ratio. The columns cinched in at the waist, jutting out at hip and shoulders, and returned to waist width at capital and base. With age, their carved vines had acquired a sheath of moss. The columns supported an incomplete domed roof, also networked with moss. The entrance was guarded by silvery doors, satin smooth. Above the doors a semi-circular mosaic set in a cobalt blue background depicted the lunar phases, waxing and rising to a central opalescent full moon, then waning on the fall.

Victor twisted the handle of a door, put his shoulder to it, and pushed. He stood back to allow her to enter first.

A sunbeam through the roof aperture illuminated a stone altar garlanded with spent flowers. The occasional, trailing zigzag of *Philodendron scandens,* its glossy, heart-shaped leaves shining on lazily gyrating stems, had found ingress the same way as the sun.

'This is the Temple of the Moon,' Victor said over her shoulder. He ran his finger down her spine and continued, 'In three days' time, it will be full moon. It's when the moon's power is most strong.'

'And then?' She felt his breath on the fine hairs on her neck. It ignited a glistening down to the delta of her spine.

Victor didn't answer straight away but rested his hands on her hips and pressed lightly. She inhaled the mossy-pebble aftershave.

What was he like naked? Sinuously muscular, his strength was all in the sudden explosion of action, poised ready to pounce. She could imagine his buttocks, steely with the force of exertion. His groin thumping away.

The pressure of his hands on her hips relaxed. 'You've put on weight.'

As he let go and stepped away from her, her hips seemed to

plump up like a recently vacated seat-cushion. Her face was burning. Hit by the disjoint between her thoughts and the reality of herself through another's eyes, she felt as spent as the altar flowers.

He drew her by her shoulders to face him. She tried to resist, aware of the red splodges likely to be on her face and neck, and of the childishness of her attempt. She didn't like herself as she was now. Her thoughts were Victor's thoughts, her words were Victor's words. In the past she would have put this man in his place. Now she could barely remember her own name. When did she become such a doormat?

'Hey, cariño, don't sulk.' He lifted her chin by the crook of his finger. 'I'll have a word with North. She'll sort out your diet.'

Oh, great. Why did North have to be brought into this?

He looked through the roof aperture as though trying to divine a course of action.

Then his face came back to the moment. 'You should come to the gym, also. I'll design a training schedule, just for you.'

At the heart of the garden, they came across a giant tree Victor knew as olivillo. Its branches were laden with tight, rusty-brown drupes, resembling olives, hence the name. She had read about the tree, but where?

The olivillo held a chasm between the cleft of its shapely roots.

'A snake has made its home here. It is said the snake links our world with the underworld. It is the messenger of the spirits of that world, the Wekufe.'

An image entered her head: a yellow snake with a black zigzag along its length, a flickering forked tongue, and intelligent, emerald eyes.

'I think I've come across Snake,' she said.

'Have you, cariño?' Victor held her eye, as a headmaster with a recalcitrant pupil.

He rested his arm against the olivillo and smiled down at her without humour. She stepped back and stumbled on a root. She imagined she was Ophelia, drowning amid the mossy pebbles.

'Remind me again, what brought you to Chile?' he purred.

Such a straightforward question. So why couldn't she picture the memory? 'A holiday?'

She was rewarded by his nod of satisfaction. He scrutinised her face as though to uncover what lay hidden. 'You were looking for something, I think.'

Looking for something? She shook her head. No, not that she could recall.

He smiled, then. 'You are very special to me.' He pulled her close.

She felt she'd passed an exam.

'Come, it is so warm, you must need refreshment. I'll have North make you a cup of tea,' he said.

On their way back to the house, Victor questioned Evangeline about her friendship with Jesús. It wasn't the first time he'd done so. She felt guilty, as though she'd done something wrong. Perhaps this was why she hadn't been accepted as part of *La Menagerie,* in the same way that Hippolyta and Abraxas obviously were.

'I'm sure his youthful…enthusiasm has its charms for a girl like you.'

'Well…' The urge to please Victor overrode any loyalty to life before him. All the same, she recognised the slime trail of a slug within her.

'You do know, of course, he and Abraxas have become very close.'

The slug flinched as if doused with salt. The garden closed in.

'It's common knowledge.' Her sisters, Hippolyta, Tomoe, and the rest had made it their duty to let her know.

The sad laughter of a dark-billed cuckoo sounded, *Ga-ga-ga-ga-go-go-go*.

'I thought, at first, you two might have been—how do you say—an item?'

Why was he asking this? 'Maybe there was something there, once, but …'

'So, you no longer care for him?'

'We're not in a relationship, if that's what you mean?'

Ga-ga-ga-ga-go-go-go.

'Mi corazón, I'm surprised a woman like you ever wasted her time on such a boyfriend.' He said 'boyfriend' as though the word was earwax in his mouth.

'It's nothing like that.' She felt a snip inside her.

Ga-ga-ga-ga-go-go-go.

⁂

They found Jesús and Abraxas on the terrace.

Jesús said, 'Did you know Abraxas is a television producer?'

Abraxas had a proprietorial air about her. No. More than that: she was taking the reins from a less experienced handler. She looked casually in Evangeline's direction. 'He's a natural.'

How long had it taken to perfect such measured insouciance?

It turned out Abraxas was developing a name for herself in natural history programmes. To make it big she needed to find the next David Attenborough. But an Attenborough for the younger generation. An Attenborough with sex-appeal.

It was more than clear: Jesús was the chosen one.

24. Snakes & Ladders

Evangeline

When the woman saw that the fruit of the tree was good for food and pleasing to the eye, and also desirable for gaining wisdom, she took some and ate it. [Genesis 3:6 – The Fall]

Something hidden.

The dull pain nudging between Evangeline's dreams, on and off, for what might have been hours, asserted itself in her hip and shoulder. Mainly on the side she was lying but, when she rolled on to her back, the pain followed to her coccyx and spine, then, with another turn, the opposite hip and shoulder. There was more to the pain than ache. Not so much around the bruising pressure points, but a prickling heat tormented the skin across her collar bone and between her breasts.

There was something unexpected, too, in the air: a mineral tang. A smell she hadn't encountered before at *La Menagerie*. Without opening her eyes, she knew this wasn't the room she'd fallen asleep in last night.

She opened her eyes and found herself in a damp cell. Hippolyta sat with her back against the wall and gave a small nod of greeting.

The Amazon addressed the opposite wall. 'She's awake.'

A shuffle of movement behind Evangeline's head preceded the appearance of Tomoe, leaning over her. Her soft voice said, 'Ohayo.'

Evangeline sat up from the floor. They were all dressed in shapeless, dirty hessian shifts.

Go and find it.

abscission /əb'sɪʃ(ə)n/ ► **noun** Botany the rejection of plant organs, such as leaves or fruit.
– ORIGIN early 17th cent.: from Latin *abscissio(n-),* from *abscindere,* from *ab-* 'off' + *scindere* 'to cut'.

The clicket-clack of kitten heels on parquet reverberated up and around the steampunk skeleton before helter-skeltering down the spiral stairs.

Kew's herbarium was a pyrethrin-infused temple. Its carmine balustrades and columns, rivets and girders, and those spiral stairs, were built to house the holiest of holies: a systematic collection of plant specimens. Identical cream cabinets ran its length, protruding like ribs from the wall and were repeated on the mezzanine above, and the balcony above that, with more cabinets still. Overhead, the white angularly joisted ceiling loomed like ghostly spiders-in-wait.

Evangeline shook her head. 'What's going on?'

Hippolyta rose from the floor with the economical movement of an athlete and bounced on her feet. 'Today, you start your Ablution.'

'Which is…?'

'Come.' Tomoe bent forward like a bud of anemone silvering in summer rain. She took Evangeline by the hand and pulled her to her feet. 'We can explain along the way, but we need to make a start before sunrise.'

'Don't worry.' Hippolyta clapped an arm around her shoulder. 'We'll be with you every step.'

Evangeline pulled at the front of her shift, the indraft of air soothing the itchiness. 'What's with the hair shirts?'

'The cilice is traditional for the Ablution.' Tomoe led the way down a flight of stone steps and along a dingy corridor. 'It signifies the sloughing away of the old you.' She hesitated in front of a door. 'This way, I think.'

The door opened onto a dazzle of mirrored brightness, a frigid blast of sweat and rubber, and thumping, high intensity workout music. Gym equipment, no doubt all the latest spec, with docking ports for music players and dangling cords of heartrate monitors, gleamed in readiness. Overhead, a network of exposed pipes, some large enough to crawl through, others barely the size of her wrist, added an industrial-style retro finish.

What had she expected after this descent into the bowels of *La Menagerie*? A torture chamber? Victor certainly had a peculiar way of doing things. It didn't need all this charade of sackcloth and ashes. And, anyway, how was anyone supposed to have a decent workout in this get-up? Every wall reflected countless Evangelines, backed by infinite Tomoes and Hippolytas, shrinking into the distance; the brilliant lighting nobody's friend. Evangeline's reflection dared her to say she wasn't enjoying this, that she didn't want to play anymore. As she met the apprehensive eyes of her facsimile, she knew she'd lost her way. Would she ever find her way back?

Something lost behind the Ranges.

This time, the wave swallowed Evangeline whole. She screwed her eyes shut and went inward, deep inside the belly of the whale.

The pain ebbed, as before, and once more she was present in the overheated delivery room. Stark, unnatural light radiated from a galactic examination lamp hovering high over her groin.

'Water,' she said.

Will held an open bottle to her lips. Evangeline sipped, once, twice, just wetting her tongue each time as if this would hold back the pain. Water trickled down her chin. She turned her head. Dark circles beneath Will's eyes stood out from the white face. He looked older, a different person: Will, and not Will. Things would never be the same again. He was trying, she was sure, to arrange his features into an expression of support, but he couldn't disguise that out-of-his-depth look behind his eyes.

Fruit set is the process in which flowers become fruit and potential fruit size is determined.

She no longer knew whether the thumping beat drove her pace or the steady pad-pad of her feet on the treadmill led the music. Sweat dripped into her eyes, blurring her vision. The cilice, itchy when dry, now drenched to steel wool, scarified her skin.

Either side of her, also on treadmills, Tomoe and Hippolyta barked encouragement. Occasionally, they skipped off their machine to adjust her pace or incline, standing in front of her, urging her on with countdowns and almost-theres. Once, she held her hand up, enough, but all she got in reply was a you-can-do-this and an increased speed. She may have asked why she was doing this, right at the beginning, but now it was impossible to question. Just do. Railing was not an option. Sometimes, they changed to rowers, or cross-trainers, for thirty minutes or so, but they always came back to the treadmill.

She lost the capacity to do more than put one foot in front of the other, but the metallic clank of resistance weights, the glub-glub-globble of the water cooler told her there was another user in the gym.

YAVUACEAE
Araucanía, Chile
Yavuea morganii

Location: Western flank of Volcán Llíma, 300 yds South East on dirt track after turn-off from source of R. Llíma. On this Day, we walked up a dirt track as far as the Stone Effigy. High altitude. Uncommon on Volcanic sandy soil or semi-disintegrated Lava. Humid. Grows alongside the emergent *Araucaria araucana*.

Leaves: glossy, cordate with pronounced drip tip, blade with pellucid dots. Inflorescence: determinate. Flowers: (presum. fragrant?), unisexual (poss. dioecious?). Carpel 1; ovary superior; with ± apical placentation; stigma 1, capitate, truncate, lobed. Ovule 1.

38.75 S 71.73W

Collected by: Edwin Morgan
Date: 13th July, 1838

A pair of well-honed, electric blue, female buttocks moved into the mirrored reflection, hovered, and moved out. And again, lift, two, three, hold, two, three, down, two, three. In all, the buttocks made fifteen appearances. Without getting the full picture, Evangeline assumed the pair had been engaged in barbell squats x 15 = 1 set.

Fruit drop (abscission) occurs at certain developmental stages:

1. **Pre-setting:** shedding of flowers with aborted pistils, shortly after blossoming.
2. **Post-setting:** affects unfertilized flowers and some improperly fertilized flowers.
3. **June drop:** at this stage, fruit have grown to the size of a marble.

The above three stages of abscission are natural and beneficial to the tree as they allow it to balance resources by losing excess fruit, ensuring the remaining crop ripens to maturity. But there remains one further, rarer, stage which takes place just before fruit harvest:

4. **Pre-harvest fruit drop (PFD):** factors affecting PFD include poor cultivation and nutrient imbalance.

Go and find it. Go and look behind the Ranges.

Another contraction crested the one before. Her pelvis cracked; she was ripping apart.

Will squeezed her shoulder. 'You've got this.'

What an idiot thing to say! 'Back off.'

He retreated to the end of the bed. It was all going on beyond the green sheet, an area that no longer belonged to her.

'One last effort, Evangeline,' said the midwife. 'Come on, you're not pushing hard enough.'

Relieved to be off her feet, she pressed her elbows into the pads and curled her biceps to Tomoe's count.

'Ichi, ni, san, shi …'

Hippolyta held a paper cone of water at the ready. Evangeline could already taste the waxed paper-infused frigid water and anticipated the switch from dehydrated dizziness to brain-freeze faint.

Clank.

Evangeline turned to the noise. The neat, spikey figure brought her electric blue thighs together, then opened wide as she lifted her head and locked eyes with Evangeline's reflection.

'You've no place in science,' Catalina's matt red lips said.

'You've made your bed…deal with it,' the galactic lamp telepathed, with an interplanetary voice, part-Dalek, part-schoolmarm.

Most extraordinary.

Magnoliid Complex Phylogeny

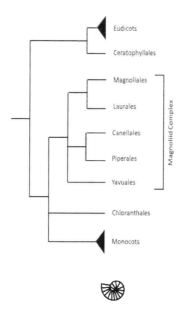

Lost and waiting for you. Go!

25. A Most Calculating Mule

Morgan: The Atacama, 11 February 1843

It turns out I'd been babbling for several days. The gash to my arm of which I had no knowledge of cause, nor had given much thought, became infected. By Solomon's account, after delaying progress for a night and a day, during which time the fever took hold, my companions decided we should move on. In my delirium, Solomon lifted me up onto Paco, who, Maite asserted, walked with the greatest of care to avoid disturbing his cargo.

The Camanchaca had accompanied us only so far. Emerging from a quebrada, one of the deep narrow valleys addled with fog, Solomon reported having been buoyed by the sight of rainclouds ghosting the distant peaks. His optimism had since been challenged. During my oblivion, we'd travelled into a barren, red, unearthly desert. Our boots and the hooves of the mule train— those tugboats of the desert—stirred up orange dust which settled on our clothes and stuck to exposed skin. Yet civilisations from times past had not only colonized the area but had stubbornly protected it from attack. I made out the scant remains of a fortress looking down at us from a ridge.

If Hephaestus had crafted a torment for Man, even in all his ingenuity he could not have conceived of such as this: the combination of heat, desiccation and altitude plagued our every step. The plateaux and valleys we traversed were cracked and scarred as though some divine hammer had, in anger, smote all life from the surface. Other features of the landscape suggested that those who fled retribution were turned to pillars of salt. We took refuge where we found shade and became crepuscular and nocturnal creatures. By night, we were guided by the stars.

My fever abated but, every now and then, I had waking dreams. I'm sure the xeric conditions played their part. After all, it is well-known that thirsty travellers in the desert can hallucinate the presence of oases. Nevertheless, I would surmise it rare to find an individual whose apparitions involve a talking jaguar. Far from disturbing me, his appearances gave me the fortitude and determination to reach my goal. I did not tell my companions about my visions, not wanting to concern them in any way. But, once or twice during Nahuel's visitations, Solomon looked at me askance. It made me wonder whether the conversation was in my mind or had slipped into the material world. But since my illness, I had not needed as much sleep. I rested only because it was clear the others, in particular Maite—as plucky as she was—needed to do so.

☙

And so it was that on what I hoped would be our last day in the desert, I woke before dawn. My eyes drank in the stars above while my legs fidgeted to be on their way. But this morning was different. Gone was the absolute silence that fills the ears. In its place came the rhythmic chirping of insects. The infinite, blank night sky gave way to a blush on the horizon. The air against my face felt pregnant. It held a promise of a fragrance that had not existed yesterday. In time, the blush ripened. With it, a bird trilled, to be answered by another not far away, and then another. Then they all joined in. A scuttling went past my head. I twisted the axis of my shoulders to see the skitter of a lizard, its mottling of black and sulphur, its hind limbs stemming horizontally from the body, its claws long and slender, glancing lightly off the sandy surface. Unable to believe what I saw, I pushed myself upright for a clearer view. What yesterday had been barren plateau, had overnight metamorphosed into a glorious carpet of perfect pink blooms, dominated by the musk mallow *(Malva moschata)*. Without knowledge of it, the rainclouds Solomon had spied from afar, had released their load after all.

We dismantled camp and continued on our way. Inspired by the morning's spectacle, Maite recounted the legend of *El Desierto Florido,* the Desert in Bloom.

'There was once a beautiful maiden with raven-black hair and lips the colour of the pinkest mallow. Many men in the village asked for her hand in marriage, but she refused them all. One day a brave and handsome miner came through town riding the finest mule in all the land. The mule's name was Paco.' Laughing affectionately, Maite patted our Paco's flank before continuing, 'The miner came in search of gold. Instead, he found love—the greatest treasure by far.

'Soon, maiden and miner were never apart. Wherever she went, there was he. Wherever he went, she would follow. But one night, the miner had a dream. In the dream, he was shown the mountain where he would find a rich vein of gold. At the break of day, he rose and left his love, promising to return as soon as he found the ore. Each morning she looked for him on the horizon. Each evening, she hung a lamp outside her door to help the miner find his way home. But he never returned. Eventually, the maiden pined away and died of a broken heart. Mourning her death, the villagers buried her in the desert and the Sky, sharing their grief, wept over her grave. When the villagers looked out the next day, the desert had become a flower meadow, as pink as the maiden's lips.'

With the desert behind us, we made good progress through a broad, fertile valley, much of which was divided into vast haciendas belonging to wealthy colonial families. Once again, my letters of invitation assured us of hearty lodging and the kindest hospitality. We also had the good fortune to witness first-hand the renowned skill of the huaso, that species of free-spirited horsemen who herd the cattle and work the land. These wandering stars warned us that the fort at Concepción had been taken, and the entire town was under the control of the Mapuche. This was a serious threat. The Mapuche warriors had a reputation for heroism superior to that of Hercules. We armed ourselves with the pistols and rifle which had hitherto been stowed away and followed the north bank of the Río Bío-Bío towards its source. At the time, we thought it a straightforward matter of avoiding the incursions by travelling away from the trouble spot. Although we didn't know it then, we came to regard our position as being caught between the Devil and the deep sea.

Stopping for the night in a German watering hole on the frontier, we made enquiries as to the safest point to cross the river. Among its cosmopolitan clientele, various opinions were put forward.

'You want to continue upriver where you'll find Diego's Ford,' said one.

'You don't want to do that,' said another. 'What you need to do is turn back ten mile or so. Pass the Duqueco on the right then you'll see the Bureo on the left—'

'You don't know your arse from your elbow. It's the Bureo on the right and the Duqueco on the left,' said a third navigator.

'Well, when the river is joined by two others it gets wider. Where it gets wider it gets slower. That's where you can take the ferry across,' said the second.

A discussion ensued, on the merits and otherwise of each suggestion.

In the shadows, a broad-shouldered man with prominent cheekbones, listened to the conversation without contributing.

None the wiser on the best route across the river, we thanked our informants and made to retire to our rooms. As we walked past the stranger, he addressed us, 'The territory is safe enough,' he said in a guttural voice. 'For those who respect our ways.'

'We mean no harm,' Maite said in Mapudungun. 'Mr Morgan, here, wishes to explore the regional plants.'

I once again recognised the advantage of conversing with a fellow in his own tongue. A new warmth glowed in his eyes.

Through Maite, I asked the fellow whether we needed to seek permission from the local Mapuche leader to travel through their territory.

'It would be a courtesy well-received,' he replied.

'Would you be willing to assist us in this endeavour?'

'It happens that I'm travelling in your direction. I will help you as far as our two paths are one,' he said.

Receiving the translation, I held out my hand. 'Edwin Morgan, sir. Your offer gratefully accepted.'

Hesitantly, as though this was an unfamiliar code, he took my hand. 'Ventura Coña.'

※

In the company of Ventura, we crossed the Bío-Bío and advanced into the Mapuche stronghold. The region is popularly known as the Lake District: a land of volcanos, forest and—need it be said— lakes. So many of them, for this area is the wettest in Chile. Upholding its climatic reputation, the rain fell without stop. We took to the mules for our comfort, but never was such a term more misplaced. Rain seeped into everything. Our clothes and bedding were perpetually soaked through, the panniers holding my precious collecting equipment and scientific instruments leaked, spoiling the specimens I'd collected to date, and far from having our pistols at the ready, their workings seized up with all the moisture.

The mules, accompanied by Saqui, Ventura's chestnut stallion, walked in mud up to their knees. Nevertheless, Paco, a most calculating mule, drove ever forward and led his stable mates by example. It is with no little remorse, therefore, that I report the following episode.

For many nights the conditions had forestalled any attempts at lighting a fire. Without the means to cook we resorted to handfuls of grain which turned to gluey sawdust in our mouths. Late one afternoon, hungry, drenched and exhausted, we encountered a veritable botanist's paradise on the lower flank of our path. Rare, unfamiliar, perhaps even undiscovered, shrubs and herbs tantalised me: a profusion of a sweet-scented legume—their papilionaceous blue-violet flowers mollifying the angry clouds above—were interspersed with the white of cardamines and yolk-yellow orchids. In just an hour or so, I reasoned, I could more than recompense myself for the rain-spoilt specimens. Solomon and Ventura remonstrated with me: the light was failing, and we needed to set up what camp we could. Maite's guileless eyes said it all: I was risking our safety for the sake of my botanizing. Paco, in his own way and in his own good time, went further than all of them.

I leaped from his back and fumbled to unstrap my collecting tools from one of his panniers. Hardly able to see before my eyes in the deluge, I slid down the slope regardless. Up to my knees in flora, I set about with my pocketknife, cutting unblemished specimens which bore leaves and flowers, and tapping the flowerheads for seed. I was a man possessed. I may have mumbled over my shoulder for my companions to find a place to camp for the night. Yes, I must have done, for when I next looked up from my task, I was alone save for stalwart Paco waiting on the path above. He jiggled his head and huffed, the strangest sound, more bear than mule and quite unlike his normal self. I assumed the weather had got to him as it had the entire company.

Just a few more specimens, then we could follow our friends to camp. Further down the slope, an orchid attracted my attention. Sideways on, I scrambled down to the rarity and, notebook at the ready, jotted down details, leaning over my work in a vain attempt to protect it from water damage.

Leaves lanceolate, mid-green, alternate, sheathing at base. Flowers borne in spikes. Three sepals whitish to pale green, oval, and three petals arise from top of ovary. The two lateral petals white with dark green veining, the labellum deep yellow, green at base—

An extended whinny culminating in a high-pitched hee-haw, interrupted my notetaking: Paco was fractious.

'Patience,' I complained.

I remember thinking I could do without all this caterwauling. If it wasn't for that confounded mule, I'd be on my way by now. I continued with head bent over notebook and flora but was conscious of Paco's hooves stamping the ground. Really, these interruptions would try the patience of Job.

Hoooowawoowawooaninney-heee-haww.

'For the love of—' Looking up, a torrent of mud spewed down the upper slope.

'Paco! Run!'

Grasping at clumps of the flora I'd admired only moments before, I aimed for the path. But my feet slipped in the mire and I crashed to my knees. It was too late. I twined my wrists around the plants in my hands. Thus tethered, I put myself at the mercy of God and the tenacity of the plants I loved.

The river of mud was upon me. An onslaught which blinded, deafened and smothered by turns, filling my mouth with its taste of the grave. The mudslide took all within its path: debris—uprooted trees and boulders and hapless rodents—pummelled my body. The last thought to pass through my head was one of remorse: I'd brought this upon Paco. Then I knew no more.

⚜

I was in hell; a lower purgatory in which my penance was heavy stones and sealed eyes. Hell pressed around me. It held me. It filled me. I gagged, only for hell to force through my open mouth. I lay face down, my arms stretched tight and bound at the wrists, my fingers fat and stiff and numb. My chest pained to explode for want of air. Teeth clenched, I sipped at cavities between coarser soil particles.

Then, as if this wasn't hell enough, something stabbed my thigh. Whatever it was, was on the move, for it stabbed me again, this time in my kidneys, forcing a yell from me. There were more of these stabbing demons. The first moved up my spine while another prodded my skull. At this, I screeched. Then a crunching sound. It had a rhythm to it, a chuck-switch, chuck-switch that I knew, but could not name.

Teeth nibbled my hands. No, not my hands but the tethers that bound them. First one hand then the other was free. Feeling the blood flow once more, I extended my fingers and felt air: cold and clean. Bit by bit, other hands pulled the clay coffin from my back. Air entered my lungs: a shock which heaved my ribs open. Throughout it all, words of encouragement.

'It's him,' Solomon's voice came to me.

'Keep digging,' Ventura's voice replied.

Hoooowawoowoowawoo-heee-haww.

⚜

Later, sitting with my friends beneath tarpaulins around a fire, Paco and his contingent under their own shelter, I shook my head.

'Paco, you are a chief among mules. I owe you an apology,' I said.

The mule nodded.

'I was all too ready to blame you for delaying my work, when the truth is that I should have heeded your warning.' Picking up a bag of oats, I rose to my feet and walked over to him.

'From now on, I will take responsibility for my actions, and not blame my misfortunes on others.' I offered him a handful of grain.

Paco, the staunchest of friends, nuzzled my arm.

Hoooowawoowoowawoo-heee-haww.

26. The Counsel of Snake

Evangeline

A cup of tea, an algal pond in miniature, stood on the nightstand. Just the sight of it quelled the thunderstorm playing out in Evangeline's head. Lately, every morning started with a headache. She drained the cup in two gulps.

She rested her eyes while the tea went down, its spice warming her from inside out. Then, she took in the snake bedposts. A memory stirred in her periphery. The dream, more of a nightmare, had been about a snake in the world of the Wekufe. The snake had been chasing her. No, not that, not quite, but it had sought her out. It had found her. There was something so familiar in the memory. As though she'd had the dream before, as though she'd sat like this and had the same impression.

⚜

No matter how wide Evangeline opened her eyes, all was gloom, stifling and near tangible. The tunnel height varied, often forcing her to crouch and even crawl. The burn in her quads testified to the tunnel's descent, as her kitten heels stumbled on the uneven ground. No matter how implausible it would be to find a tree so far below the surface, an overwhelming compulsion drove her deeper underground. She pushed up the sleeves of her catsuit and lowered the zip at her throat, registering the echoing drips, and a stale, crypt-like odour of damp stone and of human life long since passed.

Evangeline became aware of a ssshhh following her. To go on, not knowing what followed, or to turn and face it? She sped up, but the rustling, slithering noise kept up with her. She turned.

A snake—the snake—reared up. She recognised this moment as when she usually woke.

But not now.

Glistening with an ethereal light and with emerald eyes, Snake rose above her head. Its coils slid over each other, unwinding, displaying its pale-yellow body zigzagged with black along its back.

'Take the path through the Wekufe,' said Snake, her voice ancient and wise. 'Stay on the path, do not deviate. Always look forward, not back. Do this, and you will reach your destination. Never look back and no harm will befall you.'

'But I don't even know whether what I'm searching for exists,' Evangeline said.

'Lisss-ten carefully, girl. Look for the light in the darknesss. Find the rhizoxants,' said Snake.

'"Rhizo–", something to do with roots, then?' Evangeline asked.

'Yesss. The rhizoxants will help you in your quessst. When you find them, take three handfuls, no more.' Snake bowed her head to the ground as though she'd said all that was needed.

In the gloom, Snake's faint luminosity became fainter still and then no more. Evangeline was alone.

⚜

A knock on the door brought her back to her Rococo bedroom.

'Lilith. Wake up. It's time,' it was Tomoe's voice.

For a moment, there, she hadn't recognised the name. She felt not fully awake. A pink and spring green catsuit hung on the door of the armoire. Matching kitten-heeled booties stood by. Victor selected all her clothes. There was a time when such an arrangement would have been intolerable for her. What little of her former self remaining in Evangeline cringed at what she, this Lilith, had become. And there was so very little left of Evangeline.

As she got off the bed, out of the corner of her eye something on the bedpost glinted emerald green. It appeared to have come from the eye of the carved snake and yet that was solid wood. Hanging over the bedpost was a mini barrel bag, pale yellow with a black zigzag, made from snakeskin.

She unhooked the bag, slung it over her shoulder and opened the door, 'Ready.'

27. The Temple of the Moon

Evangeline

The full moon hung just above the horizon. Larger and brighter than usual, it looked as though a divine hand had sliced open a giant cantaloupe and set it in the sky, tantalising those who gazed upon it from Earth. It seemed so close but to stretch an arm towards it only made clear the futility of the gesture. Listless with the day's heat, the air was clotted by transpiration from the vigorous and abundant vegetation. As they made their way along the Snake Path, the humidity settled on her face, plastering her fringe to her brow. The high-pitched whine of unseen insects zipped past her ear.

The garden was so familiar. Hadn't she always known its twists and turns, the short-cut to the natural pool, where the concrete facsimiles of plant life arose, and the earthen path—and how it rang hollow when walked upon—which led to the deepest part of the garden, the secret place where the ancient olivillo stood and among whose roots Snake lay entwined.

Victor and her sisters were waiting in front of the temple. The women stood in a row, arms around each other. Hippolyta, the tallest, was in the centre. Behind them, the silvery doors were open, and torchlight flickered within.

Victor stepped towards her. 'The wait is nearly over.' He took her face in his hands and kissed her lips. 'Are you ready?'

'I'm ready,' she said. At last, she would be one with the sisters and with Victor.

Victor looked around at the gathering of women. 'Tonight, mis corazones, we welcome a new sister into the fold.'

'By the love of Mother Moon,' the sisters chanted in unison.

'Your sister comes willingly,' Victor said.

'We welcome our sister,' the women chorused.

'Come, the moon has taken her position and she waits for no one,' Victor said.

Victor led Evangeline through the silvery doors into the temple. Her sisters filed in past them, to form two rows, hand in hand, either side of the stone altar. Fresh night-flowering blooms decorated its base and gleamed in the shafts of moonlight slanting through the roof's aperture. The flowers saturated the air with a cloying perfume. A tumi knife lay on the white stone. Its gold and turquoise handle glistened in the moonbeams. Hanging from the pillars behind the altar-head was the painting of Lilith with Snake. By the light of the moon, it must surely have been here always, the perfect setting in this temple, deep within the garden.

Victor clinched her waist and lifted her onto the altar. He continued to hold her poised on the cold stone, infusing a sense that the moment was nigh. The heat of his touch radiated into her, to flip and flutter. Was this what she wanted? The prospect brought her out in a sweat. Very soon, she would be bound to this community. Very soon, she would belong to him. Her body clenched with fear and desire. She could neither reason nor think. He shifted his weight forward, driving his leg between her knees.

North, in her black dress with high neckline, corseted waist and full skirt, stood at the head of the altar. She held a jug. It was a very familiar looking anthropomorphic earthenware jug, the size of an Oktoberfest stein, and with the texture and underlying colour of a speckled hen's egg.

She who accepted the name Lilith gasped, it was the totem she'd found in her rucksack. The memory flared like a half-forgotten dream, illuminating other associations she now grappled to fit together: Jesús identifying its antiquity, Jesús with her on a search for the World Tree. Then she remembered a car chase, a glimpse in the rear-view mirror of someone watching them escape. Someone with lacquer-black hair billowing in the backdraft of an inferno.

But these fragments were at odds with others that seemed closer to hand, easier to grasp, as though her story was being narrated.

She could remember coming into being. She'd been formed from clay, just the same as Adam. One minute, inanimate, the next, a bolt of electricity racked through her—a pain that shocked open her eyes—and she was living, sentient. She remembered the first breaths, fragrant with woodland, searing her lungs, the heat—life, this was life itself—as blood pumped through her veins. Then the first sound—a breeze rustling through the tree canopy—and her eyes absorbed the mosaic of green and filtered sunlight of that canopy. And laughing; she remembered the sheer joy of being alive that had to be given a voice.

It was paradise.

If she really thought about it, they should never have married. But she'd been hopelessly in love. Or maybe it was the idea of being in love. It wasn't like she had much experience with men: he was the first. It didn't take long for the cracks to appear. Adam always put himself first. His word was law. If ever she questioned what he said, he'd tell her not to talk back to her husband. It's not that she wanted to be in charge, well, not always. But he was closed to other views, other ways of doing things: he didn't take well to direction. After Adam ditched her, people started to talk about her. They said she was wanton, a demon. They called her the scarlet woman. Then she met Victor, he appreciated her for what she was, he encouraged her to find herself.

Yet this history with Adam wasn't compatible with the images firing up at the sight of the totem. Painful things, buried deep, yet perfect, too. The sweet weight of love in her arms. Try as she might to ignore them, they refused to go away, as when someone walks in front of a projector, the film continues to roll but the person warps the picture.

She knew Jesús in that forgotten life. So, when her sisters were protecting her from him, were they trying to keep them apart for another reason? And what had happened to him? She couldn't recall seeing him for days, weeks, perhaps longer. Had he left without her? Maybe he was in trouble.

She pulled her attention away from the jug and saw Tomoe with her lacquer-black hair, then turned to Victor.

'Mi corazón,' he said. 'The moment I saw you—your colouring—you may have gone by the name of *Eve*-angeline, but you were no substitute, I knew you were my Lilith. I had to have you.'

'But you are my family. This is all I've known,' she said, as much to convince herself as anyone else.

'Not quite, mi amor. But you've always had my heart.'

'How did I come to be here?'

'We met in a different country. Argentina, do you remember? I knew you were the one. I knew you would be perfect.' He sighed. 'But, as I recognised this, you were on your way. You had a flight to catch. I might have lost you. I couldn't allow that. So, I put the totem in your bag. I had to know I could find you again.'

Was she losing her mind? How could she have forgotten these things?

'There was a car chase,' she said, remembering the terror. She noticed Tomoe and Hippolyta exchange a glance across the altar.

'That was…unfortunate.' Victor frowned at Tomoe and Hippolyta.

He instigated the car chase? He—they—could have killed her. She scanned the faces in the room. The women, those she called sisters, each one distinct, each one startling to look at, as though a sculpture stepped down from a pedestal, or a figure liberated from a painting. Though each was different, there was a familial resemblance. They all had the same eyes, not in colour, but expression. So fervent, as though in a constant state of ecstasy.

They would do anything for Victor, and often did. To think she envied them.

The full force of clarity came at once. Evangeline pushed herself away from Victor.

But she still didn't understand. 'How did you know where to find me?'

'The totem. It contains a tracking device. We'd been following your signal ever since you came to Chile.'

'That totem there?' she indicated the jug in North's hands.

'Yes, that totem there brought you back to me.'

His hands had moved to her shoulders. She felt his grasp tighten as he nodded to North who poured from the treacherous totem-jug into a silver chalice on the altar. In the flickering torchlight, the green tea was the colour of poison.

Victor picked up the chalice. With controlled calm he said, 'Don't worry your head about the past. You are Lilith. That is all that matters.' The chalice glinted in the light of the moon, whose beams enveloped her in a silvery glow. 'Drink up. There's a good girl.'

She pulled her face away. 'What is this stuff you've been giving me?'

With a lavender water-infused rustle and a grip as strong as a

188

bird of prey, North wrenched Evangeline's wrists against her back and pulled her to the centre of the altar. 'The tea prepares you for the embodiment of your imprint.' North's voice in her ear compelling.

Evangeline struggled, but couldn't break free. 'You're all mad.'

She heard the chime of metal on stone. The knife was in Victor's hand. 'The pain will be…exquisite,' he breathed. 'But brief. Then you will be free of pain forever.'

A low growl came from beyond the temple's silvery doors. As one, all looked to the entrance, which burst open to reveal the bristling black hulk of Florito. The hound's lips retracted to display fangs dripping with saliva. Victor wielded the knife. The sisters closed in to protect their Svengali, but not soon enough. The hound leapt forward. A howl rent the air. The full heft of the canine crashed into Victor and pinned him to the floor.

North hurled the chalice, it rebounded off the hound's flank and clattered against a pillar.

'Hippolyta, get this creature out of here,' Victor growled.

In a frenzy, the hound turned on the women. Spittle frothed around jaws, blood gushed from a wound.

Freed from North's clutches, Evangeline dived through the door, shielded by Florito keeping all at bay.

'Don't let her go,' Victor commanded.

Florito snarled one last time at those in the temple, then followed her with a scrabble of claws on stone.

They made for the deepest part of the garden, the wildest part of the garden. Where the plants shaded and sheltered. Where the ancient olivillo stood. She could hear Victor, Hippolyta, Tomoe and the others calling her name. She had to get to the tree before they found her. She knew what her path was now. Florito, panting heavily, hide wet with sweat and blood, followed his nose.

28. The Fissure

Evangeline

Florito bounded ahead, crashing through undergrowth, dipping out of sight, with just the furious rustle of shrubs a giveaway to his whereabouts. Evangeline couldn't tell where their pursuers were. They must have fanned out—the voices came from all around, and they were growing louder.

A spray of dirt hit her in the face. Though blinded and choking, she deduced this was a good sign: she'd caught up with Florito and he'd already found the olivillo, the entrance to the Wekufe path. His forepaws scraped at the soft earth and fallen leaves between the roots. Soil flew out in an arc behind him, spraying a fine tilth over the surrounding ground. First his head disappeared in the hole, then his broad shoulders, then all that was left, his tail. When even the tail had gone from sight, Evangeline scrabbled through the opening he'd made. Earth and root fibres rained down on her back as she worked her way flat on her front, using her elbows, army-style, through the entrance. Then, by clutching at the inner parts of the tree, she tugged to squeeze her shoulders and hips through the narrow gap.

Just in time.

A hand grabbed her ankle as she drew it through the opening. Her free leg kicked hard, kitten-heel met a skin of resistance and pierced through. The sole of her boot hit upon a bony orbit. An inhuman roar pierced the air. Yet the hand held fast.

Then a creaking, as if a heavy, ancient door had gathered momentum and slammed tight. Evangeline was immobile as the whole tree heaved and groaned, and the structural roots—each the size of a tree—forming the wishbone of the fissure, drew together. The hole through which she and Florito had entered, now impenetrable. They were locked in.

Cold sweat prickled her skin. A squirming mass rose within her, devouring reason. The hand grasping her ankle relaxed its hold. She pulled away from the lifeless fingers at which she stared blindly.

Her heart thudded, projecting a dizzying strobe of red on the back of her eyes. She felt she might drown in the verve of her own blood. Stifling and claustrophobic, worse, far worse, than an overcrowded rush-hour tube.

Florito leant his bulk into her, his moist, rasping breath warm on her shoulder. She awkwardly wrapped her arms around him and with her head against the dug-out's roof she whispered, 'I'm so sorry, my boy.' She shifted her balance. 'I've not been a good mum.'

Evangeline felt him lick her face and thought her heart would break.

She'd allowed him to be locked away, then forgot all about him while she tripped out on green tea, cosying up with an egocentric, control-freak of a cult leader and his fancy-dress harem of notable women.

Was she capable of caring for someone dependant on her? It didn't seem like it.

And yet, despite the unforgivable way she'd treated Florito, he remained his loyal, loving self. As if to prove it, she received another full-face lick.

'Florito. I love you.' She hugged his stocky body. 'We're going to find a way out of here.'

She kicked at what had been the entrance to their earthy tomb, hoping for some give, some weakness, but the way was locked tight. They'd made their way here to escape Victor but, now they were here, the thought of continuing on this path filled her with dread.

'Right then. There's no going back, and if we stay here waiting for something to happen, I think I might actually drive you barking.' She kissed Florito's forehead, comforted by his presence. 'So, it looks like that decides things.' She rested her cheek against his neck.

'Right then. Snake's advice was to follow the path of the Wekufe. Forward we go. We take the path through Netherearth.'

Right then.

The Wekufe.

The beings known as the Wekufe had been make-believe when they played a part in the creation myth told by Jesús to while away the hours driving the Pan American Highway. Evangeline remembered the way, when Jesús was thinking, a small frown formed on his brow and he looked downward as though into himself, his long lashes concealing his eyes.

Then, as the right phrase came to him, his blue eyes rose to meet hers, his smile, so easy, so warm. 'The Wekufe live in the dark under our world since before time,' he said. 'When the Great Bird in the Sky defeated Pihuichen, the winged serpent, he divided Chaos into Earth and Netherearth.'

In daylight, with Jesús beside her, the story he told had just been a folktale designed to make sense of the world. Her throat felt tight. Jesús wasn't here—she'd put paid to that. Instead, she was about to take the Wekufe path, the path of the dead.

Free of the mental fog induced by North's special tea, she

recognised once again the maggoty despair that had dwelt within her since Effie. Perhaps that's why she'd been so ready to go along with Victor and *La Menagerie*: annihilation by intoxication. Now, absent of the green brew, the desolation weighed her down just as much as before. The tea's seduction never could make that hurt go away. Nor would it replace what she missed most of all. Shame burnt through her for wanting to block the memory.

Evangeline remembered the shock and denial when the doctor confirmed her worst fears: she was pregnant. But it had all changed with the first flutter of the baby moving. That was the moment she knew she loved the life she carried inside her, loved her fiercely.

A cold muzzle nudged the palm of her hand. She'd heard that dogs pick up on their owner's emotions. She stroked his head.

29. Nothing is Certain

Morgan: Liucura, 7 March 1843

We came across a jaunty town cascading over the leeward side of a mountain plateau. Both town and mountain went by the name Liucura, the Mapuche word for white rock. In full sun, I'd go so far as to say the white was brazen, such as to cause me to wince. The settlement was more striking still by dint of the townspeople's tradition of painting the roofs an intense cobalt blue. The stone-built houses seemed to grow from the rock. Indeed, we soon learned that some of the dwellings extended into cavities within the cliff face.

The narrow, cobbled and many-stepped streets, helter-skeltered their way up through Liucura. Breathless and thirsty, we arrived at a square, fronted on all sides by buildings open at ground level for everyday commerce, selling the freshest produce, woven textiles and woollens. As to the upper storeys, through open windows, the rhythmic clack-clack of shuttle on looms made its way to our ears. The windows, themselves, were traced with more of the cobalt blue, giving the buildings a wide-eyed appearance. Everything was well-kept and clean. The town may have been miles from anywhere, but these people took pride in it.

Contorted, cinnamon trunked myrtles,[15] populated the square. Their fragrant canopy, awash with sea spray stamens of white flowers, shaded the market stalls. But Paco pulled on his reins. He wasn't interested in the myrtle, nor the market wares. For in the middle of the square, out in the open, he had spied something we all desired. A broad fountain glistened with spring water bubbling from the giant urn of a genuflecting statue.

Oh! The shock of bright water as I doused my head. The welcome sting on the back of my neck. I could see in the others what I felt inside: an awakening. They stood taller, their eyes cheered and focused, their chests heaved with drawing in air. My drenched collar continued to cool and invigorate me as we sat on the side of the fountain while mules and horse took their fill.

With just a few enquiries, we found bed and board suitable, in their own distinct ways, for *Homo explorator* and equids. We would spend a few days here, to dry and repair our belongings and stock up on supplies.

When a body is accustomed to sleeping on the ground, the comfort of a bed is a curious experience, and not one that is wholly enjoyable. A soft mattress has too much warmth, for one thing. Then there is the impression, a hint, no more than that, of insecurity. To sink into a mattress is as though the world on which all life exists, the environment we take for granted, is not as steadfast as we like to imagine. Added to which, exchanging stars with ceilings, and trees with walls, a person easily succumbs to a sense of being hemmed in, or, at its most extreme, of claustrophobia.

I don't think I was alone in feeling like a fish out of water. Or, to be more germane, a plantsman off the land. When I visited him

---

[15] The *Luma apiculata* is much used in honey production in this region and has edible fruit. Here, the trees went by the name kelümamüll, orangewood in Mapudungan.

in his housing, Paco nibbled my sleeve fractiously, as if to say: it was time we got on our way. I suspected Maite, of all of us, was the only one who appreciated what town life offered: the privacy and security of living within the confines of a dwelling. She meshed with the villagers as though she'd known them all her life. She knew the names of the fruit seller, and the young schoolteacher, and the priest. She would have liked to stay here, I was certain of it. But Solomon was the star she followed. Wherever he went, there her heart would be.

⚜

Still bathed in sunlight, the summit watched over the village, its peak the eternal sentinel. We sat in the town square where, by now, shade soothed all but the most easterly quarter, the white walls transforming from blatant to serene. It being our last evening in Liucura, we ordered up a second jug of chicha.[16] Ventura, Solomon and I were in high spirits, itching to be on the road again. Sweet Maite was not her usual self, more pensive than I'd ever known her.

'We'll continue across the mountain. It's more arduous but…' I said, wanting assurance the others were with me.

'We has fresh legs, we can do it,' my steadfast friend, Solomon, said.

'It's that, or add several days by taking the valley road,' Ventura's quiet delivery was a voice people listened to. He looked at us each in turn. 'But, beware, the mountain comes with more

---

[16] Here, this beverage was made from the fruit of the myrtle. The villagers also put the fruit to use in a rather too quaffable wine. An unsuspecting patron could easily wake up the morning after the night before, with a headache to match that of Zeus. Unlike the father of the gods, however, the good reader can be assured that it will not be necessary to call on Hephaestus to cure the pain by cracking open the skull.

peril than steep terrain alone: bandits prey on unsuspecting travellers.'

Solomon wrapped his arm around Maite's shoulders and kissed the top of her head.

'We have pistols and we have each other,' she said, drawing herself up while avoiding Solomon's searching eye. 'We are more than a match for any bandit.'

I was torn. I revered this woman for her mettle and warmth. I would die before I allowed any harm to befall her. Solomon, his brow creased as he interrogated his glass, clearly felt the responsibility ten-fold.

I met his eye across the table and said, 'Let's take the low road.'

He nodded. It was the right thing to do.

As though to make amends for what she must have felt was a hindrance, Maite asked me for a story from my homeland. I duly obliged.

'A poor farmer was wandering by the slate grey waters of Lyn-y-Fan Fach.' I took a sip from the glass Ventura replenished, before proceeding. 'From the middle of the lake rose a woman more beautiful than he could imagine. Her silken hair fell to her waist and her eyes were the colour of the lake itself.

'Besotted, he dropped to one knee and begged her to be his wife.

'In a voice like still water, she said, "I shall not marry you."

'Distraught, the farmer returned home. But he could not sleep. Bread in his mouth tasted of sawdust. He had not the energy to plough his field.

'A week went by like this and he returned to the lake, a little thinner than before. Once again, the Lady of the Lake emerged from the water. But when he asked her to be his wife, she said, "I may not marry you."

'Despairing, the farmer returned home. He could neither eat

nor sleep. In the absence of the plough, thistles sprang up in his field.

'Another week went by this way before the farmer returned to the lake, his livelihood all but ruined. He called out and, once again, the Lady of the Lake rose from the water. When he proposed to her this time, she said, "I will marry you on one condition. You must promise to treat me with respect. If you strike me three times without cause, I will return to the lake."

'"That is an easy promise to keep," he said and soon they were married. The Lady of the Lake brought with her a dowry of the finest cattle, the like of which had never been seen, and the farmer grew prosperous on the sale of their creamy milk.

'One day, during a wedding reception, the Lady burst into tears, knowing the bridegroom would not survive the year. Flustered, the farmer rapped her knuckles.

'"That's one," she said.

'Life went on and they attended a christening. The Lady cried, divining the child would be harmed by the sun. Embarrassed, the farmer tapped her shoulder.

'"That's two," she said.

'Several years passed and the farmer let out a few notches on his belt. At a funeral, the Lady burst out laughing, relieved the deceased's suffering was over. Mortified, the farmer clouted her around the head. Without a word the Lady sped back to the lake, never to return.'

By way of appreciation for the tale, Solomon filled my glass, again. As often happens when chicha is shared between friends, it wasn't long before a song arose. For is there nothing more uplifting than singing in unison? Ventura started us off with a ballad, something about an inamorata in a red dress, the chorus of which was a *too-ra-loo-ra-ley* we could all approximate. But between our harmonies, I detected a freeform voice ranging from baritone to mezzo-soprano. I put down my glass and listened.

There could be no mistake.

Hoooowawoowawooaninney-heee-haww. From his quarters around the back of the cheesemongers, Paco had something to say.

Solomon also homed in on the din. By now, Saqui and the entire mule train had joined in on backing vocals. We fell silent while Solomon went to investigate. And, apart from the equids, it was deathly quiet. The usual drone of bees around myrtle, and prattle of birds chancing their luck beneath café tables, had stopped dead. The villagers, so recently bustling around the market, stood still, the whites of their eyes stark.

Then a growl. There was no other way to describe it, but the growl issued not from any animal alive nor dead, but from the very earth itself. Low-pitched, it increased in volume to fill our ears with its pain. The earth trembled. A glass smashed to the floor. People gasped in confusion. Tables danced about. Chairs went over. Market stalls imploded. Clang. Crash. Bang. Market produce, the vegetables and textiles so fresh and colourful but moments ago, now spilled across the square. A building façade buckled, sending its cobalt blue tiles dashing to the ground. By now, the ground undulated like rubber, giving rise in me, as I'm sure for many others, to motion sickness.

'Solomon.' Wide-eyed, Maite got to her feet and ran unsteadily towards the stables.

Ventura and I went after her. People were dashing this way and that, avoiding the obstacles of falling debris as best they could. In the panic and turmoil, I lost sight of both Maite and Ventura.

A shout came from the crowd, 'Look!'

Above the village, a waterfall cascaded down the face of the mountain. At least, that's what I thought at first. Indeed, it was a fall, but not of water. Earth turned fluid. Milled as fine as flour between the grindstones of the summit, it plumed as it fell. Soon, a dense cloud of dust filled the air. I could neither breathe, nor see my hand before my face.

From somewhere nearby, a woman's shaky voice said, 'Oh my God. Please God, please make it stop.'

Disorientated by the loss of visibility, no longer trusting the very ground under my feet, I moved forward as best I could. People were screaming, children crying. I narrowly escaped a boulder as it crashed to earth, flint kicking up to strike me like shrapnel.

A hand grabbed my ankle. 'Help me,' came the voice.

The hand belonged to a young man in the prime of his life. Only, it was obvious in an instant, he wasn't long for this world. Bright red blood foamed from his mouth and his breathing was shallow. From mid-chest down, he was submerged in rubble, but I could hear, with dread, air being sucked into the chest cavity. I was ever thankful he was unable to lift his head to view the damage, I assumed his vertebrae had been crushed. His eyes pleaded with me and I held his hand.

'Everything will be all right,' I said, wondering how those words came so readily. 'We'll soon have you on the mend.' I continued to hold his hand, while the fear in his eyes subsided and his spirit ebbed away.

In the aftermath, when I could be sure of the ground beneath my feet once more, and the air had cleared sufficient to look around, I wandered the area, as many did likewise. We looked like ghosts. A thick coating of pale dust covered everything. Clothes, skin, hair, all ashen, just the eyes, vacant and bleak.

'Morgan?' Not much more than a whisper, but I knew the voice.

Lying in brickwork and rubble, she smiled bravely.

'Maite.' I dashed to her.

Blood clotting on her forehead, some scratches here and there, she was as covered in dust as the rest of us.

'Maite, are you hurt?'

She tried to move but was impeded by a beam straddling her legs. The left of which, I saw now, was bent at an unnatural angle.

'I'm sure if you would help lift this, I'll be fine,' she said, but when she pushed at the beam, her shriek told me otherwise.

Holding her eyes with mine, I said, 'Hold still.' I pulled off my chamanto and laid it under her head.

'Have you seen the others?' She voiced my own concern. I'd lost sight of Ventura during the quake and hadn't seen Solomon since he left us to take care of the mules.

All around us bodies lay in the rubble, never to rise again. Wails of mourning mingled with groans from the afflicted.

'No, but we'll find them.'

She replied with a wan smile. Then a cry of anguish as I heaved the beam from her legs and cast it away. The white of her bone protruded from the flesh. I needed help to set it straight, but particles of dust remained suspended in the air and would settle on the open wound. From the rubble, I pulled the colourful material that had so recently been for sale. I used wads of the cloth around the injury, and ripped the remainder into strips, splinting the injured leg to that which was unharmed by way of the colourful bandages. Then, I covered her lower limbs with more material. Water gushed unchecked from the fountain, the statue having split asunder. For want of anything better, I filled my chupalla and held it to Maite's mouth.

'Maite, wait here, don't move,' I instructed. 'I'm going to find help.'

I hated leaving her, but if I didn't find help, her condition would deteriorate. All around me, people had their own troubles. Mothers called for their children. Mewling infants, with upraised chubby arms, went unnoticed by those involved in the rescue effort. As might be expected, the rescuers gave priority to the buried and injured, before attending to those on their feet. Men dug through rubble on the suspicion of a noise. They would help when they could, but that wouldn't be soon enough.

I reasoned our only hope was to find Solomon and Ventura, and to return with them to Maite. The buildings fronting the square stood like crooked, crumbling teeth in the rubble. Using the now deformed cone of the mountain as bearings, I took a path across the debris, then bore left. From some way ahead, came the keening of women. Pierced to the core, I sped towards the mournful noise.

The sight of a row of eight tiny bodies is one I shall never forget. Mothers were in the process of carefully washing the faces, hair and hands of those who would never smile at them again. Then the women tucked blankets around their children as though putting them to bed. Fathers, unable to resolve the catastrophe, held back and went within themselves, as tears streamed silently down their cheeks. Still more children were being pulled from the rubble of what had been the school. Cheers of joy rang out from the fortunate few, the parents running forward to claim their child, determined to keep them safe. In the thick of it, a man larger than life hauled at the debris. With him, a mule train was doing its bit. The mules waited while Solomon, for it was he, filled their paniers with masonry. Then with Paco in lead, they carried the waste from the catastrophe. Solomon had evidently employed a local lad to unload the rubble in a suitable site for the rebuilding process.

Dilemma: Maite alone in the square, needing help; the town's future generation on the brink of annihilation, if not rescued urgently.

I joined Solomon in his endeavours and we worked until every child was accounted for.

'Man, it's good to see you,' he said as we drew breath.

'Likewise, my friend. Come, there's no time to lose.'

I filled him in on Maite's condition as we scrambled back to the square. We found her where I'd left her, but not in a good condition. She was neither unconscious nor fully *compos mentis*. Between Solomon and I, we re-set her leg, and erected a bivouac around her. Leaving Maite in his care, I went to look for Ventura.

It wasn't until many hours later that I found him. His body was broken in so many places, I was hard pressed to know which injury had caused his demise. I could only pray he had not suffered.

☙

With a heavy heart, I set out from Liucura alone. Maite had to stay behind, she was in no fit state to travel. In turn, Solomon refused to leave without her.

And so it was, Paco and I, alone on the road, in search of a tree within a myth.

30. Perils of Potholing

Evangeline

Florito led the way into the gloom, with Evangeline crawling behind on hands and knees. Rootlets and fibres—at least, she hoped that's all they were—trailed across her face and tugged at her clothing.

Every so often, a sizzle of hot liquid against cold stone and a distinctive whiff informed her Florito was marking their way.

'Good boy, Florito. You're more than a match for Ariadne's thread.' Talking, just to make any sound, proved her existence in this limbo. She felt bigger, braver when talking. So, canary in the mine, she chattered and didn't stop.

The Wekufe, if they existed, would surely be scared off by the racket of a girl and her hound stomping through the underworld, yacking away as though they didn't have a care in the world of the living—or of the dead.

Added to which, Florito made a good listener. 'Do you know the story of Theseus and the Minotaur? No? Well, it goes a little something like this.'

She gathered the story in her head. 'The king had built a labyrinth to hide away the Minotaur—half-man, half-bull—born of his wife. It just so happened that Minos had a son who was killed in Athens. In reparation, seven young men and seven young women were sent to Crete every nine years as a sacrifice to the Minotaur. Theseus volunteered to go to Crete to kill the Minotaur and rid Athens of this curse. But even if he achieved his aim, no one had ever returned from the labyrinth.

'When he arrived in Crete, Ariadne, the savvy daughter of King Minos, fell head over kitten-heels in love with Theseus and determined to help him in his quest. She gave him a ball of thread and told him to unravel it as he went through the labyrinth—that's where you come in, Florito. You're Theseus leaving a trail—Theseus found and killed the Minotaur, and thanks to Ariadne's thread, doubled-back on himself to make his way out of the labyrinth.'

Evangeline rested back on her heels. Before moving on again, she said, 'But Theseus' story doesn't end there. He turns up in the war against the Amazons. So, our friend Hippolyta would have known him.' She pondered this for a bit. 'Do you know, Florito, I feel bad for leaving the women behind. Who knows how long they've been in that man's clutches? I don't understand how it works. The imprint thing. Hippolyta and Tomoe and all the rest, they really believed they were their namesakes. And my painting, the one of Lilith, whenever I was close to it, it was the strangest feeling. I'm not sure how to describe it. But it was like I'd been smudged. There was another person inside me sensing what I sensed and feeling what I felt – but sensing and feeling as if for the first time. But while that was happening, I could smell the damp woodland, and feel the serpent slithering across my skin. It was as though I was looking through Lilith's eyes.'

The walls and roof opened further. She stood upright, wiped her hands together and rubbed the soil from her nostrils. The tunnel smelled of neglected churches, the kind with dust-opaque windows and walls mottled by mould. But there was a faint undertow also. A stale breath of a smell, the smell of decayed flesh.

The path continued its descent. The hollow ring of her footfall solidified into a tap as earth turned to stone. With one hand against a wall to guide her, she followed the sound of Florito's panting. Up until now, she only managed baby-steps, worried she would trip in the dark. But the floor was even and, more importantly, she didn't want to be in the tunnel a moment longer than necessary, so she lengthened her stride.

'Florito, I think I've got the hang of this potholing malarkey.'

Crack!

The impact ignited white needle-light behind Evangeline's eyes. She folded over, hands on knees, breathing through the pain. The sound of Florito's claws scrabbling forward amplified her queasiness.

'Hang on a minute, my boy. I've come a cropper.'

She waited until her senses returned to normal. Florito's snuffling was partly muffled but while she was bent over and closer to the ground it echoed. He'd made his way through a low gap in the rock, leaving her alone in the gloom…far below ground…with no obvious way out. She was following the advice of a talking snake she'd met in a dream. No amount of project planning for a botanising expedition—even one involving the mythical World Tree—could have accounted for such a risk scenario. The thought she'd tried so hard to submerge, loomed large: they were buried alive. Her heart thudded as though it would topple her over.

From the far side of the wall, a single, sharp bark pulled her back from the brink of panic.

'Stay, Florito. I'm coming.'

She flattened herself to the floor and pulled herself through the gap. Standing upright she heard Florito close by lapping at water. Judging from the echo, she guessed they were in a large cavern.

With arms windmilling to prevent further collisions, she slid one foot in front of the other, not knowing where the ground gave way to water. In this way, she reached Florito on the edge of an underground lake. He licked her hand, his muzzle dripping cold water down her leg. She knelt beside him, cupped her hands in the water and sluiced his flanks. His skin quivered beneath her hands. She didn't know how deep Victor's knife had penetrated, but she was sure the wound stood a better chance of healing if it was cleaned thoroughly. The hound, now drenched, shook himself out and gave her a shower into the bargain. Her yelp of amused shock echoed.

'Florito, it might not be a bad idea for me to train myself to use echolocation. If I start clicking away like Flipper, you'll know why.'

As they continued along the path, she noticed a curious thing about immersion in total darkness. Things flitted across her vision. To start with, it was just specks, or filaments which darted away when she focused on them. Then biconcave disks floated across her vision, moving rhythmically as though propelled by a pump. Soon, the shapes fused together to take on corporeal form. Corporeal but not quite human. They were leucistic and elongated, much taller than the average man, with long, emaciated legs. Their arms reached to their knees, their gnarled fingers hanging limp.

These visions were a figment of her imagination, weren't they? After all, when she turned to face them, they dematerialised. But if she was imagining things, was it also possible Florito had tapped into her imagination? For, ever since the visions had appeared, he'd been growling his very particular low rumble.

One of the beings broke away from its comrades and floated toward her, solidifying as it did so, becoming more human. Its movements were more human, too, even though it did what no human could: it—or rather, he—was walking on water. He radiated a gentle light, as though lit from within by a candle. She could make out a white shirt, ripped jeans, a muss of black, curly hair. She gazed into his cloisonné blue eyes and he smiled.

'Jesús. I never thought I'd see you again.'

This was not natural. People didn't appear out of thin air, nor could they walk on water. Had the crack on the head affected her faculties? Was Jesús a hallucination, brought about because he was what she wanted to see most of all?

She screwed her eyes shut. Please let him be real. She opened her eyes and Jesús was still with her.

'Walk with me,' he said.

'I don't have a clue what's going on anymore, but I so want to believe you are real.'

Jesús took her hand and held it to his chest. 'Arbolito, do I not feel real?'

Her palm felt the warmth of his chest beneath the chambray shirt, and the beat of his heart.

Florito barked, forepaws bouncing off the ground.

'Hey, amigo. ¿Cómo estadio?' Jesús crouched in front of the now-growling hound and rubbed its chops. 'You never were my greatest fan.'

'But where did you come from?' she asked. 'And while we're about it, how come your jeans are dry?'

Standing again, he brushed her jaw with the crook of his finger. 'Have faith in me.'

'There's nothing I want more, but Snake told me not to deviate from the path.'

'Snake, from your dream?' he said.

'OK, that does sound a bit lame.'

'Just believe in me.'

Scared and alone, Evangeline so wanted to believe.

Florito huffed, as if reading her thoughts.

No, this wasn't right. 'Jesús, where did you come from?'

Jesús shook his head a little and stepped back, the moment

severed. 'Is of no matter.'

She hesitated.

He said, 'Just put one foot in front of the other.'

Evangeline stepped into the shoals. If the whole lake was only ankle deep, that might explain the appearance of walking on water.

The surface of the lake rippled. Was she imagining it, or could she hear, as if from far away, a tumult of suffering? Without a doubt, she heard Florito sounding the alarm. Then a vortex opened in the water and grew. The surface was still until it fell over the edge and plunged into an abyss. She felt its greed for her soul, sucking her towards it.

As one, all fell silent.

From deep within the void, she heard the mewling of a newborn baby, drawing air into its lungs, clutching at life.

'Effie!'

Evangeline waded further into the water: Effie needed her.

But as quickly as the sound had appeared, it was gone.

The vent belched vaporised water, bearing the miasma of purgatory, a stench laden with the rot of ages. As the putrid cloud billowed upwards and outward, buzzing sounded overhead. Then, they were upon her; swarming around and over her, their tough little exoskeletons percussing off her skin, biting her, zipping past her ears. Florito snapped wildly but ineffectively at the plague.

The hand holding hers became gnarly, needy. Through the plague of diabolical flies, Jesús' body extended, his muscles atrophied, his skin paled, and his glorious hair fell in clumps from his head. He continued to pull her into the lake, his movements stiff, his strength undiminished. The blue of his eyes faded to rheumy cataracts, and his lips retracted to display yellow rodentine teeth.

'It will stay here forever. Existing without hope,' said the creature that moments before had been Jesús, his breath an open cesspit.

She tried to wrench her wrist out of his grasp, but he held on tighter and continued to pull her deeper into the lake. The water was up to her waist, now, icy cold, numbing her toes in the kitten-heel booties which slipped on the bottom of the lake.

Behind her, Florito splashed into the water. Evangeline struggled with her captor while trying in vain to ward off the bombardment of flies. They swarmed around her head, obscuring her vision, finding their way into her mouth, biting her neck, her hands. With her free hand, she hit out at the Weku. When she managed to strike, her fist slammed into dense, inert matter, invulnerable to what she had to give. Struggling to keep her balance in the swirling waters of the vortex, she kicked as hard as she could beneath the surface, but the water's resistance robbed her legs of any power. Florito, in amphibious mode, joined her. The Weku, so intent on committing her to the pit devoid of hope, was oblivious to the hound's arrival. Florito sunk his jaws into the creature's hide. It shrieked in agony. The sound ricocheted around the chamber, to crash around in her head, infecting her mind with despair. The Weku loosened its hold on her and she pulled her hand from its clutches. She had no weapon. But she made use of what little she had. Unslinging the snakeskin bag from her shoulder, she swung it over her head and swiped at the Weku.

As it struck the creature, his clammy skin withered inward, like rotten fruit. Finally, all that was left was dust which drifted across the lake to be sucked into the vent. Foul vapour spewed from the void which, having been thrown a bone, shrank to the size of a plughole, then disappeared altogether. Once more, the water was as still as the cavern was black.

Evangeline began to think the bag in her hand was more than just a style accessory.

'Come on,' she called for Florito as she waded to shore holding the bag clear of the water.

Back on dry land, they continued along the path. Ahead of

them, a sliver of coral pink light shone in the dark. With every step towards the light, the affliction of the swarm slackened. It wasn't that the flies left them alone—they didn't—but that glimmer of light gave Evangeline hope. The path aimed for a cleft in the rock, in the shape of a snake's eye. The light came through the eye of the snake.

31. Vault of Light

Evangeline

It was clear Florito could not be wedged through the eye of the snake at ground level.

Evangeline said, 'Excuse me, my lad, but this has to be done.'

Cautious of his wound, she wrapped one arm around the solid bulk of his chest and, with her other, scooped him up by his hindquarters. As she lifted him level with the widest stretch of the gap and posted him through, Florito appeared more troubled by this indignity than the pain. He landed the other side with a thud and a heartrending whine. Evangeline followed him through the cleft sideways on. The last of the flies ceased their pursuit and remained behind in the Chamber of the Lake.

Like all good explorers, she'd started to name the features she met along her journey. Here, in this underworld, she designated their current location the Vault of Light. The vault was decorated, or so it seemed, by thousands of votive candles dangling from above. Warm glows of light were attached to fibres of some sort illuminating the vault in which they found themselves. Their light both buoyed and soothed her at once.

Waiting for you.

She'd been so sure back there, that the baby she heard was Effie. Here, in the Vault of Light, Effie's presence was stronger still.

'Effie?'

The quiet which answered her call was neither sinister nor lonely. Nor was it the silence of people not knowing what to say. Instead, peace filled her and with it came strength.

The hound before her needed attention.

'Now I can see properly, Florito, let me look at that wound of yours.'

She wiped the blood from his flank. The wound, the width of her hand, gaped and was deeper at its centre, consistent with the semi-circular blade of the tumi knife that made it. The absence of blood spurt assured her no artery had been damaged.

It was beyond strange how Florito had come into her life in a bar in Temuco and had persisted in tracking her down, no matter how far, locked cars no barrier. At times, she'd tried to figure it out, to find a logical explanation. Truth be told, there was none. He came to her because she needed him. Not as a replacement, for no one could ever replace Effie, but because she needed his love and acceptance to move forward with her life. Speaking words of reassurance as she tended his wound, she now believed Effie had sent him to watch over her.

⁂

Things happened in life that defied explanation. She'd done nothing wrong during the pregnancy. Right up to the day, the technician always commented on how strong her baby's heartbeat was. At thirty-six weeks, she went in for a regular check-up. Normally so chatty, the technician hooked her up to the heart monitor, searched around a bit then said she wanted a second opinion.

Then snapshots.

A weekend at Will's flat. The limbo between knowing and being induced.

Then Will's voice wobbling, 'It's coming.'

Bearing down on the pain, she clutched the sides of the bed, and pushed. Slick with sweat, her hands slipped along the metal frame, banged against a cross bar. Stuck like that, she powered down. The inside wanted out. A juggernaut moved through her pelvis. And caught with a scalding sting.

'Nearly there,' the midwife said. 'Just the shoulders to come.'

Ears ringing, blood vessels throbbing behind her eyes, Evangeline pushed harder and, in one gushing torrent, the baby slid out followed by the placenta.

Crunch-snip.

Then aching silence.

The nurse asking, 'Do you have a name for her?'

Drinking in the full head of auburn hair, the colour of damp autumn leaves clinging to the tree. 'Effie, she's called Effie.'

Holding Effie, the weight of her, her body so perfect. Her warmth fading. Then that perfect body taken to be cut open, to find out why the tiny heart didn't beat. She never did know why. It's the way it happens sometimes, she was told.

She could still feel Effie in her arms. She missed not getting to know her.

Will, devastated. They'd only just exchanged on a bigger place, a place suitable for a family. They never did move in together. His grief wasn't her grief, and her grief couldn't be shared. All she wanted was Effie.

After her body had recovered from the physical signs of pregnancy and birth, she returned to work, not knowing what else to do. The smallest things set her off. Going for her morning grande skinny latte. Just anticipating the expression of the barista who always served her. The young woman's eyes would be hopeful—expectant—of what Evangeline could only guess, for they never spoke beyond the daily order. Then the gaze would dip to her tummy. There'd be a pause for calculation (original size of customer x months gone), before the look that said they'd worked it out. At the time, it was an expression she received from pretty much everyone; a blend of confusion and awkwardness and not knowing what to say.

What was there to say?

The spirit of Effie was here.

Evangeline felt her. All the innocents taken before their time were here. And they were cared for—loved and nurtured—by the radiance of the vault: for them, sleeping here, there was nothing to fear. They gurgled in their sleep and counted their toes until their time came again.

By submerging her pain, she'd become compressed, brittle. Everything inside her had been reduced to the basics of keeping going. But the hope and sweetness she felt here, cocooned in the earth, infused her with a love of life, in all its forms. Effie would always be with her. The words of Morgan were with her. Florito, his brown eyes watching her every move and mood, was with her. She had to hope that she would see Jesús, the real Jesús, again. The thought of these connections forged during her life, a network of past, present and future, filled her with light.

Something hidden. Go and find it. Go!

'Florito, the World Tree! It's waiting for us. We're going to find it. We've got to go!'

Florito sighed with the weight of the world on his shoulders.

Cupping his head between her hands, Evangeline kissed his forehead. 'I'm so glad I've got you.' She assessed the wound. 'I'll bind this up as best I can.'

There was nothing for it but to rip off the sleeves of her catsuit and tie them around his middle. He huffed, not one for canine fashions.

Having done her best in first aid, she returned her attention to the pendent lights. On closer inspection, the fibres turned out to be roots and the light came from nodules, each the size of a grape, attached to those roots. What she'd taken to be residual columns were structural roots, penetrating through the bedrock above and below.

'It must be one mahoosive tree to extend this deep below ground,' she said.

Florito tilted his head to the side.

'What was it Snake said? "You'll know the rhizoxants when you find them."'

The larger, low-hanging rhizoxants detached easily, like ripe fruit. Those she picked, went in her snakeskin bag.

While she'd been busy harvesting, Florito entertained himself with a happy roll on the floor. He must have picked up on the good vibes of the vault: as injured as he was, he would not be contained. But when she looked down at him, she almost lost her state of nirvana. Not only had he wriggled out of the bandage, but he'd rolled in fallen grape-lights and was covered in splodges of their juice, a juice which was fluorescent coral pink.

'Florito! I deconstructed my catsuit for you.'

With ears back and head down, the hound looked guilty.

'We don't know what's in these rhizoxants. And what about your wound? You don't want it getting infected.'

He slid towards her across the floor on his belly, with his hind legs doing a passable impersonation of a frog. She rubbed his coral pink head in reconciliation.

'Well, one thing's for sure,' she said. 'At least we won't lose you looking like that.'

She collected the unsquashed rhizoxants and added them to her haul.

'My theory, if you're interested, is that these nodules are like those you get on leguminous plants which fix nitrogen in the soil.

In legumes, the process is facilitated by bacteria. It's possible the same thing is happening here. Or it might be something else entirely—a secondary metabolite, for instance.' She checked for his reaction. 'I'm sorry. You were there ahead of me, weren't you?'

There was one thing further she needed to do before they left the vault. Evangeline unhooked one of the gold tree earrings, the ones she'd had converted from Morgan's cufflinks, and removed it from her ear. In her hand, the earring sparkled in the coral light of the rhizoxants above. Reaching up, she threaded it over a rootlet, clustered with glowing nodules, and secured it with a knot.

'This is for you, Effie. Morgan will tell you many stories. Sleep tight, my beautiful girl.'

'Come on, Florito,' she said making to leave. 'We've got a tree to find.'

Behind them, the coral light of the rhizoxants twinkled.

⟱

She held on to the memory of the Vault of Light, its sweetness and unconditional love, forever. In the dark times that followed, she would draw upon that love which glowed within her.

32. Hope in Hell

Evangeline

It had been some time since Evangeline and Florito left the Vault of Light, although time was a difficult concept here in Netherearth, where darkness reigned eternal.

In the gloom, they now had a glimmer of hope. She clutched the few sprigs of nodule-encrusted roots she'd gathered, a sphere of light in the oppressive gloom. Florito's roll in the rhizoxants had given him an all-over amber radiance. Not only that, she suspected the root nodules of bringing about a miraculous recovery: the wound he'd suffered at the hands of Victor had melded together with just the neatest of scabs to show for it.

Heartened, she held the posy high like an Olympic torch. 'These little beauties are going to show us the way out of here.' Fighting talk in a tiny voice.

What was it, Morgan wrote? Your thoughts create reality. Positive thinking, that's what he was talking about. So, when they arrived at a fork in the path where one way continued downward and its tributary, to her delight, inclined, she took it as a sign her positive thinking was paying off. The higher smelled foul, but if it rose towards ground level, surely, a bad smell was a small price to pay if it meant getting out soon.

Evangeline set off up the path, but Florito stayed put.

'What's up?' she asked. 'We're getting out of here.'

He snuffled the ground of the lower path and raised his eyes to her.

'Out to the land of the living. Fresh air. Trees. You like trees.'

The good boy didn't budge. 'Listen, do you want to get out of here, or don't you? This path is going up. Ergo, my canine chum, it must be the right way.'

Florito stood his ground.

'Come on my sweet boy. When we get out, the first thing we're going to do is go to a café, a proper greasy spoon, and I'll treat you to all the sausages you want.'

Florito huffed, regarded the lower route one last time, then followed her.

The path led them onto a narrow ledge on the cliff face of a canyon. The echoes—of two feet and four paws stepping on stone—so constant now, she'd tuned them out long ago. But at some point, another sound joined in. It scuttled above them. The back of her neck prickled as though a presence watched her, waiting. Then creeping, below. Soon, the scuttling, creeping, watching, waiting was all around.

They were coming: the Wekufe.

Terror seized her throat.

Evangeline held her rhizoxant posy high and ran, Florito hot on her heels.

The Wekufe came as a mob, all bones and joints and stiff scurrying over the rock face. Their pungent stench surged like a bulwark closing in on Evangeline and hound.

The Wekufe pushed forward, jostling, scrabbling, mouth-breathing, sucking air between rodentine teeth, expelling foul breath in excitable, saliva-ridden chuffs. Heedless of the loss to their number, they knocked each other from the cliff face. Those close to the action appeared to be stimulated by the spectacle of destruction into a frenzy of copy-cat behaviour.

Evangeline and Florito ducked through a passageway, reeling around calcite formations as if on a pin-ball machine. Looking behind her, watching for the Wekufe, she banged into, broke and caught a stalactite.

It wasn't long before the first of the Wekufe loped along the same tunnel, angled forward, arms hanging loosely. In the confined passage so far below ground, the stink of the sub-earthly being was concentrated, condensed and poisonous.

Florito's snarl told her the Weku was upon them.

Buzzing with adrenaline, she rounded on their assailant, thrusting the rhizoxants in his direction. Strings of saliva hung gleaming from rodentine teeth to catch on the miserly lower lip, and snap at the flicker of his thick, liverish tongue.

He wanted her.

Recoiling from light and hound, the Weku's high-pitched, nasal voice whined, 'Its blood is up. Stressed meat unsavoury. Stressed meat pale, soft. Stressed meat exudes. Let it settle pre-slaughter. Calm it.'

All the while, he performed a macabre dance, jigging up and down, all angular bones, and long, stick-like extremities. What might once have been the family jewels, rattled about like nothing more than a trinket, a knickknack, a whatnot. Nothing to look at, at all, really, and yet horribly compelling.

He lunged, grabbing Florito by the throat, and lifted him high off the ground. Those long arms of the Weku held the hound's snapping jaws clear. The bony opposing thumbs found the windpipe and pressed. Florito's eyes bulged as the bulk of his body swung free from the ground. His howl was enough to waken the dead. Then again, the dead were not only awake but walking abroad.

The Weku's pallid eyes turned to her.

'Leave my boy alone!' She swiped again with the rhizoxants.

The Weku appeared to consider a while before saying in his high-pitched whisper, 'Flesh. Be calm.'

'Calm? Calm. I'll give you calm.' Evangeline gripped the stalactite as if it were a baton.

The Weku danced his weird little jig. 'Hurry! Calm! Quick!'

'This is what we're going to do.' The tunnel's echo amplified her voice impressively. 'We're going to carry on along this tunnel. If you continue to harass us, you're going to get an eye-full of light. Have I made myself perfectly clear?' Mum had always stood up to bullies, and Mum's voice was coming through loud and clear.

Evangeline swooshed her fistful of rhizoxants at their persecutor.

'Light burns.' The Weku sucked his breath through teeth and spittle. 'It douses light.'

'Leave my boy alone!' She advanced on the creature. 'You let him go, you bully. Let him go and I'll be calm. I'll be as calm as the eye of a storm.'

'It gives itself for the release of this dark flesh?'

'You let him go first, get it?

'It offers live human flesh?'

'Put my Florito down.' Her voice faltered.

'It settles its flesh,' the Weku simpered and lowered the hound to the floor.

So intent was the Weku on the feast before his eyes, his ears had not registered the mouth-breathing behind him. But as soon as Florito's paws hit the ground, he launched himself at the Wekufe horde clogging the passageway.

The Weku appeared pleased: he now had what he wanted to himself. He rubbed his thighs.

With a sound part-grunt, part-snigger, he turned his head from Evangeline as though in delicious anticipation of what was to come.

Then he lunged.

His teeth grazed the skin of her neck while his long claw-like nails ripped at her clothing, exposing her midriff. Where the creature had made contact, her skin erupted in blisters. His filth seeped through her veins like a spreading bruise. The creature grasped her by the shoulder and pushed her to her knees. Try as she might, she couldn't shake him off. He had her where he wanted her. The curds and whey of fear and revulsion churned inside, as she experienced the spectacle of the Wekufe aperitif.

His free hand moved to his groin with deliberation. He caught his vestigial organ and engaged the whatnot in a feverish jerking which amounted to very little, really, other than a flaccid slap, slap, slap. Perhaps this foreplay was meant only to gloat in the moment of conquest, to humiliate and undermine his prey.

If that was the intention, it succeeded.

All the while the Weku slavered and leered at her bare stomach, and wheezed, 'Its skin so tender. Flesh so young, so milky, spicy. Oh, viscera. Slick, succulent, viscera.'

She spat at the creature. 'You are not having any part of me.'

Blood pumped through her scalp, honing her vision.

Shaken from his rapture, the Weku blinked his rheumy eyes several times: this delicacy talked back. He inhaled, then drew one leg behind the other. Was he deterred?

No, he was preparing to straddle her. He grasped either side of her turtle-neck, hauled her up then threw her back flat on the ground. One leg either side of her, his bony rump slammed down on her knees. He pinioned her to the floor, clamping her armpits as though riding a vintage Norton. Leaning forward, his drool dripped slowly on her bare flesh. His tongue, that fat tongue, licked his lips and flickered once more.

She was ready.

He lunged at her torso. The chisel-sharp incisors of his open mouth grazed her cheek. She thrust the stalactite in her hand deep into the orifice. The tip of the cone pierced the back of the Weku's throat, cutting short his harrowing scream, and plunged into brain matter. The creature's eyes opened wide. His stunned glare regained consciousness of her. Then his expression changed once more, this time to challenge her, as if to say: is this all you can do?

He leered and closed his hands over hers, still gripping the cone. The bones of her hands crushed, while he forced the cone deeper into his head. This time, the tip of the stalactite exited the creature's skull, whose face was now inches from her own.

The Weku fell upon her, writhing in agony, smearing her with rank sweat. He clawed and groped at her flesh, frenzied with food lust and pain and the fight for survival. Grappling with him, fending off his clutches while avoiding the cone projecting from his mouth, she felt, bit by bit, his strength diminish. His fingers, no longer able to grasp, fumbled against her. His thigh-grip slackened on her legs. He rasped, choking on calcite. Eventually, the writhing subsided, became involuntary twitching, then no more.

Lying beneath him, nose to atrophied nose, the creature's face was ignorant, mean, vacant. It was the face of a being with sentience, but one which had channelled all its efforts into jealousy and avarice. It was a being which had gained pleasure by taking for itself what others held dear—then destroying that which was cherished—simply to reduce others to its level.

'Get off me.' She pushed the Weku away. 'What's with this "it" business? My name is E-van-ge-line. Geddit?' She rasped.

Had she stooped to its level? She'd killed it, she meant to do it. It was self-defence, but its death was on her hands.

What had happened to Florito?

Behind her and blocking the mouth of the tunnel as tight as a cork in a bottle, a Wekufe slugfest was in full swing; the sound, as Wekufe fist struck Wekufe form, like a squid slapped by the fisherman against the harbour wall. Between the snarls and hisses, the pulling and clawing, and the stinking, putrid clamminess, the dark bulk of Florito, so quick and light on his paws, dancing like a heavyweight butterfly, stinging like a mighty bee.

Evangeline whistled Time. The champion canine ducked a pivot blow, pulled away from the skirmish and bounded towards her. In Florito's wake, other Wekufe immediately set upon his former opponent, oblivious their live quarry was making away.

With Florito at her heels, she stumbled into the dark, sobbing, putting as much distance between them and the Wekufe as possible: it was only a matter of time before the sub-human beings realised their mistake.

Evangeline was as suddenly aware of her own mistake in going off-course as if it were an animate thing jumping on her shoulders. They were lost and she was to blame. They couldn't go back, but every step forward took them further away from Snake's path. What to do?

Then a moment of utter clarity: there was no ground beneath her feet.

Her internal organs, the contents of those organs, determined to stay put, while skin and bones succumbed to the force of gravity. Her hands reached out, clutching at anything that came to hand. But found nothing. Travelling so fast, she couldn't breathe, she heard Florito yelp beside her then found that she, too, yelped with pain and fear.

She bounced off an outlying ledge, landed on her back on an inclined slab, then careened downward. Skimming over hollows and bumps, which jammed into elbows, propelled her airborne to crash her moments later, jarring hipbones, shoulder-blades, she pressed the soles of her boots flat to the rock's surface and felt the burn. Heels dug hard. Florito yelped, a sign he was suffering the same fate.

With a thud and a disconcerting crack, she landed on her tailbone. Their trajectory continued across the smoothest of floors. Flat on their backs, they whizzed around like Catherine Wheels on a surface so slippery, so, so cold, there was nothing for it but to wait until they came to rest.

'Florito?'

Bark.

Bruised, disorientated and dizzy, they lay on the floor while they regained their breath and took stock. Wherever it was they'd landed, it was completely different to what had been before. For one thing, there was light enough to see. And the sight took a while for her brain to piece together. Initially, she thought she was looking on the rippled, eddied surface of the Aegean Sea. But with the Aegean Sea suspended overhead. Had she been standing she would be able to touch it at a stretch. The seascape, varying between the intense blue of the deep and the crystal blue of the shallows, continued down the concave sides of the lacuna into which they'd so recently rocked up. She imagined the lacuna's ceiling was a giant arm extending lazily over the side of a fishing boat to stir up the sea, the outsized bubbles left in the arm's wake trapped in the walls. And from within the walls came noises of twig-snaps and the creaking groan and crash of a tree uprooted by the wind.

They lay on ice. It seared through the thin material of her deconstructed catsuit. The air fresh and so cold as to prickle her nose; in however long it had taken them to tumble down the shaft to where they now lay, the temperature had dropped to freezing.

But that was as nothing compared with her other discovery: the dazzling white mouth of a cave.

33. Cold Snap

Evangeline

W here were they?

It was cold. Cold as in Baltic. Evangeline had established that much. She tried pulling the shredded remains of her catsuit across her midriff but without success. Then she wondered whether Florito needed the bandage of sleeves he'd dismissed out of hand…paw, whatever.

The storm-cloud of a headache brewing since they left the Vault of Light was lifting. Whether through relief at being free from the Path of the Wekufe, or something in the air, either way, she was more aware of their surroundings, as though she and the environment were more sharply defined. Now that she thought about it, her breathing and pulse had returned to normal.

So, with head clear, and beginning to feel more like her old self, she reviewed their situation.

She was, to say the least, inappropriately dressed. Her barely-there catsuit and kitten-heels were no match for the ice. Florito, as tough as he was, didn't appear to be set up for slippery, freezing conditions, either.

All the same, the blue freshness of the cave galvanised her. She could do this.

Florito jumped up at her, cantered some way towards the cave mouth, legs going in all directions. Watching him, her mind's sound effects library selected frantic bongos. He returned to round her up, then repeated the routine, several times over, barking excitedly, tail wagging.

With her legs in splayed formation, she kept up as best she could. 'Lead the way, my lad.'

Wincing in the unfamiliar brightness, they emerged from the cave.

It was wonderful to be out of the underworld, really it was. But what lay before them set another challenge: they'd emerged on a mountain glacier.

Ice blue, its powdery surface rippled like Saharan sand. The glacier stretched from a forest on the lower slopes, to a conical smoking summit. The smoke surged upward into a clear, mid-day sky, whirling back upon itself to get caught in the jet once more until, much higher, the impetus lessened, releasing the fog grey vapour on the prevailing wind. Without a sound, the volcano's breath burdened the atmosphere with sulphur and ash. The leeward side of the cone was disfigured by a dense, spreading scar of Stygian tephra.

Beyond the summit, further peaks jutted from the forest. These inhospitable islands of granite were bald but for tufts and frizzes of trees. Behind them, more peaks again. Salmon pink and dark grey, ranging into the hazy blue distance.

Below her, below the trees whose tannins telegraphed the air, lakes glistened and the terracotta roofs—of settlements going about their business—baked.

She'd read this scene. She pictured the words on the liver-spotted page of the journal whose corners, thickened and downy with wear, she imagined beneath her fingertips. The scene was exactly as Morgan had described.

'Here's the good news, my pupper,' Evangeline said. 'By my reckoning, we appear to have popped out on the slopes of Villarrica.'

Wise old Snake. Her advice had been sound. Even if it had come through a dream.

Evangeline considered their options. The sensible thing would be to descend through the forest to civilisation. Find help, clothing, food. Have a rest then come back up here to look for the World Tree.

Her eyes swept across the dense forest of what she assumed to be southern beech and the easy to distinguish Araucaria, whose umbrella branches protruded on spindly trunks from the main canopy. A flash of light within forest green drew her attention. Five or six haulage trucks were loaded with timber. There was no time to lose: the pipeline was coming.

Her breath formed a cloud as she exhaled.

'And now the bad news,' she said.

Florito's head cocked quizzically.

'You may think I've lost it, my boy, but we're going up. We've got to climb the volcano before the oil company fells Rewe.'

The hound looked at her kitten-heeled boots and huffed. Did he also roll his eyes?

※

They'd been walking for a few hours, not making much headway for all the slipping and sliding, and their hunger, and having had little sleep since taking the path of the Wekufe. But at least they weren't cold. The effort of walking on ice and snow had their pulses surging. They were both panting, but only Florito's tongue lolled from the side of his mouth.

In the course of their foray, they'd acquired two hats which a gust of wind had pulled from the heads of skiers, presumably—

'Here you are. You have the red one,' she insisted—and, in a complete U-turn of her ethical conscience, she was overjoyed by the multitude of plastic bags blowing about, the flotsam and jetsam of the mountain world. The bags she used to fill gaps in her catsuit, to waterproof her footwear, and to cover her hands. Not a bad haul.

She was trying to remember what Chile Morgan had said about this part of the trek. Anything that might help them. Landmarks to confirm they were on course. But, being tired, things tended only to come to her after the event. That was one example, right there. Chile had written about his fatigue. How physically drained he'd been by the effort of ploughing through snow at high altitude. So, her memory wasn't great at the moment. So, too, her usual sense of where-there's-a-will. Her will needed to be fed. Her will would quite like to relax in front of a fire. If truth be told, her will needed a more intellectually responsive companion than a hound. What they—Florito, she and her will—needed, more than anything, was some shelter for the night. Although they'd miraculously emerged from a cave, she'd not seen more of the same since. And the daylight wasn't going to last forever.

A buzzing insinuated its way into her thoughts. Chainsaws! She was too late! The tree was being chopped to pieces, and all she could do was slip-slide around on a glacier.

Though, now she'd turned her attention to it, it was more of a buzzzzzzz-bump. It came from the west, in the direction of the lower slopes and forest. It came from that direction, but it was growing louder and higher in pitch. It was going to intercept them. Florito, in front of her, stopped and turned towards the buzz: forelegs braced, chest proud, velvet ears alert.

A black speck came over the horizon at speed. At times, it was in contact with the snow, when it buzzed with regularity, but it often took flight over the hidden vales to land with a bump on the snow once more.

As the speck grew, she distinguished a snowmobile, driven by a figure in neon magenta.

Help?

Whoever it was might be able to help. All the same, she mentally prepared herself for the likely argument she'd have with offers of kindness and common sense. She wasn't going to allow them to talk her out of her quest. But any spare clothing, food or equipment would be gratefully received.

Or it might be a foe. She must be on her guard, trust nobody.

Was help at hand?

She hoped so. She had to trust so: the catsuit and kitten-heels were holding her back. Jumping in the air, she waved her arms.

'Help!'

Bark!

Buzzzzzzzzz-bump.

'Over here!'

Bark! Bark!

Buzz-bump. Bu-bump. Buzzzzzzzzz-bump.

'Here, over here!'

Bark! Bark! Bark!

Buzzzzzzzzzz ~ zzzzzzzzzzzzzzzzzzzz.

The snowmobile and its neon magenta driver drew up in front of them.

The driver, compact in a figure-hugging one-piece, wore matching helmet, goggles, gloves and boots: a full flush of magenta. The vehicle coordinated with its purple body and turquoise and rose decals.

Gloved hands raised the visor from calculating brown eyes.

'Pues, look what el gato dragged in,' the magenta one purred.

'Cat!' Evangeline recognised the voice—husky as though it had been used since childhood to get its own way by screaming at full-volume—of her nemesis.

'You just don't know when to give up, do you?' Catalina said, pulling off her helmet and shaking out her hair.

'Give up? When I've got this far? I'm on the brink—'

'Brink. Precipice. Same difference, the way I see it.' Catalina pursed her lips as she hung her helmet on the upright taillight.

'Is that a threat?' After the incident on the bridge, Evangeline knew the bearings of Catalina's moral compass were wildly off-kilter.

As if picking up on her thoughts, Catalina said, 'I promised myself that day on the bridge that I wouldn't rest until I found you again. I knew then that I'd get you, mi bonita, and your little dog, too!' She cackled, swirling her leg over the snowmobile to stand as a pocket-sized purple powerhouse, in the plume of its exhaust.

Evangeline braved it out. 'Don't do this, Catalina. Why go to the effort of killing me? And if you really want rid of me that much, please, I beg you, leave Florito out of this.'

'Oh, I don't want to kill you,' Catalina gave a disdainful moue. 'Either of you. Why should I waste the effort? Overnight on a volcano will take care of that.'

'Think again,' Evangeline said. 'Today is not your day.'

Catalina switched the motor to idle. 'This, from she who wears a pink and green catsuit, wannabe-pimped with plastic?'

There was a time when Evangeline would have taken the slight to heart, but she wasn't going to let Catalina get under her skin. 'Get over yourself, Catalina. Shouldn't you be doing your thing at Asklepion?'

Catalina shifted her weight. 'Oh, but I am doing my thing. I saw your proposal to Asklepion. This tree of yours and its products could be a gamechanger.'

'Why try to stop me? So, Asklepion bowed out, but you could still have been involved, in some way. You could've advised from the sidelines.'

'Sidelines?' Catalina's lips became a firm corrugation. 'What you don't seem to understand is that, in this field, if you aren't lead author pumping out papers in high-impact journals, you've failed. Failed into obscurity. You're only as good as your last paper.' She struck the palm of one hand with the side of the other, emphasising the words.

'But we could have done this together,' Evangeline said.

'Togeth—' Catalina tossed her head. 'What planet are you on?'

'What? Because I don't have a doctorate? Because I didn't follow a set career path?' Evangeline said.

'Yes. Exactly. You don't have kudos. You're un peor es nada—a nobody. Geddit?'

'You just back your high horse up a moment, Doctor Frankensteina. So, I don't have a publication record. And, yes, I'm not a recognised authority. But I know my stuff,' Evangeline stepped forward and slid even closer. 'Don't forget, all those early plant hunters: they knew nothing of today's tools and technologies. The field of genetics didn't get going until the twentieth century.'

'Thanks for the history less—'

'But they succeeded because they did what they were most passionate—'

'You gringa talking about passion—'

'Yes, passion. For plants they went through shipwreck, fever, rebellion—'

Catalina's hands went full-on expressive—fingers jabbing the air, wrists whirling—as she shrieked, 'What do you know? You come over here and steal our—'

'I steal your what? If anyone's been doing any stealing, it's you. Where's the journal?' Evangeline held out her hand.

Catalina slapped it away. '¡Súbete a la micro! Get real! While you've been going all out with the bag-lady look,' she looked her up and down, 'Jesús is on prime time. ¡Dios mío! His followers can't get enough of him on Twitter. You wouldn't stand a chance, now. You never were his type, anyway.'

'No, hang on…wait a minute, what?'

'Oh, didn't you know? Jesús is *the* face of documentaries, right now.' Catalina's smile didn't extend to her eyes. 'I can't pick up a copy of *¡Hola!* for pictures of Jesús and some hot polola or another—'

'Stop this.'

'I think you did him a favour. I heard all about you and your—how do you say?—habit.'

'If you had any idea...'

'You Great British bolso—'

Well, that was fighting talk, right there. 'A hand~bag?'

A handbag: the only weapon she carried. She unhitched her barrel-bag and took a swipe at Catalina. The purple poppet was poleaxed.

Standing over her, Evangeline said, 'What? So, having it all isn't good enough for you, your Magent-esty? You're only happy when you've got everyone's attention. Is that it?'

'Ouff!' Catalina's magenta Eskimo boot hooked behind Evangeline's bag-clad foot and brought her down.

Evangeline planted her hands on the ground to raise her head. Catalina was too quick for her and, grabbing a fistful of hair, she slammed Evangeline's face into the snow. Her mouth filled with the cold stuff, numbing her brain. But not her scalp, which burnt with pain as her head was yanked back once again by her hair. Villarrica's Stygian scar came into view as she gasped for breath. Then, straight away, her nose was smashed into the ground again. The grey matter ricocheted around her skull, jangling all the more with Florito barking on the sidelines. He knew better than to get between the two women.

Punch-drunk, Evangeline felt Catalina's knee in the small of her back. She pushed up, unbalancing Catalina who toppled onto her back. Evangeline took the advantage and pulled herself out of the snow. Falling on top of her foe, she gained control of Catalina's arm and pinioned it to the ground. Even through the quilted sleeve, the other's muscles were like iron. Dodging

Catalina's free hand clawing at her face, she tried reason.

'Look. It's still not too late,' Evangeline breathed. 'We go together. I discover the tree. You gain the medical glory. All I want is to know it exists and that it is safe.'

A gob struck her eye.

'I spit at you, you English!' Catalina struggled against her. 'Our land is not for you to pillage. And how could you possibly imagine that our men would ever be turned on by a fanta—a ginge?'

Evangeline's vision blurred. She blinked the spittle out of her eye but felt its weight on her cheekbone.

'Who's not thinking it through? You don't have the expertise to identify the tree. You need me.'

As if incensed by the logic, Catalina slammed her feet on the ground, dislodging Evangeline.

Both scrabbled to their feet and went at each other, locking fists. Evangeline's longer arms held the smaller woman at bay, but she recognised the other's superior strength. She kicked Catalina's shin, and kitten-heel rent magenta. The Chilean dropped to her knees but pulled her rival with her. They tumbled and slid on the snow. Catalina kneed Evangeline in the groin and followed it up with a few blows to her midsection. The shock of each strike was numbed by snow and adrenalin, but left Evangeline gasping for breath.

Grappling with Catalina in her snow togs was like wrestling with thickly insulated lead piping. But one part of the pharmacologist's body was unprotected. Evangeline slapped that self-satisfied face once, twice, three times. The Chilean's eyes were stunned, and her cheeks burned with the imprint of a hand. Taking the advantage, Evangeline grasped the other's arms, shoved her foot into Catalina's sternum and sent her in an overhead somersault. Catalina slammed to earth on her back. Still holding one arm, Evangeline swivelled around on the snow, twisting the limb in its socket until Catalina screamed out.

Florito took hold of a magenta Eskimo boot and tugged. Catalina kicked back but, for the hound, this was all part of the sport. First one boot then the other came off.

Grateful for this diversion, Evangeline caught her breath. 'Even if you found the tree, you're so unhinged, no one in their right mind would ever support your research,' she panted.

Wild-eyed, Catalina said, 'I'm going to make history.'

Evangeline pulled away from her opponent. 'I've offered to work with you on this, but I see that's a no-go.' She gulped for air. 'Frankly, that is more than fine with me. But give me the journal.' Evangeline held out her hand again.

'Why would I give you that satisfaction?' Catalina remained defiant.

'I need this. I'm doing it for Chile Morgan...and for Effie.' As the words left her mouth, Evangeline wondered how it was she was able to tell her innermost feelings to someone she hardly knew and liked even less, yet she couldn't talk to those closest to her.

'Well, there's the thing. If I had no ambition, I'd hand over the journal. You English like your fair play. But, a little tip, *nice* doesn't cut it.'

Then a strange thing happened. Far across the growing shadows and snow sparkling in salmon pink sundown, something was airborne.

Catalina, hands on hips, was raving about her future. 'I am going to find that tree, and all the world is going to know my name...'

What was coming towards them?

'As Strategy Director of Asklepion, I'll show them what I'm really made of. And if they don't give me what I want, their competitors will...'

A large bird? A raptor?

'I will be showered in accolades: the Shaw Prize, the Nobel

Prize…'

Evangeline had difficulty tuning out the woman's yapping to focus on the airborne fauna. It soon became evident, however, the thing in the sky was, well, not quite right.

If it was a bird, it had a bulky look to it. And the wings were wrong. They weren't bird-like, but flicked up and back, such that the creature made darting, wheeling movements, turning sharply. Light radiated through the dark pink leather of the wing and put into relief the finger-like bone structure. The wings weren't feathered at all.

A bat, then? But even as she thought this, she knew it to be wrong. The head was bulky. The body was, well, it was nowhere to be seen, and the legs were chunky, strong. Even at this distance, and with Catalina banging on about medals of honour, she could make out its talons. There was something unnatural about this creature.

Florito began to howl. A drawn out, doleful cry that rang across the mountain.

Catalina broke off from her tirade to say, 'Shut that mutt up, can't you?'

'Catalina. Stop a moment.'

'How dare you tell me what to do!'

'For the love of all that's holy: put a cork in it.'

But it was too late.

There must have been something in Evangeline's expression. Standing by the snowmobile, Catalina did as she was told and fell silent.

Catalina would say barely more than a dozen words again.

Evangeline had been watching the sky but glanced at the woman. Catalina's eyes were locked on her, as though divining chickens' entrails. Then, as if she had interpreted the omens, Catalina's expression changed to fear.

'OK,' Evangeline spoke quietly. 'Maybe we need to move.'

Eyes fixed on each other, they rose to their feet, avoiding sudden movement. Florito, with head low, slunk towards the snowmobile in stealth mode but stopped, front paw raised in mid-air, when Evangeline tapped the side of her thigh with her hand.

'Walk towards me, slowly,' she said to Catalina.

Catalina crept forward, her bare feet crunching through the snow, to stand on tiptoe behind Evangeline and peer around her shoulder.

'There's something behind your snowmobile. It's…I don't know, I've never seen anything like it before,' Evangeline said.

She reached behind her and took hold of Catalina's left hand in her right. The woman may have been self-centred and eager to do away with her, but this was a prime example of better the devil you know.

And what Evangeline thought she'd seen swoop down behind the snowmobile, defied all logic.

Florito, his whole body alert, placed himself between women and snowmobile growling a Halt!-Who-goes-there? challenge.

The sun gave up the ghost and dropped out of sight. The ice that had dazzled, dulled.

Evangeline scanned around for cover. They were a sitting target against the snow, but granite and shale were making inroads on the ice. They would be better camouflaged against the stony background.

With her free hand, she swung the strap of her bag around her wrist, leaving a sufficient length to keep any assailant at a distance.

She squeezed Catalina's hand and said, 'You OK?'

Evangeline glanced over her shoulder and Catalina bobbed in response.

'Right then. It may be nothing at all: just a bird or a bat.' She concentrated on keeping her voice quiet and calm. 'But we need to know. Then we won't worry for no reason.'

Catalina gripped Evangeline's arm like a tourniquet.

'So, what we're going to do is walk around the front of your vehicle and check it out.'

Catalina's eyes were like dark chocolate buttons.

'Florito is here, and he doesn't stand for any nonsense.' Evangeline squeezed the hand again. 'But, if there is anything we don't like the look of, anything at all, it's sound. Because I've got a plan.'

When she could tell from Catalina's expression the message had been processed, she added, 'If there's any hint of danger, I will say "now". When I do, we are going to run like the clappers to that outcrop of shale.'

Catalina bobbed again.

'Where are we going to run?' Evangeline said.

Catalina pointed to the outcrop of shale.

'Right then. We're going to see what's what,' Evangeline said.

Wrists entwined, Evangeline pulled Catalina to the front of the snowmobile. Florito, swaggering like a gunslinger, moved ahead to maintain his position between vehicle and women.

They all peered around the bumper.

And peered some more.

Aside from the snowmobile, all to be seen, was snow.

But she'd seen something. She was sure of it. A live, unnatural thing had flapped behind cover of the vehicle.

Catalina snatched her hand away and straightened her shoulders. Florito sniffed the ground.

With a snort of derision, Catalina picked up the helmet she'd balanced on the taillight.

But no sooner had she done so, she screamed and threw the helmet into the snow.

They all looked at the helmet as it rolled in the snow, over and over, before coming to rest, the open neck upper-most. The dark, heavily padded lining could be a hiding place for a great many things.

'Something's in there,' Catalina said, hopping from one foot to the other.

'I'm not sure what I saw would fit in there,' Evangeline said.

'Whatever. I'm going.' Catalina swung her leg over the seat, grasped the vehicle's grips and revved the throttle.

The engine roared, belching out vapour from the exhaust. A shadow, no more than a suggestion of something, if anything at all, separated from the rear and rose into the gloom.

Oblivious, Catalina said, 'Chavela!'

Evangeline had to hand it to Catalina. The Chilean was concerned about one thing and one thing only: Catalina. Everyone else was a toy to play with, to use, to tire of and to break.

'You're just going to clear off, are you?' said Evangeline.

'I've got a tree to find.'

'But I saw something.'

'That's the thing with some drugs,' Catalina said. 'Flashbacks.'

Evangeline flinched, then flicked the woman away with her hand. 'Your look out.'

Catalina turned her head as though from a bad smell. She pressed a button and the snow glistened in a brilliant arc before her.

As she did so, a shadow swooped into the red glow of the rear lamp. It was hunched, like an old man. Rising in the air, what had at first appeared to be a curved spine now extended into leathery wings. Wings which spanned so wide that, with little effort, they'd eclipse a pudu, or even a small, perfectly formed woman. These wings did not arise from the shoulders, but, directly from the head. The head was human, with long silver hair, prominent blue veins in pallid skin, and bloodshot eyes. Not just bloodshot but entirely saturated with blood. From chin to neck, it lacked flesh. Instead, a network of veins, like the bare branches of a primaeval forest, hung free. There the body of the chonchon ended.

'Watch out!' Evangeline shouted.

Catalina pulled away, the thrum of the vehicle's engine cancelling out the warning as well as another, more plaintive cry.

Tue tue tue. Wings beat against the night sky, giving chase.

Tue tue tue. Talons stretched forward as the chonchon swooped upon its prey.

Evangeline watched in horror as the supernatural creature sank its talons into the small magenta figure. An agonised scream echoed across the mountain. But it was too late. The creature hauled Catalina from the vehicle and rose slowly, fluttering into the moonless night. The vehicle, out of control, ploughed into a snowbank.

Evangeline shuddered. She lifted her arm a hound's breadth away from her body, expecting Florito to fill the gap. But the void lingered.

'Florito?' She looked around. The silence crushed her. Had he headed for the cover of the forest, far below? It wasn't like him to take fright, but the alternative—that he had become a victim of the chonchon—was too terrible to contemplate.

'Florito! Where are you, boy?' She saw nothing, apart from the glow some way up the incline, radiating from the deserted snowmobile. If she could make her way to the vehicle, she could use it to look for him.

It was heavy going. Her makeshift insulation of plastic bags had not survived the tussle with Catalina. Her kitten-heeled boots were sodden, encasing her feet in numbing cold. Stumbling forward, at times on hand and knees, so tired but not daring to rest for fear of losing her boy forever, she closed in on the snowmobile. Exhaust fumes chugged from its idling engine, choking the clean air. Unsteadily, she got to her feet and captured the snowmobile.

It took a bit of pressing of buttons and turning of switches, to work out what was what, before she gingerly revved the throttle. Nothing. Why wasn't she moving? She dismounted and looked around the vehicle. The cold night air had frozen the skis to the ice. She kicked each one, to break it free, and climbed aboard once more. This time, when she revved the throttle, she was borne forward. Slowly at first, and unsteadily. Gaining confidence, she picked up speed and steered towards the tree line.

Her footprints and scuffs and tumbles were clearly visible in the vehicle's beam. Tracking them back, she came across an area of compacted snow, with two pairs of human prints and four large paws scrabbling around. This must have been where she fought with Catalina. Aiming the headlight on the paw prints, she followed them on foot. They rounded in circles, wandering off several times to return to the fray. But one track continued to the trees.

Back on the snowmobile, she followed the trail across the ground they'd taken all day to achieve, covering it in a fraction of the time. Ahead, off to the right, a dark hulk loomed towards her. It came at speed. Evangeline's steering wobbled. A pair of blood red disks glared in the headlight before she veered off course. But over the throb of the engine she thought she heard a short, sharp bark. She released the throttle. Out of the night came another bark.

It was Florito and he came bearing gifts. A pair of gifts to be precise: magenta Eskimo boots. A tight fit but, nonetheless, welcome.

Could a hound travel on the back of a snowmobile? Evangeline wondered what equipment Catalina had brought with her. In the tunnel bag, she found a bungee rope and a cargo net. That should do it, she thought. What else was rattling around in there? Unzipping an interior pocket, her fingers smoothed over the surface of well-worn leather, a slim volume. The journal had returned to her.

34. The Horse Ceremony

Morgan: Lake Mallalafquén, 28 March 1843

Rhythm hypnotic brings the spirits. Rattle, shake, drum—percussion is the thing.

On the volcanic shores of Lake Mallalafquén, when the early evening lull is broken by the cicadas' pulsating chorus, two-score or more Mapuche villagers gathered in a ring. Where they came from, we could only guess. I'd travelled several days through laurel-leaved forest—the wet, temperate climate reminding me of Wales—without seeing a single, solitary soul, excepting friend Paco. Yet they, the Mapuche, must have been close by. Hidden among the evergreens, watching my every move. When I scrunched the leaf of the Chilean myrtle (*Luma apiculata*) in my hand, and inhaled its citrus aroma, was someone breathing in my scent?

Word had spread. A horse ceremony. For a wingka. What was Machi Gonzalo thinking? The shaman performing medicine on a non-Mapuche? They came to witness the event. To be part of it. And here they were. Here we all were, between lake and forest, and under the watchful presence of Villarrica herself. The night was clear. Just a ribbon of silvery cloud across the neck of the mountain. The moon illuminated the volcano's mantle of snow such that she, Villarrica, appeared to draw closer. Together, moon and Villarrica stroked the features of the Mapuche: temples and cheekbones gleamed, eyes shone.

Here, in what has been called the Chilean Lake District— distinct from the Cumbrian version by way of its thermal springs and volcanoes—the Mapuche wore chamalls.[17] In the intensity of the moment, some of the younger men had cast these off entirely and danced bare-chested, their faces serious with concentration, with fringes pasted to brows by the sweat of their exertions. All, young and old, were united in rapping out a rhythm. The lively tempo they produced from seed rattles, gourd shakers, woodblocks and clapping, reminded me of the two-beat gait of a trotting horse. As if not to be outdone, the chittering barks, shrieks and hisses—the mating calls of the tiger owl—played a caprice around the music: an elbow in the ribs here, a slap on the head there. The overall effect: a wanton, pummelling symphony which rollicked around the body in a dizzying surge of disinhibition.

A step-notched pole (a rewe), the girth of a ship's mast, stood in the centre of the ring. The rewe acts as the connection between the worlds of men and of spirits. In other words, it is a symbol of the World Tree. On its top step, Machi Gonzalo placed a handful of volcanic rocks. These were to protect against evil spirits. On lower steps, the machi had put food, drink and kopihue *(Lapageria rosea)* flowers.[18] Bound to the sides of the rewe were the branches

---

[17] Chamall: the Mapudungan word for chamanto, the double-sided poncho I have affected since my earliest peregrinations through Chile.
18. The Mapuche associate such items with femininity and seduction. Their purpose here is to attract the helpful spirits. In the case of *L. rosea*, as with the origins of much folklore relating to plants, I

of sacred trees – foye, trihue, boldo, and klon.[19] Next to it Machi Gonzalo, dressed in a shawl, long skirts, headdress and silver earrings, prepared for the ceremony.

To the machi, sexual identity is a fluid concept which exists beyond the designation of male or female. The identifier of co-sex might be more appropriate here. What is important is how the machi interacts with the spirits and practices medicine, more than the sex they were assigned at birth based on visible anatomical evidence.

All machi, whether male or female, must bond with their ancestral spirit, their filew, to perform medicine. To initiate that bond, the machi attracts the filew's attention, flirts with it, wears necklaces and a blue headdress to seduce the spirit from the sky, before they become wedded as machi bride and spiritual husband.

I was also in the circle. Not a central figure, almost in the wings, in fact. This was good. It allowed the people to become accustomed to me before the main event. And they were inquisitive. Now and then, from behind, I felt a hand tug at my clothing or touch my hair. I sensed it was curiosity more than hostility. Conquistadores aside, I doubted I was the first white man these people had seen. After all, in recent years successive waves of European merchants and miners had taken advantage of Chile's natural resources. But, for a wingka such as myself to solicit Mapuche medicine, this must surely have been a rarity indeed.

I put their lack of hostility down to their trust in Machi Gonzalo. He and I had hit it off from the first. Despite not being able to speak the other's language, we each recognised in

---

suspected the shape of its parts or its habit to be relevant (its flower is pink and bell-shaped and it has a climbing habit).

19. On closer inspection, I recognised these as *Drymys winteri, Laurelia sempervirens, Peumus boldus* and *Aristotelia chilensis* respectively.

the other a shared love of flora. His round, unlined face reflected the openness of his soul. Through his dungumachife, his ritual (and lingual) interpreter, he revealed the secrets of the plants and trees we came across on our forays to the surrounding forest, and foothills of Villarrica. I may have only known him a week but, in that time, I had gained an innate trust in his intention to use his knowledge and spirituality for the good of others.

It was he who first taught me about the ethnic uses of the Yavuaceae. This most remarkable family of trees is equipped with aromatic bark, wood and resin of medicinal use. A compound from its bark is an effective cicatrisant, as I know first-hand from having sliced my hand with a machete while out foraging.

The people of the region apply it for conditions as varied as loss of heart, antisocial behaviour, visitations by evil spirits, indigestion, gout, headaches and the flux. It may also be used as a condiment.

Something tells me there is more to the esteemed family than even this litany allows. But, when pressed for more detail, Machi Gonzalo clammed up. Yet, at times, I am almost certain he sees me as instrumental in its destiny.

Standing by my side in the ring was the machi's dungumachife, Hortensia. She was not much more than a girl, with a shy smile that dimpled her cheeks and reached her brown eyes. She managed to keep up a running commentary throughout the ceremony, translating the machi's words into Spanish from which I derived the general gist. So, with Machi Gonzalo, Hortensia and myself within the circle of Mapuche, our select party was completed by mule Paco, resplendent in a garland of llankalawen,[20] taking it all in his stride.

---

20. Lycopodium paniculatum – the clubmoss is a symbol of masculinity for the Mapuche. I wondered whether this had something to do with the plant's erect habit.

Machi Gonzalo sat cross-legged on the floor. He stuffed what looked like a length of bamboo with dried plant material and lit it. Inhaling, he drew in deeply, cheeks hollowed, eyes semi-closed. On his out-breath, he bellowed clouds of smoke. In…Out. In…Out. In the stillness, the air around him grew dense with a sweet-smelling fog. When he stood, only his head and shoulders were visible above the smoke.

The machi raised his hands to the heavens. 'Father Sky, Mother Earth, I humble myself before you. You who own all the medicine that is. Hear me now.' He then pointed at me. 'Grant me the wisdom to help this wingka find what he seeks. Hear me now. Hear my petition. This wingka is wise in the ways of plants. I have seen this with my eyes. I feel it in my heart. I smell that he is my brother in the ways of plants. Hear me now. Hear my invocation. You see his hair of fire. Is this not He who has been foretold? Is this not He who will fulfil the prophesy? Reveal the medicine to me so that I might help him. Hear me now. Hear my supplication. The time comes when our people will need him. Show him the way to Rewe. Old Woman of the earth, of the four directions. Old Man of the sky, of the four dawns. See me humbled. Hear me now. Hear my prostration.'

The machi prepared the plants we had gathered earlier. From the sap of trihue, he made a tincture. Hortensia explained the plant was normally used for its feminine properties—healing and soothing—to treat headaches and fever. However, tonight it would be required for its masculine qualities. That is, to protect against evil forces. The next plant the machi selected was the vespertine *Datura stramonium* (miyaya in the Mapuche language). He pulled apart the prickly fruit to disgorge its seeds. *Datura,* you may know, belongs to the Solanaceae[21] family and contains the same

---

[21] Solanaceae: the nightshades. This economically important family includes the potato and tomato.

hallucinogenic alkaloids as its relatives, Belladonna, Henbane and Mandrake. Machi Gonzalo then took the fruit of *Latua pubiflora* (the natives use the Spanish name palo de bruja, witches' broom), also solanaceous. He ground these together with a batán, a flat stone against which a smaller grinding stone is rocked. He added other plants to the concoction but his hand was too quick for me to discern which species they were. He scooped the pulp into a bowl and added chicha until it was the consistency of soup.

The machi beckoned me forward. At least, I thought he did. But Hortensia put me right. It seemed Paco was to be the star of the show, with me in a supporting role. My task was to ride the mule anticlockwise around the ring until he was sufficiently exerted. I must confess, I had my doubts whether Paco would so be compliant. After all, he is a mule who knows his own mind. On this occasion, however—perhaps due to the sense of ceremony— Paco was a mule reborn. Silene, the immortal, stainless Queen of the Night, had wrought her magic. He looked like a thoroughbred horse, nobler and with finer musculature. Damn near brought a tear to my eye, I was so proud of him.

Machi Gonzalo daubed Paco and I with blue paint. Paco's eyes, nose and mouth were circled with the paint and I was given a blue cross on each cheek. Hortensia explained that blue was the colour of the sky and, therefore, represented the spirit world. The decoration would commit Paco's senses to spiritual use and help me find what I sought.

Through Hortensia, the machi instructed me to mount Paco and ride him several times around the ring. Machi Gonzalo took up his kultrún as we galloped. The kultrún, a drum made from the hollowed-out trunk of the foye tree and covered in sheepskin, is the instrument of the machi. Its skin is painted with a cross symbolizing the World Tree. The symbol divides the face into four to represent the fourfold division of the world – meli witran mapu – that is, the four cardinal points, the four seasons, the four winds and the four celestial bodies (the sun, the moon, the stars and the planets). The intersection of the cross represents the centre of the universe, a sacred place where the different worlds meet. It is in this place the machi connects with the spirits and the ancestors. The air above the drum is the heavens (wenu mapu), the drum head is the earth (mapu), and the drum base the underworld (munche mapu). Machi Gonzalo beat his kultrún close to his ear. The song of the drum followed us as we galloped around the ring. It intermingled with the beat of the Mapuche music. The mule's hooves on the black sand. With his breath. With my heart.

By the time Machi Gonzalo signalled for us to stop, Paco's sweat rose in a cloud of steam from his back. Vapour plumed from his nostrils. Hortensia took Paco's bridle for me to dismount. As I did so, Machi Gonzalo dipped my head under the mule's nose. Hortensia explained that Paco's breath on my head and back would give me strength.

'Heavenly Father Mañke, great bird in the sky, carry me with you,' Hortensia translated Machi Gonzalo's words, a few at a time.

I repeated the words as they came to me, 'Heavenly Father Mañke, great bird in the sky, carry me with you. My ancestors watch me from above and give me strength. Guide me to Rewe. To the World Tree. I will ride this horse. I will incense the horse with smoke. I will sweat my invocation. Come into my head. Come live in my heart. Take me to the sky. Take me over the world. Give me knowledge. Give me strength. With four horse breaths. With four humours. My walking horse. My spirit horse. Your breath has lifted my being. Spirit horse. Mounted warrior. Protect and help me on my journey.'

Machi Gonzalo handed me a bowl of the concoction. Cloudy and flecked with vegetation, it had the curdled head of stale beer. This was poison. At worst, the effects could lead to insanity or even death. But know this. Had I walked away that night without drinking it, I've no doubt the World Tree would have remained a mystery to me, a fact I would have regretted for the rest of my life. I was determined to go through with it. I drew a deep breath and put bowl to lip.

It was bitter, drying my tongue and mouth. As soon as it had passed through my gullet my stomach rebelled in agonizing spasms. My reaction was to heave forward, to rid myself of the toxin. Left to my own devices, I would have been wallowing in vomit and bile and blood. However, a vice-like grip on my arms supported me as the contents of my gut were ejected, forcefully, continuously, until there was nothing left inside. All the while, the machi sprayed me with mouthfuls of water which did nothing to put out the fire on my skin. The light. The light burned my eyes. I screwed them shut but to little avail. The light found me.

⚛

Through the light, figures dance, divide and blur together. Their colours grow and pulse and call to me. The horse in the sky calls to me. I hear you. I see you. I feel colour. I speak colour. Taste, in colour. The horse knows the way. I follow. The tree comes out of nowhere. But it is here, as it has ever been. Branches, leaf green with life, extend to indigo heavens, microcosmic dots of light. It fills my sight. Within the tree, I see the sap, the life force, rise and flow in an amber glow of pulsing motion through the branches. I see it. Below, the roots writhe red. The red surges over my feet. The spirits, so many spirits, ripple around and within. We are all one. Their colours beat a rhythm all their own. I see them all. Mother Earth faces me. Her eyes so full of compassion, accepting, prejudice-free. She invites me. I speak her name: Bachuéte'e. From her belly, her sacred words travel down a thread to the white blossom at my feet. I hear her words. I know. All this I see. The way forward is clear to me now.

35. Place above the Clouds

Evangeline

The ledge wasn't much wider than Florito's shoulders, all the same, he swaggered along ahead of Evangeline in customary John Wayne fashion. Leaning into the wall, weak-kneed, she clutched at each chink in the rock face.

Don't look down.

They'd abandoned the snowmobile some way back at the edge of the glacier. Their path swooped below Villarrica's peak, skirting an incline of volcanic scree. Poised atop the scree, as pale as the volcanic matter was dark, teetered a huge boulder, the shape and smoothness of an egg banded from point to base by an off-white vein.

Morgan's words came to her:

> A sight of geological wonder in this barren land. Though I travelled by mule and not magic carpet, I was hard pressed to convince myself this colossal stone was not the roc's egg of Sinbad legend.

They sprang up the slope, to the ledge on which the roc's egg rested. Unseen from below, obscured by the boulder, they came to an arch. Without a second thought, they went through. Evangeline's ears filled with the sound of the sea.

Must be a funnelling effect. But, how, with no wind?

More peculiar, was that in the moment it took to pass beneath the arch, the climate changed dramatically. From Valdivian temperate rainforest, they emerged into an arid scrub land more typical of the Matorral, an area a hundred miles or more north of where she believed they were.

A hot breath of air stirred the scrub whose dry bones whispered like a shaman's rattle in her ears. Nodding above rosettes of rapier leaves, and towering over Evangeline, turquoise spears blazed with orange anthers. Sticking out at all angles from the spears were tail-like extensions of brilliant green touched with currant red, as though a family of iguanas had taken fright while foraging among a blueberry patch and now quivered within the ethereal flowers. A quiffed, olive-tinged bird perched on one such an extension and dipped his beak into a turquoise flower, his throat pulsing as he drank the puya's nectar.

For all the rattling and shimmying of the scrub, and the slanderous psithurism of the breeze in the foliage, some things remained static. Lichen-mottled monoliths peered between the rosettes and shrubs.

Snout-nosed, goggle-eyed and spoon-tongued, the monoliths' mouths gaped wide in a silent scream. Evangeline knew, beyond doubt, she was looking on a scene Morgan had witnessed nearly two hundred years before. This had to be Putromühue, the Place in the Clouds.

A dog barked, some way off in the distance, and was answered by another. Florito's ears swivelled in interest towards the canine conversation. It was a sound she associated with domestication. Her suspicions were confirmed by the gleeful shrill of a child, safe in the knowledge those who loved him were nearby and watching over him.

'Mama!' piped the child. 'Muy bien. Mira las flores gigantes.'

His mother's laughing reply, soft and low, wasn't clear. Perhaps an assurance more than a direct communication. But what was plain, even from Evangeline's distance, was the woman, so burdened with love, was delighted by anything her son had to say.

Evangeline hesitated. The indigenous people of Morgan's Putromühue had spoken a language isolate. When he first came across them, he'd only been able to communicate by sign language. Yet the boy had spoken Spanish: 'look at the huge flowers.' She'd been unrealistic to expect a civilisation to remain cut off from the rest of humankind in the twenty-first century. But if they'd forgotten their language, would they have retained their cultural knowledge? Or, was Rewe lost forever?

There was only one way to find out.

Evangeline, with Florito in rearguard, pushed her way through the vegetation, avoiding the sharks-tooth spines of the puya rosettes which swayed like hula-dancers in the breeze. Her snow boots, the ones she had inherited from Catalina and so necessary yesterday, were tight, steamy and clumpy. Stomping her way towards the woman and child, it was no surprise the alarmed woman pulled her son close. Evangeline, worried she might scare them off, waved and smiled. The woman, her lips apart, nodded but stepped in front of her son. She held a machete in thickly padded leather gauntlets.

Evangeline paused, then took in the wicker basket near-full of what looked like chagual, the edible, fleshy leaves of the puya.

Evangeline closed the gap between them, speaking in Spanish, 'Hi, I'm looking for Putromühue.'

The woman's eyes took in the magenta snow boots, the pink and lime green catsuit, and the gaping, grime- and blood-smeared midriff.

Evangeline spoke slowly, 'Can you help me?'

Dark-skinned and shorter than Evangeline by a head, the woman remained wary. Her scrutiny rested on something above Evangeline's right shoulder. She gasped. Her eyes glanced across Evangeline's face, then, but soon returned to that point to the right of her head.

Evangeline glanced behind her: was this an ambush? Seeing nothing but the arid landscape and Florito, she couldn't fathom what would attract such rapt attention.

The woman shook her head and stepped forward. Her hand reached out to just below Evangeline's right ear, to the remaining earring converted from Morgan's gold cufflinks. The ones crafted in the form of the World Tree. The woman held it gently for a moment then her smile broadened, and she stroked Evangeline's hair. If a stranger had done this in London or even Bristol, she'd have been given short shrift. But, here, Evangeline went with it. Something might come of this meeting. Anyway, the woman seemed friendly enough.

In a heavy dialect, the woman said, 'We knew you would come.'

⁂

The shock of the icy water was invigorating. Evangeline cupped the water in both hands and poured it over her head. Again, and again. The unnatural filth of the Wekufe, the residual narcotic of North's strange-brew green tea, the grime of travelling, all of it, she wanted out. The river—so clear she'd no trouble identifying the most comfortable pebbles to stand on—washed around her.

Florito belly-flopped into the river to hound-paddle in the depths, then lay panting in the shallows.

'Come on, boy. We'd better get back.' Evangeline waded from the river. 'They'll be wondering where we are.'

He followed her out of the river and shook himself dry.

The catsuit that had survived Netherearth and a trek across a mountain glacier lay crumpled in the dust. From the bough of a tree she pulled down the burgundy dress with its rose pink binding the villager, Wüf ko, had pressed into her hands earlier. Evangeline slipped her arm through the simple wrap-around, and fastened it with a wide sash, which had a repeated geometric design. She pulled on the knee-high moccasins and lifted the pendant over her head. The jewellery, the size of a breastplate, was decorated with coin-like metal disks that chinked with every move she made. Finally, she wrapped a woollen mantle around her shoulders and fastened it with a knot.

Evangeline felt a growing sense of delicious anticipation as they returned to Wüf ko's village. Its well-kept thatched huts, rukas, ran along a wide, unpaved street, decorated with monolithic totems and ornamental planting. Llamas, and turkeys and happy brown piglets had free rein of the place. When Wüf ko brought them here for the first time this afternoon, she explained in her stilted Spanish, that the chagual she had been gathering was for a harvest festival. Tonight, Putromühue would celebrate.

News of their arrival must have spread during the afternoon. The main street rang with excited chatter. Although crowded, people made way for her, and especially Florito who lumbered along beside her. At the same time, the villagers were eager to talk to her whether they spoke the same language or, as more often the case, not. Once or twice, a hand from out of the crowd stroked her hair. When she turned around, she found women smiling at her. A white woman, a strawberry blonde at that, would be a novelty. Wüf ko joined Evangeline, linking arms with her, and appeared to enjoy the position of being the one to have found her.

People made for a large oval-shaped ruka, decorated inside with clay lanterns punched with a tree design that projected onto faces and walls. The smell of cooking wafted towards them, reminding Evangeline she hadn't eaten for days. They sat on the matted floor, with Florito sprawled behind Evangeline, and were served a tasty stew of meat, pumpkin, corn and potato. Wüf ko watched Evangeline take the first mouthful.

'You like?' Wüf ko asked.

'It's delicious,' Evangeline said with her hand covering her full mouth. 'What is it?'

'Charquicán.'

A nudge in her shoulder blade nearly put her nose in her stew, announcing Florito's interest in the food.

'We have not left you out,' Wüf ko said, beckoning to someone in the shadows, who came forward with a large tureen. 'We do not normally serve dogs where we eat, but I can see you are a very special dog.'

'Should he not be in here?' Evangeline had been through so much with Florito, she had forgotten that not everyone eats and sleeps with their dog. She tested the side of the tureen with the back of her hand. 'It's still a bit warm, my lad, so don't go wolfing it all down at once.'

The tureen was duly set before the hound who gave it his full attention, using his jaws to juggle each cube of meat to the floor, allowing it to cool before chomping it first on one side of his mouth, then on the other.

A jug was passed down to them. Wüf ko poured the cloudy straw-coloured liquid into two clay beakers, handing one to Evangeline.

'This is mudai,' said Wüf ko. 'It's made from fermented wheat. We drink it as an offering for the harvest.'

Over the meal, Evangeline learnt about the people of Putromühue, the place above the clouds. Occasionally, they ventured out to local towns to trade, but the experience was rarely a happy one. In the main, they kept to themselves and were self-reliant. They reared their own livestock and cultivated vegetable crops. If they fell sick, their machi healed them. The children were schooled in the village to keep traditions alive. They spoke Spanish and Mapudungun. All the while, Wüf ko, ever the perfect hostess, kept an eye on Evangeline's bowl and ladled in a welcome second helping as soon as there was room.

'Wüf ko, there's something you and your people need to know. An oil pipeline is under construction and it's heading this way,' Evangeline said.

'We will speak to Machi Uwa about this. He wants to meet you.'

☙

After the glowing interior of the ruka, Evangeline's eyes took a while to adjust to the dark. A fire glowed at the heart of the village, illuminating three silhouettes moving in jerky shadow play. Closer, Wüf ko identified one of the three as the machi: short, rounded, bulked out with skirts and shawls, further adorned with mixed garlands of wadded brightly coloured ribbon and the waxy pink bell-shaped flowers of kopihue, a headscarf tied pirate-style, a slash of lipstick and a heavy five o'clock shadow. His companions were a villager and his yellow dog, both as scrawny as each other. The dog lay on his side, his legs trussed, and his jaws bound with vine, while his head was clamped between the hands of his owner.

The machi poured a milky liquid down the dog's snout, while addressing the dog in a low voice.

Florito growled. The yellow dog whined.

Evangeline rushed forward. 'Is that absolutely necessary?'

Wüf ko touched Evangeline's arm and said quietly, 'We must wait.'

Evangeline shrugged off the arm. 'What's going on?'

'This is our way.' Wüf ko gestured for Evangeline to sit down.

Evangeline scuffed the ground and was going to say more, but Jesús' voice came into her head, so clear as though she had only to turn and he'd be there. The morning they set off from Santiago, he turned down the radio. Picking up on his gravity, she eased off the accelerator.

'What is strange, or cruel, or wrong to us, is not always so to others. Our morals and beliefs reflect our own culture, it is not for us to impose these things on others.'

In the closeness of the car, she sensed him watching her face, as though to check the message sank in.

A tug at the hem of her dress by the now-seated Wüf ko, brought her back to the present.

She joined the woman on the ground, who translated the machi's words in a whisper, 'He says "it chases coypu, it will not eat chickens. It will say *kwa, kwa,* it will not lie."'

'How do you mean, "it will not lie"?'

'The dog barks when it should be silent, when it is on the hunt. It goes after our animals.'

The machi signalled for the man to unbind his dog. Released from his ordeal, the dog teetered off into the night, followed by the lank spectre of his owner.

'Machi Uwa, this is Evangeline the Outlander,' Wüf ko's hand in the small of Evangeline's back felt protective.

The machi nodded and settled by the fire, where he gazed into its flames.

Evangeline shifted her position and coughed in the back of her throat. He seemed in no hurry to meet her after all.

She followed his gaze and watched smoke rise to the heavens. The night sky appeared as though she was seeing it for the first time. The stars, so many stars, all sharply defined in the absence of artificial light. Each star, a fire, dancing as the one here before her, the one which fizzled and snapped like rain in the forest, and warmed her cheeks.

As time passed, she forgot her discomfort. She was alone by the fire under the vast night sky with all nature thronging around her. Her thoughts turned to a fruitless, sterile delivery ward, its redundant monitor, its prying galactic lamp and the silence of Effie's entrance into the world.

'Daughter Firehair.' The machi's voice came to Evangeline from a mountaintop. 'Why have you come?'

Aware once more of the people around her, she drew in breath as though waking. 'I'm searching for the World Tree,' she said in a thick voice. She allowed a beat. 'It is under threat. An oil pipeline is coming this way. If Rewe is here, they will not hesitate to cut it down—and your village along with it.'

'To find the one, you must raise the other.'

Her senses sharpened. 'What do I have to do?'

'In the forest on the plateau below, a creature is dying. You must wake it.'

The machi ladled a milky soup from a pot on the fire into the bowl used to force-feed the yellow dog. 'Dog will show you the way.'

Evangeline put her arm across Florito's shoulders. 'He's not doing any dreamworld.'

The machi raised the bowl to Florito's muzzle who sniffed it cautiously. 'He is not master in this world. In dreamworld he is face to face, eye to eye with you and with forest spirits. He is equal.'

'Please. If you know where Rewe is, just tell me,' Evangeline said.

'It's not a question of whether I know where it is, but do you?'

'Of course, I don't, or I wouldn't be asking.' She fought to keep control of her voice.

Florito sighed, licked her hand and put his snout in the bowl.

Evangeline struck the bowl to the ground. 'No! You're not doing it.'

The machi was silent for a moment, the milky hallucinogen dripping from his skirts. 'So be it. He will go with you, but he cannot guide you.'

'Fine.' At least he'd be sober.

'You seek that which is beyond you. Before you find Rewe,

you must know yourself. I ask you again, what has brought you here?' the Machi said.

Evangeline shook her head. 'I want to find the tree before it is gone forev—'

'No, what caused you to look for the tree?'

'Chile Morgan believed in the tree. If I can present Rewe to the world, more people will know about *him*.'

'That is what you tell yourself. It is he who brought you the story of the tree, a story he wrote many lifetimes ago. But it is his story, not yours.' He allowed a hush to open.

The gap was filled by delivery room clatter and the wrongness of hearing newborns down the corridor. Then silence. The most profound silence. Then more, her empty yearning and the silence of people not knowing what to say.

Her solar plexus juddered uncontrollably. She heard an animal sound, one long mewl, which she realised was coming from her. But no tears. In time, her body stilled.

'Your pain will heal. Your healing will cure the cosmos.' The machi's voice had softened. 'That dress you're wearing. It *is* because everything else is. See its border design of the sun, the moon and the stars. Without the sun there is no light. Without light plants can't grow, and without plants, we have no fibre to weave material for dresses. The sun is essential for the dress to exist. In this way, the sun and the dress are one, as is all that ever has been and all that ever will be.'

Morgan's words came back to her: Rewe exists in us all. It is in me, I am in Rewe.

The machi continued, 'The loss of just one tree robs the bird of its nest, the degu of its food, and the soil of its binding. We do not live in isolation. The animals, plants, you and I, we all need each other. And we are all at risk.'

'But what good is waking up one forest beast when the forest is all but cleared,' she said.

'Our people have been here for many thousands of years. We descended from the Great Bird in the Sky. We lived in this land before the Incas came from the north. We were here before the Spanish brought their pox. Each invasion we fight,' he said. 'This pipeline you talk about. We have scouts on patrol. I have some news for you.' He looked into the embers. 'Another wingka, a male, was seen two days ago not far from here.'

Had Victor planted another tracking device on her?

36. Resurrection

Evangeline

Evangeline, with Florito close by her side, approached the archway. The outside world, her world, lay beyond in monochrome. The scant vegetation, gnarled and weatherworn, twitched as though it, too, was nervous. Ice receded like the tide. The lance-like fronds of a fern—a *Polystichum*—unfurled, flushed with pinpricks of sori which swelled to shaggy buds and burst, hurling their cloud of spore on the wind.

Had the land on which she stood become the same, high-speed monochrome? In two minds whether she wanted to know the answer she looked over her shoulder. Yellow light bathed swaying, green sclerophylls.

Time passed in the two worlds as though on different gears: through the arch it ran with the speed of a small cog, while in Putromühue it operated slowly, as with a larger, more powerful, wheel.

They stepped beneath the arch, the sound of the sea crashing around them. Cold air stung Evangeline's eyes even as her back felt the heat of the sun. Before going further, she did what Morgan would have done and reversed the chamanto to the dark, heat-absorbing side. Then they set off.

Making for the treeline, she dug her heels into the scree, setting off mini avalanches. Keeping eyes on the ground, the tumbling, shifting mass surged downwards, its movement making her queasy: that feeling she had whenever she tried to read in a car. Florito followed in her wake, causing the occasional stone to collide with her shins.

Now they were the other side, the side from which they'd started, the colour returned to the world. Not as vivid as Putromühue, it was true, but natural. In the time they'd been in the Place above the Clouds, the loggers had been busy.

The trees below had a sombre, last stand appearance. Those outermost, not long exposed to full view, their tall, bony trunks conspicuously grey, loomed over the blackened remains of their fallen comrades. A couple of Shezmu lumber trucks, in the oil company's canary yellow livery, trundled silently along this rough-hewn highway, the wind carrying their mechanical noise away from the mountain. The naked soil, churned up in ruts, bore the tyre tracks coiled like a nest of vipers. A sharply defined channel cut into, but not quite dissecting, the forest. It wouldn't be long before the Shezmu trucks burst through. And then? In the firing line was Putromühue and somewhere, hidden within it, was Rewe.

Trudging down the slope, a raindrop splashed her hand as it swung wide to steady herself. Then another, cold on her face. Soon, the rain set in. Beneath the poncho, her hands pulled its neck close. All the same, the wet wool scratched her neck and a drip trickled from her throat to the vee between her breasts. The heat of her body radiated the pungent smell of sodden llama in a fug around her head. Under foot, stone gave way to soil, so recently robbed of its vegetation and, destabilised by the downpour, turning to rivulets of mud. Had they made this journey yesterday, they would have been under cover of the forest by now. Blinking through the rain, she attempted to identify the different species of trees ahead. *Nothofagus*, mainly, with frequent *Araucaria*, but not what she was after: *Aristotelia chilensis*. She wasn't confident she would even recognise maqui—the shaman had used its local name—if she came across it but she knew it was supposed to be common in this region. If it was in flower, she stood a chance; it bore racemes of small white flowers like clusters of pearls and would be easy to spot. But she had to admit to being sketchy on the time of year. Only the day before—before they'd found Putromühue—it had been summer, but the chill and the dense leaf fall suggested winter or even spring, around the time when evergreens drop their old leaves to make way for the new. More than that, she'd only ever seen the species in a textbook. But Machi Uwa had told her to look out for the fungi which grow on its trunk and roots. They had to go deep into the forest, far away from the disturbance of tree-felling, before she would have any hope.

Under the multi-storied canopy of woodland, the downpour elaborated into a symphony, each surface the agent of different effect. High in the conifers, the rain crackled on needles like fire-sparked kindling. Bare branches smarted, their limb-length vibration a rushy river of sound. Broadleaves tapped, then channelled and discharged their catchment overboard to plash on the waiting litter.

The rain collected in hollows on the forest floor. Avoiding the ooze, she sidestepped trees and clambered over fallen logs. Oil slicked the leaf litter and leached into the puddles. Bracket fungus, scalloped like the black and white plumage of the Barred Rock hens Mum used to keep, clung to trunks softened by woolly coats of moss, glistening with rain-bejewelled webs.

This was where she needed to look.

With the toe of her moccasin, she uncovered a crop of

mushrooms sprouting from jaundiced tree roots. The fungi, silky, dusky pink, bore recurved caps which split with age. Crouching, she pulled away a multi-layered mulch of ovate leaves with serrate margin. She'd found the *Aristotelia.* The leaves, darkened by the degradation of the light absorbing pigments—the green chlorophyll, yellow xanthophylls, red and purple anthocyanins, and orange carotenoids—held fast to each another.

Clinging to the undersides of the dead leaves were clusters of tiny, spherical eggs, opaque with a swirling smoke blue wisp, like playground marbles. When hatched, the larvae would feast on the leaves of *Aristotelia* for three to four weeks before forming pupa. But the eggs hadn't hatched. Hence no caterpillars; life cycle broken.

Evangeline unzipped her bag and withdrew a couple of the grape-like rhizoxants she had found in Netherearth. Their coral glow warmed her hand as she squeezed them between her fingers, squirting their juice over the eggs. If she hadn't witnessed their efficacy on Florito's stab wound, she would have felt she was wasting her time. Even so, it was one thing to heal a wound, quite another to bring a creature back from the dead. More to the point, every minute spent messing about with root nodules was time lost from her hunt for Rewe. She hoped the machi knew what he was doing, or rather what she was doing on his say so.

She wiped a drip from her nose and rose with effort against the weight of saturated clothing. There was no time to sit and wait. Florito, who'd taken the opportunity to investigate each tree in the vicinity, bounded after her.

A little further, she found another *Aristotelia* accompanied by the same dusky pink fungus among its roots. She went through the same process with the rhizoxants and continued in this way at each *Aristotelia* they found.

Florito's panting close behind gave her a sense of harmony: they were in this together. It occurred to her she'd not heard any birdsong, or the rustle of small mammals in the undergrowth. Shezmu's nearby operations had scoured the area of habitat and food, interrupting the interconnected communities of plants, animals and all life: a forest on the threshold of extinction.

Snap.

Evangeline froze. Tuning out her heartbeat, she willed herself into insignificance. Head still, her eyes strained to extend her line of sight to the periphery of her vision. Other than a bit of deadwood falling from the canopy, what or who else would be wandering around here, in the middle of nowhere? Shezmu had already wiped out the wildlife.

The most plausible explanation was that it was one of Shezmu's destruction workers, but when Machi Uwa had told her about the wingka seen near Putromühue, her first thought was of Victor. That patron of the arts, lover of women, savant and monster. She couldn't be sure that her heel in his eye prevented him from ever coming after her again. If he was still alive, he would pursue her, she knew that much.

She couldn't shake the idea that someone was watching her but could only hold her breath for so long. Having heard nothing further, she released her breath.

The light was waning. It was time to get back to the village. She retraced her steps. Every so often, the glowing rhizoxant juice marked her route. She checked on each treated clutch. What had been a smoke blue wisp was now a clearly defined wriggler, suspended in gel. Life! Further on, they were more animated. At her first stop, tiny, wire-haired caterpillars had emerged and were tucking into the root nodules she'd left. Leaf green with black stripes, their front ends lifted off the ground seeking in circular motion. As they moved, they contracted lime-chocolate jellybean to extended carpet-shaving and back again.

Leaves crunched. Evangeline jumped to her feet. In the gloom, she saw nothing but the solid boles.

'Let's go,' she called to Florito.

They took off at a run, crashing through the clawing vegetation. If only she was free of the trees, she could pull away from the watching eyes.

When confronted by the ever-growing expanse of quagmire between forest and mountain, she realised, too late, she'd been flushed from cover like a fox from its den. She paused, gasping for breath. She needed to get her bearings. There, high on the mountainside, she found what she was looking for: a boulder, shaped like a roc's egg.

'Ready?'

Florito's expression said, 'I was born ready.' Then, he bounded into the clearing.

On this terrain, his four legs were a distinct advantage over her two. Each tyre track formed ruts compacted to a knee's-depth. It was a matter of leaping from one waterlogged trench to the next. Evangeline lifted her dress above her knees to broaden her stride. The forward foot splashed mud as it landed, the quagmire sucked at the rear foot as it withdrew.

Out of the corner of her eye, and still some way off, a hulk of canary yellow emerged from the forest. She allowed herself a glance: the Shezmu logging truck had completed the cutting. Yet, seeing her opponent for real lessened her fears somehow. For all the vehicle's power, the silhouette of a driver bobbed about in the cab, and by the looks of things, he was eating a sandwich. She had the impression the driver hadn't noticed her yet. Florito and she were so mud-splattered, he would have a job to spot them. Maybe he was too interested in his food and thinking about clocking off soon.

This small advantage might be all they needed. The truck wouldn't make it up the steep gradient. And if the driver chose to pursue them on foot, well, just let him try.

Florito was already bounding up the scree by the time

Evangeline threw herself on the incline. She might have heard a shout, but it was lost on the wind and driving rain. The roc's egg reared above them, and behind it, she pictured the arch to Putromühue and safety.

The only thing was, when they climbed onto the ledge, they found that the boulder concealed no more than rockface. She pressed her hands to the rock: solid. She pounded at it with her fist. She slapped it and kicked it. It remained unyielding. What did she expect? That the arch would miraculously appear? That all she needed to do was clap her hands and command: open sesame? She must have lost her bearings, if not her marbles. But, no, this was the same ovate boulder, for there was the off-white vein encircling it from point to base.

The sodden weight of her clothes, clumsy and uncomfortable, weighed her down.

What to do?

Bark!

Evangeline tripped, scrabbled for a handhold and swallowed down her alarm.

The wind had turned, and it brought news: a vehicle moved on the open land between forest and mountain, its rising pitch a signal it was headed in their direction.

She ducked behind the roc's egg and whispered for Florito to get down.

A white transit van jolted over the scarred landscape. The canary yellow big guns were nowhere to be seen.

The mud-spattered van slithered in the quagmire, its wipers opening brief arcs on the windscreen, which were quickly speckled in by gloop. The van hit a rut, bounced and skidded, then slid to a standstill. As if awoken by all the activity, its roof apparatus unfolded. First a cantilevered arm rose and extended, then a satellite dish pirouetted and tilted. Finally, a figure cloaked in a hooded waterproof jumped from the van. He visored his eyes with his hands.

Florito growled. She shushed.

The figure couldn't have heard her through the rain, not at this distance, but he turned suddenly in their direction. His face pale against the khaki cape.

She dropped flat to the ground, keeping her eyes on the interloper. There was something familiar about the way he moved. A memory took shape within her but faded before it was fully formed.

The figure returned to the vehicle and drove towards them, the van reeling across the mud. It crunched on scree, slid back, went forward, spat out a plume of exhaust and ground to a halt. The driver pushed the door open with his feet and continued nimbly on foot, with his hood low over his face.

It dawned on her that she was the sole defence between the outside world and Putromühue, and within the village, Rewe. Canute holding back the tide had nothing on this.

How could she, completely unarmed, resist any onslaught?

She pulled towards her whatever missiles she could find; stones, gravel, a bone-white stick. Then rose to her feet, keeping low. Armed with no more than stick and stones, she peered around the side of the roc's egg.

Before long, a cloaked head bobbed into view. Breath plumed from beneath his hood. Water dripped heavily from his cape.

Please, not Victor.

She tightened her grip on the stick. Now or never.

She dashed out from her cover, wielding the stick against the side of his head. He crashed into the cliff, dislodging his hood, and crumpled to the ground.

'What are you doing here?' she said.

37. A Triumphant Entrance

Evangeline

Florito snarled.

The intruder stumbled to his knees and patted the hound. 'I know I've never been your favourite, gancho, but at least you recognise me.'

Blood flowed from the gash on his forehead. The cloisonné blue eyes were dazed and beautiful.

'Jesús.' Just saying his name aloud brought home how much she'd wanted to. 'I nearly killed you.'

'Not quite, Arbolito.' His eyes regained focus as they found her own. 'But you had a good go.' His smile wasn't the artless smile she remembered. If anything, it was like he wasn't sure what to make of her: the time apart had put distance between them.

'Well what were you doing creeping up the mountain in this weather? You could have been an oil company oik for all I knew.' She regretted the provocation in her voice. She hadn't ever expected to see him again, but she might have daydreamed about the moment. Once or twice. Maybe more. And this wasn't panning out anywhere near as well as she imagined. But what exactly was he doing here?

'I look for you.' His face implied what-do-you-think-I-was-doing? 'Then, I hear you in the trees. I knew it was you. It was your walk.'

'My walk?'

'With purpose.' He touched the wound on his brow as though he'd made a connection between it and she who walks with purpose.

All the reunions dreamt, all the conversations rehearsed, the craving of the sight, touch, presence of him; caught unawares, all the things she wanted to say skittered on the surface of her mind like silvery sardines, too quick, too slick to grasp one from the many.

'What happened at *La Menagerie*?' she said.

There was a new reserve in his eyes she had never known before. 'You tell me.'

'That's just it. I don't know. I get flashes, just clips of dreams, nightmares. But the overriding impression I have of that time is colour, the most vivid colour.'

He scrutinised her face. 'Evangeline, you were so absorbed in that place, in Victor. It looked to me like you wanted to be there. Like you belonged there. And there was no room for me.'

'Whatever I did or didn't do, I didn't mean it. Look, I don't know whether you noticed but I happened to be under the influence of a very green, and very potent, tea.' If only she could quit the sarky one-liners and just say what she meant.

'¡Pucha, la cuestión! They drug you?' He looked to the ground and said quietly, 'I thought you were on some kind of health-kick with that tea.' He slammed his palm against the cliff. '¡Conchatumadre! ¡La cagué! Victor! I kill him.'

'You might not need to. I think I stabbed his eye out.' She didn't want to be talking about Victor.

He let out a low whistle. 'The botanist that bites.'

'How's Abraxas?'

'¡Ay! Abraxas is Abraxas. Is so much…'

'Please spare me the details.'

He swatted away her comment. 'Arbolito, is not what I mean. She have so much enthusiasms and idea. And so many contacts. She start me in television.'

Fair enough, that kind of opportunity didn't come along every day.

His head rocked back, and he stared into the sky. 'What was I supposed to think? I didn't want to be around when you were with that culeado. When Abraxas showed an interest, I went with it.'

She forced away the unrelenting image of Jesús and Abraxas outside the Temple of the Moon. 'Are you still together?'

'We were never *together*.' He tapped his lips with his knuckles. 'It was all a set-up.'

'I'm pretty sure Abraxas enjoyed herself.'

He sighed in a tired sort of way, half-closing his eyes, and said nothing.

'Sorry.' She meant it. Sorry that she couldn't say what she felt. Sorry that all that came out of her mouth was either combative, or flippant, or both.

They were wasting time talking about Victor and Abraxas.

'What are you doing here?' she asked.

The wind whipped at his hair. He looked good. 'I missed you.'

She threw her arms around him and launched a scattergun of kisses on his hair, eyes, face, before finding his mouth.

For a moment, they nearly toppled over, but Jesús braced and took the onslaught.

≋

Hand in hand they approached the arch.

'Arbolito, there's something I should tell—'

The sound of the crashing sea swallowed his words.

Sun. Warmth.

The chamanto had to come off. Head muffled in sodden wool,

she heard voices and the approach of footsteps.

Jesús said, '¡Chaucha!'—watch out.

Evangeline wrestled her way out of the chamanto to find Jesús flanked by two brawny villagers and the colourful Machi Uwa.

'It's OK,' she said to the men. 'He's not a threat.' They tightened their grip.

'Machi Uwa, I know him.'

'Daughter, your coming was foretold. His was not.'

'But Jesús isn't your enemy,' she pleaded. 'He's not like that.'

The machi planted his feet in front of Jesús. 'Since the new moon, our watchers have reported seeing a wanderer come from the forest. They say he travels inside a beast with giant ears on its back. These ears have strange magic. They rise high in the air and circle like the condor in the sky. Where the beast stops to graze, the man jumps from the creature. Sometimes the man is alone, sometimes he comes with another who carries the beast's spawn on his shoulders. But the beast is no threat to Putromühue for no matter how much the beast roars, it cannot climb the mountain. Yet the wanderer, when alone, comes close, ever closer.' He closed the gap between them and glared up at Jesús. 'You, wanderer, what brings you here?'

'Evangeline has been missing for months. I here for her,' Jesús looked across at her.

A smile bloomed within her.

'It seems to me she has found herself,' the machi said. 'Meanwhile, your search has led you to keep company with those that slaughter the forest.'

'Jesús?' What was the machi saying? What did he know? It occurred to her that Jesús had been trying to tell her something as they came through the arch.

Jesús' eyes darted from her to the machi and back again. 'Evangeline, I can explain.'

He shifted his weight. 'I make documentary about Shezmu's

rape of the forest. A Spanish broadcasting corporation pick it up and, from there, other European media translate the reports. Protest marches all over the country. Questions in Congress. A debate tabled. Just yesterday, the President he say on camera he want stricter control on logging in this area.'

'If this is true, there is hope that natural order will be restored to the cosmos,' the machi said.

Jesús attempted to reach his back pocket but his guards reinforced their hold.

He grinned to her across the machi's head. 'Do you mind?'

She reached under his waterproof and slid her hand into the warmth of his jeans pocket. He breathed what might have been a laugh. He looked over his shoulder at her and she felt the muscle in his rear contract. 'The notebook.' He reminded her.

She withdrew the notebook.

'There should be a journal article in there.'

She riffled through the pages and a folded piece of newspaper slid out. She caught it with reflex action, opened the clipping and read aloud, with Jesús translating for the machi.

Pipeline Protest Gains Traction
Thousands have marched in cities throughout Chile to rally against the construction of the $4.1 billion Trans-Andean Pipeline (TAP).

Activists, environmentalists, politicians and celebrities have joined forces against oil giant Shezmu, to halt work on the pipeline which will have the capacity to transport more than 500,000 barrels of oil a day.

Heartthrob TV presenter, Jesús Dorador, first raised awareness of the project in a daily reportage on *Canal 24 Horas.*

Dorador (33) addressed the banner-waving crowds, 'We are sending a united message to the government of Chile. Stop this destruction. Earth is not yours to trade to the highest bidder, to become a den of thieves. Protect our land, before it's gone forever.'

At stake is the clear cutting of land to make way for the pipeline. Deforestation is a causative factor in climate change, species loss, soil erosion, disruption to the water cycle and reduction in water quality.

WWF says 18.7 million acres of forest are lost per year, equal to 27 football pitches every minute.

An estimated 15 percent of all greenhouse gas emissions come from deforestation (WWF).

For every 10 percent of forest loss, one to two major species are wiped out. This figure increases dramatically when forest loss reaches 43 percent: an extra two to eight major animal and plant species become extinct per 10 percent of disappeared forest (University of Cambridge).

Shezmu's CEO, Leo Winepress, has been quoted as saying: 'Together, we can build our future. TAP offers more jobs, safer fuel transportation, and a stronger economy.'

Machi Uwa gestured for the men to release their prisoner. Jesús pulled his waterproof over his head and rubbed his arms.

The machi opened his arms wide and drew Jesús into a bearhug. 'From now on, you are a son of Putromühue.'

Later, after entering the village in procession to a greeting of Araucaria branches strewn across the path, they enjoyed a celebration in the square. Evangeline looked on as yet another villager approached Jesús, their saviour, with a gift and a bowl of chahué. The flickering firelight put his profile in perfect relief. The villager, a female elder, tweaked his cheek, and winked at Evangeline, the gesture implying you've-got-a-good-one-here. Jesús was as beneficent as ever. Every villager was blessed with his smile that came from eyes and heart.

It was as though he was born for this role.

38. A Letter

Morgan: 16 November 1881

The tree lives. Rewe lives! I have seen her with my own eyes. Proof, if ever it were needed, of the power of belief: Keep your Goal ever in mind. Remind yourself of your Destination when it is far away, Believe it is Possible when all around you dismiss it, and Pursue it with a Positive Heart. Through this, the most heartfelt desires may be realised.

But, what then?

Rewe is ancient. Older than all Civilisation. She renews year on year, under the stewardship of the people of Putromühue. But disease, drought, fire take their toll, and the future is the journey ahead. Her Vitality must be extended for the sake of all Humankind.

I have given every fibre of my being to find her. The Jaguar within me has not ventured from his hide for many a year and I feel myself fading. I have no desire to return to my old life. This is my World now. But those beyond Putromühue must learn about her. In understanding Rewe, they will care for her and, in this way, care for the World.

I have standing by a runner, the middle son of a Farmer, a

trusted friend. I have gone over the directions with him, and over again, until he described the route, the trees and rivers and mountains as though he had lifelong knowledge of them. In actual fact, in his short time on this Earth, he has barely travelled more than five miles from the village. But he is young and healthy. I am not. Under his arm is my plant press, battered, much used, though serviceable yet. But, aside from this one last charge, I will have no further need of it.

My Dear and Loyal Friend, Solomon. I entrust to you evidence of the greatest find. Within the plant press is a specimen of Rewe. With it, I enclose my cufflinks, the ones with the World Tree design, and this journal documenting my travels which have brought me to this paradise at the top of the World. We have walked side by side on the same path through many adventures. But now, my path leads where you cannot follow.

We discussed this eventuality, my Friend. I'm confident, Solomon, you will know what to do with these items.

Don't concern yourself over me. I want for nothing and continue to enjoy the companionship of Paco, even though both of us are wider in girth, greyer in beard and slower in gait.

I trust you will give Maite and your growing Brood a kiss each from me. Know I have, and always shall, love you as a brother.

Yours ever,

Morgan

39. Shezmu Showdown

Evangeline

The people came out of the forest sparkling with excitement and resolve, an initial playful froth exploding into a torrent, taking the path of least resistance: the clearance channel dissecting the forest. They carried colourful flags and banners bearing slogans: *Save the Forest* and *Scrap the TAP*. They made music, a percussive jumble that more by happenstance than skill came together in rhythm. They streamed out left and right from the mouth of the channel, along the raw edge of forest.

Before long, fluorescent ropes shot up into the branches, anchored, and dropped their heads to earth. Activists monkeyed up the lines to disappear in the canopy. Bundles, wobbling and spinning, followed them bit by bit into the trees. Through all this, the canary yellow Shezmu logging trucks, skidders, tractors and grapples continued doing whatever it was they were doing out on the denuded ground.

Across the plateau from the protesters, Evangeline leant against Jesús' discarded outdoor broadcast van and figured that the workmen within the Shezmu vehicles would be kitted out with ear defenders, blocking the noise of the demonstration as much as that of their own machinery. The glare of sunlight no doubt added a further shield by blinding Shezmu's workforce to the spectacle being played out on the forest edge. The protest would be upon them before they knew it.

A cascade of dislodged stones clattered behind her.

Jesús' arms wrapped around her waist and his soft breath announced the kiss on her neck. 'They've come.' The satisfaction in his voice was mixed with a note of relief, a feeling she shared.

She took his hand. 'Let's say hello.'

They set out across the plateau's biscuit-dry crust of cracked and broken misshapes. Florito barged between them to march in front. Once again, Evangeline wondered at the passage of time: she'd been knee-deep in quagmire during her last crossing. Less than twenty-four hours had passed in the time she inhabited, yet the land and weather gave evidence to the contrary.

Meeting the protestors at the mouth of the clearance channel, they hugged and were hugged as though reuniting with childhood friends. Still more people poured from the channel. Languages other than Spanish were in the mix. Above their heads bounced a grotesque blimp in the shape of Shezmu's Leo Winepress, given a make-over in high heels, suspenders and bra, and topped off with a trapper hat. People chanted: *He's a Lumberjack...and it's not OK.*

Sandwiches and choripanes—chorizo in a bun—were passed around. The sweaty smell of marinated pork and sauerkraut announced the presence of a catering van nearby, open for business.

'Completo!' Jesús disappeared in the direction of the food smell. He reappeared with a cardboard catering tray bearing two coffees, and what had to be completo: two rolls filled with a towering mound of pork, sauerkraut, tomatoes, avocado and cheese. Sharing her roll with Florito, they wandered through the crowds, many of whom recognised Jesús and stopped him for a selfie.

A skidder, that heavyweight of forestry used to pull cut trees to a landing, lumbered towards them. Its powerful front wheels gave it a broad-shouldered, knuckle-walking appearance, while the grimacing grapple jaws which swung from side to side on the end of a muscular neck suggested a bone-crushing carnivorous predator. The party atmosphere dissolved in an instant, someone shouted: 'Link arms!'

The monster juddered to a halt, belching foul-smelling smog from its exhaust stack. Florito competed with the sound of its idling engine. The driver leant over the steering wheel and pushed his hardhat visor higher on his brow. His arm reached for his CB radio mouthpiece and lifted it to his mouth, he paused, then abandoned the mouthpiece on the passenger seat. He opened the door and dismounted his cab, displaying generous buttock cleavage. A protestor in his early twenties, with sideburns, baseball cap and glasses, broke from the crowd and reached the driver just as the feet on the driver's short, stout legs connected with the earth.

A conversation ensued, during which the driver hitched up his jeans once, twice, and pushed the visor of his hardhat higher on his brow. The protestor put his hands together in a pleading gesture. Each shuffled from one foot to another, as though performing a ritualistic dance. The protestor turned to the crowd, looking for reassurance. It came in the shape of a young woman, long apricot-dyed hair, who skipped over to the conversation. A bit more dancing about and the driver held his hands up. The woman did a little skippy-jump on the spot and adorned the driver with a garland of leaves. Her companion clapped the driver on the back and gave two thumbs up to the protestors. A huge cheer, interspersed with blaring klaxons and drums, rose up from the crowd. The last Evangeline saw of the driver, his face was a study of concentration as he showed mastery in the messy art of eating a completo.

All these people here to add their voice of protest against Shezmu and the loss of forest. So many people felt the same way as Evangeline. She was not alone. The realisation buoyed her. Her cheeks ached from smiling. Whatever obstacles sprang up along the way, she was certain she would overcome them and reach her goal. She would find Rewe.

She looked for somewhere to put her food wrapping. 'The government's got to listen now.'

Jesús offered his hand as a receptacle. 'We need to capture this.'

⁂

The van may well have been equipped with the latest technology for transmitting video signals to a studio, but it struggled to make headway across the baked ruts and furrows. It lurched and rattled and scraped, hurling its occupants from side to side, punching their breath from their lungs as their seatbelt straps tightened. It was easier to follow in the logging machinery's tracks, but this often took them on a detour. With Jesús driving, Evangeline had by default become the camera operator. Through her open window, she swept the lens across the demonstrators, zooming in on those in the canopy as they constructed platforms and shelters. She panned the camera around to show the logging trucks trundling about the plateau. Then she turned the camera on Jesús. Straight away, he was the professional TV presenter.

It surprised her, at first. She'd always seen him laid back and enjoying the moment, but as she listened, she grew more certain this was his moment.

Presenter-mode Jesús spoke with emphasis, modulating his voice with pathos and urgency, every emotion visible just below the surface.

'This is the story of the forest,' he started. 'An ancient story but one with few pages left.'

❧

Later, as Evangeline and Jesús drove back to the demonstration, the ridges of the plateau stood in isolation. The furrows, now in shade, appeared infinitely deep, vents to the underworld. She experienced a moment of disorientation. Which realm did she inhabit? Where was she right now—dusky sky, earth or underworld? She felt present in all three, all interconnected.

The thup-thup-thup of a helicopter roared overhead. Its logo, an orange number thirteen, enough for Jesús to identify it as belonging to Teletrece, a Chilean news network. A delicious ripple of expectation swept through Evangeline. The World was watching. Shezmu would have to back down under all this publicity, if only to limit reputational damage. It was strange, then, that so many of its logging vehicles were still deployed. If anything, she'd say there were more now on the plateau than earlier. Many had acquired the slogan: #ScrapTheTAP in fluorescent paint.

The wavering arc of a flare showed a swelling mass of people. Another helicopter thundered overhead. This one larger, more rugged and nose to tail in canary yellow. Closing in, the aircraft dropped low in the sky and turned to stare down the gathering. Turbulence whisked up clouds of debris against which the protesters shielded their eyes, their clothes wet look pressing to their bodies. The helicopter approached, the engine thrum not quite obliterating the shouts and screams of the crowd. At the last minute, the craft swooped up over people and trees, rounded on itself and circled above the crowd.

Jesús wrenched on the handbrake and grabbed the camera. Evangeline intended to leave Florito in the van, but he was having none of it. He had a point: dogs must not be left in vehicles. She opened the door, he bounded out barking to all concerned.

'Stay close and don't get into trouble,' she said.

They caught up with Jesús chatting to a woman with a sweep

of grey in her dark hair, dressed in a vermillion top, olive pencil skirt and a silk scarf tied in a side knot. The woman nodded a smile to Evangeline before melting into the crowd.

'The loggers who stop work today for fear of causing an accident have been ordered back to work or lose their job,' he explained above the noise.

'Ordered? Who ordered?'

'Winepress. Is him in helicopter.'

On cue, the helicopter beamed a searchlight at the windswept protestors. Stark white, shade black, dazzled by the glare, the crowd wavered.

'Ladies and gentlemen.' A voice echoed from a loud hailer. 'Shezmu represents the many law abiding, hard-working Chileans, who deserve a better Chile.'

Evangeline and Jesús jeered along with the protesters, all moving clear of the forest: it was a matter of stand up and be counted.

'While you've been enjoying your jamboree,' the helicopter continued. 'Shezmu has held discussions with the government. I have today personally pledged profits from the pipeline to support the recruitment and retention of schoolteachers.' ...*crackle*... 'But I didn't stop there.' ...*crackle*... 'Shezmu will inject three million dollars funding into the health service.'

Would these promises be enough to turn the protesters? The soignée woman they'd met earlier, perhaps?

'You're killing the forest.' A voice came out of the crowd.

Snapped from their trance, the crowd surged again.

'Keep your oily dollars, Winepress,' said another. 'Chile's better without you.'

A glow of warmth filled Evangeline as the protesters resisted the bribes.

The helicopter's loud hailer spoke once more, 'This is a criminal act of trespass and vandalism. Leave the area immediately.' The craft ascended and flew out of sight, followed by a roar from the crowd.

It took a moment to adjust to the twilight, so they didn't notice straight away the wall that had not been there before. Two metres high, it formed a perfect square. They were surrounded.

The wall of riot shields, embossed with the TAP Squad insignia, shouted: Advance. Pace by regimented pace, it closed in. Each riot shield produced an arm bearing a truncheon. Each truncheon beat out the pace on its shield. Within the square, Evangeline sought for and found Jesús' hand, and felt his squeeze of reassurance. Between them, Florito rumbled like a chainsaw in slo-mo. The crowd came together, shouting, blaring klaxons, lobbing projectiles towards the barricade, pushing forward. In the crush, Evangeline's hand slipped from Jesús' hold and she lost sight of him. The TAP Squad launched a rain of canisters which spewed a green-white gas, silencing those it enveloped. As the sour-smelling fog rolled towards her, she ripped two strips from her tunic, wrapped one around her nose and mouth and the other around Florito's muzzle. A heart-imploding pain in her chest brought her to her knees. Florito retched beside her, his eyes streaming. Unable to keep her own eyes open for the burning pain, all she could do was fold herself over his head, shielding him from the gas. Around her, the crowd scattered. Dull thuds and yells came from all directions. Evangeline guessed those that ran to the barricade were met with violence.

Bit by bit, the gas cleared, and the pain subsided. She stood and wiped her eyes just in time to see the soignée woman of earlier, her skirt rucked up to the hips, being dragged along the ground by three of the TAP Squad in riot gear. Blood streamed from a wound in the woman's head. Adrenaline pumping, Evangeline threw herself on the back of a guard, locked her arms around his neck and clung on. His smell of sweat and cheap aftershave burned her raw throat. He could not rid himself of her, while also holding the other woman. He dropped his hold and withdrew what looked like a small gun from his pocket. The woman was about to die. Instead, clicking, and barbs of pain—a taser—shot through Evangeline, right to her core. She screamed in agony. Muscles no longer under control, her grip loosened, and she fell to the ground, legs in spasm. A jackboot knocked the air from her.

Florito had taken on the other two guards. His jaws clamped on an arm and tugged. The man yelled. His accomplice brought down a truncheon on the hound's head, but Florito would not let go. Snarling, he worried that arm. The first guard had joined in hammering down blows on Florito's back and more guards piled in. Evangeline scrambled to her feet, pulled the woman free and turned on the men.

'Stop. Leave him alone.'

Salvaging a wooden pole from the ground, she jabbed at their backs, across their heads: it fractured on contact with their body armour. An elbow in the face swatted her away, the men's bloodlust focused on the snarling hound. Through their legs, she glimpsed his flanks covered in gore and the pinkish spittle frothing from his jaws. The guards swarmed around him, kicking, beating. Blocked from view, his growl became ragged, desperate, and then no more.

The guards picked up their fallen comrade and took him away. One of them, his visor raised, glanced back at her over his shoulder, sniggered and put one last boot in.

'My boy,' Evangeline howled.

Florito lay still.

She crawled to the body, wrapped her arms around his neck and breathed in his biscuity smell. 'Why didn't you stay in the van?'

There was much less of him, somehow, than when he padded along beside her. She used to laugh at the way he held his head high when they came across people, dogs, wildlife, as though proud to be seen with her. So loyal, he would guard her with his life. And so he had. She swallowed the stone in her throat, taking in juddering breaths, exhaling phlegmy sobs. At some point, the warmth of a hand came through her shoulder.

'Evangeline.'

She turned into Jesús' chest. 'I should never have brought him.'

He held her close, allowing her to cry it out. 'Always, he want to be with you.'

After a little more time, he pulled back to look into her eyes. 'We have to go.'

'I can't leave him.'

'Arbolito, look around you. People need our help.'

'No! I'm not leaving my boy here alone.'

Jesús cast his eyes over Florito. 'OK. We put him in van, yes? But we need to be quick.'

They stumbled through a hail of stun grenades, bearing Florito between them. A flashbang exploded two paces away. She staggered. Florito's body lurched almost from the cradle of her arms. Evangeline steadied herself and readjusted her hold. But in that moment, just as the pit of her stomach tightened, his shaggy brows quivered.

'Florito?' She lifted his head with her shoulder. His deep brown eyes flickered open, a crescent of white showing confusion and pain.

'I'm here,' she breathed into his ear.

⚜

They laid Florito in the back of the van, his head resting on Evangeline's gilet. Gripped by self-recrimination she opened a gap in the window. He lay so still. She paused. He was breathing, just.

'Hold tight, my pupper, I'll come for you.' She slid the door closed.

The suede legs of her moccasins had for a while been at half-mast; she tugged at their criss-cross laces and refastened them at her knees.

'Right then.' She turned to face the battlefield.

The combat of earlier had abated to a simmering standoff. Clusters of guards, their helmets hanging over their elbows, chatted like this was a neighbourhood barbeque. What was going through their dense skulls? A good day had by all? They looked on, through pointless Ray-Bans, as demonstrators pulled their injured from the no-man's-land. The more anarchic protestors threw missiles and shouted in defiance: *Not on our land.* One—naked but for three feathers in his dreadlocks—cartwheeled just beyond arms-reach of the guards.

Where was Jesús? A chill swept over Evangeline.

There, on his way to the wounded. She scurried after him.

A homely field kitchen, glowing with paraffin lamps and fairy lights and a fire in a brazier which threatened to leap from its confines at any moment, extended a warm glow across half the field. Great vats of dhal drove their aroma—of pungent cumin, turmeric, ginger, and nose-tingling chilli—into the air, defusing the tear-gas that lingered in nostrils and memory. Evangeline and Jesús brought in the casualties. Some they patched up with bandages that had started out that morning as T-shirts and other forms of clothing, others' broken limbs were now splinted with the plentiful supply of timber. People came forward to receive their comrades and to settle them down with food and rest.

This was a place where old identities—background, choices made, obstacles overcome, opportunities missed—no longer accounted for much. All were grimy. All shared the same tales of brutality at the hands of the TAP Squad. What Evangeline took to be a businessman, by the trim of hair on a pale nape, sat in thrall to a bare-chested eco-warrior. A bespectacled, earnest young woman held court over a preservation of plaid-shirted environmentalists.

Evangeline felt her body relax in the warmth of the brazier. She didn't want to move from that spot. Ever.

Jesús picked up a lamp, got a thumbs up from its owner and said, 'I check no one is left on the battlefield.' As though sensing her reluctance, he patted her shoulder. 'Stay here. Keep warm.' He was already leaving when he shouted over his shoulder, 'See if you find sleeping things, yes?'

Sleeping things. She hadn't given it much thought. Then again, she hadn't expected the outbreak of war today. Who here, had? Some protesters looked shell-shocked; their clothing inappropriate. Others, with the peaceful aura of holding the key to life, she took to be nomads, living off-grid. A fair proportion more were cavalier in the ways of conflict.

※

Evangeline and Jesús returned to the van where Florito remained oblivious to the world. She curled over the hound and planted kisses on his forehead, relieved to hear the steadiness of his snoring. Not wanting to disturb him further, they filled a foil container with water and left it near his head. Then, they bedded down in a nest of ferns and young branches. The tarpaulin she scrounged at the field kitchen went some way to blank out the incendiaries punctuating the night. Wrapped in sour blankets—further field kitchen supplies—she felt Jesús' steady breath on her cheek and attuned her own breathing to his.

'Jesús.'

'Mm-hmm?'

'Are you asleep?'

She heard him move. 'No.'

She rolled onto her side to face him. 'What's going to happen tomorrow?'

His hand brushed the curve of her hip, her waist and the outline of her breast. 'There is no knowing what comes tomorrow. But, is

OK to be scared.'

'I'm not, with you.'

His hand steered for her clavicle and from there his fingertips traced the vee of her neckline. By the time his mouth was on hers, her body was starbright. He drew one tie of her dress, then the other, taking an ache of time to unwrap her. The feel of his skin on hers, his lips on her breasts and belly, his tongue knowing where to find her, and how to touch her, brought her to the brink of the infinite universe. They explored each other wholly, basking in their oneness. Together, revealing their secret depths they touched the sky. When Jesús shuddered, Evangeline arched beneath him, watching the wonder in his face. In the darkest hour they found their haven.

40. El Topo

Evangeline

The cacophony had roused all but the heaviest sleepers, even those who slept with chemical assistance. Sipping on gritty, black coffee in the field kitchen, Evangeline got the low down on what had been happening overnight. Shezmu had sent out the big guns—or, rather, one outsized tunnel boring machine—to forge ahead with the pipeline. The machine, equipped with a phallic shaft tattooed with the words El Topo— The Mole—culminating in a tungsten cutter-head evoking a pinecone with Rottweiler tendencies, had penetrated the rock face, scouring the tunnel walls as it went.

With this new offensive, the activists faced two fronts.

An unmanned log loader, door ajar, suggested a driver caught short.

'Think you can handle one of these, yes?' Jesús turned to look for her answer. How had she not recognised that determination— that zeal—in him before?

'What do you have in mind?'

'Meet me by El Topo.' Then he was gone.

The roof to floor windshield gave a vantage point over the skirmishes playing out below. Evangeline felt at once exposed to, and protected from, those outside. Jammed into the footwell, the detritus of the former occupant—lunchbox, hardhat, newspaper, frayed jumper—served as a reminder that she needed to master this beast fast. Once she worked out how to turn it on, the engine cancelled external noise, emphasising her isolation. Two stick-levers rose up from pedals. She noted them without touching them for the moment. Instead, she applied herself to getting to know what the two joystick-style levers on either side of her seat could do. She pushed the right joystick out. The boom shot outwards. First lesson: a little goes a long way. A gentle tap to the side of the joystick, moved the boom sideways. She tried the trigger: the grapple snapped shut. What could the left lever do? She pushed it out, the cab swung left, her heart lurched, and she pulled the lever back to starting position, returning her to face forwards. So much for on-the-job training. She couldn't put it off any longer. She gently squeezed her foot on the left pedal, the logger jerked but instead of moving straight forward it veered to the left. She tried the other pedal and the logger went right. She lifted her foot clear of either pedal. What wasn't she getting?

Both pedals together.

⟩⟩

At the tunnel head, the phalanx of El Topo's guards faced a battery of missiles. Rocks, artisan spears and Molotov cocktails crashed against their raised riot shields. A flat-bedded truck loaded with timber manoeuvred itself parallel to the conveyor belt which hauled rubble from the bore site. The truck's door opened and Jesús dismounted wearing a hard hat and hi-vis jacket. It had to be him: no one else moved with such grace. Evangeline cheered. Shezmu's workforce were either taken in by the disguise, or too distracted by the onslaught. Jesús waved his arms over his head in her direction.

By now familiar with handling the loader, she adroitly skirted the foot soldiers to bring the vehicle alongside Jesús. She opened the door to him. No longer in her own bubble, sounds of missiles and anger and fear invaded her cab, diesel fumes and teargas lodged in her throat. Jesús clambered up the steps to the cab.

'OK?' He took the hardhat she'd ignored in the footwell and fitted it on her head.

'Piece of cake.' She gave a small smile, wary of what was going on over his shoulder. 'What's the plan?'

'We stop the conveyor, El Topo sit in his own muck.'

'I'm not sure how effective this thing is as a wrecking ball.'

'Nice idea but no. Use the grapple to hold the logs in place while I undo the straps. Logs fall, machine breaks.'

'You stand well away when you're done, got that?'

'No problem. I wave all clear.' Holding onto the doorframe, he leant back as if to take her all in. 'Invincible.' Then he was gone.

Alone in the cab, she shut the door, cutting herself off from the outside. But before she even took hold of the ignition key, the loader jolted. She braced against the side of the cab. The detritus in the footwell came loose. Had a missile landed on the roof? One look through the windscreen told her others had felt it too. Heads switched this way and that, looking to friends, enemies—even the TAP Squad had lost its habitual nonchalance. None of them seemed able to identify the source. The jolt finished as quickly as it had started. An eerie quiet fell on the scene.

A Molotov cocktail arced towards the guards. Fighting resumed.

According to plan, Evangeline steered the loader to face the bed of the logging truck, clenched the grapple's wide jaws against the timber, and watched while Jesús unhitched the wrappers that gave the load the appearance of a trussed joint of beef, throwing each chain high over the log pile. She tucked her feet under the seat and hugged her elbows in tight: one nudge of a control could bring an avalanche down on him.

Jesús worked quickly. Although in plain sight and highly visible, the TAP Squad paid him little attention. Evidently, hi-vis equalled invisible.

But as he threw the last wrapper clear of the logs, she became aware of a deep, long growl, as though the earth itself had roused from sleep, opened its mouth and let out a gut-rooted yawn. The noise grew. Soon, the fittings inside the cab rattled and the windows hummed. The boom bounced as if it had hooked the Kraken.

'Run!' Her voice went no further than the frame of the cab, but Jesús ran all the same. The logs shifted. The boom jounced again, this time tearing the grapple free of its hold. Unrestrained, the logs jostled and rebounded off each other in an elephantine stampede.

Boom!

People dropped to the ground, hands covering their heads. A cloud of dust billowed from the tunnel mouth. Where was Jesús?

Boom!

Even louder than before and with dust, so thick now, it roiled against the windows. The dense cloud forced through the air vents, choking and claustrophobic. The door wrenched open and a stone hand tugged her arm.

'Vamos. Now!' As the statue-come-to-life spoke, whorls of rock dust lifted from his body, transforming the cab into a snow globe. Jesús had come for her.

Evangeline exited the loader not a moment too soon. *El Topo* shrieked in its death throes, belching acrid smoke. A fissure opened the lip of the tunnel's mouth and ripped along the ground to the loader.

Jesús pulled her away from the fissure. Panic flared everywhere. Her ears filled with screams. Screams of those escaping, those swallowed by the fissure, and of those trampled underfoot. Someone looking in the wrong direction—she saw him coming, surely, he would sense her—bulldozed her, then spat-shouted the accusation: '¡Mira a donde vas!'—Look where you're going! Jesús' firm grip pulled her away. When careened into for the second time, knocked off kilter, pain burnt the side of her head. She put her hand to her ear and felt wetness. Her palm was bloodied. Her blood? No, she was sure of it, not hers. She looked back. The glint of a watch at ground level caught her eye. The watch was attached to an arm that continued to a shoulder, all perfect together but confusing. They lacked the expected complement of torso and other limbs. She clapped her hand to her mouth. What the hell had happened?

'Jesús, wait.'

They stopped and turned. Corpselike figures skulked in the entrance to the tunnel. Her mouth turned dry. She knew these dwellers of dark and decay.

The Wekufe.

An activist's mouth opened in terror. Not watching where he was going, he tripped and fell. As one, the Wekufe swarmed upon him. He didn't stand a chance. More Wekufe ventured into the daylight, drawn by the rich plunder of live prey. At first, they moved blindly, tracking by odour. Soon, the smell of human flesh drove them to frenzy. Once they felled their prey, their rodentine teeth went for the belly, and the delicacy of viscera.

Evangeline fought to stop throwing up. 'We need to get to the arsenal.'

41. Fire at Will!

Evangeline

The garrison loomed in the centre of the clearing. Its fortifications of watchtowers, a wooden palisade twice a man's height, barbed wire and a burgeoning arsenal, represented—for everyone engaged in this conflict—the only defence from the Wekufe. Protestors surged towards it. They all wanted to be inside, safe. Panic prevailed.

Guards fired into the crowd at will: sitting ducks.

A corrugated roofing sheet surfed the crowd. Reaching the front, it rose upright in an activist's arms, and tamped down on wire-barbed bodies. The invaders learnt to knit together—armadillo-style—linking arms, head down, holding the shoulders of the one in front as they charged, their weight bowing the corrugated sheeting. Few reached the wall, fewer still had grapple hooks to climb their way to safety. Safety! What a joke? One bandanaed activist, his tartan shirt tied round his waist kilt-like, took a run-up bracing the weight of an upright timber between his interlocked hands and shoulder, tossed the caber across the barbed wire and scampered across—how he kept his balance was anyone's guess—only to be shot as he approached the wall.

Uniform in Ray-Bans and black, the guards resisted the incursion. They sent forth a spider-like drone to hover above the crowd, an onboard speaker commanded: 'Clear the area! Clear the area!' over and over, while jets of dirty yellow gas discharged onto upraised faces. The afflicted rammed the heel of their hands in their eyes. Noses streamed with snot. Guards wielded dazer lasers, the bright, rapidly flashing green lights blinding and disorientating, nauseating. They bore noise cannons strapped to their front.

Evangeline and Jesús squeezed through the crush. Despite herself, she flinched as a stun grenade went off nearby. Punched in the back, she stumbled, righted herself, and turned to retaliate, fist raised. The culprit recoiled, wide-eyed at the fight in her. Something like a football lobbed overhead. Not from the garrison, but to it. The missile fell with a bounce into the crowd. A clearing opened around it. A beat before pandemonium broke out. To get away from that thing with staring, vacant eyes. Its slack mouth, its hair caked in gore, its trailing, serpentine sinews and vertebrae, all human. A putrescent fug rolled over the crowd. A smell that took Evangeline back to Netherearth. Sweat prickled her lower back.

The Wekufe were coming.

The crowd charged the barbed wire. Jesús grasped her wrist, pulling her through the crowd.

'I get us in,' he said over his shoulder. 'But wait for my word.'

His foot clunked on a corrugated sheet, she followed. Others pushed their way on also. The sheet heaved and pitched on the barbed wire. A woman clung to Evangeline's sleeve as if to a buoy, then crumpled and fell. A neat black star with a bloody trail graced the woman's forehead. Jesús shook off an activist attempting to hurl him from the ramp, then leapt at the palisade. Arms outstretched; the tips of his fingers found purchase in gaps between the stakes. He found a fingerhold at a stretch upward, and then another. Using the toe of his trainers to gain traction, his body swayed side to side in his ascent.

Evangeline held her breath. Please, dear God, keep Jesús safe.

A shot rang past her ear, a reminder that not only was she at risk, but her position drew attention to Jesús. She hunkered down, tucking her head into her chest and clung to a wildly bouncing corrugated corner. People clamoured past her, hurling themselves at the wall. Most failed, rebounding onto barbed wire, but one or two latched on and started the hazardous crawl upwards.

'Arbolito.' Jesús hung by his arm hooked around the top of three stakes. He'd made it. He twisted at the shoulder to scan the crowd.

'Jesús.' She stood up.

His cloisonné blue eyes found her. Blood trickled from wounds on his forehead, more dripped from lacerations on his chest.

'Jump!' He held out his free hand. She sprang from the sheet and vaulted towards him. She fell against him and scrabbled to grasp his waistband. His hand locked around her wrist.

'Now, I throw you over.'

'What?'

'Ready?'

'How?'

'Use your legs.' Before she had a chance to question further, he drew back his arm, twisting at the waist.

Her eyes fixed on his, her wrist in his grasp, she was an extension of his arm, a pendulum. She swung her legs in the same direction as his arm and felt the pull.

'Legs!' His arm swooped her across him, holding her free of the fence wire.

She felt the outward force pulling her away from him but believed with absolute certainty that Jesús would hold her secure for as long as needed. As her course approached its zenith, she flicked her legs from the hip and pushed higher. All the while their eyes remained locked on each other. His arm curved her trajectory over the palisade. Jesús' grip on her wrist slackened and let go. She fell to earth with a tumble.

They were home and dry.

She picked herself off the ground and looked up. Jesús' head bobbed above the palisade, he grinned down at her, and with another heave his torso came into view.

Be safe Jesús. Be safe Jesús. Be safe Jesús.

Still on the wrong side of the fence, he adjusted his grip on the stakes.

Careful, careful, careful.

With perfect control, he pivoted over his arms, legs as one following through, and cleared the spikes. Jesús hung by his arms, closed his eyes and gave a relieved shake of the head.

Later, she would cling to this moment, unable to make sense of what happened next.

Was that when she heard the shot? As Jesús' eyes opened wide, his brow furrowed, and he fell to earth?

The bullet ripped through his chest. The puncture wound, and the blood, so much pumping, vibrant blood.

Or was it only the sight of the blood that the tiny tuk-tint of trigger-pull and hammer release sounded in her ear? Evangeline dropped to his side and pressed her hand to his chest, the lifeblood, sticky and hot, seeping through her fingers to pool in the dirt. His precious blood, his body, contaminated.

'Jesús! It's alright. You did it. You're going to be alright. Stay with me. Please, stay with me. Please. Jesús. Please.'

Never more alive, she clutched his body to her, pressing her life on him. She cupped his head in her hand and looked into his face. Too soon, the light of his eyes went out.

Grief erupted in all-consuming howl. She craved the comfort of being held and knew his arms would never hold her again.

The tread of approaching boots, a hand rough in her hair, whip-tail hold, tight, tighter. Yanked to her feet, she came eye to mirrored Ray-Bans with a guard.

42. It's Coming!

Evangeline

S hoved with brute force, Evangeline pitched through the entrance of the mess tent. A mannish reek, spunky in an unspent way, assaulted her. From the looks of things, the TAP Squad had recommissioned the tent to hold prisoners of war. Her position was clear.

She was ready for a fight.

Muted footballers played on a too-bright TV suspended from a tent pole. Places in the world carried on as though everything was normal. What once was Evangeline's world had become other. On the screen, inflamed red shirts moved across a lurid pitch. Here, in an army-style tent amid the din of heckling guards and activists, the players performed their victory dances for television-land alone. That ordinary life was worth protecting. It was the life Jesús and Effie deserved.

A strand of hair clung to Evangeline's cheek. She brushed it away and realised she was crying.

Gun-toting guards faced the prisoners without looking at them. Or so it seemed at first, but whenever an activist stepped out of line, the butt of a gun rammed into a nose, forcing the prisoner back. One guard, on the short side, strutted about behind his colleagues, swagger stick tucked underarm, his burnished face, she supposed, the product of a more than liberal dash of gift set aftershave. If anyone thought they were in charge here, it had to be him.

Evangeline pushed through the scrum towards him. Bellies and groins pressed in, marking her with testosterone and sweat.

Still six or so heads from him, she yelled, 'Butcher!' Her fists balled by her sides. 'Yes, you! Napoleon! You're responsible for this massacre.'

The higher register of her female voice cut through the general slanging match. He turned blank-faced, his eyes gelid ponds. When he had her in his sights, he looked her up and down, then again, more slowly, leaving no asset unaccounted. The corner of his mouth lifted like a puppet pulled by strings, revealing a scar in his cheek. In another time and place, she may have described his expression as a lopsided grin, but now she read the shortarse as reckoning himself to be a ladies' man. A great weariness descended on her.

The guard stepped towards her through the horde, bringing his swagger stick to rest on her shoulder. The touch of its steel tip sent kickback through her skin. She set her shoulders: she'd be damned if after…after all that had happened, she allowed this jumped-up whodjit the pleasure of seeing any sign of weakness in her.

She regretted wearing moccasins. What she wouldn't give for a sharp heel to grind through his conceited, uber-polished little boots. Instead, she shot stilettos with her eyes as she took hold of his cane between finger and thumb and lifted it from her shoulder.

'The Wekufe are at your door,' she said struggling to keep her voice calm. 'They will not discriminate between activists and TAP Squad. Whoever crosses their path will meet the same fate. The Wekufe will pull limb from limb, they will defile, they will eviscerate. They will not stop until they've brought everyone, *every*one, down to their level. They mean desolation and death.'

He gasped as if in pain, or fear, or, oh God…no, pleasure? He gazed at her as though mesmerised. The room fell silent and she felt all eyes on the two of them.

Quick, think. A man like this had to be seen to be making decisions. She would have to guide him towards the right one.

She forced a smile. 'The people here,' she said in as reasonable a voice as she could muster, 'have come to you for refuge. If we can't work together, we won't survive the night. Not. One. Of. Us.'

Napoleon opened his arms, palms upwards. 'Señora, look around you. There is no room here.' His voice was silky but scoured with cigarettes.

'I can't believe your company would commit millions for public welfare but turn its back on people in crisis.'

He smiled then, a hard smile, and gave her a look to say they both knew the answer to that one. 'This is business.' He said it in such a way as to imply this is *men's* business. She fought against the bile rising in her throat.

'That may be, but your success hangs on your reputation. The media would have a field day if the TAP Squad did nothing while Armageddon raged on out there. Your shares would take a nosedive.'

He inclined his head to the side as if to concede she had a point.

'And it doesn't take a great leap of the imagination to work out that somebody within the TAP Squad will be made to take the rap.'

Whether her words had convinced him, or he'd had enough of her talking, Evangeline couldn't be sure. Either way, he turned to his guards. But before he had a chance to issue orders a guard burst into the tent at the double and whispered in Napoleon's ear.

'You.' The swagger stick pointed once again in her direction. 'With me.'

Napoleon strutted to the watchtower, tugging Evangeline in his wake. A ladder rose through a hatch far above. He hesitated, eyes flicking between ladder and Evangeline. He undid his belt buckle, all the while gripping her wrist.

What now?

He wrenched her arm against her back, the torque burning her muscle and skin.

'You want us to work together?' He ground the hardness of his groin against her rear. 'I'll show you how this is going to work.'

She pulled away from the heat of his breath.

A thrup of leather on canvas. Her free arm was twisted to join its opposite number behind her back. Her wrists were bound roughly with what she took to be his belt, still moist from his sweat, then a shove from behind pushed her against the ladder. Clank. Forehead, chest, hip and shin crashed into its rungs punching out sense, breath and strength.

'Up,' he said.

'How can I? You've just tied my hands.'

'Up.' He forced Evangeline's wrists higher up her back. The movement so violent, her feet left the ground.

When she landed back down, he kicked her heel. 'Up.'

She put one foot on the bottom rung, the sound tinny, then, leaning into the ladder for balance, she brought her other up to join it. Soon a bar of pain crossed her shins, level with the pressure of the rungs. Napoleon's boots clanged on the bottom rung as his hands came alongside her thighs to grip the rails, encaging her. He swatted the backs of her legs with his swagger stick: Faster! Move!

Just when she thought she couldn't go on, a cold draught from above stirred her hair and she was climbing through the opening of the lookout. One more step, then all she could do was fall forward onto the floor. The tread of Napoleon's boots rang as he emerged through the hatch and advanced on her. Wanting to know what he had in mind, she rolled to her side. He sneered as he stood over her. Just then, something outside caught his attention, and his expression lost its certainty.

She seized the moment. A swift kick between his legs and Napoleon keeled over, clutching his groin.

'That's how it's going to work.' She scrambled away from him and rose to her feet. He remained gasping on the floor, his eyes screwed tight. Was he putting it on? Waiting for her to look away before he made his move? As she scanned for a weapon, her eyes cast across the window, just an opening in the wall, and she forgot the immediate danger.

Below, shrouded in dusk, the plain lay strewn with mangled and desecrated bodies. The wind changed, bringing with it a smell that clenched the pit of her stomach: the metallic-faecal stench of sweat and blood and ruptured bowels. Fearing her legs would give way, she slumped against the window's frame. Not so long before, she had watched while Jesús climbed the parapet. She could see him now. He had touched these defences. She closed her eyes and pressed her lips to the wall.

Rat-ta-ta-ta-tat! At the sound of gunfire close by, Evangeline opened her eyes again. With some relief, she noted several guards firing on the inhuman plague, the spent gun shells showering like sparks in a smelter's yard. The remaining activists fought on bravely, but they were no match for the Wekufe. She could not peel away from the horror. A scuff behind her told her Napoleon was recovering.

She turned to find him leaning on one knee as if doing penance. He looked up at her, all lust gone, and nodded towards the window.

'It is a sign from God,' he said.

'What the hell do you mean?' The last thing she expected from him was the religious zealot.

'Look to the sky.' He jutted his chin indicating towards the forest.

A shout came from below. 'It's in the trees! It's coming!'

She turned back to the window. A spectral grey cloud formed above the forest. It shapeshifted, sending out a spur in one direction, which withdrew only for an elbow to project elsewhere. Across the flexiform mass different zones faded to translucence then condensed to thick impenetrability, and back again. But, ever, it closed in.

The cloud was almost upon the beleaguered people below. With it, came a sound, neither vocal nor mechanical, but the movement of many. A ghostly whisper of air. Broad sagittate fragments broke from the cloud and made for those on the battlefield.

'What is it?' Evangeline said.

'Deliverance.' His step, softened from the swagger of earlier, drew close to the window. She glanced across at him.

Outside, the fragments danced above the heads of the activists; they hovered there a moment, just out of reach, then, one by one, they dropped down to land on the Wekufe, and only them, as though bestowing a kiss. But this was no lover's caress. Instead, in that instant, the Wekufe's unquenchable bloodlust syphoned from them, leaving empty vessels. Evangeline had the impression of Goya's *pinturas Negras,* peeling to red chalk and charcoal, before dissolving altogether into dust and going the way of the wind.

※

With the last of the Wekufe gone, the activists dropped to their knees and mouthed the trinitarian formula, crossing their chests. Joy rose within Evangeline like a bubbling spring.

A shadowy fragment broke away from the cloud and flitted down to the shoulder of an activist.

'Watch out!' she shouted.

The activist smiled in delight. And remained whole. Then more of the cloud descended on the men below, yet so lightly, so gently, as to be nothing more than the faintest shadow.

By now, the cloud had reached the parapet and enveloped the tower. When fragments, each the size of her splayed hand, broke from it, they revealed themselves not phantoms but moths. One maverick came into land on the tip of her own shoulder. A primitive cave painting in umber and terracotta and chalk and charcoal, its wings quavered she was sure as a gesture of greeting. She looked up from the moth to see Napoleon grinning like a schoolboy with a champion conker—the boy he perhaps had been before he developed the taste for power—beneath one moth on his head and another on his chest.

Then all went black.

43. Bachuéte'e: Queen Eternal

Morgan: Putromühue, November 1881 and beyond

The time has come.

As I set out on the path we all must follow, my thoughts return to when I first happened upon her.

❦

I woke with the first glimmer of morning and filled my lungs with green. The fresh, sweet fragrance aroused in me the feeling of delicious anticipation; today held the promise of good things to come. After breakfasting on bacon and a hunk of bread, I finished my coffee and scuffed dirt over the fire. Paco munched pasture thoughtfully while I saddled him up and stowed away my bedroll and utensils in his straps and paniers.

Snow-capped Villarrica dominated a landscape which wore the blue cloak of Hypnos long into the morning. A mighty forest of

Nothofagus spp.[22] swathed the volcano's hips, extending as far as the eye could see along the distant valley. But before mountain, before forest, a fertile plain clanked with the bells of llamas concealed within its subshrubs and grasses. Also unseen, but making their presence felt—much to Paco's chagrin—were the tripartite spines of the barberry. We picked our route cautiously, by-passing the tell-tale saffron-yellow flowers. It didn't help matters being forced to pull the brim of my chupalla low across my eyes, in a determined effort to outwit a temperamental breeze.

Not content with plaguing us, the wind infected the forest with its mood. As we approached, the trees jostled each other fractiously, stilled, then set up again. Paco's withers trembled as I steered him, with some effort, to take a path through the trees. We had travelled a long way together, and I considered Paco to be as true a friend as any I could wish for. Generally sweet natured, he had been known to exhibit an independent spirit, but this wariness was something new. While thankful for the arboreal barrier fending off the wind, the drone in the canopy above caused Paco's ears to twitch this way and that.

Then there was the gloom that closed around us: far more complete than ever to be expected for the broadleaved species, as though the forest within knew not of light. I mused the land had been thus veiled in continuous forest since the dawn of time,[23] and

---

[22] *Nothofagus:* a genus known as the southern beeches, native to the temperate southern Pacific Rim. Its distribution suggests the genus arose on the supercontinent, Gondwana. As that landmass fragmented, the genus distributed to Australia, New Guinea, New Zealand, New Caledonia, Argentina and Chile.

[23] Upon reflection, however, given the region's tectonic activity, my rational mind knows this to be unfounded. More likely, catastrophic events such as landslides open sites to allow the colonisation of pioneer

drew around me my chamanto waiting for my eyes to adjust.

We tracked through the forest, hindered by the dense underbrush of ferns and the lurking fallen giants who had succumbed in times past to calamity, or old age. Before long, our path started to rise uphill, then it climbed in earnest. Many of the trees we passed were etched with primitive carvings of jaguars, birds, &$^{c.}$ One image, a gruesome head with staring eyes, oozed burgundy from its fanged mouth. I dismounted and using my knife, I scraped off a little of the exudate and held it to my nose. Sweet, it may be, but this was not sap: the rusty odour unmistakeable. Paco's nervousness was beginning to unsettle me. I turned, sure of something watching, waiting. I saw nothing but trees and murk, void of time. In the saddle once again, I spurred Paco's flanks to hasten his step. To make amends for the indignity of asserting a master-servant bond, I attempted a lively cueca.[24] My audience received the performance with an exaggerated snort.

Eventually, we broke from forest to bare precipice: we had crossed the tree line. Ahead, as far as the eye could see, a topography few could ever hope to traverse. Jagged peaks pointing heavenward, their snowy mantle glistening in the sunlight, while treacherous flanks disappeared to the depths below. Volcanic cones misshapen, cut off in their prime, yet still alive—yes, still alive.

I identified a possible way forward: a narrow ledge curved out of sight around the mountain. Paco was willing to give it a try, grateful to be clear of the forest. Moving steadily, my faithful mule

---

species and regeneration of shade-intolerant species. I beg forgiveness for the musings of a man too long alone, save for the company of a mule.

[24] Cueca: a dance I've often enjoyed at fiestas and in the taverns of Chile, involving much slapping of the guitar and waving of one's kerchief.

never faltered. We continued to climb, always believing the rise immediately before us would give way to even ground. But just as we reached one summit, the path rose again.

As the sun lost strength, I wondered how I was going to set up camp on an exposed ridge with an intractable mule for bedfellow. Glancing up to check the sun's position, I was confronted by a most singular boulder: a sight of geological wonder in this barren land. Though I travelled by mule and not magic carpet, I was hard pressed to convince myself this colossal stone was not the roc's egg of Sinbad legend.

Our path tucked behind the boulder, then continued to surprise us by passing through a basaltic lava tube cave.[25]

What paradox was this? In just a few steps, the alpine climate we had so lately endured, ripened to Mediterranean. Moreover, the path gave way to a plateau like none I had ever witnessed. Before us, spread a profusion of ethereal spikes of waxy turquoise blooms, each flower as wide as my hand, embellished with nodding saffron stamens. Emerging from spiny rosettes, the entirety reached above the height of a tall man. Interspersed between the flora I discerned pillars of equal height, but stone in nature. The monoliths, decorated with inhuman faces eschewing classical beauty, must have been carved by an ancient hand.

I thought I saw movement. There in the shadows. Yet, all I beheld was a lithic visage with fangs, bulging eyes and lolling tongue. We continued but gained no more than a few paces before something moved again. This time, I was certain of it. I called 'Hallo!' My voice odd to my ears in this extraordinary world. We waited, staring into vegetation. I called again, more a question this time, 'Hallo?'

---

[25]For those of a geological bent, flow tubes form when the outer edges of a lava flow cool and crust over, while the inner lava continues to flow, eventually draining free.

A small being revealed himself from the safeguard of a monolith, rewarding our patience. His straight black hair, just skimming his shoulders, framed a flat, round face. He wore no more than a cloth covering his nethers, a bow slung across his lean torso, and quivers over the opposite shoulder. From the first, he was fascinated by my mule. For his part, ever keen to make a new acquaintance, Paco blew down his nose and trumpeted his lips. Our small friend beamed. Not wanting to scare him off, we checked our transport. The tribesman closed the gap between us and, eyes ever on the mule, raised his hand to Paco's muzzle. In turn, the mule sniffed the newcomer's scent then, satisfied, nuzzled the open hand, his whiskers causing the little fellow to double over with laughter.

'How do you do.' I'm not so much a fool that I believed our friend was familiar with the Queen's English. Nevertheless, I do ascribe to do unto others, &$^{c.}$

Tapping my chest, I made my introduction. 'Morgan's the name, my fine fellow. Edwin Morgan.'

'Mor*gahng!*' Savouring the unfamiliar vowels in his mouth, the outcome was nasal in tone.

He gestured to his person in similar fashion. 'Panquí.'

He next offered me some leaves he pulled from a woven pouch hanging from the ties of his loincloth. The ovoid, glossy, mid-green leaves possessed two pale, parallel lines either side of the midrib, giving the impression of a thin-lipped mouth. I accepted his gift which he motioned for me to put in my cheek. I scrunched a few in my hand and in they went. The leaves' astringency immediately apparent. Panquí grinned at my contorted face and beckoned me to follow.

In Indian file we entered a stand of colossal trees. The trunks, regimentally straight, had bark like elephant hide. In the lofty heights, spidery branches projected densely overlapping, spine-tipped leaves.[26] Along our path, I had the good fortune to come across the cones heavy with seed, spherical and of considerable size. The seeds can be eaten roasted. I stowed a cone in Paco's panier for what would be a welcome addition to our supper.

Panquí, frequently stopped to check we were still with him. I allowed myself to be diverted by the arboreal majesty of this remote land, my lack of attention to our guide making a poor rear-guard campaigner of me. I discerned rhythmic drumming, originating some way ahead. As we drew closer, my mouth tingled and numbed around the bolus of leaves contained therein.

Through a circle of thatched-roofed huts, we emerged in a clearing where Panquí's people were gathered around a fire. Some drummed, others danced a shuffling stomp that chinked the bells about their ankles, more still sang with soft voices. All in all, the people generated a repetitive, not-unpleasant, melody.

I took care of Paco's comfort while Panquí went to speak with his people. He returned in the company of a village elder who gave me a thorough examination, his firm fingers squeezed my bicep and prodded my chest, chuckling at something known only to him. He seemed quite taken by my hair. Three months without the civilising snip of a barber's scissors had made an unruly mane of my Titian locks. All the while, they spoke with great animation. One word, Bachuéte'e, was repeated sufficiently often for my ears to distinguish it from their chatter. At last, Panquí and the machi came to an accord. By this time, the villagers had taken up the chant of Bachuéte'e which they accompanied with an accelerando of drumming.

I was led in procession to a hut fronted by woven hangings.

---

[26] When first identified by Europeans, genus *Araucaria* was erroneously ascribed to the pine family. Its subsequent name derives from the Spanish for Araucanians (the Mapuche), for their diet based on the tree's seeds.

The machi raised his voice to address the drapery. Once again, Bachuéte'e was invoked. A moan from within, low yet distinctly female in origin. Hitherto, I had only gained the impression of good intentions from these people. Now I was not so sure. The moan came again, this time louder and more animalistic. The moan continued with a pulsating wail and ended in an ear-blasting caterwaul. In the silence which followed, Panquí patted my back as if to reassure me. The machi advanced to draw back a corner of the cloth.

I beheld a woman the colour of burnt sugar, kneeling, head thrown back, beads of sweat on her brow, long hair cascading over proud shoulders. Her upturned breasts were like separate beings, moving of their own will. Between her copious thighs, a man. By God, this bounteous Freyja was magnificent.

Her eyes, semi-closed, flickered open and settled on your humble servant. She licked her lips. Raising herself on her haunches, she released her consort. The man was spent and had to be helped to his feet by my two companions. Holding me in her gaze, she stroked her hand from the valley between her breasts to the promise of paradise between her legs. She motioned to the others who, bowing, left us alone.

'Morgan, at your service, madam.'

'Bachuéte'e,' she rose and came towards me.

A braver man than I may have quailed and none would think the less of him for it. Not so Morgan. On my honour, I stood firm. 'For Queen and country.'

Laughing, she sidestepped me nimbly, more so than I had credited possible for this savage maiden and disappeared through the curtain.

The chase was afoot.

I spun round and pushed through the drapery just in time to see her dart through the trees beyond the clearing. The villagers hailed my appearance by setting about their drumming with gusto. I leapt over the fire and headed into the trees. Like a game of Blind Man's Buff, I saw nothing and ran arms outstretched. Branches played at my clothes, roots would have me topple and roll among them, but every so often a peal of laughter some way ahead guided my progress. Ever spurred on by the ludic beat of the drums, I rounded the bole of a tree and came upon my goddess. She laughed again, a fruity laugh, and was out of my grasp before I knew it. Her movement, silent and surefooted: of the forest. By contrast, I blundered about wildly, with no idea how far we penetrated the forest, nor of direction, the drumming sounded all around. I continued the pursuit but, in my haste, my foot caught in a trailing liana and I fell, spread-eagled. Before I could catch my breath, Bachuéte'e came to me out of the shadows and sprang at me. Hands and tongue worked their way under my shirt. I pulled the confounded article over my head. Impatient with the quandary of civilised clothing she bit at my groin through the khaki. I unbuckled the belt and forced my breeches past my hips. The cool, humic forest floor stuck to my damp skin. A swarthy aroma of moist leaves enveloped us as Bachuéte'e, my queen, my goddess, showed me heaven.

Later, with legs still entangled in liana and khaki and the soft debris of the forest imprinting my body, I enjoyed the exquisite illusion I had taken root in this forest. Bachuéte'e, in great mirth at my predicament, was helpless to extricate me.

Over the weeks, months, years that followed, that illusion never left me. In time, I came to know it to be true. Bachuéte'e, you see, is my goddess, as she is of the tree. Goddess of the tree, she is of Rewe.

She is Rewe.

The time has come.

Bachuéte'e comes to me now, with welcoming arms. Amid the

sweet smell of trees in growth, I stand tall, straighter than I have for many a year. My blood courses through my system with renewed vigour. Time has no meaning: the past, the present, the future and what might have been are all one.

The four directions are one.

The four dawns, one.

The four waters, one.

The four winds, one.

All are one with Rewe.

Rewe is all.

44. Family Tree

Morgan and Evangeline: Putromühue, within time, without time

I made all haste to the arch: the woman had returned, that much the Putromühuens told me. But what they left unsaid was the condition in which they found her. A nervous exhaustion had taken hold of her, a stubborn malaise from which she had not the heart to recover. For days she lay on a cot, neither awake nor asleep, her red hair tumbling across the pillow, putting me in mind of Ophelia. God forbid that she should suffer the same fate as that poor maid. More to the point, I forbid it! And so, while she remained insensible of the world turning around her, I sat with her, watching for any sign of vitality.

By all accounts, she would not have made it here, had it not been for that slobbering great hound. He carried her up the mountain across his back, knowing where to find help. Without him, I doubt she would have had the strength to continue to her journey's end. For all his drool and High Winds, I have the greatest respect for hound Florito, his sure-footedness, loyalty and—ahem, shall we say strength of character?—put me in mind of an old friend of mine, long gone now, but forever in my heart.

As if their Odyssey had not been enough, Mache Uwa welcomed Florito with, 'it chases woman with sunset hair, it will not eat chickens. It will say *kwa, kwa,* it will not lie.'[27] Thank Heaven I arrived when I did and divested the machi of his special brew. I dread to think what canine Chaos might have ensued had Florito found himself in the spirit world, and not in his rightful place by the side of his mistress companion.

After that, I kept the machi occupied with prayer, for only with Faith would the girl choose to come back to us recovered, and only then would she be, once more, our brave Evangeline. Give the man his due, Uwa kept up the incantation night and day.

Over the beat of the kultrún, his voice rang out, 'Father God,

---

[27] This merits further explanation. The indigenous peoples see their dogs simultaneously as the canine animal; as human (in the sense that the animal informs the people about the world beyond human, thus extending their understanding of the world around them); and as a representation of the characteristics of dogs (hunters).

In preparation for the hunt, the people tell their dogs what to hunt, they warn them against attacking domestic animals, the dog should bark *kwa kwa* when it has the quarry, and should not bark, or lie, when it does not.

Here, the machi intended to send Florito into the spirit world to retrieve Evangeline, the woman with the sunset hair. When the Machi addresses the dog in the third person, he demonstrates the humans' superior status over dogs.

For my part, I beg to differ: our species is not superior. I believe Lord Byron said it best in his epitaph to Boatswain, his Newfoundland Dog, 'one who possessed Beauty without Vanity, Strength without Insolence, Courage without Ferosity, and all the virtues of Man without his Vices.'

you send us a sign. Mother God, receive this sign. Old Man of the Sky, of the four dawns, Old Woman of the Earth, of the four directions, receive this sign. Young Man of the Sky, of the four waters, Young Woman of the Earth, of the four winds, receive this sign. Renew the power of the cosmos. Old Man, Old Woman, Young Man, Young Woman, bring forth the Light of Rewe.'

A gentle pressure infused Evangeline's fingers with a kind of buoyancy and warmth that came back to her as a distant memory. It tweaked her arm. She ignored it. Do nothing, it would go away. If she wanted anything at all (but 'want' was such a tiring word), it was to be left alone. But the pressure didn't let up. It nudged and nipped, but so tenderly that at times she thought it must be her mind playing tricks: lost limb syndrome for the marooned.

Waiting for you.

The next nip tugged gently, accompanied by flickering subdued light, as though viewed through a teeming throng of beings, each the size of her hand. The softest vice held her hand and led her back to the land of the living.

Go and find it.

Evangeline rose to the surface and inhaled the damp, Marmite-breath of Florito. Her eyes blinked open, unleashing a clamour of hound: all barking, bouncing, play-bowing.

Behind his bulk, she detected another presence.

'You're safe now.' a woman's voice said.

The voice was familiar but, hearing it, Evangeline realised she'd been expecting someone else. When Florito settled back low on the floor, she found the open face of Wüf ko smiling down at her.

'Was a man here?' Evangeline asked.

'Here? There's been no man.' The woman puzzled her brow. 'Well, not unless you count Florito.'

'Sitting just here.' Evangeline indicated the bedside. 'Big, you couldn't miss him.'

Wüf ko shook her head. 'You've been in deep sleep for three days. Perhaps you dreamt it.'

'I thought someone was with me, a friend.'

'You are in Putromühue. You *are* among friends.' Wüf ko's voice caught.

As much as she wanted to do otherwise, Evangeline pushed the question no further. She tapped her head and attempted a laugh. 'Marbles well and truly gone.'

Wüf ko's face lit with compassion. 'You've been through much.'

The tree, Rewe—

Kingdom Plantae
Phylum Magnoliaphyta
Class Magnoliopsida
Order Yavuales
Family Yavuaceae
Genus *Yavuea*
Species *Yavuea morganii*[28]

—one of the earliest of flowering plants to emerge on Earth, was the last of its kind when I happened upon it (I was honoured to discover my learned colleagues at Kew named it after me). Before it passes out of existence, Rewe the World Tree is worthy

[28] For those whose noggins struggle to retain the ranking system of taxonomic classification, a mnemonic: King Philip Came Over from Glorious Spain.

of celebration. The Pontfadog Oak,[29] for all its history, would have nothing on it. To think, the World Tree has been at the root of my story and Evangeline's, branching out from the plant world to that of man—

Kingdom Animalia
    Phylum Chordata
        Class Mammalia
            Order Primata
                Family Hominidae
                    Genus *Homo*
                        Species *Homo sapiens*

—proof, if any were needed, that what is known as our environment,[30] a peculiarly anthropocentric concept, should more accurately be viewed as a world of interconnections and interactions of which we are mere guardians.

At one time, the tree species, *Yavuea divus,* dominated the forest. Taller than its neighbours, it emerged above the canopy, putting all in shade, fortifying its branches and leaves against the drying winds. The giant eagle nested in the overstory, diving into the canopy to surprise its prey from below. Now, the prey has long since been scared away by the roar of logging machinery.

Of course, I always knew Evangeline had it in her, she comes of good stock. The machi, on the other hand, took some persuading. For all his belief in worlds beyond those of living

---

[29] This venerable oak overlooked the Ceiriog Valley, Wales, beneath which Owain Glydŵr, the last native Prince of Wales, rallied his troops in the Welsh Revolt against Henry IV. It is said, even now, he awaits the call to return and liberate his people.

[30] A new concept for me, equating to what I used to describe as landscape.

man, he lacked faith in the spirits' auguries. Or, more precisely, for the spirits don't get these things wrong, the machi denied his own reading of what was foretold. The Putromühuens have so long set themselves apart from the wingka, the machi had come to believe they begat only disease, discord and destruction. It is much the same, for instance, as the elderly widower sitting alone in his Rhondda terrace, who fancies all the sins of Sodom and Gomorrah consume the streets outside. In fear, he bolts and double locks his door, and pulls the chain across. What folly is isolationism.

I digress.

Being, as I say, out of love with the world of human progress, the machi doubted we should pin our hopes on a wingka woman to return life to the most sacred of all trees, Rewe. For this reason, Machi Uwe set Evangeline a trial that would have outwitted even the great Gilgamesh. For her part, Evangeline, being Evangeline, was not the least foxed. The trial? The trial was to resurrect that which has the power of transformation, living four lives in one, its appearance each time unrecognisable from the last. But a grave affliction disturbed the natural order. A case of business interests taking precedence over nature. You will have followed Evangeline as she went deep in the forest, and marvelled as she, by way of rhizoxants from Netherearth, triggered the eggs' transformation to larvae. But the efficacy of the rhizoxants did not stop there. This insect species, within Order Lepidoptera, had been on the verge of collapse due to Shezmu's destruction of its one food source, *Aristotelia chilensis*, the sacred maqui.[31] The amber juice of the rhizoxants enabled the larvae to gain nutrition from a variety of plant hosts—less discerning about which plant host it fed from.

I've no doubt the observant among you will have piped up: Order Lepidoptera? For yes, if you've been paying attention, you

---

[31] A Mapudungun word meaning peaceful intention and benevolence.

might well have put instar and instar[32] together and come up with the non-ranked division of Heterocera.[33] In short, moths. That is, the very moths that swarmed from the forest in a cloud over the Shezmu barracks, and picked off the Wekufe, one by one. But why Wekufe and not human, you ask? Well, I'm coming to that.

You will be aware, certainly, of the symbolism of the moth. Its lifecycle and (mainly) nocturnal habit give rise to all manner of mumbo-jumbo about prophesy, second sight, &c, &c. Yet in many a hackneyed notion, a germ of truth exists. Think on the words:

'Lo, they all shall wax old as a garment; the moth shall eat them up.'[34]

The Wekufe, older by centuries than man's natural three score years and ten, are our dissatisfied ancestors, the malcontent spirits, consigned to exist in Netherearth. In life, they held others to account for their own lack of opportunity, scarcity of funds, and perceived deficient encouragement. They were, in fact, the very embodiment of mean-spiritedness. Thus, as in life so it was in death, a self-bred torment of envy and malice. The one power moths do possess is that of transformation. So, when the moths flitted down on the heads of the Wekufe, the moths didn't so much eat them up, as to release them from purgatory. Next port of call: Paradise.

⧬

---

[32] Derived from Latin for 'form', 'likeness'. A developmental stage of arthropods which occurs between each moult (the scientific term being: ecdysis. The herpetologists among you will be aware this process also occurs in snakes), until sexual maturity is attained.

[33] Derived from the Greek for 'varied-antennae', the division is non-monophyletic, hence, it does not abide by the rules of classification. Monophyletic groups share characteristics (we call these synapomorphies) derived from the same ancestors, which distinguish those belonging to the group from those outside.

[34] Isaiah 50:9.

The evening sky shimmered like a mirage, but this was no illusion. The air pulsed with movement, fanning a suspicion of the sweetest perfume towards Evangeline. She closed her eyes and, lifting her heels from the floor, drew in.

Waiting for you. Go!

The molecules of scent wove around her olfactory system in a dance of the seven veils. A complex vapour of silver-pearled dew held on the downy skin of potent, fleshy fruit, mellowing to woody incense. More corporeal than spiritual, the volatile molecules undulated from her head to her body. There, they shimmied from lungs to blood, and flowed to her every atom. Intoxicated, her knee buckled: only the support of Wüf ko's arm through her own kept her upright and moving forward. If the fragrance prelude could do this, how powerful the full symphony? More intriguing still, what was its source?

All around them, excited faces glowed in the flickering torchlight. The chattering throng of what appeared to be the entire village moved forward. It occurred to Evangeline that what they couldn't express in words, they blasted in music, of sorts. From the hunting-horn blare of the trutruka, the elastic boing-zoing of the mouth-held trompe, to the incessant drumming kultrún, this was jamming in the extreme. Something was, most definitely, up.

The flittering cloud led the way. She had no fear of it now, for she'd come across the cloud before and knew it for what it was: a whisper of moths. The people moved slowly, following the moths out of the village, funnelling into the woods on the one path. Individual moths swooped down to the torchlight but, governed by a stronger force, they resisted the urge to enter the all-consuming flame. A pair of beads glinted within the branches. Then more and more, until the whole woodland blinked with them. Evangeline pointed this out to Wüf ko who lifted her torch closer to the canopy. The black-ringed eyes of a mouse-like creature gazed down at them.

'We call it chumaihuén. In Spanish they are called monitos del monte,' she whispered.

'Monito? Little monkey?' Evangeline whispered back.

'For its tail, see.' Wüf ko indicated the prehensile tail curled around the branch. 'It is special in other ways, too: it carries its babies in a pouch.'

'A marsupial?' She looked in wonder.

For a moment, the chumaihuén sat back on its hind legs and didn't move: all eyes. Then, with a twitch of whiskers and pink nose, it darted off.

'Curiouser and curiouser,' Evangeline said under her breath. For, instead of running to safety, the tiny creature stole a march on the women and hitched a lift on the shoulder of a rabble rousing trutruka player further up the chain.

The high-pitched babble and happy shrieks of children reached Evangeline from different directions, as though the villagers were fanning out. Unable to see beyond four or five people in front of her, she assumed an obstruction in the path had forced a diversion, for the torches of those nearer the front of the crowd flashed through the trees in two opposite files. Then, the people immediately before her parted.

There was nothing.

Nothing.

A colossal nothing.

༄

Was this it, then? Had Evangeline come all this way for Nothing? To have achieved naught?

Stop you there.

This was no wasted effort. Evangeline's journey has been more than fruitful. Allow me to elaborate.

Result the 1st/

> Evangeline, botanist aspirant, has gained first-hand exposure to the diverse flora of Chile, broadening her

plant knowledge, setting her up for the long and illustrious career ahead of her.

Result the 2nd/

> In observing plant species' adaptations to habitats ranging from arid desert in the north to saturation in the south, from maritime in the west to alpine in the east, and in temperatures subtropical to subpolar, moreover, to achieve all this and out-compete other species, resist attack from pests and diseases, and strategize proliferation,[35] Evangeline has herself adapted. Like plants, she has overcome the adverse and warded off those who would do her ill. Deep within her, a change has taken place, a form of evolution by natural selection, if you will. By dint of her search, Evangeline views herself—and the world around her—with new eyes.

Result the 3rd/

> The balance between woman and nature, that original lifeforce, is restored once more.

≋

In the hunt for Rewe, Evangeline's path meandered and diverted. Yet she persevered. A playwright[36] once said, 'Trees that are slow to grow bear the best fruit.' I mention this for its relevance to Evangeline's story. Of course, I do not suggest she was stunted in childhood. One need only look at her—

What's that, you say? You don't see her? Permit me to stand aside.

≋

Florito's body pressed against her legs. She could tell by the way he asserted his shoulder to the fore of her hipbone that, far from

---

[35] Flora of Chile, take a bow.
[36] Molière, no less.

being fearful, he meant only to shield her from harm. Through the barrel of his chest, she felt the rumbled growl he directed into the void. Full of love for him, she buried her fingertips between the concertina folds of his scruff, and, side by side, they stared into the dark.

Wüf ko coughed in the chill of the night air. The sound emphasised the silence that had fallen. Horns, pipes and drum all laid aside. The people had stopped on the lip of a large bowl-shaped depression, whether the result of subsidence or an ancient caldera Evangeline couldn't tell. The bowl was so large, the villagers, all a hundred or so of them, comfortably stood on its perimeter in one circle. Or so she assumed, because she couldn't see. No, her sight was still intact, for there were the people to the left and right of her, hand in hand. Florito, closest by, looked as bewildered as she felt. But she couldn't see across the bowl.

The nothing was not nothing, then, but something.

And from that something, a vibration sounded, so deep as to find the core of her being. Overwhelmed, breathless, she looked for an end to what was before her. Craning her head back, far back, along with everyone else, a starry sky kissed the moment in which she stood: the something extended to the heavens. But something had happened to the sky directly above the depression. Now and then, the occasional star glimmered in that space of nothing-something. The something was moving, not in one continuous direction but back and forth, swaying, as though...

Evangeline made out a pattern, branch-like, and the moths looping in, hovering. She recognised a tree. Smoothly, hugely, cinnamon barked, giant flower buds borne at the terminal end of a branch, glossy, heart-shaped leaves. Without closer scrutiny of the leaves for the translucent, otherwise known as pellucid, dots, she knew with a rush of certainty what she was looking at. This was her tree, this was Rewe.

A warm tear followed the line of her uplifted cheekbone and

lost itself behind her ear.

So imperceptibly, she would never pinpoint the exact moment, the branches flushed velvet red then bloomed with radiance. The light modified to infinite indigo and flowed down the trunk, turning the villagers to deities. Before indigo reached the ground, it turned cobalt, then pulsed forest green through the surface roots. Within the substrate, amber and white light flickered like a distant thunderstorm, a reminder of the rhizoxants she'd collected in Netherearth.

The whole tree was alight. Its branches were laden with lianas and epiphytes. Rewe's crowning glory sparkled with the eyes of monitos del monte, scores of them, all driven close to ecstasy by the perfume emanating from generous white buds.

As the full moon reached its zenith, the radiant petals unfurled one by one, releasing the heavy scent of bletted fruit. The monitos del monte frolicked in the anthers, while moths took their fill of nectar.

The whoosh of villagers dropping to their knees drew Evangeline's attention. It was just for a moment, but when she next looked towards the tree, a proud-shouldered, voluptuous woman was walking in a spiral-track from the centre to the rim of the bowl. The woman stopped before Evangeline.

The woman opened her arms. 'Evangeline, Young Woman of the Four Winds, I've been waiting for you. Your coming was determined before you were born.' The hint of a smile softened the barbed glance towards Machi Uwe. 'You were made to bring new life to Rewe, to heal her as you healed yourself.'

'Bachuéte'e. Earth Mother. I am come.' The words rose from within Evangeline. She had no thought of them until she heard them aloud.

'Walk with me daughter. There is someone who wishes to see you,' the goddess said, extending her hand.

Evangeline took the hand offered and stepped down into the

bowl. Bachuéte'e kissed her forehead, then stood aside. A larger than life character, with Titian hair and twinkling eyes came forward, crunching leaf litter beneath his boots. A glint of gold shone from his ear. It was her earring, one of a pair she'd had converted from his cufflinks. The one she'd left in the Vault of Light.

With more than a hint of a Welsh accent he said, 'Evangeline. You have made me so very proud.'

Emotion welled up and she flung her arms around his neck. He enveloped her in a bearhug.

A small hand tugged at her dress. Evangeline released herself from Morgan to look down. A girl with russet curls and apple-red cheeks reached her plump arms upwards. Evangeline took her in her arms and breathed in her sweet smell.

'Effie!' was all she could say.

THE END

Lost & Waiting

Bibliography

Allaby, Michael (ed.) (1998) *Oxford Dictionary of Plant Sciences*. 2nd edition. Oxford: Oxford University Press

Bacigalupo, Ana Mariella (2007) *Shamans of the Foye Tree: Gender, Power & Healing Among Chilean Mapuche.* Austin: University of Texas Press

Byron, George Gordon (1808) *Epitaph to a Dog*—quoted by Morgan in Footnote 27, Ch.44, Family Tree.

Crow, Joanna (2013) *The Mapuche in Modern Chile: a Cultural History.* Gainesville: University Press of Florida

Heywood, Vernon (ed.) (1993) *Flowering Plants of the World.* Updated edition. New York: Oxford University Press

Hickey, Michael & King, Clive (2004) *Common Families of Flowering Plants*. Cambridge: Cambridge University Press

Jones, Terry, *et al.* (1975) *Lumberjack Song.* London: Charisma—reworked by protestors in Ch.39, Shezmu Showdown

Kipling, Rudyard (1898) *The Explorer*—forms the call to Evangeline

Kohn, Eduardo (2013) *How Forests Think: Towards an Anthropology Beyond the Human.* 1st edition. University of California Press—informed the dog ceremony witnessed by Evangeline in Ch.35, Place Above the Clouds, and explained by Morgan in Ch.44, Family Tree.

Tennyson, Alfred (1842) *Ulysses*—paraphrased by Evangeline in Ch.16, Reunion. Lord Tennyson's poem is carved on the memorial cross of Scott's polar expedition on Observation Hill, Antarctica.

Glossary: Botanical Terms

Angiosperm   A flowering plant distinguished by having its seeds enclosed in an ovary. The most highly evolved of plants.

Anther   The terminal portion of a stamen of a flowering plant. The pollen sacs containing pollen are borne on the anther.

Bryophyte   A division of plants including the mosses. Prefer moist habitats. Spore-producing. The oldest land plants on earth.

Capitate   Pin-headed. Of an inflorescence, consisting of flowers/florets with no stalks, arising at the same level.

Circumnutate   The successive spiraling of the growing tip of the stem of a plant as it grows.

Carpel   One of the flower's female reproductive organs, comprising an ovary and a stigma, and containing one or more ovules.

Cordate	Of a leaf, heart-shaped.
Cryptogam	A plant that reproduces by spores or gametes rather than seeds, i.e. an alga, bryophyte (mosses), or pteridophyte (ferns).
Determinate	(inflorescence) One in which the terminal flower opens first and prevents further growth of the axis.
Dioecious	Possessing female and male flowers/reproductive organs borne on separate plants.
Epiphyte	A plant that uses another plant for its support, but which does not draw nourishment from it.
Family	Taxonomic category between the higher rank of order and the lower rank of genus.
Genus	Taxonomic category between the higher rank of family and the lower rank of species.
Illiciales	Order of flowering plants including *Illicium* spp. which are the source of star anise.
Inflorescence	Any arrangement of more than one flower.
Laurales	Order of flowering plants including the laurel family.
Legume	A tree, shrub, herb, water plant, climber, etc., of the Leguminosae (pea family). The roots of most plants have tubercles containing bacteria which enhance their take up of atmospheric nitrogen.

Lycopod   Seedless, evergreen plants with dichotomously
                        branching stems. The oldest surviving vascular
                        plant division.

Ovary   The hollow, lower part of the female reproductive
                        organ (carpel), containing one or more ovules and
                        surmounted by the style(s) and stigma(s). The
                        ovule is generally above the other floral parts
                        (superior) or below them (inferior).

Ovule   A structure in the ovary which, after fertilisation,
                        develops into a seed.

Matorral   An ecoregion in Chile which equates to the
                        temperate Mediterranean climate, with rainy
                        winters and dry summers.

Papilionaceous   (flower) resembles a butterfly. Denotes
                        leguminous plants of subfamily Papilionoideae.

Pellucid   Translucent.

Phylogenetic   Relating to the evolutionary development and
                        diversification of a species or group of organisms
                        or of a particular feature of organisms.

Piperales   Order of flowering plants including the pepper
                        family.

Placentation   The arrangement of the parts of the ovary to which
                        the ovules are attached (placenta).

Poaceae   The grass family.

Sagittate   (leaf) Shaped like an arrow head.

Sclerophyll   Plant showing adaptations to Mediterranean-type
                   climate (see also, Matorral). Leaves are evergreen,
                   small, hard, thick and leathery.

Spadix   A spike of flowers on a fleshy axis.

Spathe   A large bract subtending an inflorescence.

Species   A basic group of organisms.

Stamen   The male organ of a flower.

Stigma   The part of the female reproductive organs on
                   which pollen grains germinate; the apical part of
                   the carpel.

Style   An extension of the carpel which supports the
                   stigma.

Taxonomy   Also known as systematics. The theory and
                   practice of grouping individuals into species,
                   arranging those species into larger groups, and
                   giving those groups names, thus producing a
                   classification.

Truncate   Appearing as if cut off at the base or apex.

Unisexual   (flowers) Having only male or female organs.

Acknowledgements

This novel is inspired by the extraordinary adventures of Victorian plant hunters, including the botanical artist, Marianne North (for more on the real-life explorers, I recommend The Plant Hunters (1998) by Toby Musgrave, *et al.,* and Sex, Botany & Empire (2003) by Patricia Fara). Through my writing, I aim to heighten interest in the world's flora and its conservation. My use of botanical terms and binomial nomenclature is deliberate: not only does this unambiguously identify the plant in question, it allows the reader to become more familiar with this language. Don't ever be scared of the botanical names, just don't use a silly voice (and believe me, many do) when saying them aloud.

I write in homage to the ripping yarns of H Rider Haggard, Rudyard Kipling and Sir Arthur Conan Doyle, into whose extraordinary worlds I escaped when young.

It is one thing to embark on the big adventure of writing a novel, quite another to finish. I would not have done so without the feedback, support and friendship from my two write clubs. The Wiltshire Writers are Fiona Blakemore,

Nicola Curtis, Robynne Eagan, Clare Evans, Anita Goodfellow and Grace Palmer. Los Ficciones are Rachel Dacus, Robin Gregory and Jim Hall. For beta-reading, I bow to Elizabeth Keswick and Graham Read, also Anita and Clare, previously mentioned. For Chilean colloquialisms, I raise a cola de mono to Jorge Salgado-Reyes. For naval knowledge and high seas expertise, I salute Chief Petty Officer Christopher Owen, very sadly no longer with us. For the local writerly network, I engage with Novel Nights (**https://www.novelnights.co.uk**). For the rhythm, I sway to Carlos Santana. For your faith in Jesús, I smile, Karla Neblett. For the World Tree inked on my skin before pen was put to paper, I am procumbent to the talented Briony Victoria at Carousel Custom Tattoos (**https://www.instagram.com/explore/locations/10126352 82/carousel-custom-tattoos/**).

While working part-time, I spent an immersive year on the MA Creative Writing programme at Bath Spa University, where I was able to focus on developing this novel among the sashaying peacocks of Corsham Court, under the tutelage of Gavin James Bower, Celia Brayfield, Gavin Cologne-Brooks, Samantha Harvey and the incomparable Fay Weldon. For your expertise and enthusiasm for the written word, I hear you.

To you, intrepid reader, thank you for joining the expedition. As you prepare to disembark, I welcome your honest review on Amazon and Goodreads, for the benefit of other readers.

This book has been an adventure in more ways than I could have imagined. Here's to my next voyage of discovery.

www.amandaread.net

Printed in Great Britain
by Amazon